I0756164

THE TEMPLE
OF THE
THREE WHISPERS

BOOK NINE:

THE TEMPLE OF THE THREE WHISPERS

BRIAN HARMON

The Temple of the Three Whispers
Book Nine: The Temple of the Three Whispers

Published by Brian Harmon
Cover Image and Design by Brian Harmon

ISBN- 978-1-945559-38-9

Don't miss these other great books by Brian Harmon!

***The Temple of the Blind* series:**

The Box (Book I)
Gilbert House (Book II)
The Temple of the Blind (Book III)
Road Beneath The Wood (Book IV)
Secret of the Labyrinth (Book V)
The Judgment of the Sentinels (Book VI)

***The Temple of the Three Whispers* series:**

The Lady of Cedric's Cove (Book I)
Circles in Hermes' Footsteps (Book II)
Misplaced in Mysteria (Book III)
The Denselands (Book IV)
The Impassible Wall (Book V)
The City Beyond Memory (Book VI)
The Keeper's Dollhouse (Book VII)
Priestess of Ruin (Book VIII)
The Temple of the Three Whispers (Book IX)
Whispers in the Murk (Book X)

The Rushed series:

Rushed (Book 1)
Rushed: The Unseen (Book 2)
Rushed: Something Wicked (Book 3)
Rushed: Hedge Lake (Book 4)
Rushed: A Matter of Time (Book 5)
Rushed: All Fun and Games (Book 6)
Rushed: Something Wickeder (Book 7)
Rushed: Evancurt (Book 8)
Rushed: Relic (Book 9)

***Hands of the Architects* trilogy:**

Spirit Ears and Prophet Sight (Book 1)
Pretty Faces and Peculiar Places (Book 2)
Broken Clocks and Amber Threads (Book 3)

For Mom

Chapter 1

Gina awoke with a start, her hands clasped over her mouth. Did she scream again? Or did she manage to hold it in this time? If she woke up her stepsisters in the next room, they'd be mad. They were always mad at her, always snapping at her and calling her a freak, but they were especially mean when she woke them up. It wasn't as if she could help it. Sometimes the screams slipped out faster than she could wake up. Especially on nights like this, when what she awoke to was the awful feeling of something foul and grotesque slithering under the sheets with her.

This one had wrapped itself around her thigh, cold and clammy and vile, a horrid, twitchy thing, damp and spongy and pulsating against her naked skin. It was creeping higher, its countless feelers wriggling up under her nightshirt, prodding and groping. And there was nothing she could do about it. She could *feel* it, yet somehow she couldn't *touch* it. She couldn't slap it away or brush it off. She couldn't get away from it.

The first time this ever happened, she fled shrieking into the hallway, waking everyone up and making a spectacle of herself. Throughout the entire ordeal, the thing never let go, never stopped its squirming and squeezing, a hideous and squelching thing the pallid color of a corpse, without limbs or a head or any other discernable features, little more than clumps of flesh strung together into tangles of boneless hands. It was wrapped around her arm, clinging to her, but no one else could see it. When her stepmother took hold of her arm to examine it, trying to understand what was wrong with her, she placed her palm directly on it, yet never felt anything. And likewise, the thing clinging to her showed no reaction whatsoever to anything or anyone else. It seemed to only exist to *her*.

Until it didn't, that was. One second it was there and the next it was just simply gone, vanished inexplicably, leaving no evidence to prove that she wasn't making it all up.

Her stepfather was still alive then. He wasn't the kind of man who was ever really cut out to be a father. He wasn't the warmest or most loving. He was kind of awkward when it came to children. But he wasn't unkind. And he was patient. He shooed her sneering stepsisters, Jessie and Janie, back to their room and took her back to bed. Like with all the other times, he assured her it was only a bad dream, only her imagination. And even back then, she couldn't blame him for not believing her. She even wondered if he might be right. Because no one else could see them. No one else could hear them like she could. Not one other person could feel them. Only her.

Night terrors, he called them. Products of some sort of repressed trauma. Probably a buildup of confused emotions attached to her mother's passing when she was old enough to remember her, but still too young to know how to deal with such a thing. An incomplete grieving process. He was no psychiatrist. He had no understanding of the human mind or how emotional trauma worked. He could only make guesses. But he tried. And even back then, she appreciated the effort.

The accident took her stepfather not long after that. And although her stepmother was never cruel or abusive in any way, she was easily exasperated by her various episodes and didn't know how to deal with them the way he did. She looked for the simplest and most likely explanations and doggedly stuck to them, which were usually that she was doing these things out of angst or a desire for attention or to express some kind of pent-up frustration. She was convinced that the best course of action was to simply ignore it all until she finally grew bored and stopped. It became an insurmountable rift between them that left her an outsider in her own home until the day she packed her bags and left.

As for her, Gina wished desperately that they'd been right, that all those things were only bad dreams and her own overactive imagination. She'd give *anything* for them to only exist within her mind. She wanted nothing more than to only be making all those things up because of some misguided desire for attention. But they *weren't* nightmares. She wasn't making them up to get people to pay attention to her. She never even *wanted* any attention. She was genuinely terrified of the things she saw and heard and felt.

Because they were *real.* And some of them, she understood even way back then, were *extremely* dangerous.

And here in her bed on this most unpleasant of nights, this one clinging to her trembling thigh was starting to burrow its way into her panties.

She clenched her teeth and squeezed her eyes closed. She couldn't let herself scream. Screaming would only make everything worse. But it was so difficult. She could feel the tears slipping down her face, but she couldn't let herself cry. Not a sob. Not a whimper. Any unnecessary sounds could agitate her sisters. They were right there in the next room, right on the other side of the wall.

Then, as the things so often did, the horrible thing simply melted away, vanishing back into the night, as if it were never there at all.

She let go of the breath she'd been holding and gulped down a gasp of relief. Once again, the things in the shadows had left her unscathed. But it was only a matter of time, she was sure, until something found her that wasn't nearly so harmless.

She wiped at the tears and then grabbed her pillow and pressed it over her face to muffle any gasps or sobs that might yet bubble up.

Nobody was shouting at her at least. She couldn't sense anyone stirring in the house. That was good. That meant she probably didn't scream. It was always bad when someone woke up. If she was lucky, one of them would yell or pound on the wall, telling her to shut up. But sometimes they'd get extra mad and burst into her room, berating her. The worst of times, they'd open the door and throw things at her. Jessie once hit her in the face with a heavy spiral sketchbook, leaving a scratch under one eye that seemed to take forever to go away.

But sounds weren't the only thing that sometimes escaped her when she awoke like that. Shamefully, she reached down and felt at her underwear, making sure she didn't wet herself again. That was even worse than screaming.

Fortunately, she was still dry.

This time.

She sighed with fresh relief and then rolled over and hugged her pillow.

Why did she have to be like this? She never asked to be different. Why did she have to be born if this was what her life was going to be like? She hated it. She couldn't even escape these things in her sleep!

(*I'm always with you.*)

She sniffled and opened her eyes. What was that just now? An old memory? Something from a dream? There was no one here in her room. She'd know if there were. It was impossible to sneak up on her.

Somewhere in her head, she imagined a vast space of blinding white and a woman with long, white hair with an iridescent shimmer trailing behind her.

That wasn't a real memory, she was sure. It must've been something from a dream she had once. Or maybe something she saw in an old movie?

Wherever it came from, she found a little bit of comfort in it.

Again, she closed her eyes and buried her face in her pillow.

Sleep settled over her like a warm and soothing blanket, taking away her fear and her tears and her frustration for a while, leaving nothing but a calming haze of peaceful nothingness.

And yet, something wasn't right.

She couldn't seem to wake up. It felt as if she were floating in an endless fog, adrift in a sea of nothingness.

Had something happened to her? Did one of those monsters finally get to her?

No… She'd forgotten something. She'd become confused and distracted. She needed to clear her mind.

She wasn't eleven years old anymore. She was twenty-six. She didn't live in that house. She hadn't seen her stepfamily in eight years. She left for college one day and never returned. She chose a new life for herself, a life where she could be alone, where she wouldn't be a bother to anyone.

Until the goddess came to her.

(*I'm always with you.*)

The goddess…

A subtle voice inside her head, whispering encouraging things to her whenever she felt defeated and vulnerable. Ada. The Great Beholder.

She remembered now.

She'd been through *so* much worse than those foul, grabby things that occasionally slithered into her sheets at night. The Vertical Design building and Janon Tane. Tristesse Lane and Gwilym Glum. Cedric's Cove and Hochog. She'd survived the Denselands and crossed the impassible wall and descended into the Temple of the Three Whispers to the depths of the glass labyrinth…

That was where she was. The glass labyrinth.

And she didn't come here alone.

Where was Nicole? Did she lose her? A sharp pang of fear shot through her, sobering her a little. How could she forget Nicole? She was supposed to be keeping her safe!

She tried to reach out, to search this strange, inky darkness for her, but she couldn't move her arm. Her hand wasn't free. Someone was holding it.

A great wave of relief washed over her as the pieces clicked into place inside her confounded mind. Nicole was still there with her. She hadn't lost her. That was a relief.

But why couldn't she see anything? Why couldn't she *move*? Where were they? The more aware she became, the more she understood that something was wrong. She couldn't sense the labyrinth around her. It was as if everything were out of focus.

She tried to think back. She was leading the way through that chamber of mirrors. But not *actual* mirrors. "Mirrors" was simply the word she found for them, inadequate to really describe them, but closer than anything else she could think of when she first sensed them. There were no reflective surfaces of any kind. It was more like the phrase "smoke and mirrors," referring to deceptions and illusions, like in a magic show. She was surrounded by pathways that were twisted and overlapped in dangerously confounding ways, almost as if they were designed to distract and mislead her.

Right… It was coming back to her now. It was a dangerous place. Like tiptoeing through a minefield. One wrong step and they could have fallen through one of the many cracks and ended up almost anywhere. Or even nowhere at all…

Was that what happened? Had she messed up? Were they lost?

She tried to turn around, but her body wouldn't respond. She seemed to be stuck in agonizing slow motion.

This wasn't the glass labyrinth, she realized. It was the space between the cracks. A transition space. A fissure between realities, she supposed.

This was what existed within that split-second gap when she passed from one side of the glass to another.

She was *inside the looking glass.*

And she didn't know how to get out!

Already, the fog was closing in around her again, enveloping her, as if she were being sucked into a suffocating quagmire. She had time enough to feel a great rush of fear and wonder if she'd ever wake up again.

Then sleep swallowed her once more.

Chapter 2

Nicole turned and looked around, puzzled. She was standing in what appeared to be a narrow city alleyway, the sort of grimy place where shady things always seemed to be going down in the movies, with towering brick walls stretching high into a gray and dreary sky above. It didn't look like anywhere she'd ever been. She didn't think there was any such place in Briar Hills. It looked like a scene from some supersized metropolis. There were overflowing trash cans surrounded by bags of garbage, discarded cardboard boxes and crates full of empty glass bottles for as far as she could see, but little else. It seemed to go on forever in both directions, with no sign of any street or sidewalk. There were doors everywhere, but none that would open. They were all metal and windowless, without any handles or locks, as if they were all nothing more than fire exits. It all looked so strangely…*wrong*…

What was this place? And why was it so quiet? This looked like something that should only exist deep within a huge city, but there were no traffic noises, no roar of construction equipment, no hum of air conditioners or furnaces, no voices, no distant sirens, no droning airplanes passing overhead. There weren't even any *nature* noises. No barking dogs, no singing birds, no chirping of insects. And in spite of all the garbage surrounding her, there were no bugs crawling around, no roaches, no rats, no flies.

There weren't even any *odors*. Despite all the trash, this place didn't stink. There were no traffic exhaust smells or faint asphalt smells or even dank concrete smells. It didn't smell like *anything*.

She couldn't remember how she came to be here. Or even

exactly where she was before she was here. In fact, she couldn't remember a lot of things. The past few days were a blur. She remembered Brandy's wedding. Something happened there, she thought, but she couldn't recall what. Everything after the ceremony was a blur of weird emotions and flashes of half-thoughts that made no sense in her head.

She'd lost her shirt somehow. She was wearing shorts and sneakers, but only her bra on top. She felt like she could almost remember doing something with it… But everything was so hazy. And it didn't seem to matter all that much. She wasn't technically indecent. And it wasn't like there was anyone around to offend, anyway. But she was also filthy. Her hair was a tangled mess. And there were strange, black stains smeared on her clothes and skin.

Unsure what else to do, she started walking, her gaze drawn upward. Those dingy brick walls towered over her, making her feel small. There were a few doors up there, too, she saw, handleless and inaccessible like those down here at her level, most of them useless even as emergency exits. Only a few of them had fire escapes. The rest simply opened onto empty space. If someone were to try stepping through one, they'd only fall to the cracked asphalt below, and very few of them were close enough to the ground to not be a fatal drop.

She stared up into that dizzying brick chasm for a moment, at that dreary stripe of hazy sky hanging above, an odd feeling of déjà vu creeping through her. It reminded her of something, but she couldn't remember what. Someplace unsettling. Someplace damp and dreary. Someplace *depressing.*

Why were there no windows?

Her foot struck an empty liquor bottle, sending it clattering across the concrete. It was surprisingly loud in the odd silence. It startled her. But it was a much-needed reminder to watch where she was going before she tripped and fell into a pile of garbage.

She turned and looked back the way she came, then forward again. There was a gap in the wall up ahead. A way out, perhaps? It was too narrow to be a street. It looked like another alleyway, just like this one. But it should lead her to the front of whatever these buildings were. Maybe she could find someone inside who could tell her where she was. Or allow her to use a phone.

She pressed her hand against the fabric of her dirty shorts, trying to remember what happened to her cell phone. She should have it on her. She never went anywhere without it. But her pockets were all empty.

Why couldn't she remember anything?

She reached the adjacent alley and peered around the corner, only to find that it was the same as this one, narrow and dreary and littered with piles of garbage, with no end in sight.

She turned down it anyway, unsure what else to do, and continued walking. It couldn't go on forever, could it?

Of course it can, she thought, the words drawing a deep frown on her smudged face. A strange memory circled around inside her head, half-surfacing, teasing. An endless cobblestone street… Hallways stretching forever into darkness…

She stopped walking and pressed the heels of her hands against her eyes, frustrated. What was happening to her? What was this place? And how did she get here?

It couldn't be real, she decided. It made no logical sense. Why would there be no useable doors? Why were there no windows? Was it a dream? Was she asleep somewhere?

Was she *dead?*

No. That didn't feel right. This was something else. Something *wrong*. She shouldn't be here. What was she doing before she was here? She pressed her hands more firmly against her face, as if trying to push the truth into her brain through her eyeballs. She needed to remember. It was *desperately important* that she make herself remember. She wasn't sure how she knew this, but she did. She needed to snap out of it.

And it was right there… Just below the surface… Just out of sight… She could almost reach it.

She lowered her hands and opened her eyes.

The glass labyrinth.

Everything was still a haze, but she remembered there being a glass labyrinth. But not *actual* glass. It was only the same stone as the rest of the temple. Gina only described it as glass because of the strange way her psychic eye was able to peer through it.

She blinked at the litter-strewn scene still stubbornly laid out before her.

Gina… She remembered the wedding reception. That weird feeling of loneliness and melancholy. The barely-there. Andrea and the mysterious spear. The horsemen running them off the road. Most of it remained a blur, but she remembered *Gina.* She was just with her. Inside the glass labyrinth.

But where did she go? She was right here a moment ago.

Or…not *here*, she supposed… Because she still didn't know where "here" was… This place…these narrow alleyways with their towering walls and useless doors… This was obviously somewhere else. Unless this, too, was a part of the glass labyrinth…

For that matter, was it really only a moment ago that she was in that other place? Or did that all happen a long time ago? She couldn't be certain… Everything felt so…*distant…*

She needed to snap out of this mental fog. Something had obviously happened. Was it that empty room they found, the one Gina said wasn't empty at all, but rather full of *mirrors* or some shit?

(*Mirrors… But not mirrors. Not light. Not reflections. More like how magicians use them. Optical illusions. Forced perception. Tricks of the mind. Deceptions…*)

That sounded so weird, and yet it was exactly the sort of thing Gina kept saying, wasn't it? Crinkled-up spaces. Know-it-all goddesses. Broken time.

(*Holes… Gaps… Different from the cracks that let me move back and forth… Those were just doorways. This is like a freeway interchange. There are so many ways we can go from here. So many places we could end up. One wrong step and we could go somewhere impossible to come back from.*)

Was that what happened? Did she fall through a hole of some sort? Was she lost? Was she trapped in this place? Was that why none of the doors would open? Was that why the alleyways just went on and on?

Her heart sank at the very thought. Had she fucked up

again? Her heart was already beating faster. What if she couldn't find her way back? What if this garbage-filled nowhere was her entire existence now?

What should she do? What *could* she do?

"What've you gotten yourself into this time, Nik?"

She gasped and twirled around. "Keith?" But all she glimpsed was a shadow disappearing across the wall into the other alleyway.

She ran back and looked, but it was just as deserted as it was when she was last here.

Was that only her imagination?

No… It was all flooding back to her now. The long journey from Briar Hills to Cedric's Cove to the Denselands to the City Beyond Memory, everything she went through, every pitfall she stumbled into. And every time she got herself into trouble, Keith came to her rescue, saving her from the barely-there, from Tristesse Lane, from that deranged abomination of a hospital. He even saved her from Hotdog's monstrous, shambling corpse.

She stood there, her stomach sinking as the rest of it came back to her. Fesh tears welled up in her eyes.

Keith *did* always come to her rescue…even in that awful meadow… Even after the terrible way she treated him, he was her knight in shining armor.

But Keith was gone. He wasn't coming to save her this time. Or ever again.

Her knees felt weak. She turned and propped herself against the dingy bricks. The air suddenly felt very heavy, as if some great weight were crushing down on her.

She lost Keith. She lost Andrea. She lost Brandy and Albert. She even lost Gina.

God, she was such a fuckup.

No wonder she found herself in this endless, back-alley hell, tossed away along with all this garbage.

This was exactly where someone like her belonged.

Tears streamed down her face as she sank to her knees on the grimy asphalt.

She belonged here.

Chapter 3

There was so much blood…

It was everywhere. Splashed on every wall and ceiling. Pooled in gory puddles on every floor. Soaked into every carpet and cushion. Dripping from every piece of furniture in every room.

And it was all over Albert's hands.

He stood over the woman's broken, lifeless body, his breathing labored, his pulse racing, his eyes wild. His every nerve felt electrified with adrenaline. Had he ever felt such a rush before? It was intoxicating. *Addictive.*

He wanted more.

But this one had stopped screaming. It wasn't fun anymore.

He turned his blood-spattered face toward the *other* woman, the one cowering in the corner.

She let out a terrified sob. She was shaking her head, begging him, but she wouldn't run. She couldn't. Her knee was broken. He did that, too…though he couldn't quite remember it…

Somewhere in the far back of his mind, he kept wondering how he even came to be here in this place. There were holes in his memory. Great, fuzzy gaps between all the blood and screaming. And it seemed to him that he kept moving around, not just through the house, but to entirely different locations. He was somewhere else entirely before, with the *other* woman, the one carving up her own brother, before he strangled the life out of her.

That felt so long ago now… What had he been doing all this time?

His gaze dropped to the fireplace poker he was gripping in

his hands, at the blood dripping from its iron tip. Everything was so hazy, but he could almost remember picking it up to defend himself from something. Except…that didn't make any sense… He had no need to defend himself. *He* was the one doing the killing. *He* was the monster here.

He frowned, confused. Something didn't feel right. Why was he doing this?

"Why did you stop?" whispered a familiar voice in his ear.

Warm hands slipped around his waist, sharp black nails gently scratching at his belly, drawing lines in the blood splashed on his skin there. The feeling sent a storm of half-remembered sensations coursing through his muscles like an electric charge. Conflicting emotions clashed within him. His body reacted with a strange mix of lust and revulsion. He wanted to turn around and take her right then and there, but he also wanted to run as far away from her as possible. He wanted to embrace her, but also to throttle her. He wanted to *rape* her. And he wanted to *gut* her.

He looked down at those dainty hands, at those black nails, and felt a distant pang of fear. What was he doing? This wasn't him. He never wanted to do any of these horrible things.

Then he looked at his own hand, at the golden band on his left ring finger.

He felt as if he could remember *two* women, one raven-haired and one fair…but he couldn't remember which was which…or even their names…

He felt her lips brush against his ear. "I want to watch you break her bones. Let me hear her scream." She closed her teeth around his lobe and bit him. It wasn't a gentle nip. There was a sharp pain. The sensation should have helped clear his head, but instead everything seemed to grow even fuzzier. His head was swimming. He couldn't think straight. "Show me what's inside her."

What was inside her… Yes… What an exhilarating thought. It excited him. It made his entire body quiver with anticipation.

He blinked down at his bloody chest and belly, confused. Was someone talking to him? Was someone just here? He felt almost as if someone were touching him. There was a pain in his earlobe that wasn't there a moment ago.

What was he doing again? He couldn't remember. Everything was so confusing.

(Keep going.)

Right… He was having some fun…

(Show me what's inside her.)

Yes…

Again, he lifted the poker and turned his empty eyes on the injured woman cowering in the corner.

Another terrified sob escaped her. She was shaking her head again, pleading.

Somewhere deep inside, his heart ached for her. That poor woman… How could anyone be so cruel as to harm someone so helpless and afraid?

Somewhere much *less* deep inside him, however, some part of him that didn't feel like him at all was bristling with perverse anticipation. She was so very scared…and so very vulnerable. She was *trapped*. And she was all *his*.

He raised the bloody poker high above his head and relished the sound of the woman's terrified, begging shrieks. The sound excited him in ways that were almost *sexual*. He was practically panting as he stood over her.

He couldn't wait any longer!

He brought the poker down, aiming not for her head—that would end the fun far too soon—but for her shoulder. The very sound of it whooshing through the air was exquisite. And what followed…the thud of iron against meat, the crack of her collarbone snapping, the piercing scream of agony…

What an absolutely intoxicating feeling. So much *power*.

He was going to make this last as long as possible, relishing every grisly second of it, every splash of blood, every snapping bone, every agonizing scream…until there was nothing left…

And then he'd go out and find someone new to play with.

Chapter 4

This was weird.

Corey found himself drifting through the endless expanse of deep space, surrounded by a myriad of colorful stars and vast clouds of cosmic dust and gas. It was beautiful beyond words, like something from a high-budget science fiction movie. Or even those incredible NASA photos that circulated online. Truly breathtaking.

But everything about it was wrong.

He couldn't really be floating around in space, obviously. He'd freeze, for one thing. And he wouldn't be able to breathe. Those were the first two basic principles of space that silly cartoons always ignored. And depending on what movie you were watching, his head might explode for reasons he never quite understood.

Besides, there were no stars in the Denselands. The skies out here were perpetually empty.

(On second thought, how much could he really depend on the scientific principles of being stranded in space without a protective suit in a world where there was no sun in the sky and yet everything wasn't frozen over?)

He was going to have a lot to talk about once he finally found his way back to Violet.

But then again, that wasn't exactly a guarantee, was it? Entirely the opposite, in fact.

(You know there won't be time for you to escape if you stay here. There's no 'one percent' about it.)

That was unfortunate. He would've liked to at least have been able to tell her about all the cool things he'd discovered.

But he had no time to dwell on that right now. He had a job to do. Everyone was counting on him.

But first, he had to figure out how to get down from outer space…

Which way *was* down, anyway? One thing you never thought about in science fiction movies was the complete absence of the simple concept of up and down outside the artificial gravity. How did the ships all end up oriented the same way? Was there some kind of universally agreed-upon axis?

But he was getting distracted again. Floating in space was a very cool sensation. Not many people ever really experienced zero gravity. It was something he never thought he'd get to scratch off his bucket list, even if it wasn't real. What he needed to be focused on, however, was *why* he was floating in space right now. He wasn't supposed to be adrift in the cosmos. He was supposed to be fixing Austin.

He was with him there in the bloodlike-liquid-soaked terminal, slowly but steadily wiring him into the temple's bizarre circuitry. He was only tying strings onto spikes, but that was just an oversimplification of a truth so complex that his brain couldn't handle the actual reality of it. What he was actually doing was the equivalent of hard wiring a broken starter in order to fire up a machine infinitely more complex than his old Dodge Ram. But something wasn't right. He was finding more and more connections that should've worked, but wouldn't. At first he thought it was something he was doing wrong. But that wasn't possible. He had the sentinels' infallible blueprints inside his very brain, after all. Something else was happening. And when Austin began malfunctioning as well, he began to realize that it was far more than a damaged component he was dealing with.

Something had sabotaged the system.

Back in the carriage, on their long journey from the Lucianna Mysteria to the heart of the Wood, Albert and Brandy told them about all they went through to open the carriage house. Among so many other wondrous sounding things, they mentioned something they described as an "infection" that attacked and killed the caretakers of the property. His thoughts kept returning to that as he pondered the concept of some kind of computer virus interfering with the upload. Was that what he was dealing with here? Something capable of infecting both biological lifeforms and sentinel tech? How was he supposed to combat something like that? He was only a human. And admittedly not the most prime of example of one, either.

He wasn't going to be able to fix this problem with strings and spikes, no matter what they really were. This was something far deeper, something way down in the sentinels' queer programming. Tackling it from the outside would be like trying to fix a programming glitch with a screwdriver. It simply wasn't how it worked. So he changed his approach.

He had no idea how it was that he knew how to do that, and yet here he was. He'd plugged himself into the system, not just physically, but mentally as well. He should be *inside* the machine, deep in its very *programming.* From here, he could act like an administrator, accessing things others couldn't. That was how he envisioned it. And that was where he should be right now.

So again, why the hell was he floating through space?

Had he done something wrong? Had he fallen into a trap of some sort? Had he screwed up and *electrocuted* himself instead of merging with the machine as intended? Was he *dead*? That didn't seem right, either. First of all, electricity had nothing to do with the sentinels' technology. He found himself understanding somehow that it didn't exist in their original universe. It was actually a fairly recent concept. Which was weird, because didn't the human brain work on electrical impulses? Did this temple predate human beings? Or did their biological functioning change along with the properties of the universes they inhabited?

Focus, Roly Poly.

He frowned at the words as they passed through his head. That was what Violet would say to him if she were here. She was the logical one. The voice of reason. The one who kept them grounded. And she was usually right.

He had so many questions. *Too* many. It was distracting. He kept getting off track. He needed to focus on one thing at a time. And the first thing he needed to do was figure out how he was supposed to do *anything* while lost in the far reaches of space, of all things.

No. This wasn't space. He'd already established that. He'd be dead by now if he were in actual space. The real question wasn't what he was supposed to do in this place, but rather *what was this place*?

He closed his eyes and allowed himself to drift. He hadn't moved. Not physically. He was quite sure he was still back in that terminal room with Austin's broken body. Only his *consciousness* was here. If he really looked closely…

He tried to put his hands on his stomach and found that he couldn't.

He could *imagine* doing it. But he couldn't feel his body. Because he didn't have one. Not here. He couldn't have a body because he wasn't really here in this place. Because this wasn't a place at all. Was it a dream? An altered state of consciousness? Some kind of higher mental plane?

No. He did what he did in the terminal in order to enter the machine because something was preventing him from doing his job in the physical world. His intention was to go *inside* the machine. And that was where he was now. Not physically. He hadn't just crawled inside the components of the sentinels' stoneworks like he did while climbing through the inner workings of the temple before he arrived at the terminal. He wasn't floating around inside a huge hard drive. He was in much deeper than that. This was more like slipping into the data flow of a network. He was inside the very *coding* of the machine.

He opened his eyes and looked out at the stars all around him.

Coding…

Was it possible…?

He turned around, scanning his surroundings. There were stars everywhere. From faint little pinpricks of light to great, colorful balls of distant fire. But they weren't stars. They weren't burning. They weren't shining. That was merely what he was perceiving them to be.

Each one of those countless stars was a single piece of raw

data.

The most basic element in a computer.

A bit.

A switch.

Painted across that vast, black canvas were patterns of shining stars. *Constellations.* Not strings of stars, but strands of data. Words. Information. *Programming.*

And if he were to move around within this vast universe, repositioning himself in relation to those stars, the orientation of them would change. The constellations would differ. Strings of bytes would become strings of code. They'd turn into syntax. They'd become *commands.*

That was what he was looking at. This was a mental representation of what would be an equivalent to a modern-day computer program.

But this was no computer. Computers were comprised of hardware and software. This was neither. Or perhaps it was both at once? He wasn't sure. It wasn't like anything he'd ever encountered before.

He wasn't even sure what *he* was at this point. This wasn't his body. He didn't travel here. He didn't get up and crawl through the temple's access tunnels or crawlspaces to get here. He came here by sort of *plugging himself into* the strings. His physical body was back in that terminal room with Austin's. This was…just *something else*, he supposed. Something *different.* Something new. Something outside the physical world he was accustomed to existing in. None of this was real.

And yet it *felt* real. At least, this sensation of floating through empty space felt real. He could even get used to this. It was so quiet. So relaxing…

Focus.

"Right," he muttered to himself, though he couldn't decide if he actually heard the word leave his mouth or if he only imagined it.

He had a job to do. Now that he'd determined what this place was, he found himself faced with a much more confounding problem. Just how the hell was he supposed to do anything here? He was literally a speck of dust drifting through the temple's programming.

It was a matter of scale. A person couldn't affect stars any more than an ant could push over a house.

This was a conundrum.

He might have to think about this for a while.

Chapter 5

"Two on the left," warned Everett.

Above him, Violet shined her light up and to the left. A shimmer of reflected light revealed two of those gossamer strands. "I see them." She shifted her weight and repositioned her foot, making her way up the opposite wall.

He followed as close behind her as possible without getting in her way, his eyes remaining fixed on the spot where her light illuminated the dangerous threads even after she aimed it the other way.

They were so hard to see in this darkness. Without Alice's help there was no way they'd be able to spot all of them. Especially while trying to move quickly. And they didn't have the luxury of taking their time.

The *graymother* was coming.

It wasn't a mother to anyone or anything. It wasn't even a she. Nor was it a he. Nor was it gray. The name was simply a broken interpretation of whatever bizarre language Alice used, phonetically similar, perhaps, but altogether wrong. He couldn't remember exactly how the word she planted in his head sounded. And even if he did, he wouldn't be able to pronounce it. He didn't think a human mouth could make the sounds she used when she warned him about it.

It was surprising just how *eerie* the concept of a monster with a name no tongue could speak was. It gave him a chill that somewhat surpassed his raging curiosity.

The graymother was insanely ancient. Alice described her as a relic of a universe long dead and forgotten even when this place was being built. It was something utterly alien, unlike anything else in any existence as far back as even the oldest of things could recall, a remnant among remnants.

And they were deep inside its territory.

"One on your six," he reported.

Violet paused and shined her light above and behind her. "I don't see it."

"About four feet above your head, I think?"

"Got it," she replied, her light reflecting off the fine strand in a shimming, iridescent streak. There was plenty of room. She probably wasn't in any danger of touching it anyway, but it was better to be safe than sorry. Clearly, she thought so, too, because she was careful to keep her body tucked in as she climbed past it and higher into the rough, shadowy heights of the cavern.

This place was so weirdly unlike any other part of the labyrinth he'd seen. He supposed those so-called "sentinels" just built the place around the graymother's nest or hive or whatever this place served as. The way everyone spoke about them and the Keeper, it was probably in the design from the beginning. There was no such thing as an accident where those guys were involved. Even the puzzle box told him that much.

There was no end to all the wonders he was discovering!

"One above you," he warned. "Move to the other side."

"Thanks." She spotted it and immediately began making her way around the stone and up onto a ledge on the opposite side, where she stopped and flexed her aching hands. "How high does this place go?"

"Alice doesn't know, exactly. She says it has weird properties or something. It's both bigger and smaller than the space around it?" He frowned down at her. "That doesn't make any sense, but that's what she says."

"Nothing about *any* of this makes sense," she grumbled, then turned her light up at the rough stone above her. "That way looks kind of sketchy."

Alice was saying so, too. "That way," he said, pointing farther to the left. "It's a little tighter there, but we should be able to fit."

"What's the deal with that graymother thing? Is it still chasing us?"

"Alice says it's below us somewhere. Seems like it's not sure where we went. It's probably waiting for us to touch another of those strands. Like a spider waiting to feel a vibration in its web."

Violet shuddered visibly at the analogy and he made a mental note to not compare it to a spider in the future.

She stood up, sweeping her light back and forth, her eyes peeled for more of those razor-thin filaments, and began climbing again. The space he pointed to was pretty cramped, but it looked like she could squeeze through it pretty easily. And he was pretty small himself, so if she made it he was fairly sure he would, too.

It was probably just as well that he lost his backpack to that zombie bear in Gutler's Weep. Like his flashlight, it probably wouldn't have survived the trip through the void and back, but even if it did, he probably would have had to abandon it here.

He watched as she wriggled her head and shoulders into the gap and then pulled herself upward, distracted for a moment by the sight of her perky butt stuck out toward him in those tiny shorts. (A fairly new feeling, if he were being honest. He'd never been all that distracted by girls before. It wasn't like he was ever around any of them growing up.) Then, just as quickly, her dirty socks disappeared into the hole and the blinding flashlight beam was shining back at him.

"Can you fit?"

"I think so." He was already climbing, pushing those distracting thoughts from his head. It was because of how weirdly close everyone kept getting, he knew. Back in that cool, old-growth type forest, Olivia hugged him and then clung to his hand while he led her back the way he came. (He was trying not to think about that weird breeze that blew her dress up and revealed…well, he was *trying not to think about that.*) And then he found Andrea and she was clinging to him the same way. Then they lost Andrea and *Violet* was clinging to him like that. It was a lot of intimate contact for someone who'd barely ever had a proper conversation with a girl. And then there was that kiss…

Again, he was trying not to think about that.

(Doesn't mean we're a couple or anything.)

Right. Just an emotional reaction. The poor girl was buried alive when he found her. That had to be a disturbing experience. He was lucky she wasn't talking gibberish and pulling out her own hair.

He squeezed through the gap. It was tighter than he expected. Apparently he was a little bigger than she was. At least in his shoulders and waist, he supposed, because those areas scraped the rough stone, scratching him a little. Most guys were bigger than him, so he always thought of himself as pretty small, but Violet was even tinier.

She was crouched over him, ready to give him a hand if he needed one, but he was okay. As soon as he was clear, she stood up and shined her light upward again.

Alice spoke up again in that strange, not-quite-there way she communicated. A clear warning to be careful. But before he could relay it, Violet hissed and twirled around, clutching at her elbow.

Another of those nearly invisible filaments was stretched in front of the stone there, unseen as she focused her light upward to check their path.

"Oh shit, that's not good…" she groaned. There was blood dripping down her arm where it bit her, but that wasn't what she meant. The cut was the least of their problems.

Somewhere beneath their feet, something seemed to shift. That odd sensation of the temperature dropping—not *on* his skin, but *in* it—swept over him again. There was another hole beside her, beneath which was a sizeable drop down into the cavern, farther down than her light reached, and something about that darkness seemed to shiver at the approach of something dreadful.

"Up," urged Everett as that strange simultaneous sensation of both an ominous hush and an unsettling din of discordant murmurs and whispers settled in the air around them. "It's coming."

She was already moving, her light sweeping the space above for more of those iridescent shimmers even as she climbed the raw stone.

He began climbing after her as soon as there was room for him to find a footing. "There'll be several behind you on the way up to the next ledge. Keep close to the wall."

"Gotcha!"

This wasn't good. They were lucky the first time. The graymother was somewhere far away. By the time it reached the place where she triggered the first filament, they'd climbed far enough that it couldn't be sure which way they went.

The graymother was deaf and blind, Alice told him. It used the filaments to find trespassers. If they'd avoided them, they could have avoided detection. Now they'd tripped another one, setting off an alarm throughout the nest. It knew they were still here. Worse still, it knew which direction they were going. It was going to get easier and easier to find them.

"Got it," he muttered under his breath at her. "We messed up. Thanks for the pep talk."

Above him, Violet climbed up onto the next ledge and shined her light around. She was visibly shaken, and he could hardly blame her.

"Some on either side of you," he called up to her. "Keep to the middle and go up the wall straight in front of you."

She nodded and hurried on.

They were moving too slowly. This wouldn't end well. He should focus less on watching out for Violet and more on saving himself. Worst case scenario, if the graymother were to catch her, he might be able to use the distraction to get away.

He climbed up onto the ledge and stopped, frowning at himself. What a terrible thought! Why would something like that even cross his mind?

He looked down at Alice, still cradled in the crook of his arm.

It wasn't him at all, he realized. It was her. *She* was suggesting that he stop worrying over Violet and save himself.

"That's not going to happen," he grunted as he stood up.

"What?" asked Violet.

"Nothing. Just thinking out loud."

"Well, less thinking and more climbing."

"Right." He glanced down into the darkness below, at the flickering glint of those trembling filaments. The graymother wasn't far behind. They might not be able to reach the top in time. But that didn't mean he was going to betray his friend just to save his own butt.

He'd find another way.

Chapter 6

Brandy stood squinting into the blinding sunlight, bewildered. In front of her lay a long stretch of dirt path nestled between walls of tall prairie grass and wildflowers.

It was hot. Sweltering. She blinked at the blinding sky hanging over her, clear and blue. The sun was burning overhead, as blistering as it was on her wedding day. There was no wind to soothe the heat, either. The only sound was the droning of insects in that towering grass.

She turned and looked behind her, only to find the same scene laid out in that direction.

"What the fuck?" she muttered to herself. How did she even get somewhere like this? Wasn't she just drowning in a pool of disgusting ichor in the depths of that awful labyrinth?

She looked down at herself. She was still covered in that foul, brownish slime. It was oozing down her belly and legs, dripping onto the dirt at her feet. She could still feel the burning claw marks on her breast and her lip was still sore and swollen where that bitch bit her. Even the partial puncture wound on her belly was still there. All proof enough that she hadn't imagined any of that stuff. But then what was *this* weirdness? When did she get outside? And back into a world of sunshine and grass, no less? She left sunlight behind way back in Wevenwert.

She was still wearing her shorts. She still had Albert's tee shirt knotted around her chest. But now one of her shoes was missing. A quick glance around revealed it wasn't lying anywhere nearby. Had she lost it while sinking in the ichor?

She was going to be stark naked again by the time she found her way back to Albert. That was just what this shitty adventure was missing.

At least the ground here wasn't very rocky… That was one small takeaway. But just what the hell was she supposed to do now? How was she supposed to find Albert if she didn't even know where the fucking *labyrinth* went?

She looked at the flashlight in her hand. It was still glowing, though it was difficult to tell the difference out here. She turned it off to save the battery, then tucked it into her shorts pocket. One less thing to worry about, she supposed.

The more she processed this odd change of scenery, the more hopelessly lost she felt. She might not have understood much of anything since she made the mistake of setting foot in the pervert's sleezy museum, but everything she *did* know was telling her this couldn't be real. There was no grass in the second temple. There was no *sun*. There weren't any insects that could be making all that noise.

The witch must have done this. God, she hated that little whore.

She stood up on her toes and stretched, trying to see over the grass, but it was too tall. There weren't any buildings or trees on either side for as far as she *could* see, nothing tall enough or close enough to stand above the weeds. Nothing but that blinding blue sky, as if the field went on forever. And yet the path she was standing on appeared to be manmade. It was a uniform width, flat, mostly barren, as if someone had come through and cleared it for the specific purpose of making a way through the grass. But it wasn't a road, precisely. It was too narrow for a vehicle. And there were no ruts worn into the earth to indicate tires.

There didn't seem to be anything to do except pick a direction and start walking. She certainly couldn't stay here, that sun would bake her if she didn't find some shade. She could already feel herself sweating. And she couldn't remember the last time she put on deodorant. Or sunscreen…

She muttered a curse under her breath and reached up to twirl a lock of her hair, that old thoughtful habit she'd carried with her since childhood. But her poor hair had gone stiff from

.y ichor. It felt revolting.

)isgusted, muttering more curses at her lousy luck, she started walking.

She looked down at her mismatched feet. Wearing only one shoe felt weird. It was uncomfortable. When Albert lost his shoe, he just tossed the other one away without taking time to think about it. But that was in the temple, where the floors were smooth and flat. She couldn't decide if she should do the same or keep it on so that at least one foot would stay protected from any sharp rocks or thistles or other hazards on this rough dirt path. Like this, she could at least limp across any rough terrain.

But it *felt* downright silly.

She tried to think of what Albert would say about this situation. He'd have some sort of rational deduction about it, she was sure. But she couldn't think of what it might be. To her, the closest thing she'd seen was that ruined alternate reality place they kept finding themselves in back in the hotel, the one with the blood-red sky and the baren landscape. Except this was sort of the opposite. Instead of being sent from a world of summer heat and beautiful sunshine to some kind of apocalyptic nightmare, she was sent from a world of utter darkness to a blazing summer field.

Was this just the way it was here? They entered the first temple through the city sewers and exited into the Wood. Maybe since they entered this one from the Wood, it exited back into their world? That would make a certain sort of sense, she supposed. Maybe… But if that were the case, then what was she supposed to do? The first temple opened onto the burning mountain. If there were any mountains here, they were too far away for her to see from this path. Maybe this was like the long passage they had to follow after Nicole ignited the fire in the tower room. Maybe she just had to follow the path.

Yeah, that felt like the sort of reasoning Albert would probably come up with if he were here.

If he were here… Her heart ached at the thought of him out there somewhere, probably at the mercy of that slutty witch. She couldn't even reach out to him without being attacked again.

She'd definitely changed her mind about the pervert's offer. If given the chance, she'd gladly hand that bitch a one-way ticket to hell.

But there was nothing she could do about it right now. There was nothing she could do about *anything* from here. All she could do was trudge onward, limping along in her one remaining shoe, seething with hatred for that nasty little witch and aching for the feel of her husband's arms around her again.

Chapter 7

Erin descended the stone steps, deeper and deeper into the mysterious vault, one hand crossed over her bare chest, the other clinging to her cell phone as it illuminated the path before her.

How far down had she gone? It felt as if she'd been on these damned stairs for at least an hour. Her legs were beginning to ache.

Every now and then, she'd shine her light back the way she came, paranoid that someone was going to see her. She was stark naked, after all. A part of her couldn't stop imagining that some creeper could have seen her wandering through the woods and followed her here, that he was even now watching her every move from the cover of the perpetual darkness that had been chasing her this whole time.

Why did she have to be naked? What purpose did it serve? A strange part of her mind seemed to *almost* remember something about traveling naked through a stone structure. Something about the ever-shifting nature of those spaces…and the stubbornness of the human brain getting in the way of something… But the thought was as alien as that freaky faceless statue that demanded her clothes. It didn't feel like her *own* thought at all, as if it came from somewhere else entirely.

Not for the first time since she drove past Crump's city limit sign, she wondered if it might be possible that she'd merely gone crazy. Wasn't it a much simpler explanation that she'd suffered some strange, mental breakdown rather than actually encountered an antlered monster in a freaky dark space at the back of a mysterious bar that supposedly existed on the fringe between the worlds of the living and the dead? Much less the part where she was sent on an otherworldly quest to retrieve an ancient, mystical key at the cost of her very life? One of those things just seemed considerably less likely than the other. But then, if she were merely out of her mind and hallucinating all this stuff…then where was she right now? Was she locked up in some padded room somewhere, heavily medicated, drooling onto her straitjacket? Or would the real her still be wandering free out there somewhere, perhaps imagining these seemingly endless stone steps while tromping down the up escalator at a crowded mall in her birthday suit?

There was a deeply unpleasant thought…

And yet somewhere deep down, she *knew* that what she was seeing right now was the truth. Strange as it all was, this was the reality of the universe.

But this certainty had barely crossed her mind when she stopped, confused. Not for the first time, she felt an overwhelming sensation of being somewhere else right now, surrounded by the same smooth, gray stone, but in a flat corridor rather than on stairs. She was holding her cell phone, letting its flashlight illuminate the way downward, and yet at the same time her hands were empty; she was guiding herself through the darkness by sliding her hand along the stone and her bare feet along the smooth surface of the floor. She was both naked and wearing a fancy dress.

(*Hurry!*)

There was something desperately important that she had to do, both here *and* there.

(*Have to find it…*)

She continued downward, an unpleasant chill washing over her. Why did she feel so unsettled about all this? Was it because of what Horatio said about her impending demise? Was it going to happen today? Down here in this darkness?

No… That didn't seem right. There was still something she was supposed to do *after* this.

(*We have this little tradition in our family for weddings. We give these to the bridesmaids on the special day. It's a sort of good luck charm.*)

She frowned at these words as they flickered through her mind and then faded away again.

"What is happening to me?" she whispered into the eerie silence.

When she drove away from the Elysium Fog that day, Horatio's instructions still fresh in her befuddled brain, she thought she knew where to find the thorn. She hadn't yet realized that the antlered weirdo didn't give her all of the information, that he expected her to spend a year fumbling around before she located it. But she *did* know what she was supposed to do with it. Her job was to protect it, to keep it safe from anyone or anything that might want to sabotage the Keeper's cycle. And then, when the time was right, the thorn's true owner would be revealed. (For some reason, she always pictured a wedding whenever she thought of it. Did it belong to some future bride?) Her job wouldn't be done until she passed it along.

And then she was supposed to die.

It seemed like a shit deal, if you asked her. And she wasn't looking forward to finding out how that part was going to go down. But it was getting to the point where almost anything would be better than all those frightful things she'd been seeing and hearing this past year.

Ahead of her, the bottom of the steps finally emerged from the stubborn darkness. A larger space awaited her down there. And while her burning muscles were grateful to see a level surface again, her stomach tightened with uneasy anticipation. Was this what she'd spent the past two years searching for? Was this where the thorn was hiding?

She paused on the final step and shined her light into the pitch-black passage stretched out before her. The surfaces were all the same gray stone, but for some reason, the floor was covered in perfectly still, murky water.

The sight made her skin crawl. She was expected to go in there? *Naked?* A shiver of revulsion passed through her at the thought. How deep was it? What sorts of things could be living in there?

But there was no other way to go but back.

She stood there a moment, refusing to continue. Was it worth it? Why was she even doing all this? It wasn't as if there were some grand reward in it for her. The only thing she'd been promised for all this unpleasantness was an early death. And yet she just kept going. She told herself it was because of the scary things she was beginning to see, a mounting fear of it getting worse, but was any of this her choice at all? Looking back on it all now, it felt more like a compulsion. It was as if someone had planted the idea in her head that she had no choice but to accept what was happening.

Was it possible that Horatio did something to her? Did he brainwash her somehow? Was he tricking her? Was she being used?

She shined her light back up the steps, nearly convinced that she should retreat and run as far away from this place as possible before she could sink any deeper in this mess.

Except...then what?

She didn't understand any of this. Her world wasn't perfect by any means. She didn't have a family to go home to. She'd made a great many acquaintances but not friends. She didn't stay in one place long enough. And she certainly never had anyone she could take with her. She'd never felt cut out for a long-term relationship, never really thought about being a mother or growing old with anyone. But this was the life she chose. Maybe when she was older, she'd crave something different, but for now, she was *happy*. She was exactly who she wanted to be. She was young and she was free and in control of her own life.

Or so she thought.

But did she have any kind of control at all?

If she climbed those stairs again right now, reclaimed her clothes and crawled back out into that sweltering forest, what would be waiting out there?

She could circle around that freaky cemetery, make her way back to the sawmill, get back behind the wheel of her Corolla and drive away. She could ignore Horatio and all those awful things she'd been seeing. And she could *keep* stubbornly ignoring them, regardless of what came at her. For the rest of her life if need be.

But what sort of life would that be?

This was all so damned confusing.

Again, she shined her light into that murky water. This was a threshold, she somehow realized. This was the point where she either plunged onward or ran away. A decision that might affect not just the rest of her life, but also whatever came after…

She closed her eyes and took a breath. She cleared her head.

Again, that strange sensation of being somewhere else came over her. She stood in a darkness that wouldn't go away when she opened her eyes. She was still barefoot but no longer naked. She had something to do…something to find. Not the thorn, but something else, something she was having trouble remembering. Something she wouldn't have to worry about until later. Except it was *already* later? And all of *this*… Breastbroke…the haunted cemetery…the giant's palm and the faceless statue…and of course the flooded passage… It all felt so strangely *distant*…as if it all happened a long, long time ago…

"What do I do?"

The words sounded strange somehow, almost alien. She frowned at the question, confused, as if she weren't the one who asked it. "Just keep going," she replied, though she didn't know why she was saying this. She didn't have the answer. That was why she asked the question.

And yet at the same time…

She remembered that feeling. Like she was going mad. Like the entire world had turned upside down and inside out and she was caught in the middle of it all, stumbling and tumbling and trying to find her feet. She remembered standing at that threshold, teetering on the point of no return, needing to know if she was doing the right thing. But there was no one to tell her the answer. Not there. Not then.

"Just keep going," she said again. "Face your fears. Cross the water. Find the thorn. One thing leads to another."

"But he said I'm going to die."

"Not today. Not for a while."

"Still…"

"Death isn't the end." It felt so strange, talking like this, both to herself and to another, in both the present and the past, the words passing from her lips and into her memory. "It's only the beginning. The truth of it all is waiting for you."

"I'm afraid."

"Everything will be okay. I promise."

She opened her eyes and stared down at the murky water. "I promise," she said again, her head churning with conflicting thoughts.

What was that just now? For a moment, she was some other place…some other *time*…far away from both here and now…

Everything would be okay.

She reached down with her foot and dipped her toe into the water. It was cold. The feel of it against her bare skin made her gasp. But it was only a couple inches deep.

She stepped all the way down, submerging one foot, then the other. The stone floor was the same as the steps, but had a strange, almost mossy sort of feel against her bare soles. A layer of settled silt? Or perhaps some kind of algae? It wasn't pleasant, but it could be much worse. If she'd let it, her imagination could have run wild with any number of horrifying scenarios.

(Everything will be okay. I promise.)

She gathered her resolve and set off down the flooded passage, unaware of just how *not okay* everything would soon become.

Chapter 8

Before you go, I have something to give you. A gift from me.

The Sentinel Queen's words that night remained branded into Wayne's memory, as did the feel of her alien hand as her far-too-long fingers closed around that part of him. He remembered feeling frozen in place, his body seemingly reacting of its own accord. He was mortified to discover that he was rock hard, practically throbbing as those freakishly long fingers stroked him. He didn't want to be touched like that. Not by *anyone* much less *her*. It felt wrong. *She* felt wrong. She wasn't even *human*. And yet he was unable to fight her, unable to even utter an objection. He'd never felt so helpless in all his life.

He remembered everything going fuzzy and distant as he was gently lowered to the earthen floor of that awful tunnel, his mind flooding with images of women he'd known, confusing him, distracting him as she lowered herself onto him, taking what she wanted without his consent.

When he awoke later, he was alone and dazed and *wet* and *unclean*. He felt violated. He was angry and confused.

And for what?

When he returned to the City of the Blind later that night and confronted her again, she confessed to manipulating his mind. She possessed some sort of strange power of seduction, able to fill anyone who laid eyes on her with involuntary arousal. Something about her purpose as "the Mother" and her duty to look after the Temple of the Blind.

I did what I did to put myself with child, she explained in that strange, psychic voice that spoke inside his head instead of to his ears. *I intended to birth a new breed of children, a new race of keepers for the Temple of the Blind, with you as their father.*

Now, as he stood here in this strange room within these bizarre, translucent-white walls, her haunting words flooded back to him as vividly as the night she spoke to him.

I succeeded in becoming pregnant, but still I failed. I can feel my deathwatch ticking. I will be dead within hours, alongside my last son, and with me will die your child. I've begun a life I cannot complete and I am deeply ashamed.

His child. Inside her. Like him, she never had a choice. She never had a chance to live.

Or so he thought.

Beside him, Olivia squeezed his arm and crowded closer to him. "She called you 'daddy,'" she whispered.

The little girl sitting on the bed was still smiling that bright smile at him. She *did* call him "daddy." But…how was that possible? He'd only been intimate with three women in his entire life. He was still with Olivia and he would've heard about it if Gail had become pregnant. Dunnen was a small town. Things like that tended to get out. The only child he'd ever come close to having was the one conceived within the belly of the Sentinel Queen that night. But the Sentinel Queen was dead the very same day as that encounter. She said herself that she'd run out of time. And Albert, Brandy and Olivia all claimed to have felt the exact instant of her passing with their psychic abilities, a strange and sudden sort of lonesome feeling that struck them all at the same moment. She didn't live long enough to have given birth. And even if she had, this child was older than that one would have been.

"I don't understand," he said.

"Don't you?" asked the little girl.

"Am I supposed to?" He wasn't being sarcastic or facetious. It was an honest question. *Should* he understand? Was he missing something? Because he simply didn't understand how she could be alive when her mother died long before she ever should have been born.

"You died the night I was conceived," she explained, "but the Keeper repaired your body and kept it functioning until your soul returned."

"…kept me alive…" he muttered to himself.

"You're not one of *those* rare gems," he recalled the scarecrow man telling him while marveling over his ability to return from the dead. "Your body is mortal. It heals only so much. Yours is a power of the soul, for sure. In order to come back, I'm betting you'll have to have a functioning vessel to return to."

Albert and the others explained it to him after he woke up, how the Keeper told them he repaired his body and kept his heart beating and his lungs working, allowing him to come back, not so unlike the way the doctors resuscitated him after the accident when he was just a boy.

"My mother couldn't be saved," she explained, her smile softening a little. "Her life was tied to her purpose within the stoneworks. But the Keeper was able to remove her body before the door was opened and keep it functioning long enough for me to be born."

He looked down at Olivia, but he could find no words. It seemed perfectly possible, when she explained it like that. If he could come back from the dead that night, why couldn't the same trick help the Sentinel Queen's unborn child to survive? And she *did* look like him. He couldn't stop seeing Wendy in her fair little features. But if this were all true, then…

"She's your daughter," sighed Olivia.

A daughter? Just like that, he was a father?

That couldn't be right. It was some kind of trick. This was a temple. Wasn't it far more likely that this was some sort of monster in disguise? A distraction? Or even a trap? Something to do with that "Priestess of Ruin" Andrea was talking about?

He shook his head. "That was five years ago," he told her. "You're too old to be her."

"Time works differently here," she explained. "And so does the aging process of the Faceless Ones. Even I don't know exactly how old I am. There's no concept of time inside the Keeper's Compendium."

"The what?" asked Olivia, confused.

"This place he gave me is a safe haven, sealed away from

the rest of the world, a fragment of a long-dead universe, frozen in time, preserved. The Compendium has a lot of things preserved. It's like his own private museum of bygone worlds."

"Wait..." said Olivia, confused. "If it's so safe, how did *we* get here?"

"Daddy's psychic bond to me opens a door. No one else could do it except the Keeper himself."

Wayne's head was already spinning. Compendiums and psychic links? He didn't understand anything. But she kept mentioning the Keeper. That ugly little creature who was responsible for everything, according to pretty much everyone who seemed to know anything. The same creep who kept putting him and Olivia in danger. He'd put them through so much already. Why *wouldn't* he throw a curveball like this at him, really? That it was "the Keeper's will" was probably the most believable part of the whole story.

"But none of that really matters." The little girl hopped off the edge of the bed and walked toward him. "I've been waiting my whole life for you to find me."

He had to resist the urge to take a step backward as she walked toward him. This was too sudden. Too *weird.* Was he supposed to just accept this without question?

"Your daughter..." Olivia said again, trying to wrap her own head around it.

"She doesn't look like a sentinel..." he observed. Her body wasn't disproportionately elongated like theirs. And she most definitely had a face. She had full lips, a perfect little nose and ears. She had *hair.* And unlike her wall-crawling brother down in the depths of the first temple, she even had *eyes.* They were brown, like his and his siblings'.

She reached out with her little hands as she approached him. There was something odd about the gesture, something slightly awkward. And the way those eyes didn't exactly seem to meet his...

"Wait..."

"She's *blind,*" whispered Olivia.

"I'm much more human than sentinel," she explained. "I

inherited most of my physical attributes from you. But while I *have* eyes, they don't work." She crossed the room and took hold of his hand. It was a smooth gesture. Careful, but accurate, without any searching. "But I also inherited some of my mother's psychic abilities. I don't need to see. And I was able to call out to you and bring you here with her inner voice."

The very voice he'd been hearing for some time… He stared down at those little hands clinging to his. She was a pretty little thing. And she just kept smiling that sweet smile. But there were so many *bad* things in this darkness…so many *scary* things. How could he be sure she was what she said she was?

"It's fine to be cautious," she assured him. "I'm your daughter, but I'm also a stranger in a strange world. But although this is the first time I've been able to hold your hand, it's not the first time we've met. We've been together many times. In your dreams."

"My dreams?" He remembered Nora's Lilac Grove, how the scenery was familiar, how images came flooding back from dreams he'd been having.

Was it only because she mentioned it, or did it feel like he'd held these little hands like this before?

"Have you really been here in this room this whole time?" asked Olivia, concerned. He knew exactly what she was thinking as she looked around. It was a fairly nice little room, for being somewhere in the depths of a temple. But it was hardly a place for a little girl.

"The Keeper gave me this place so I'd stay safe. He's provided me with everything I need. It gets lonely here, but it's necessary." She looked up at him with those distant, unseeing eyes. "Because he needed me to be here when you arrived. I'm supposed to show you the way."

"The way to what?" asked Wayne.

That sweet smile never faltering, she replied, "To the place where only the dead can go."

Chapter 9

Andrea felt the tips of those blades press against her throat and squeezed her eyes tighter. Would it hurt for long? She didn't want to hurt anymore. Was there pain in the Murk? Was there suffering? Was there fear? There was no heaven, she knew that. Not out here in the middle of the endless Wood, at least. Not beneath that poisoned sky. She'd already learned that awful truth. There were no spirit highways out here. All that awaited her was a lonesome and empty eternity.

As she hung there, waiting for the inevitable end, an image materialized in her mind. A great, coiled shape in the darkness. She wasn't sure what made her think of it, but it reminded her of a snake.

She didn't like snakes. That wasn't what she wanted to see in her last moments of life.

But the image was persistent. It grew clearer and clearer. An unmistakable serpent emerging within her mind. She could see the individual scales glinting even in the darkness, a faintly iridescent sheen sliding over them.

A head rose up from the center of those coils, enormous yellow eyes staring back at her, as clear as if she were looking at them in broad daylight.

Was this giant snake *Tia*? Was this her true form? A fitting shape for a sneaky, deceitful bitch. Or was this merely some kind of metaphor for the betrayal that was waiting for her from the start?

Real or imagined, that terrible serpent opened its mouth with a chilling hiss, its gleaming fangs dripping venom.

"Goodbye," said Tia.

The snake's enormous head lashed forward with incredible speed, straight at Andrea's unprotected face, fangs flashing in the darkness. Startled so badly by this vivid vision, she screamed and opened her eyes.

Tia was still standing there, those awful blades still pressed to her throat, her own eyes wide open.

Andrea hung there, helpless and confused, her body trembling with fear. Was that some sort of manifestation of her fear? Her brain's way of making one last effort to kickstart her fight or flight response, pointless as it may be strung up in these chains? She supposed it wasn't entirely surprising, considering some of the weird things her brain came up with when she was facing something cripplingly terrifying.

Except…why was her startled surprise mirrored on Tia's face?

"That snake…" she whispered.

Andrea frowned. Was she able to read her mind? How did she see something she imagined? *Was* it her imagination? She didn't know a lot about this weird world beyond her own reality, but she was fairly sure there wasn't an actual giant snake coiled up in front of her. Unless the snake and this Tia woman were one and the same, of course. Unless she was a *literal* serpent.

Why was she imagining snakes?

She was *terrified* of snakes.

And why did her imagining snakes make this madwoman stay her hand when she was determined to murder her?

Tia chuckled. Then she *laughed.* The sound of it seemed to expand like a balloon, transforming into something crazed, her lips spreading into a smile that was strangely *mad.* She reached up with a hand that was again perfectly human and ran it through her hair in that too-familiar gesture even as her face twisted into something barely recognizable.

Andrea stared at her, confused. What was happening right now? Had she missed something? Why was the self-proclaimed chaos goddess going bonkers?

The chains holding her suddenly dissolved again, dropping her with another startled shriek.

"Ow…" she groaned as she rose to her feet, wincing at the fresh scrapes on her skin. "Can you stop that?"

"What are you up to…?" muttered Tia, ignoring her.

"What are you talking about?"

She turned those wild eyes on her, that unsavory grin still pulling at the corners of her mouth. "Could it really be?" she wondered.

"Be *what*? You're not making any sense."

"It *could* be that…" she seemed to decide. "If so… Oh, that would be *so* much fun!" she squealed, ignoring her.

"Seriously, what's gotten into you?"

Tia's gaze shifted off into the distance again, that mad expression unwavering. "The Murk Serpent…" she breathed in an unsettling sort of mad giggle.

Andrea didn't like those words. "Murk" had brought her nothing but anxiety since Horatio first said the word to her. And she simply didn't want anything to do with "serpents" under *any* circumstances. Those two things didn't belong together in the same breath, in her opinion.

"If he's waking the guardians…" she muttered to herself, her face twisted into a strange mix of conflicted emotions. She turned and walked a few steps away. "A trick? He's a clever little shit. But would he go that far just to throw me off?" She turned around again and shook her head, those messy curls bouncing over her bare shoulders. "No. That's too much of a gamble for him. There's no *other* reason… Nothing else would make sense. And yet…"

"Are you on something right now?"

But Tia only let out a surprising squeal and started jumping up and down. It was a surprisingly childish display. And somewhat obscene, the way her boobs bounced around when she did it.

She *really* didn't understand why they were naked.

"This changes *everything*!" breathed Tia, a great, almost *insane* grin spreading across her freckled face. She looked almost *perverse*, as if she were getting off on whatever this was she was blathering on about. Then, without warning, she snapped her attention back to Andrea, her gaze piercing, making her take a step backward in surprise. "I've changed my mind," she decided. "I won't kill you. I want to see how this turns out."

"How *what* turns out?"

But Tia didn't answer her. Instead, she lunged forward and grabbed her, startling a surprised scream from her. But instead of plunging those deadly knife fingers into her throat, she *hugged her.*

It was a strange feeling, not merely because their naked bodies were suddenly pressed together in an unnecessarily intimate manner, but because this woman was ready to literally *murder* her only a moment ago. Her entire personality seemed to have inverted itself without warning. And it wasn't a quick hug, either. It went on for an uncomfortably long time.

"I'm starting to think you need some *serious* therapy," she grunted.

Finally, Tia let go and Andrea breathed a sigh of relief to finally be free.

"Take this," said Tia, grabbing her hand and pressing something into her palm.

When she looked down, she saw that she was holding Stella's favorite ring, the one with the white stone that she always wore.

"Call it an apology if you want. Or compensation if you'd rather. I don't really care. Either way, you can think of it as a good luck charm. It's special. And *irreplaceable*, so don't lose it."

"Okay…" she said, staring down at it. It was kind of strange seeing it there. It was the first time she'd ever seen it without her. A good luck charm? Not that she couldn't use one after the week she'd had…but could she trust anything this woman said anymore?

Then, with a frightful bark of a laugh, Tia grabbed her wrist and yanked her forward.

She let out a startled yelp and stumbled. In an instant, everything had changed again. A familiar pitch darkness had enveloped her. She was blind. And there was smooth, cool stone beneath her bare feet. She stumbled forward, still clutching the ring she was given in one clenched fist, confused.

She couldn't remember Tia letting go of her wrist. It felt like she'd missed something there. Did she black out for a second?

No… It was just that bizarre way that all the weird things out there—and Tia was definitely the weirdest of them all—moved around. She wasn't going to understand it. She might as well not even try. "Where am I now?" she asked instead. She reached out with her hands and found the flat, smooth surface of a wall right beside her.

Was she back in the labyrinth again?

"Go down," said Tia, her voice seeming to come from multiple directions at once. "All the way to the bottom."

"Now you're *helping* me?" Her head was spinning. Make her way downward? Like, to the very lowest levels of the temple? Was that where the exit was?

"Oh, I wouldn't call it *helping*, sweetie." She was suddenly right in her face again, an ominous, looming presence in the dark that was as familiar as her obnoxious laugh but at the same time not even remotely human. "I'm still going to make sure no one opens that door." She pushed her up against the wall, mashing those obscene breasts against her. "It's only the *killing you* part I've changed my mind about. *You*, I can see now, are going to be *much* more fun alive than dead. At least for now." Then, bewilderingly, she kissed her.

It wasn't a peck on the cheek, either. She mashed her lips right up against hers and shoved her tongue all the way into her mouth.

Andrea tried to scream, but it was difficult with her mouth full of batshit crazy chaos goddess. All she could manage was a very startled and revolted mumble.

Then, just as quickly, Tia backed away again.

"Oh my god!" cried Andrea, wiping at her mouth, disgusted. "Stay away from me!"

"I'm going to keep fucking up the Keeper's plans as long as possible. The next universe is going to belong to *me*."

"*Gross*! Where'd you learn to kiss? *Obedience school*?"

Tia let out one of her loud and painfully *familiar* Stella laughs. It echoed strangely, as if she were moving around.

"I can't even see! Where's my flashlight?"

But she didn't respond. Everything had gone silent.

Andrea turned around, her arms out, feeling the space around her. "Hey! This isn't funny! I don't know where I am!"

But somehow she already knew that Tia would be of no more help. She'd already vanished.

She was alone again.

"You're such a spaz," she sighed, still confused. Then she frowned. "Hey! What about my clothes?"

Chapter 10

Gina cried out and sat up in bed, her heart racing, her hands clasped over her mouth. Something had her. Not just some foul, squelchy, corpse-fleshed thing slithering under her clothes or wrapping itself around her thigh, but something far worse. Something with *teeth*. She felt them clamping down on her, piercing her. There was real, tearing pain in her belly. Something was ripping her open. She was being eaten alive!

The pain wasn't real. She knew in an instant that it was only a nightmare, one she'd had many times before. But it was already too late. Caught in the horror of the dream, her fear took over, wrenching screams from her before she had time to wake up.

Her eyes flashed to the corner of the room, to the shadowy, writhing shape clinging to the ceiling there. It would have looked almost human, with arms and legs and even a face, if humans could be crumpled up into a ball like that and cling to the wall with freakishly long, dislocated fingers and toes. It stared back at her with soulless black eyes from the middle of a strangely warped face. It was always there when she awoke from that particular dream. It caused it somehow.

She'd read about mythical beings called mares—the origin for the very word "nightmare"—who instilled horrifying dreams in their victims and fed off their fear. She wasn't sure if that was a real thing or mere superstition, but this thing seemed very similar to those stories.

Either there were many of these things out there or, far more likely, she supposed, this one had been following her for a considerable portion of her life. She'd lost count of all the times she'd awakened to its presence. Always in the corner across from her on the left, always staring at her with those empty black eyes. Even when she moved into a new apartment, it was always able to find her again, always perched in the same place, staring at her from the same perspective.

It wouldn't harm her, she knew. Experience had taught her that by the time she awoke, it was done with her. It would fade away on its own and leave her be for a while. Months or even years might go by before she saw it again.

Much more concerning was the fact that she'd done it again. She'd woke up screaming.

Already, she could hear footsteps.

She woke them up.

They were going to be mad.

She pulled up the blanket and covered her face as the door flew open. She could almost hear Janie's shrill voice telling her what a freakshow she was. Or Jessie hissing at her in that obnoxious stage whisper she used so that her mother wouldn't hear her telling her she should just kill herself already if she couldn't be fucking normal for one night.

But no one shouted at her.

In an instant, someone was beside her, *hugging* her, of all things.

"Are you okay?" worried Piper. "What happened?"

"What's going on?" shouted Seph. She was standing in the doorway, holding one of her aluminum painting easels out in front of her as if it were a dwarven war ax. She was wearing one of her oversized, threadbare tee shirts she slept in and little else, her raven-black hair a mess, her glasses on crooked. "Did you see something? Where is it?"

Gina blinked at them from behind her blanket, bewildered. She'd only just moved into this apartment a few days ago. After losing the job at Vertical Design, she couldn't afford to keep hers. Seph and Piper were nice enough to let her move in with them. They upgraded to a three-bedroom unit in the same building they were already living in and split the rent and utilities three ways so that she only needed a part-time job to pay her share. But she'd been dreading this exact situation. It was only a matter of time before her freak side made an appearance. Then they'd see how much trouble she was to have around.

Seph scanned the room, but didn't see anything to warrant a panic, so she rushed to the window and peered through the curtains at the street beyond. "Where'd it go?"

If anyone else could actually see what frightened her, it was Seph. She had a very rare gift. Like her, she was able to see things very few others could. If she hadn't noticed the thing in the corner…

Sure enough, when she glanced back at it, it was already gone, vanished back into the unknown from which it came. It was odd… It always felt as if her ability to see those things had attracted them to her, and yet it almost seemed as if they made themselves scarce when Seph was around, as if they were for some reason avoiding her. But she couldn't fathom why they'd act afraid of her…

"Did something happen?" pressed Piper. She, too, had been jostled from her bed, still in her bright pink matching pajamas, her blonde hair tied back in girlish pigtails.

"No," she muttered, embarrassed by all the fuss. "Nothing. A bad dream. I'm sorry."

"You sure?" asked Seph. She'd lowered the easel but was still peering out the window, suspicious. "You can tell us if you saw something."

"That's right," agreed Piper.

She nodded. They were both so kind to her. It was rather awkward. She wasn't used to people treating her so well. But it wasn't as if they had any reason to doubt her. Unlike her stepfamily back in Indiana, these two *knew* there were real monsters lurking out there. They'd seen their own share of nightmare-inducing things. Deceitful demons. Undead zombies. Relentless mall wraiths. They knew she didn't have to make things up. "It happens sometimes. I'm sorry. I didn't mean to wake you."

"There's nothing to be sorry about," Piper assured her.

"That's right," agreed Seph. She straightened her glasses and looked around the room, still making sure they were alone. "Don't hesitate to tell us if you ever think you see something."

Again, she nodded. "I've always had night terrors. As far back as I can remember. Not as much now as when I was little, but it still happens. I can be…difficult to live with."

"That's bullshit," Seph informed her. "You're not difficult."

"That's right," agreed Piper. "You can't help it. You see all that creepy stuff all the time. We get it."

"I know all about seeing creepy stuff," Seph reminded her.

"Or *hearing* creepy stuff," Piper added.

"That too," said Seph.

"We're here for you. If you ever have a nightmare, you can come to my room. You can sleep with me if you need to."

"She's not a *child*, Pips."

"I *know* that! But sometimes you need to not be alone! Doesn't matter how old you are." She wrinkled her nose at her. "And put some pants on, Persephone."

"I'm covered up just fine! Not everyone can stomach going to bed looking like a freaking *care bear*."

Gina smiled a little behind her blanket. She liked these two. They were nicer to her than anyone else had ever been. And it wasn't simply because they believed in the things she could see. They were good people.

But how much could they really take? How long before being awakened in the middle of the night by their weird roommate became too much to bear? How long before they began resenting her?

How long before they hated her?

She closed her eyes and forced back the tears, refusing to let them be seen. She didn't want them to push her away. She didn't want to be left all alone again.

Except…they never pushed her away.

She didn't move in a few days ago. She moved in *three years* ago. Her nightmares had been far fewer than in the past and they'd treated her the same each time. Hugs. Assurances. A quick search to insure she was safe. They believed her wholeheartedly and they genuinely worried over her.

She loved them. They were the closest thing to a *real* family she'd ever had.

She opened her eyes and blinked up at the stone ceiling.

Right… She was in the glass labyrinth, far away from home. Deep inside what Albert had dubbed the "Temple of the Three Whispers." Beneath the false streets of the City Beyond Memory.

She could feel the passageways tangled up all around her again in that strange, knotted way. And she could see again. The space around her was illuminated by Nicole's flashlight. She was still with her, still holding her hand.

The last time she awoke, she was trapped in the in-between space, with no idea how to get out, unable to move or see or even sense these broken surroundings. But now they were on the other side of the mirrors. They'd made it through. They'd survived the journey. And even better, it seemed as if they were safe. She sensed no danger in their immediate vicinity. That first time, she must have simply become aware too early. She found herself between the two sides, caught in a state of transition. Perhaps her fear of losing Nicole had affected her, causing her to become aware of that strange, transitional space.

She could guess about such things all she wanted, but she had no way of knowing anything. And she seriously doubted anyone would ever be able to explain it to her. The important thing was that they'd reached whatever was beyond the mirrors and Nicole was still by her side.

She sat up, relieved, and wiped at her face. There were cold tears on her cheeks, all the way down to her ears. So many emotional memories. Was that a product of the glass labyrinth's bizarre mirrors, too, or only her own traumatized mind at work? It was difficult to be sure.

But it was over now.

Everything was fine.

She sniffled and leaned over Nicole. "We made it," she said, giving her a gentle shake. "I think it's okay now."

Except everything wasn't okay at all.

"Nicole?"

Again, she gave her a shake, more firmly this time.

But no matter what she did, Nicole wouldn't wake up.

Chapter 11

"Snap out of it."

Nicole blinked hard and wiped at her face. Keith?

She straightened up, confused, and looked around. That wasn't her imagination. She was sure of it. That was clearly Keith's voice just now. But there was no one there. She was still alone. She even glanced up at the doors overhead, half-expecting to see one of them standing open, a painfully familiar face peering down at her…

"You're not giving up on me again, are you?"

That was absolutely Keith's voice! But where was it coming from? She couldn't seem to track it for some reason. She turned all the way around, searching, her gaze darting to every rubbish bin, every garbage bag, every cardboard box, trying to spot someone hiding behind one of them. "Who's there?" she demanded.

What was happening here? She didn't understand. It couldn't really be Keith. Keith was *gone*. She'd gotten him killed. He wasn't ever coming back. This was something else. Some kind of trick. It had to be.

But when she turned around again, she saw someone disappearing into another alley. The sight made her heart leap. She felt such an overwhelming surge in her chest that it left her dizzy. Her thoughts drifted back to that morning five years ago, when the five of them stumbled out of that spirit tunnel and found Wayne lying there on the ground, his wound all patched up and very much alive.

Had it happened again? Had someone snatched him from death's grasp the moment she walked away? Had he miraculously returned to her? A drunken sort of haze washed over her at the thought, and she stumbled after him, desperate to see him, to hold him. She needed to tell him again how sorry she was, that she never gave up on him and never would.

But was that really him? She had only that one brief glimpse. It was impossible to have seen whoever it was with any certainty, yet a part of her was utterly convinced that it couldn't have been anyone else. He was still missing his shirt, his arm still wrapped, looking just like he did when she left him in that miserable corridor.

She ran after him, desperate to confirm it, but when she reached the alley where she glimpsed him, he was again nowhere to be seen.

She hurried forward, refusing to give up. He definitely went this way. He was *just* here. She saw him!

Unless she didn't…unless she was only imagining that she saw what she thought she saw…what she *wanted with all her heart* to see…

Some part of her knew this was madness. Did she really think she was following Keith? He was *dead.* He was gone. Whoever this was she was trying so hard to catch up to, it wasn't him. But she couldn't help herself. She wanted it so badly. She *needed* to find him. She owed him too much. She owed him her very *life.* And she had *so much* to apologize for.

She rushed around another corner and stopped, breathless. There was nothing more than the same endless, garbage-strewn concrete stretched in front of her.

But when she looked back the way she came, she again caught sight of someone just vanishing from sight.

That was definitely him! She was sure of it. His grown-out hair. His bare shoulders. His bloody shirt wrapped around his arm. She ran after him, pushing herself to go faster.

Where was he leading her? And why wouldn't he let her catch up? She wanted to see him up close again. She wanted to hug him again. She wanted to tell him how sorry she was for everything again.

When she reached the place where she glimpsed him, however, he was gone. There was no one in sight, dead or otherwise. Had she missed her chance? Was she too late? She rushed ahead to the next alley, but he wasn't there, either. Where did he go? Why couldn't she catch up to him? She looked back the way she came. Maybe she went too far. Maybe she passed him.

She stood there a moment, a mild panic welling up in her, trying to decide what to do. Should she rush down this way and see if he was in the next alleyway? Or should she keep going straight? Or did she go back and double-check? If she went the wrong way, she might lose him for good. But if she lingered here too long, she might also lose him.

A frightened combination of a gasp and a sob escaped her as she plunged forward, hoping she was making the right choice.

She felt like a little girl who'd found herself separated from her parents and lost on a crowded street. Except of course that there was no crowd here. Three was no one at all. She was utterly alone. Utterly *lost*. It was unsettling. And it was terrifying.

She called his name, shouted it, her voice echoing through the towering walls, but he wouldn't answer. Where did he go? Why wouldn't he let her catch up?

She reached the next alley, but he wasn't there, either.

She wiped at her eyes, frustrated. Seriously, how many times could she possibly fuck up? What was wrong with her? Why couldn't she get anything right?

Then she heard a noise break through the unnatural silence around her. It sounded like a door clicking closed. She turned and scanned the space around her, her heart leaping, unsure if she should be excited or concerned.

Her gaze landed on one of the upper doors, at the top of a rickety looking fire-escape. It looked exactly like all the others, metal, windowless, but *unlike* the others, it had a handle.

She didn't think about it. She couldn't. If she thought about it, she'd no doubt realize how insane all this was and *then* what would she do? There was nowhere to go but to follow this one desperate hope. She hurried over and climbed the ladder, making her way up the three stories to where the door waited, ignoring the way the old metal groaned and rattled under her weight.

Was this where he went? Was he waiting for her inside? Or would she only find the door locked, as unopenable as all the others?

Why was everything so weird? Where was she? Was this another of Glum's tricks? It didn't feel the same as that dreary street, though. It didn't have the same feel to it, like the barely-there's queer version of her apartment. The sky above was a dull gray, but this place wasn't cold or dreary or dark or drizzling. It was just…sort of suffocatingly empty.

Maybe it was more like that nightmare hospital? That maze of hallways was like this. An endless, inescapable tangle of impossible corridors.

Why was everything *mazes*? What was up with that?

She stood in front of the door, her heart pounding. There was something wrong about all this, but she didn't know what else to do. She wouldn't get anywhere just wandering around.

She reached out and grasped the knob. It turned. The door creaked open. Her heart gave a hopeful sort of flutter in her breast. Something new at last!

Except everything inside was darkness.

Was this really where she needed to be?

"Keith?" she called, her voice echoing strangely. It was less like calling out inside a building than into some bottomless mineshaft.

She opened the door wider, trying to let more light in, trying to see what was there. She didn't want to go into the dark. The dark was frightening. Maybe she should stay out here.

But then Keith's voice drifted out from inside: "Hurry. Keep up."

"Where are you? I can't see you."

But he didn't answer her. She could only hear his footsteps inside. He was there, walking away from her, deeper into that darkness.

Desperate to find him, she steeled her nerves and stepped through the door, letting it close behind her.

Everything went black.

"Oh shit…" she hissed as she found herself creeping forward, utterly blind. This was stupid. Something bad was going to happen to her. And she had no one but herself to blame.

What happened to her flashlight? She had one before. In fact, it was Keith's. Did he take it back?

No… She remembered now. Gina was holding it. She asked for it. Something about navigating the stone and the glass. She didn't ask any questions because she wouldn't understand anyway.

"Don't stop," warned Keith.

She snapped to attention, her eyes darting blindly through the darkness. Which direction did that come from? Where was he?

"It's not safe here."

A little to the left? She took two steps, then stopped again. She couldn't see a thing!

Didn't she have her phone? Keith returned it to her along with her clothes after he rescued her from the meadow. It was in her pocket.

But of course her pockets were empty. She'd already checked.

She crept forward, her hands out in front of her, feeling her way deeper into the darkness. She hadn't bothered even looking for a light switch. Somehow, she very much doubted there was one. There weren't any in Glimmering Sunrise Place. Why would there be? Those places weren't real. Even the light wasn't real.

Where was she? She hadn't encountered any walls or furniture. The space in front of her had been completely empty, as if she were walking through some vast, empty room. There was nothing but the floor, hard and cold and flat, like concrete. A warehouse of some sort? But wasn't she on the third floor? How many levels did empty buildings like warehouses usually have? And how easy would it be in the dark like this to simply walk off a ledge?

Keith even warned her that it wasn't safe here. What did he mean by that? Why wasn't it safe? What dangers was she stumbling into this time?

"Keith?" she tried. "Where are you?"

But Keith didn't answer her.

Where was he leading her? And why wouldn't he wait for her? Maybe he was mad at her. No one would blame him. She squeezed her eyes closed in the oppressive darkness. She felt weirdly disoriented, almost nauseous. That hazy, confused sort of feeling was washing over her again.

No… Not again. She'd been feeling this way all along. She just didn't notice it for a while. Everything felt foggy and dream-like.

"Keith?" she called again. Then, in a softer voice, "You're scaring me."

"Am I?" he whispered into her ear.

She let out a startled cry and jumped back. "Keith?"

A horrible, icy feeling was suddenly creeping through her body.

He was standing right in front of her. She could *feel* him there…

Except that didn't feel like him at all. It felt like someone else. Someone bigger. Someone far more dangerous.

"Anun amum ut mu," sighed Keith, those familiar words filling her with such utter terror that she was instantly sick to her stomach.

"No…" she gasped, taking a step back. It couldn't be. Not again. "No!"

"Anun Goar Nangup."

Chapter 12

Albert dropped to his knees and retched.

What the hell was wrong with him? Why was his head filled with such awful thoughts?

It was bad enough seeing all that blood and horror, but why was he imagining that he was the one doing all those gruesome things? And why would he feel as if he were *enjoying* it? That was the worst part of it all, that feeling as if all those hideous deeds were giving him some sort of erotic pleasure. The very thought of it made him sick.

It was *her*. Dolly. Shanzer's twisted little slave. She was the one doing this to him. She was inside his head, affecting his brain. But he didn't know how to make it stop. How did you fight something that was in your mind?

"What a pathetic sight," she whispered.

He shot to his feet, his heart leaping. He couldn't let her get control of him again.

But when he turned around, she wasn't there. And everything had changed. He'd moved. He was standing at the top of a staircase he'd never seen before, looking down at a carpeted floor stained deep red with blood.

So much blood…

He took a step backward. He didn't want to go down there. He didn't want to see any more of whatever awful scene was waiting for him there.

Dainty arms reached around him again, shiny black nails glinting in the lamplight. He cried out, startled, but found that he couldn't move. His feet seemed to be stuck to the floor, his muscles rigid.

"Just like all the others…" He watched those black nails slide up and down his exposed belly, gentle, strangely intimate. It was entirely too much like Brandy did when they were snuggling in bed together, as if she knew exactly what she were doing, like a perverse imitation of her. "Why do they always fight it?" Those nails slid upward, past his belly to his chest. "You know you want it. *Everyone* wants it. Somewhere inside, whether they admit it or not, everyone's like me."

"Bullshit," he managed.

"That's what they *all* say…" Those nails traced their way around his nipples. Behind him, he felt her body press closer. Her probably poisonous lips brushed his bare skin, kissing him. "They all denied it. Every single one of them. But if that were true…" A shiver of revulsion raced through his paralyzed body as he felt her tongue slide up his spine. The sensation made him feel dizzy, not very unlike the way Brandy sometimes made him feel, but in an entirely different way. Not with pleasure, but with *disgust.* Much like the way certain smells could take you back to a moment in time, regardless of whether the smell was lovely or putrid. She licked him all the way up between his shoulder blades, to the nape of his neck, the sensation hot and cold at same time. Was it only his imagination, or was her tongue unnaturally long, like in that freakish delusion the bogey forced on him back in the Lucianna Mysteria? "If that were true…" she said again, "…then why are you always so easy to control?"

Everything went out of focus. For a moment, he felt himself falling, tumbling through a confusing kaleidoscope of blurred images and muted voices.

Then the nightmare began again.

Blood spattered across his face, hot and slick, the smell of it both overpowering and strangely exhilarating. His heart was pounding. Something about the sound of the blade plunging into soft flesh, shrill screams turning to desperate gasps. He could feel the strength slipping from those groping hands. He could see the life slowly fading from those wide, terrified eyes.

The thrill of it…

Sick…

Twisted…

Exquisite…

"No!" He squeezed his eyes shut, desperate to block out the horrible imagery. "Let me go!"

"You can stop pretending," she cooed at him, her lips brushing against his neck. "I know the *real* you."

"I'm nothing like that!" He was back where he was before, standing at the top of that staircase, looking down at the blood-soaked carpet below. This time, however, he could see someone lying down there. It was only a hand. The rest was thankfully out of view, but there were plenty of details for his deductive mind to take in. It was a woman's hand, small and delicate, with fancy nails and jewelry. There was something about that hand, something about the bracelet shining through the blood. It looked *familiar.* He could see that hand in his mind, clawing at him, trying to fight him off as he forced himself onto her. Flashes of faint memories danced through the back of his mind. A lock of auburn hair. Red lips parted in a terrified scream. A torn dress. Begging and screaming and sobbing.

"Your body says otherwise," whispered Dolly.

When did she reach those awful black claws into his shorts? Why was she touching him there? And why was his body *reacting* to her? There was nothing *arousing* about this woman. She was a literal monster. His skin crawled at this horrid woman's touch. No part of him should be enjoying this. He wanted to run away. He wanted to *vomit.* And yet he was still riveted to this spot, unable to move, unable to stop her and unable, it seemed, to make that wretched, betraying part of him stop encouraging her!

"*This* part of you remembers," she purred.

Remembers *what*? This bitch wasn't making any sense. She was crazy.

And yet, *did* he remember? The auburn-haired woman with the bracelet… Begging him to stop as he forced himself onto her…violating her in every horrible way he could imagine…

"That's not real!"

"Of course it is."

"It's not!"

"You think you know what's real?" she asked him. "Is *this* real?"

He uttered a startled gasp. What happened? Where was he? He looked down at his hands to find them covered in blood again. And on the floor at his feet lay another woman's motionless body. He staggered backward, away from it, but tripped over something. He landed hard on his back, only to find himself lying on a bed. Dolly was sitting naked astride him, her hips moving rhythmically. "*This*?" she panted.

"Get off me!" he grunted, horrified. He thrust his hands out to push her away, but in an instant he was back in that first bedroom, his hands clenched around the crazed woman's throat, strangling her. He tried to yank them back, but he couldn't. They seemed to be moving on their own. And it wasn't just the one woman. He found himself jumping from one place to another, a new victim choking in his monstrous grip with each disorienting transition, over and over again.

"What about this?" asked Dolly. Once again, *she* took her place being strangled by him, but unlike the others, she never screamed, never cried, never lost that deranged smile.

He tried again to wrench his hands free, but they wouldn't listen to him. In an instant she was no longer on her knees in front of him, but lying on her back. He was having his way with her, his body thrusting with such feral intensity that it felt as if he meant to break her small body in half.

"Do you want *this* to be real?"

"Get out of my head!"

He stood alone in the darkness, his body trembling, gasping for breath. It felt as if he'd just been through a marathon. He felt so tired he could barely stand.

"You can't make me leave," Dolly whispered into his ear.

He turned around, thrusting his hands out, trying to shove her away, but there was no one there.

"These aren't just random hallucinations."

Again, he twirled around, this time swinging his fist without realizing he'd advanced from merely pushing to punching. This was no mere woman, after all. Was she ever even human?

"I told you, these are my *precious memories*."

(*I wouldn't share this with just anyone.*)

Memories… She said something like that before, when she first showed herself in these nightmare delusions.

(*It's* you *who's in* my *mind now.*)

Did that mean all of these awful visions were *real*? Were all of these people her victims?

(*I can make her do anything I want. I can make* you *do anything I want. And there's nothing you can do to stop me.*)

"That girl is nothing like she appears to be," he recalled Lucianna warning them about her, way back when they first returned to the hotel. "She's an incredibly powerful witch. And she's immensely evil."

When did he move again? He turned around, still searching for the source of her mocking voice, only to find himself standing in a long corridor of mismatched doors. It seemed to go on forever.

Again, he couldn't move. His body was frozen.

And again, those dainty arms were wrapped around him, those gleaming black nails pressed against his belly.

"I've broken a *lot* of toys," she giggled. "I made them do such…*creative* things to each other."

(*She possesses powerful psychic abilities. She can manipulate people, force them to do whatever she pleases, turning them into helpless puppets.*)

"You're sick," he groaned.

"You all say that, but in the end, you always play with me. You always bend and pose just like I tell you to do. My pretty little dolls. Over and over and over again. Every single time."

(*Nothing about her is as it seems, not even her age. She's much older than she appears. And she's a raging sociopath with far too much blood on her hands to ever wash off.*)

Wait… Was there a separate atrocity behind each and every one of those doors? Were they literally doorways into this monster's past crimes? Was that why each one was different?

How many people had she murdered? How long had she been at it?

She was suddenly standing in front of him, those sharp,

black nails curled around his neck, her nose pressed against his. "You'll bend, too," she whispered. Then she kissed him. "Any way I want you to. You'll see."

Chapter 13

It was a matter of perception. This was the conclusion Corey came to as he drifted through the vastness of space, surrounded by a machine language literally written with the immensity of the stars.

The human mind was as amazing and versatile as it was limited in its ability to grasp the unexplainable truth of an environment far more complex than it was ever made to comprehend. It was a contradiction of itself. An oxymoron. The average human being couldn't do complex mathematical functions in his head, but the kind of processing that must go into the intense reality of even the most basic of *dreams* was not only astounding but literally done in his sleep. In the absence of understanding, the brain could fill in the gaps using nothing more than raw imagination.

This was no different. The proof was in all that he'd learned with Austin. They'd already established that things weren't as they appeared to be. He looked like a man, but was in reality an ancient piece of extremely advanced technology utilized by the sentinels in order to activate the Keeper's machine exactly as intended exactly when the time came. He wasn't really a machine dressed up to look and behave like a man. He was something far more complex than the human mind could never fully comprehend. He appeared as he did because of common context clues, expectations, and the adult mind's habit of ignoring things that didn't align with its core beliefs. Those weren't strings. Nor were they wires. They were much closer to what this place was. Lines of computer syntax made physical. And those spikes protruding from the wall in the corner of the room, the "contacts," he'd called them, were neither spikes nor contacts but *receivers*. They and Austin were like computers on opposite ends of a network, sending and receiving data, but on a monstrously complex scale, unfathomable by modern scientific understanding. And this was the information highway connecting them.

This place was the same as those bloody strings. Each star was raw data. Each constellation was a line of code, mapping not space, but function. A complex line of an ancient, alien computer language spelling out an incredible program that he couldn't begin to imagine.

Again, he opened his eyes and looked around. It looked so real. But it wasn't. This delusion of floating through space was a metaphor of his mind, a representation of the sheer scale of the sentinels' incredible machine, a machine the size of a major city across, multiplied by its labyrinthine interior that stretched endless miles both down into the earth and up into an impossible sky, then folded over on itself in countless narrow corridors and winding paths, and then multiplied *again* across unfathomable spans of time through countless lifespans of universes across all three planes of primary existence represented by the natural, the supernatural and the unnatural universes, all woven together in one place.

Of course he felt like a speck of dust floating through the endless expanse of deep space. This was a task that was simply too big. He couldn't imagine it. He was floundering in the void, lost and incapable of even perceiving a way out. The human mind was as adept at holding one back as it was of finding a way forward. But if he wanted to be of any help to Violet and the others, he was going to have to find a way to overwrite that particular part of it.

Perception. Imagination. Understanding. Like pieces of a jigsaw puzzle, they could paint a complex picture, but only if he found a way to piece them together. The first step in that process was going to be to *change* his perception into something he could actually imagine himself interacting with.

A different perspective. A different set of tools. A different *mindset.*

It was an almost laughable idea. Overwriting his own instincts, his brain's self-preserving hardwiring. But the indisputable fact was that he wouldn't be here if he couldn't do this. The sentinels wouldn't have bothered giving him the information if they didn't know he was capable of utilizing it.

This was the will of the sentinels. This was what they expected of him when they injected their knowledge into mankind's genetic code. It was the only reason he was able to understand all this madness. And more than anything, it meant that he was capable of doing this. Regardless of how impossible it might seem, he had everything he needed to succeed right there inside his brain.

He closed his eyes and cleared his head. He needed to push the concept of space out of his mind. Because there was no space. There were no stars. There wasn't even *him*. This was something far closer to digital than physical. Beneath this grand starscape lay something far different and much closer to the truth. This wasn't a place at all. That was why it presented itself as *space*.

This was the sentinels' equivalent of a massive computer program, infinite in its scope and extension, buzzing with the possibilities of innumerable dimensions waiting to burst into existence. His mind struggled to make sense of it, groping and grasping for any kind of recognition, jumping at imagined patterns, piecing together false perceptions in a desperate effort to find something familiar. He imagined phantom shapes and structures, patterns on the horizons and had to force them out of his mind lest he find himself back in that hopeless abyss, floating among impossible stars.

But it wasn't easy. His instincts fought him, struggling to take control, to lead him back to something familiar, even if it meant making something up. He was fighting with himself, struggling to break free of those old mindsets. It was surprisingly exhausting. He felt as if he were going around and around inside his head, circling like a plane with a malfunctioning landing gear, trying to find a solution before exhausting its fuel. Someone else would have already given up and let himself sink into this impossible void.

But he was stubborn. And more importantly, he was *curious.* He *wanted* to be here. He wanted to know more about this place, about the sentinels' machine, what it was, how it worked. And as he embraced this wanting, he found that something emerged from the syntax. Lines of code materialized as a stream of thought within his consciousness. And in that code he saw himself.

Because the sentinels knew he would be here one day to receive their instructions.

He wasn't merely here as one of the Keeper's infinite backup plans. He was crucial to the design from the very beginning. He was the final variable in the sentinels' ancient equation.

And in this moment, that meant only one thing to him.

It meant that he was going to find a way to do this.

Chapter 14

"Left," warned Everett.

Violet swung her light to the left and saw it there, close to the floor, a shimmer of iridescent light sliding along one of those fine filaments. Not for the first time, she wondered if stepping on one of those would merely cut her or if they were actually sharp enough to slice off her toes. The thought was enough to send a shudder through her body. She knew she was going to miss her boots, but not *this* much.

"There's one directly above the wall in front of you."

She saw it, too. It was high enough that she should be able to climb up and slip under it without any trouble, but she needed to stay wary.

Why did they have to be so hard to see? She'd tried using her glass shard to see if it would make the dangerous things any easier to see, but it was no use. She still didn't understand how the shard worked, or what it was about the hidden places it showed her that it worked on, but so far it hadn't been much help here in this city of stone.

That chill inside her skin was still with her, a sharp contrast to the sweat that she felt gathering on her skin with all this climbing. And that deeply unpleasant murmur was still there, too, less heard than sensed, like the booming undertone of the base from a distant blaring speaker. It almost seemed that she could feel the vibrations of those creepy voices inside her *eyeballs* of all things.

She climbed up to the ledge, then paused to peer ahead. No filaments lying across the floor. None crisscrossing the opening above. Only the one above her head. Carefully, she pulled herself up and crawled forward, her eyes peeled.

Why did these things have to be so hard to see?

"Now you," she said.

Everett was already making his way upward. Couldn't he shove that doll down in one of those pockets or something? It looked so awkward packing her around like that. But then again, maybe she wouldn't like that. She supposed if she were the one giving them directions, she'd probably be a little miffed to just be stuffed into some sweaty shorts and left there.

"Careful," she warned, pressing down on the top of his head, making sure he didn't suddenly lift himself upward and directly into the dangerous thread.

(There was plenty of room, but those things were really freaking her out.)

"I'm good," he assured her. "Alice says we're getting closer to the top. I think she's showing me a kind of map. It's a little confusing, but this whole place gets narrower as we go up. There's several paths leading back into the labyrinth up here, but she still says the topmost one is what we want."

"Whatever she says." She was well aware that she set out into the world *looking* for all the weird things out there, but things had gotten a lot more complicated than she ever imagined. She was starting to pine for the days when *Corey* was the weirdest thing she knew.

The path in front of them was narrow, but it widened out after a bit, making it easier to move around.

"It's clear up ahead," reported Everett. "But don't get too close to the wall on the right."

She shined her light in that direction and saw that there were several shimmering strands stretched along the rough contours of the wall, making reaching the opening above it impossible. To the left, there was a gap and a path leading back down, which they'd already determined wasn't where they wanted to be. The only way to go from here was straight ahead.

She stopped as a hard shudder passed through her.

"I felt that, too," said Everett. He looked back the way they came. That not-quite-heard muddle of murmuring, whispering voices was swelling.

The graymother was getting closer. They needed to move faster. The wall in front of them was twelve feet high and not as rough as some of the others, making it more difficult to scale, but it was wide enough for them both to climb at the same time. She took the left side, giving him room, and gestured for him to climb beside her. The more they were able to stick together like this, rather than having to take turns, the better. There was a rough column of stone separating the ledge above them, but it was the same space beyond. When she shined her light up there, she saw it illuminating the walls on both sides. And there was no sign of those deadly strands.

She scurried up over the ledge and then crouched there, sweeping her light up and down, searching for any hidden threads blocking the way forward. There was a very vivid image in her head of standing up and having one of those silky strands bury itself in her skull and it was probably going to haunt her nightmares any time they weren't already preoccupied with revisiting that damned *coffin.*

She didn't see any of those webs, but she remained cautious. Just because she couldn't see them didn't mean they weren't there. They were practically invisible, especially when they were close to those stone surfaces.

She stood up, cautious, and crept past the column. Everett was already standing there, his head tilted to one side, probably listening to his creepy little girlfriend…

There was no opening for them to climb up from here. Instead, the path split. She shined her light into the left passage. It looked tight, but she shouldn't have any problem with it.

"Left or right?" she asked, hoping Everett's creepy little friend still knew the way.

"There's a taller shaft leading farther up over here," he said, pointing to the right. "Alice says it's the fastest—whoa!" He took a step away from her, startled.

"What happened?" she asked, starting to move toward him.

"Stop! Careful!"

Only now did she see it. Several of those barely visible filaments were stretched between the stone pilar and the wall, separating them. "Oh shit..." she gasped. An unpleasant tingle washed through her nerves at the thought of how close she came to walking right into it.

There was no room to pass safely between them.

Again, she lifted the glass shard and peered through it, hoping it would reveal some hidden opening she could slip through, but still it refused to show her anything useful.

It was her fault. It was her idea to climb together. She could see that there was a single space beyond the stone column, but not the razor-thin strands separating it into two spaces.

"We have to go back," she breathed, aiming her light down at the ledge they'd just climbed over.

"Not a good idea," replied Everett.

She didn't have to ask him why. She could see the filaments out there shimmering in her light. Each and every one of them was vibrating.

A strange, darkling shadow passed through the gloom below, like the outline of a massive shark just beneath the surface of the water.

The graymother was right down there, circling, crawling through those many holes, searching for the disturbances in its web.

"We're out of time," realized Everett. "We have to split up."

"Not happening!" she snapped at him. The last time he left her alone she ended up almost eaten by hounds, kidnapped by the Priestess of Ruin, brutally murdered in some kind of recurring dream reality and buried alive!

"Everything's connected here," he said. "We just keep going up, like Alice says, and we try to keep moving toward each other. Maybe it'll even confuse it, make us both harder to find."

"You don't even have a light!" she reminded him.

He stood there a moment, blinking back at her. He knew she was right. Without her, he'd be blind. But then his expression brightened. "But I have Alice!" he countered. "She'll tell me where to go."

"That's a ridiculous amount of faith you're putting in a literal haunted doll."

He beamed at her. "Yeah. I know."

"You're weird," she told him.

"Just go that way," he told her. "Keep moving up. I'll keep talking so you can hear me. There's, like, a *million* ways to go in here. We'll be back together in no time!"

"We better be," she told him.

A strange sensation flooded the space around her, one she couldn't properly describe. For some reason it made her think of subsonic sounds. Corey had talked about those before, theorizing that perhaps certain portals might be located using them. He hadn't gotten around to experimenting with it, but she knew that sounds below the range of human hearing, when blasted loud enough, couldn't be heard but could still be felt. Something about *this* feeling made her think of it. It was like a shiver passing through her extremities without any apparent cause, like a vibration passing through the air around her.

"Hurry!" he urged.

Reluctantly, she turned and rushed toward the passage on the left. She'd go through there, then up the first chance she found. Then back around to the right again.

But again, she stopped. "Shit!"

Everett was heading toward the passage on the right, but he stopped and looked back, concerned. "What's wrong?"

She swept her light back and forth. Just like the space between them, this passage was filled with shimmering, vibrating filaments.

She looked back at him, boiling fear filling her gut. "I'm trapped…"

Chapter 15

Brandy groaned. She was dripping with sweat. Her hair was plastered to her face. Her glasses were fogged. It was only getting hotter the longer she was out here in this field.

How long had she been walking? Nothing had changed. She still hadn't seen so much as a tree over that tall grass. There didn't seem to be any end to this sweltering path. Even the sun hadn't changed position in the sky, as far as she was able to discern.

She'd untied Albert's shirt and had it stretched between her raised arms, trying to shield herself as much as possible from the punishing sun, but she couldn't tell if it was helping. She was probably just going to end up getting her tits sunburned, too.

Why was everything so fucking *uncomfortable*?

She looked back the way she came, uncertain. Did she do something wrong? Was she supposed to go the other way? Or was she only going in a big circle? It wasn't like she'd be able to tell. There were no landmarks to navigate by. There was nothing here but that tall grass. Everything looked exactly the same.

Hours ago, back on the other side of the wall, she recalled Nicole talking about how she, Andrea and Gina found themselves in places like this. Simple, unassuming stretches of space that simply kept going on and on without end. A gloomy street. A dreary apartment hallway. A monstrous hospital. Was this like that? Was she only going to end up walking herself to death in this stifling heat?

She turned her gaze out into that grassy wilderness. She supposed there was nothing keeping her from simply turning off the path. Could that be the answer? Was the way out somewhere over there? Or would she only get herself hopelessly lost if she tried to push her way through that tangled mess?

She was still clomping along in just the one remaining shoe. She was probably going to turn an ankle or something like this, but for now it felt as if she were at least protecting one of her poor feet from this raw terrain. And if she did, in fact, end up having to force her way into that field, she might need even that little bit of protection. There was no way to know what she might step on.

She trudged onward, panting and sweating and hating every second of this miserable experience. She didn't even care that much for the outdoors under ideal conditions. She hated when it was hot and buggy. This path wasn't even particularly *pretty*. Everything just looked overgrown and wild.

She wished she knew where Albert went. Was he safe? Was he even still *alive*? (No. She couldn't let such an awful thought take root. She couldn't bear it.) If she tried contacting him again, would that gothic whore still intercept her? Not that it mattered. There was no way in hell that she'd be able to get herself all turned on in this blistering heat. There was nowhere out here to even get remotely comfortable, much less put herself in the mood to fuck.

She couldn't decide who she wanted to beat to a bloody pulp more: the pervy shaman or his slutty assistant.

Her arms were getting tired. She dropped them to her sides and squinted up at the burning sun. She supposed it *was* helping a little, because she could feel the temperature increase when she stopped shading herself with the shirt.

She used it to wipe the sweat from her face and neck, then draped it over her head.

That didn't work very well. It felt like it was just capturing the heat. And everything below her neck was still exposed to the sun. She'd *definitely* burn her poor tits like this.

She stopped walking as a new sound made itself heard over the droning of the insects. Low and deep. Drawn out. Guttural.

A growl? From somewhere in that tall grass?

She scanned the edge of the path, her heart pounding. Did

she imagine it? Maybe there was a stream or a pond out there beyond her sight and it was only a bullfrog or something.

But why would there be only *one* frog making any noise?

No… That wasn't the sound of any bullfrog she'd ever heard before. It was a far more menacing sound. A growl. Or even a snarl.

"Just my imagination," she muttered under her breath, hopeful. But she didn't believe for a second that she only imagined it. Something was out there. Because why *wouldn't* there be something out there? Wasn't that how all this worked?

Uneasy, she knotted Albert's shirt around her again and continued onward, her eyes and ears wide open for any more signs of danger.

What was this place, anyway? Was it a part of the temple? Some kind of illusion set up by the sentinels to test her? Or was this a product of that slutty witch's magic? Without any idea where she was, she couldn't even imagine what manner of dangers might be lurking in that grass. Could there be hounds creeping around out there? Or another psychic predator? Or something far worse that she had no reference for yet?

With every step she took in her one remaining shoe, she lifted herself up onto her toe and stretched, straining to see as far as possible out over that grass, searching for anything she could use as a marker. If she were lucky enough to be where the sentinels intended her to be, then there would be a way out. That was their thing, wasn't it? Testing them? Judging them? Making them prove their worth before allowing them the decision to open the Keeper's next fucking door?

It was the best she could hope for. Because if she'd left the temple entirely, if she were outside the sentinels' designs, then she was already fucked and there was nothing she could do about it. She very much doubted that the pervert's pet bitch would include an exit if this was her doing.

But there was nothing out there that she could see.

What was she supposed to do?

She turned and looked the other way and froze. It was only there for an instant, but she was certain she just glimpsed something ducking down into the grass, out of sight.

Her stomach rolled over. What the hell *was* that? It was too fast to get a look at it. She couldn't make out the shape. Was it a head peeking up? If so, it was something much taller than she was.

This wasn't good. There was nowhere to hide out here.

She continued onward, faster now, her head down, hoping to stay out of sight.

Was that another growl she heard? Or was that only her own stomach gurgling with fear? She felt like she might throw up.

She lifted her head, daring to peer farther out over the grass. Maybe it was nothing. Maybe she really was letting her imagination get the best of her.

But when she looked forward, there was a strange figure standing on the path ahead of her.

She stopped moving, a scream caught between her teeth, struggling to escape.

It was humanoid, but unnaturally tall and thin, less like a person than some kind of freaky Halloween decoration, with wide, hunched shoulders and a narrow, emaciated torso. And it was unnaturally *dark*, too, for something literally standing in the sun. She could make out no features whatsoever. It was little more than a silhouette against the sundrenched background.

Whatever it was, her gut was telling her it definitely wasn't friendly. She turned to run back the way she came.

But there was another one behind her.

Or was it the same one? It was the same distance away, posed exactly the same.

She turned and looked back at the first one. Was it closer now than it was before?

"Oh fuck…" she whimpered.

This wasn't good. Her every instinct was telling her that she was in terrible danger right now.

She didn't have a choice.

She fled the path and set off into the tall grass.

Chapter 16

Erin's teeth were chattering. She wasn't sure how long she'd been walking through this flooded corridor. She never thought to look at the time on her phone, so looking at it now wouldn't tell her anything. But it had been long enough that the cold water splashing up her legs as she walked felt as if it had drained all the heat from her body. She could feel the goosebumps on her arms and chest. Her feet felt numb.

Again, why did she have to be naked for this? She didn't understand it. It was only making this entire ordeal more uncomfortable.

And she hated that mossy, slimy feel of the stone beneath her bare feet, as if something gross were growing down there. But so far she'd managed not to slip and fall, a small but welcome wonder in this otherwise cold, black place.

She shined her light back the way she came again. She'd lost count of how many times she'd done that. There was no good reason for it. There was nothing back there. It wasn't just that she couldn't hear any splashing or that there weren't any ripples racing toward her on the water's surface. She found that she simply knew she was alone. It was almost as if she *remembered* being alone here. Although she wasn't sure why. She couldn't remember something that she hadn't finished doing yet. And she'd certainly never been anywhere like this before. But regardless of any of that, looking back made her feel better. It made this cage of darkness she'd found herself caught in feel a little bigger.

When she pointed her cell phone forward again, she saw that the passage was widening. Was she nearing the end? Had she almost reached the thorn? She was eager see what it was. It had been haunting her thoughts all this time, after all. What did a thorn of Yggdrasil look like?

But for some reason, she also felt a mounting sense of dread as she watched those stone walls yawn open before her. It felt as if she were about to be swallowed.

She gasped at the feel of the water climbing past her ankles. It wasn't merely the walls that were receding. It was also the floor and ceiling, meaning the water was now getting deeper with every step.

This was going to get *very* unpleasant. She was already shivering. Was it cold enough for hypothermia to set in? And why *was* it so cold, anyway? It was a hot summer day out there. The sun was burning down on the forest not all that far above her head. She was *sweating* when she crawled into the cave. But of course the answer to that question was simple. It was a cave. Caves stayed cool in the summer heat. And this water was likely being fed by an underground spring.

She let out a hushed squeal as the water crept up her thighs, a merciless blanket of cold enveloping her screaming skin.

She looked back the way she came again.

Someone was standing in the water back there, little more than a shadow at the far reach of her flashlight. The sight startled a terrified scream from her.

"Who's there?" she demanded. "What do you want?"

But there was *no one* there. The figure was gone.

She stood there, clutching at her hammering heart, listening for the sound of splashing feet in the water. But there was no sign of anyone. There weren't even any telltale ripples in the water that weren't likely to be her own.

"What the fuck?" she gasped. Was that real? She couldn't have just imagined it. And yet it was only there for an instant. She wasn't able to make out any details. It was just a shadowy shape looming in the darkness far back where her light didn't reach.

And then there was the strange way her brain insisted that she somehow *remembered* being alone down here. There couldn't be anyone back there because there *simply wasn't.*

So it could only be her imagination.

And yet she knew what she saw.

Whatever it was, she didn't like it. Not one bit. Even more unsettled about being down in this frigid darkness, she began backing away, the biting cold of the water climbing higher up her bare thighs. Why did she come down here? What was she thinking? She should've run the other way as soon as she saw the name Breastbroke on that old map!

This was madness.

And now she was afraid to even go back. She splashed onward, her teeth clenched against the torturous cold that washed up her hips, numbing her body.

It was so cold! Why did it have to be so *deep*?

Again, she looked back, but there was still nothing there. She heard no splashing other than her own. Was it even possible for a human being to be back there? Was it some kind of ghost, instead? Or something far worse?

Nothing, insisted that strange part of her brain. *There was never anything there.*

This was a *really* bad idea. Why would she do this? What was she thinking?

There was nothing ahead of her for as far as she was able to see. How far was it to the end of this flooded tunnel? And would the water only get deeper? Would she eventually just drown down here?

She should give up on this insanity and go back. That was the obvious thing to do. That was the *smart* thing to do. To hell with the antlered freak and his thorn. But she was too afraid of whatever she thought she saw back there a moment ago.

Maybe that was the idea. Some kind of illusion to frighten her into pushing forward.

But when she looked back again, she glimpsed something moving under the water.

A terrified scream escaped her and she rushed forward, the water surging up her torso, the stinging cold biting into even more of her tender flesh.

Something brushed against the back of her leg, wrenching another scream from her.

What was that? Where did it even come from? This whole thing was basically just one long tunnel stretching all the way back to the cave entrance. There were no other passageways for it to have crawled out of. Was there something in the water this whole time? Something she waded right past without noticing? It didn't make sense. And even if it did, she couldn't think clearly through the blinding terror gripping her right now.

Again, something touched her. This time, it felt like fingers grasping at her naked butt in the water. She let out another scream. She forgot about the cold. It simply didn't seem to matter anymore. She lurched forward, plunged into the water and began swimming, desperate to get away from whatever was there.

Immediately, however, she realized that she had a severe handicap. Her phone! She thrust her arm up over her head, paddling with just the one hand while kicking. It was the only light she had. Phones these days were more water resistant than they used to be. A splash here and there wouldn't do it any harm, but if she let it get too wet she could end up *blind* on top of it all!

Why was this happening? Was this part of Horatio's plan? Did he know this thing was here? Did he know those things were in that abandoned cemetery?

She never should've set foot in that bar.

That place had brought her nothing but nightmares.

Something appeared ahead of her. A raised platform in the middle of the room. A sort of stone island. She could climb up out of the water!

She pushed herself to swim faster.

But a hand seized her ankle and yanked her backward, plunging her beneath the surface before she could scream again.

Chapter 17

"What do you mean, where only the dead can go?" asked Olivia, tightening her grip on Wayne's arm again. Why would she say it like that? Did she intended for him to die again? Because she absolutely wasn't okay with that. Her heart couldn't take it.

"It's exactly how it sounds," replied the little girl. She was pulling on Wayne's hand, leading him back toward the bed. "Sit," she urged. "You're tired. Both of you."

"We don't understand," Olivia pressed. Her head was spinning. There was too much happening at once. She was still reeling from the revelation that the Sentinel Queen's doomed, unborn baby had survived and grown into a beautiful little girl. "You make it sound like he's going to have to die again."

"Of course," she replied without hesitation. "That's why he's here. He's the only one who can reach the spirit terminal and make it back again."

And make it back again…? She looked up at Wayne, her heart sinking at the memory. The way he kept coming back to her… She knew that wasn't just a fluke. *Four times* he'd been to the other side and back. It was obviously significant to why he was here.

There are answers waiting for you on your journey, she thought, recalling the words Sandy spoke to them way back when they first started this nightmare. Answers about what made them special. Answers about what really happened five years ago in the first temple.

(*Don't you want to know more about who the two of you really are?*)

"Spirit terminal?" asked Wayne. He looked dazed, and she couldn't blame him. He just found out that he had a daughter.

He needed time to process that. *She* needed time to process that. She was going to marry this man in just a few months and she wasn't anticipating gaining a *stepdaughter.* What did it mean for them? What were they going to tell their families? How would they even begin to explain it?

"It's like a switch that needs to be flipped before the Oblivion Door can be opened," explained the little girl. "One of several scattered throughout the stoneworks. Your friends are out there working on the others, but this one is yours." She climbed up onto the bed and gestured for them to sit beside her.

Wayne, still distracted, did as he was told. "Oblivion Door," he repeated, nodding. "Our friends. Right."

Olivia sat next to him, still refusing to let go of his arm. "Andrea and the others," she surmised. "That's why we were all separated?"

"That's right. Every one of you is a part of the Keeper's machine. You each have a very specific purpose in his design."

"So we keep being told..." muttered Wayne.

Olivia reached around him and hugged him, but she kept her eyes on the girl. Such big words for such a young child... It was a little bit eerie listening to her talk. She sounded so much older than she looked, and yet that face she was making as she smiled up at him was so childlike and innocent. She really did look like just an ordinary little girl excited to see her daddy.

She looked so much like him, from the texture of her hair to the shape of her nose and mouth. And yet she wasn't even entirely human. She was the Sentinel Queen's daughter. Did that make her the Sentinel *Princess*?

But then...that was just a silly name that Albert gave her, wasn't it? No one else called her that. Everyone else had called her "The Mother."

So then... was she "*The Daughter*"?

This was too confusing. "Do you have a name?" asked Olivia.

"Sentinels didn't have a concept of names," she replied. "Their psychic natures made it irrelevant. If you were a sentinel and there was another sentinel over there, you'd just know exactly which sentinel it was. Your minds would touch."

Olivia wrinkled her nose at the thought. That sounded like a complete and utter lack of any kind of privacy to her, like your whole life was a public record.

"You know things about the sentinels?" asked Wayne.

"Some. There's a certain amount of knowledge that just sort of passes its way down. It was given to me when I was conceived, passed from my mother along with her half of the genetics, just as it was passed to her from her father when *she* was conceived. We also gain some knowledge from our human parentage, but not nearly as much. And more so in the case of Mother, who was actually carried to term by hers. In our case, I don't have your memories, but I know you well enough to visit you in your dreams and call to you across the broken space of the stoneworks."

It was so strange, listening to her talk like that… She was like Nadia, back on the train. So young and childlike, but full of wisdom beyond her apparent years. Except this girl looked even younger than Nadia.

And she was still stuck on the idea that the poor girl didn't even have a name. It seemed like she should have a name.

"It's a lot to take in," she said, one hand holding Wayne's and the other patting it, as if *she* were the parent and *he* were the child. He was staring down at those hands, that dazed look still on his face. They looked so small compared to his, so delicate. "It's okay to take your time. We have plenty. There's always extra time in the Compendium."

Olivia leaned closer to her. "Can you see what's going on out there in the labyrinth? Everyone else who came here?"

"Not *see* exactly," she replied, those dark and beautiful eyes turning toward her but staring through her rather than at her. "I can't watch what they're doing. But I have a special connection to the stoneworks. To *everything* the sentinels built. And I have a special connection to *Daddy*. So I have a good idea of what's going on at any time as long as Daddy's in the stoneworks."

Wayne was still staring down at the girl's tiny hands, but every time she said "Daddy" she saw him blink, as if dust were getting into his eyes. He was having a hard time processing it. And it was no wonder. Another man might've been completely freaking out right now. After all, it wasn't just that he had a daughter he never knew about. He had a *sentinel* daughter. A product of being what could only honestly be called *raped* by that faceless monstrosity in the first temple. And who by all rights never should've survived gestation. That was a lot. And yet here she was, alive and well, pretty as a picture and sweet as could be, clinging to her daddy with joy painted on her face, but talking like *Sandy* did back in that creepy trailer park…

That was a lot for *her* to take in. But she couldn't let herself be distracted. She had questions she *needed* answers to.

"Are they all safe?" she asked. "Our friends? Everybody?"

"No."

Olivia's heart dropped. No? She didn't even hesitate. And that sweet smile didn't falter for even a second, as if the subject held no interest for her.

"No one's really safe," she explained. "Things can go wrong. And you never know what the Keeper's plan really is." She was still staring through her, but her smile began to fade a little. "Some of them have been hurt," she explained. "All of them are scared. It's confusing and frustrating. There's been a lot of tears and screams. Some of them have left the stoneworks altogether for periods of time, slipping through the cracks, struggling with obstacles and distractions. And there are things out there causing trouble, too. Intruders. Enemies of the cycle."

"Like the scarecrow man," she surmised.

"There was a man with you for a little while," she said, her smile fading even more. "Thin. Bloodied. A boat captain?"

"Keith!" Olivia realized, nodding.

Now her smile had gone away completely. "He didn't make it. I'm sorry."

Olivia pressed her hand over her mouth, horrified. "Oh god…"

"Keith's…?" breathed Wayne. "No… That can't…"

But Keith was such a nice guy… So kind and considerate. A real gentleman. A rarity in the world these days, it seemed.

"But he's not *really* gone," the girl added, her expression turning thoughtful. "The Wood has a way of swallowing people who die in it, but he's different. He's a part of the Keeper's plan, too. He had an important job to do while he was alive and he finished it. Now he has another important job to do."

Olivia was shaking her head. No. That wasn't right. Why should Keith have to *die* to do the Keeper's job? Why should *any* of them have to die? It wasn't fair. It wasn't *right.*

"I can't say what will happen next for him, but I know that the dead have important roles to play, too." Those distant eyes drifted back up to Wayne. "Just like the first time, when *you* were there to make sure everyone made it home."

Olivia pressed herself closer to Wayne, her heart aching. She didn't care what kinds of roles the dead had. Why did good people have to die just for the Keeper's sick plans? There were plenty of people out there who were *already dead*, after all. There was apparently a whole *world* of ghosts out there. "The Murk," Andrea called it. He couldn't have found *anyone* who was already dead to do it?

It wasn't fair.

"But he's the only one?" she asked, her voice timid, almost afraid to hear the answer. "Everyone else is still…?"

"No one else has died," she assured them. "They're still out there, looking for each other. And for you, of course."

"That's good, at least," sighed Wayne.

"You'll see soon enough," promised the little sentinel princess, smiling at her again. "Everything's going to work out."

Chapter 18

Andrea wiped her mouth again. She *spat* again. Stupid, nutjob chaos goddess slobbering all over her like that. *Gross.* She didn't even like girls, much less crazy, lying, supernatural, back-stabbing bitches with mental disorders. She wouldn't like it very much if Nicole did that to her, either, but she probably wouldn't feel *grossed-out* like this.

She did that on purpose, too, she knew. She said she'd been around pretty much *forever.* She *had* to know how to kiss after all that time. No, that whole *world's sloppiest kiss* was just the sort of thing that would've tickled Stella to no end. She'd be laughing her butt off at the thought of her spitting every few steps, trying to erase the memory from her mind.

Again, she felt her heart ache a little at the thought of yet another friend exiting her life. She was still clutching the ring she gave her, still rolling it around in her palm, feeling it. For some reason it felt significant, like some sort of final lingering ember of another dying friendship.

A good luck charm, she called it. Like the lying, slobbering nutjob cared anything about her luck. A part of her wanted to hug it close to her. Another part of her wanted to turn and fling it into the darkness where no one would ever be able to find it again. But she merely slipped it onto her finger and closed her fist.

Stella was gone. She could never come back again. It wasn't possible to go back to the way things were before. Because that was all a cruel lie. There never was a Stella. There was only Tia. And Tia wasn't even human. She was a monster.

Why did everyone always have to change?

The others would probably change, too. Nicole. Brandy and Albert. Olivia and Wayne. Her best friends in the world. The people she'd grown closer to than anyone else. They went through all that stuff five years ago together. They dealt with it together. They bonded over it. That was the sort of thing that turned friends into family. But still everything changed. Brandy and Albert were married now. Olivia and Wayne would be married in just a few months. They'd probably have kids soon. They'd grow up. They might all grow apart. The idea made her want to cry, but there was nothing she could do about it. What if they all left her behind just like all her other friends?

What if she ended up all alone after all?

"Stop it," she whispered to herself. This was no time to be feeling sorry for herself. It wouldn't matter what all her friends did if she got herself killed here today because she was thinking up depressing scenarios for her future instead of focusing on not falling into a pit of spikes or something.

She felt her way along the stone wall, one hand pressed against it, the other out in front of her, searching for obstacles. With each step, she prodded at the floor with her bare toes, searching for pitfalls.

She was no stranger to darkness. The house she grew up in was backed into the woods on the outskirts of the city. Her dad owned seven acres of the forest bordering the plot where Gilbert House lay hidden and her bedroom looked out onto it, opposite the brilliant dusk-to-dawn light that illuminated the front and side yards. Even with the window open, it was too dark to see her hand in front of her face when she turned out the light at night. It was terrifying when she was little. She couldn't stand being in there without a nightlight, but when she was older she appreciated the darkness. She found it relaxing. In fact, it was a little hard for her to get used to how much brighter it was when she moved into the dorms her freshman year, and even more so when she moved into her current apartment with Nicole, where there was a bright streetlight shining right into her window every night. Sometimes she still missed the darkness of her old bedroom. But that was a different darkness. That was *familiar* darkness. There was nothing familiar *or natural* about *this* darkness. This darkness felt almost *alive*, like something hungry and evil watching her every step.

This was *stupid*. How was she supposed to get anywhere in this massive labyrinth when she didn't even have a flashlight? She was completely blind whether this passage was filled with murk or not!

Something was going to eat her. She just knew it.

And she had to be *naked* again, on top of it all?

Stupid Tia…

She could feel tears welling up in her eyes again and she wiped them away, frustrated. She *hated* this. Why did she keep ending up alone? It wasn't fair!

And what was she even supposed to do? Tia told her to make her way to the bottom. Like, the bottom of the whole temple? The lowest possible floor of the labyrinth, deep down in the depths of the earth? That sounded like the absolute scariest place she could possibly go! She was already in a deadly ancient stone deathtrap built by a bunch of giant, faceless, stretched-out, psychotic freaks and filled with a nightmare menagerie of vicious monsters. Now she was supposed to go check out the *basement*? She'd *really* rather not.

Besides, did anyone actually expect her to find her way *anywhere* in a city-sized labyrinth? "Sure," she grumbled to herself. "Just keep going down. Super helpful as long as I actually find some freaking *stairs* or something. *Stupid*."

She stopped walking and listened. Did she hear a noise just now? A voice, perhaps?

She stood there, holding her breath, waiting for it to come again.

There was only silence.

Just her imagination. She continued walking.

She sniffled and wiped at her nose. On top of everything else, she was probably going to catch pneumonia running around naked in this place.

Was everyone else having as hard a time as she was? She was probably the only one with chaos goddess cooties.

She turned and spat again.
So gross!
What was wrong with that woman?

Chapter 19

This was bad.

Gina wiped at her eyes, frustrated. Why wouldn't Nicole wake up? What was wrong with her? Was it the mirrors? Had they done something to her? Should she not have brought her to the glass labyrinth?

She wished the goddess would talk to her again. She could really use some divine wisdom right about now. She wasn't even sure at this point if she'd done anything right since stepping off the boat and into that scary forest. What if she'd been making the wrong decisions all along? What if *everything* was completely fouled up and it was all her fault?

Maybe she was right all those years ago. Maybe she was cursed.

And yet, she supposed it didn't matter. Regardless of *how* she ended up in this situation, she was stuck here. There was nowhere she could go. Because it wasn't as if she could just leave poor Nicole behind. Never in a million lifetimes could she be so heartless. She'd never be able to live with herself. And moving forward wasn't an option. No one was going to come to help. No one else could reach them here in the glass labyrinth. And she certainly wasn't strong enough to carry her. She wasn't moving from this spot until Nicole woke up.

She cast her psychic gaze across the surrounding space. It was still broken out there, still disjointed and folded, still ever shifting and overlapping, still full of mysterious voids and things that filled her with that unspeakable, primal dread. But there was nothing concerning in their immediate vicinity. They were safe staying here for the moment.

With a considerable amount of effort, she lifted Nicole's shoulders and head up and slid her legs under her, propping her slightly so that she'd be more comfortable until she finally woke up.

At least, she desperately *hoped* she woke up. She didn't know what she'd do if she didn't. She couldn't bear the thought of it.

She could use that hateful psychic part of her brain to monitor her. It was how she knew she was only sleeping. She could sense her rapid-eye movement, her heartrate, the rhythm of her breathing, even the subtle changes in her brain activity, all without having to touch her or even being able to *see* her. It wasn't something she'd ever told anyone about. It always felt like the sort of thing people wouldn't want to know about her. After all, it wasn't merely medical-type things she could sense. She could tell if someone was getting angry or uncomfortable or embarrassed. Most people couldn't lie to her. She could always tell when the women around her were on their periods or if someone had an embarrassing rash or any number of other private issues. And she *always* knew if someone was feeling sexually aroused. (That was one of the easiest, to be honest.) Those things had always felt like a terrible invasion of privacy. It felt sneaky, almost voyeuristic. It felt *sleezy*.

She didn't see those things on purpose, of course. If she could turn it off, she would've done it in a heartbeat. But she couldn't help it. It was just another part of her awful curse. And yet there were times when even the worst of her awful abilities came in handy. Like right now, for instance.

Nicole wasn't dead. She wasn't in any kind of coma. She wasn't physically injured in any way. Even her brain was functioning properly. She seemed to simply be asleep and dreaming. She didn't seem to be in any danger at all.

But she wouldn't wake up. And she didn't know why.

She stared down at her for a moment, unhappy. She hated not being able to help. And Nicole had already been through so much. Between the barely-there and Hochog and his scary god and all that unfortunate business with Keith… She'd even lost her shirt. Not that being exposed seemed to bother her in the least, but still…

She lifted the flashlight and looked at it. It was Keith's. That was one of those little details she always seemed to know about things, almost like a psychic handprint. It was the same one he was carrying when they left the boat. He'd managed to bring it all the way here. The idea was strangely profound. It was only an object. A thing. And yet she wanted to protect it. She wanted to keep it safe. For Nicole. And maybe for herself, too.

Her thoughts drifted back to their time aboard the boat. He was so kind to her, right from the start. He never questioned her when she said she sensed things in the water. He followed her instructions without hesitation.

(*Glad we have* you *aboard or we'd be literally sunk by now.*)

She felt a sharp pang of sadness deep in her heart at the memory of him.

(*That was incredible. You're really something else.*)

She squeezed her eyes closed as another tear slipped down her cheek. This was all so difficult. She barely had time to get to know Keith and she was heartbroken. What if she ended up being unable to save Nicole after all they'd been through together, after this kind woman had repeatedly saved her life, all the kind words she'd said to her?

She felt so desperately helpless right now.

Maybe life was actually easier when she didn't have anyone who cared about her. Maybe she was too fragile for a world where people were so kind to her that she couldn't bear the thought of losing them.

No… That wasn't true. That was a selfish and cowardly thought, nothing more than a childish fear response to the pain she was feeling in her heart. These were her friends. And she'd never possessed anything more precious in her entire life. She wouldn't give that up. Not for anything.

She needed to be braver than this.

For Nicole's sake, she needed to be stronger.

Somewhere in the surrounding corridors, something was moving. It didn't walk or run or even crawl or creep. It sort of oozed and distorted. And at the same time, it flickered and shifted.

It wasn't getting closer. Not yet. And it was a big labyrinth filled with small spaces like these. That was her biggest advantage. They were like specks of algae floating around in a vast lake, unlikely to bump into each other.

And yet she knew instinctively that it was only a matter of time. Eventually something would be drawn to her.

Again, she looked down at Nicole. She was such a strong woman, so assertive, so stubborn, so determined. And yet losing Keith like that had wounded her, taking much of that away, leaving her weak and vulnerable. It was difficult to see her like that.

Nothing had changed. Her heartrate was the same. Her breathing. She was still sleeping, still dreaming. It was as if she were under a spell, bewitched by a fairytale villain to await the arrival of her prince.

Except her prince had already been slain…

What an awful ordeal. Gina wiped away another tear, then reached down and brushed away the hair stuck to Nicole's peaceful face. Her skin was cool to the touch. She wished she had a jacket or something to lay over her.

She wished for a lot of things. She'd always wished for things. Maybe if she'd been born strong like Nicole, she wouldn't have needed to.

She switched the flashlight off to save the battery—she didn't need it—and then tucked it back into the front pocket of Nicole's shorts.

She wouldn't leave her here alone. Not willingly. But she couldn't pretend that she had any kind of control in this place. She wasn't strong enough to stand and fight the things prowling the glass labyrinth. If one of them showed up before she woke up, she might have to make a difficult decision. She might have to lure it away to keep her safe. She might have to use herself as a distraction. And then she might never be able to return for her.

If Nicole were to wake up alone, she'd at least have the flashlight.

And she *would* wake up. She *had* to.

She didn't know what she'd do if she didn't.

Chapter 20

"Anun Goar Nangup..."

Nicole fled through the inky darkness, her heart thundering with terror. Why the hell was she hearing those words again? Why were they being spoken in *Keith's* voice? She refused to believe that it could be Keith. But that filthy Hotdog Creep was dead! He couldn't still be prowling around. She didn't merely drop the bastard off a roof this time. She fed him to the hounds. She saw the gore fly when he fell into that enclosure. There shouldn't have been anything left of him to get up and stalk her.

No... Hotdog was definitely dead. He was *more* than dead. He was only bloodstains and hound shit by now. This was the other guy again. His boss. Goar Nangup himself. His evil presence found a way to seep into her brain after she pureed Hotdog Zombie. Something about that black filth that spewed from the asshole's body along with his rancid blood. He took control of her, puppeted her like some kind of toy and made her walk back to that awful meadow that killed Keith. She thought that was the end of him, that whatever foul hold he had on her had dissolved when Keith pulled her out of that delusion, but he hadn't gone anywhere. He was still inside her head that whole time, just waiting for his chance to strike again.

She was so *stupid*. She was so desperate to see Keith again that she let that gross Lovecraft monstrosity get into her head. Why would she think that a *literal ancient god* would leave her alone just because her boyfriend happened to come along and carry her back out of that meadow? Was it even possible to evict something like that from inside your head? She couldn't possibly defend herself from that.

Where did the door go? This was much farther than when she came in. She should've run into the wall by now. Was she even still inside that building? Or was this somewhere else?

This was all so fucking confusing!

"Anun amum ut mu…" chanted the monstrous thing with Keith's voice from somewhere ahead of her. She screamed and fled back the other way.

Why wouldn't this thing leave her alone? It didn't make any sense. Ada and Gina both told her she wasn't special in any way. She was the last person some moldy old god should be obsessed with.

Again, she fumbled with her pockets, searching in vain for her phone or a flashlight. *Any* source of light in this god-forsaken darkness!

Where was Gina? What happened after the room with the mirrors? What couldn't she remember? Did something bad happen to them both? Was that why she was trapped here in this place? And for that matter, was this darkness even a *real* place? Or was she only caught in her head again, like before? Another nightmarishly realistic dream?

"Why are you so much trouble?" asked Keith, his voice calling out from right behind her, startling another scream from her.

She covered her ears and ran. "Stop it!" she shouted. "You're not him!"

It was such a dirty trick, using his voice against her. And not merely his voice, but his *words*. Those familiar things he'd said to her.

"Of course not," he replied, this time from in front of her, sending her fleeing the other way again. "How could I be him? You *murdered* him."

"*Shut up*!"

Maybe it was better that she was caught in this darkness. Hearing this monster mimic Keith's voice was unbearable enough. If it looked like him, too, she wasn't sure she could stand it.

She should've found *something* by now. If this were a *real* building she'd walked into, she probably would've collided with a wall by now. Was there *anything at all* in this darkness? Or was it like those hallways in Glum's dreary illusions? An impossible, endless expansion of space that she could never hope to reach the end of?

Something caught her foot. She tripped and fell hard. She screamed. She cursed. Something had her. She tried to pull free, but something was clamped around her ankle with a monstrous grip. "Let go!" she grunted. "Get your filthy claws off me!"

But the thing with Keith's voice wouldn't let go. Its grip only tightened, pulling her in spite of her struggles. She was being dragged backward through this pitch-black nothing, powerless to fight it.

"Anun amum ut mu," hissed the hideous and agonizing mockery of Keith's voice.

"Fuck you, asshole!" she shouted at it.

Keith's familiar laugh echoed through the empty silence, the sound of it breaking her heart. But it wasn't Keith who was laughing. *Goar Nangup* was laughing. He was laughing in Keith's stolen voice, mocking her. *Torturing* her.

"Anun gan tezul um shog."

There was nothing in this darkness to grab onto. She clawed at the floor, desperate to escape the monster's grip, but all she managed was to break another nail on the unforgiving concrete, a sharp blade of pain biting into her finger.

"Poh epog napug tok sa."

She cried out, frustrated. She *hated* this. What was she supposed to do? Everyone kept telling her that this was all the Keeper's plan, that everything would work out, and yet there was nothing she could do. She couldn't even free herself from this thing's grip. She didn't want to die in this horrible darkness, but she *certainly* didn't want to die to this epic dickhead of a fucking so-called *god*.

"Jang huf pahag na go. "

"*Oh, just shut the fuck up already*!"

"Just hang in there, Nik," whispered Keith's voice. But it didn't come from behind her, where the unseen thing was dragging her by her ankle. It came from right in front of her face.

"Keith?" she gasped.

"It's okay," he assured her.

She reached out in the darkness, desperate to lay her hand on him, to feel his skin again. But where was he? She couldn't find him.

"It'll only hurt forever," he sneered.

Nicole stared into the inky darkness, her heart sinking. She wanted to curse at the foul thing, but when she opened her mouth, all that escaped her was a terrible, mournful sort of scream.

It wasn't fair…

"Anun Goar Nangup," hissed the cruel mockery of Keith's voice.

Chapter 21

Albert was caught in a nightmare loop of bloody atrocities, unable to wrench his mind free of the witch's hideous control. Over and over and over again, he witnessed horrible acts of inhuman cruelty. Brutal murder. Agonizing torture. Gruesome mutilation. Violent rape. She showed him every grisly detail, every scream, every spray of blood, every final, gasping breath. Sometimes he was the one doing the killing. Sometimes he was merely watching the horrors unfold with a strange, morbid fascination that wasn't his own and made him sick to his stomach.

But in every bloody scenario, there was never any sign of *her*. He never watched *Dolly* murder anyone. She only showed herself when she *wanted* him to see her, when she wanted to *play* with him. When she wanted to remind him that *she was in control.*

The witches own dainty hands never seemed to get bloody. It was always someone else, usually someone close to the victim. Friends, family members, loved ones simply turning into homicidal monsters out of nowhere, as if possessed.

Was it precisely *because* these were her memories that she played no visible role in them? Was she not present because he was watching from *her* perspective? Something about this realization made it all feel that much more dreadfully real. And he didn't want to believe any of this could be real.

Those poor people…

She called them "toys." "Dolls." And she bragged about how she played with them until they broke, "bending" and "posing" them in any way she desired. Lucianna said she possessed terrible psychic powers capable of controlling people, and it certainly looked as if she simply set her sights on her chosen victims and then forced them to act out her sick fantasies.

But were all these horrible visions truly "memories" she'd made over the years? There were so many…each one more gruesome than the last.

She appeared to be a young woman, still a teenager, even, but some of the people and places she was showing him were from time periods stretching back decades. Their hair and clothes and even the décor of their homes changed from one blood-soaked scene to the next, bouncing through time, in no discernable order, but some clearly from all the way back in the seventies…the sixties…the fifties…and even earlier…

(Nothing about her is as it seems, not even her age.)

Not merely a witch, he somehow managed to realize through the endless series of nightmares playing out before him, but a wicked old hag straight from the pages of a fairy tale, complete with a magic spell to keep her eternally young, exactly the sort of villain who feasted on the roasted flesh of careless children, for all he knew.

It was chilling to think that someone this deranged might have been wandering around free all those years, doing as she pleased, probably in no danger of ever being caught. What homicide investigator in his right mind would go looking for a mind-controlling witch as a prime suspect? It literally took an even more powerful witch to bring her reign of terror to an end. The more he saw, the more terrifying the idea of this woman's mere existence became. There was absolutely no way to defend against a force of evil like her. And what *other* monsters might be out there, roaming free through their world, doing as they pleased?

Who *was* Dolly? Was she even human? Was she always deranged, or was she a normal child once upon a time? Dolly wasn't her real name, he was certain. Shanzer called her that, he realized, likely a name he gave her as karmic punishment, informing her in no uncertain terms that now *she* was the doll to be played with.

All of these thoughts traveled through his mind like a passing breeze, a force of habit for his logical mindset. He was the puzzle solver, the mystery sleuth, ever observant, always on the lookout for those little details. But on the surface, he was going through hell. The scenes playing out before him were only getting worse.

The witch wasn't content to merely make her victims slaughter each other. She seemed determined to destroy them utterly, body and mind, making them do horrendous things, like making the poor woman in that first room *eat* her brother's butchered corpse. Time and time again, the horrors didn't end with the beating of the victim's heart, but went on and on for hours. Or even days.

"Do you like what you see?" purred Dolly. She was pressed against his back again, one hand caressing his chest, the other shoved down the front of his shorts. "Do my toys excite you?"

"No," he growled. Why couldn't he move? What was she doing to him? She wasn't even really here! She told him herself that this version of her didn't exist. It was some kind of psychic shadow of the real Dolly. Shouldn't he be able to fight her at least a little? What kind of power was this?

"No? But this part down here says something different."

"Get your hands off me!" That wasn't him. She was doing something to make him respond to her. She had to be, because there was nothing sexy about any of this horror show. And *she* made his skin crawl.

"Mmm… You're cute when you're mad. I like it." He felt a stabbing pain down there. Those black nails, sharp as talons… And all he could do was stand there and let her do it. "Show me more," she mocked in a breathless whisper.

Then the nightmares started again. Blood splashed on every surface. Screaming and begging and crying. Warm flesh turning cold.

And he was forced to experience every sadistic detail.

Chapter 22

Well, this was a *little* better, Corey thought.

He was no longer adrift in the cosmos. His feet were on solid ground. The concepts of up and down had returned. But spread out before him was an empty, sprawling city, with eerie, deserted streets and towering skyscrapers blotting out the hazy night sky for as far as he could see.

It made sense, he supposed. It didn't take a genius to see where *this* metaphor came from. From a city of stone to a city of lights. From a black forest to a concrete jungle. From a labyrinth of darkness to a labyrinth of streets.

He was no longer one man adrift in the whole of the cosmos. But he was still only one man in an entire city.

At least he could move around, he supposed. He started walking, making his way down the middle of an empty street that seemed to stretch out forever into the distance.

Like that beautiful starscape with its clouds of cosmic dust and gas, this definitely wasn't real. There were no people to be seen. No parked cars. There weren't even any streetlights. The only light here at all was shining from various illuminated windows and those were lit up so brightly that he couldn't even see through the glass to whatever was on the other side. And everything was eerily silent. There were no traffic noises, no electrical humming, no distant drone of machinery. There weren't even any pigeons or rats, no stray cats or barking dogs. The only sound was the whispering of the wind through the countless buildings. It was as if nothing living existed here, and yet there was litter. Papers fluttered past him. Plastic bags danced across the pavement. Colorful flecks that looked like pieces of confetti drizzled down from the empty heights, like lingering remnants of some recent parade that obviously never took place here.

The entire scene was unsettlingly wrong. The more he took in, the more wrong it all appeared. There were things missing that he couldn't quite put his finger on. The smell of it all, for one. What was a city supposed to smell like, exactly? Every city was different, each one had its own certain bouquet. Exhaust fumes. Construction dust. Smoke and pollution. Food and coffee. Animal waste. Sewer gasses and garbage. Some cities had a sulfur stench, like rotten eggs. Others smelled strongly of nearby bodies of water, whether they be rivers, lakes, canals, swamps or the ocean. But this place didn't smell like *anything*. It was like the silence. Abnormal. Unnatural.

Did his mind create this entire place? Or did his mind merely plant the seed and the machine ran with it? How much of this was him and how much was the program?

What a fascinating concept.

Don't get distracted.

Right. He needed to focus on what was important. Violet would yell at him if she were here. Again, he had so many questions. And again, they were getting in the way of what he was supposed to be doing.

Why was he here? What did the sentinels expect him to do?

And where was Austin? Was he in here somewhere, too? Lost in these crazy codes, buried in the syntax? Or did he only exist outside in the physical realm, waiting impatiently for him to fix this problem and go back to work?

More and more questions. And there was no one here to offer him any answers. Only time could give him that. And time made no promises to anyone.

He lifted his face and stared up at those towering skyscrapers. This was still so big. How was he supposed to find whatever he was looking for with an entire city to search? It didn't feel possible.

But then again, he had to remind himself of what he was doing here. He wasn't searching for some lost treasure. This wasn't a video game. He didn't need to find a key to advance to the next level. He was here to fix the corrupted code.

But where did the code go? There were no stars visible in this sky. Either the lights were washing them out or, like the forest outside the walls, there weren't any up there to see. And really, what would be the point in the code still being in the stars? If he couldn't do anything with them while floating out in space, he sure as hell wasn't going to be able to do anything from this street. The code would've moved, too. It should be somewhere he could access it. Was he going to have to search all these buildings to locate some kind of computer terminal?

He stopped walking, realization dawning on him. He stared up at the lights glowing in all those windows. Those patterns were familiar, he realized. They were the same as the constellations. Instead of stars, they were presented as illuminated panes of glass. And the patterns they spelled out across those vertical surfaces were the code.

"I see," he said aloud. His voice echoed back at him from several different directions, reminding him how eerily and unnaturally silent this "city" was. It was surprisingly creepy. But creepy had never really bothered him. He didn't scare easily. If anything, the creepiness of this place only fascinated him more. He couldn't wait to tell the story. (Assuming he ever got the chance.)

He turned around, scanning the countless illuminated windows in all the buildings lining all the streets stretched out around him. He'd located the code…but what was he supposed to do with it?

The terminal was compromised. Something was changing the orientation of the wiring. Strings that should connect to a specific contact were suddenly incompatible, threatening to short the whole system out. He'd already ruled out human error. The sentinels' blueprints would've ensured against that. The problem would either be with the terminal or with Austin, which meant that something in the coding was damaged or changed. But while he could recognize the lights as code, he had no idea how to read an alien machine language, much less recognize and repair errors.

Then he saw it. A light in an upper-floor window was flickering. That didn't look right. Why would there be a bad bulb or ballast in a world he basically just imagined into reality?

He started walking toward the building and glimpsed another farther down as he moved closer. And when he reached the intersection ahead of him, he saw several more flickering lights farther down the street.

That was it. That was where the machine was damaged. That was the syntax he needed to rewrite.

But how, exactly, was he supposed to fix it?

He approached the nearest of the affected buildings and counted the floors. Assuming there were no shenanigans with the physics of this imaginary city and that the number of floors inside therefore matched the number of floors outside, he should find the problem on the ninth floor.

The front doors were unlocked. Inside, a gloomy hallway led directly to the elevator. The silver doors seemed to stare back at him.

Easy enough.

He looked back at the empty street behind him once more, then stepped inside and let the door close behind him.

Chapter 23

Everett stared at the dangerous gossamer filaments dividing the space between him and Violet. She'd found herself cornered, with nowhere to go but back the way they came. She'd have to climb down and around the column of stone. And the graymother was right down there somewhere.

The way for him was clear. He should just leave. Make a run for it. There was no sense in both of them getting caught.

He squeezed his eyes closed hard and shook his head. *That's not happening!* he thought at Alice. He wouldn't leave Violet behind. Not for any reason.

When he opened his eyes again, she was already standing over the ledge, her light aimed down into the darkness below them, where the graymother's filaments shimmered more brightly than ever. Each one was vibrating. He could hear them, even. Soft, subtle, but ominous. Almost less a sound than an unpleasant *feeling* in his ears. It was as if they were trembling at their master's approaching presence.

"I've just got to climb around," she reasoned, turning her attention to the column of stone separating the two sides.

"Webs," he said, pointing up at the stone. He hadn't noticed them when he first climbed up here. They weren't in his path. Alice wouldn't have bothered warning him about them. But they were stretched up toward the ceiling at an angle so that if she tried to sidle around it, she'd hit one.

She cursed at the sight and turned her light on the space below her again. She was going to have to climb down and then back up on this side. She was quick and agile, more than capable, but again, he glimpsed something darkling in the gloom below.

The graymother was close.

They should've been up another level by now. They were taking too much time. They couldn't afford to wait for her.

"Stop that!" he muttered under his breath. They had time. The graymother didn't know where they were. If it did, it already would've been here. He couldn't see it, couldn't hear it, couldn't even fathom what sort of thing it might be, but it was obviously in its own environment. It had every advantage.

When he glanced over at Violet again, she was already out of sight and making her way down. She'd be next to him in less time than it would take to argue with Alice over it.

She dropped down the last few feet. He heard her bare soles hit the floor. He watched her light sweep across the walls, glinting off those humming filaments.

Then another of those deeply unpleasant shudders passed through them and they both froze.

Did it hear her?

Somewhere in that bizarre, soundless cacophony of voices, he swore he heard someone scream, though he wasn't sure how he'd know the difference. It was such a chaotic mess of muddled sounds.

"What *is* that thing?" she whispered.

"Hurry," he whispered back. "Don't stop."

She grasped the flashlight in her mouth and quickly scaled the stone wall. It felt agonizingly slow, standing at the top, waiting for her, feeling that overwhelming presence rising closer and closer, but it only took a few seconds, then she was over the ledge and kneeling in front of him.

Now all they had to do was keep climbing toward the top.

She snatched the flashlight back out of her mouth and shined it down into the space behind her, paranoid that the thing was already rushing up at them.

"Let's go," he urged.

But as she was getting to her feet, another of those fierce shudders swept over them. To Everett, it felt as if it passed through the stone beneath him, up through the soles of his feet and all the way into his brain. The intensity of it startled her and she stumbled back a step. For a moment, she teetered on the edge, about to fall.

He grabbed her arms and steadied her, but when she tried to grab him back, the flashlight slipped out of her hand and struck one of the strands.

It felt as if an underwater bomb had gone off. Something unimaginable belched upward from the depths below them, filling every nook and cranny of the porous stone. That hushed muttering became an impossible screeching and shrieking that seemed to pass right by his ears and bore directly into his brain.

The graymother was coming. There was no way they were going to be able to escape it this time.

Not both of them, anyway.

"Oh shit," squeaked Violet, terrified. She'd felt the same dreadful sensations that just bombarded him, he could tell. And she knew what it meant.

There was only one thing to do.

"Go," he whispered. Still gripping her arm to steady her, he yanked her forward and pushed her toward the passage on the right. Then, before she could stop him, he jumped off the ledge and landed on the stone below with a jarring thud that stung his feet and made his teeth knock together.

"*What're you doing?*" she hissed down at him.

"Get to the top!" he shouted, not bothering to keep his voice down.

"Get back here!"

But he couldn't do that. If they tried leaving the nest together, they'd both die here. Her only chance was for him to distract the graymother. He hurried to the nearest hole and slipped down into the space below it, not daring to even look back at her.

The darkness quickly became overwhelming, but he found that he could still make out his immediate surroundings. He didn't think Violet's light reached this far. He was fairly sure Alice was showing it to him.

In one of his shorts pockets was his knife. He pulled it out, extended the blade and slashed at one of the strands as he ran past it.

It didn't cut it. As far as he could tell, it didn't do anything to it. The blade sort of bounced off it as if he'd just slashed at a lead pipe instead of a whisper-thin thread. Except it made no noise whatsoever when it connected. What it *did* was send out another of those weird, shuddering shockwaves.

That was definitely going to get its attention.

(This is a terrible idea.)

"No, *your* idea was terrible. We don't betray friends!"

(Pointless.)

"Just keep showing me where all the webs are!"

There were more paths leading up, but he was afraid climbing higher would lead him back to Violet, which would only lead the *graymother* back to her as well, so he opted for a narrow path between two large openings.

(Above.)

He ducked down, slipping easily under it, but felt himself teeter a little on the uneven floor. The sensation made his heart leap with fright. He couldn't see the empty space on either side of him, but he could sense that there was a significant drop there. If he fell into one of them, he likely wouldn't get back up.

(Below.)

This one was trickier. He imagined one of those ultrafine filaments stretched across the path in front of him, waiting for him to trip over it, possibly losing his foot in the process. He slowed down, carefully stepped over where Alice was telling him it was, then hurried on his way again.

Somehow, he understood that he'd passed the opening on the left. There was a wall there now. But the dangerous drop on his right was still there. And worse, the path was getting narrower and more uneven, his footing more treacherous.

Behind him, however, the stone walls felt as if they were being pushed apart. A terrible presence was bearing down on him, something far too big to actually fit in the space it was occupying, making him think of a genie crammed inside a tiny lamp.

He wasn't going to get out of this one, he realized. It was too close. He was completely exposed.

But he protected Violet. That was the important thing. He could be happy with that.

He wondered if he was too far from home to find his angel. He probably was. He didn't think even angels could follow him all the way out here. That was a little sad. But he wouldn't change it. Not for the world.

(Be careful!)

The ground he was running across was too uneven. There was a low spot in the stone. He stumbled and lost his balance.

Everett fell.

Chapter 24

Brandy couldn't see a thing in this grass. She never knew it could be so difficult to walk through *grass*, of all things. But it kept tripping her. And there were prickly, thorny things in here, too. They kept clawing at her as she shoved her way through, scratching at her bare skin, catching on her shorts and shoelaces, poking through her sock with almost every step. And still that punishing sun was beating down on her. How did this stuff tower over her and yet still offer no shade whatsoever? There was sweat running down her face, dripping from her nose and chin, stinging her eyes, making it hard to even see.

This was pure misery!

What *were* those creatures back on the path? Where did they come from? It was as if they just appeared there. She looked back again. They didn't seem to be following her, though she wasn't sure what was stopping them.

Something caught her foot and she fell, a vulgar curse escaping her.

She pushed herself up onto her hands and knees and stared at a fresh scratch beading blood on her little finger. This was fucking *awful*! Why was this happening to her? It had to be the witch's fault. That hateful little bitch!

She sniffled and wiped at the tears welling up in her eyes.

Maybe she should just stay like this for a little bit. Keep quiet. Listen for movement. They could probably hear her tearing through the grass, gasping for breath, hissing at every scratch and scrape those damned thorns carved into her skin. Maybe they'd lose track of her and wander off.

But the thought had barely crossed her mind when she

heard another of those menacing growls somewhere dangerously close behind her.

She scrambled back to her feet and rushed onward, her heart pounding, fresh tears streaming down her face.

This was the *worst*!

She was going to murder that fucking witch the next time she saw her.

She looked back again, convinced that whatever growled at her must be right on her heels, about to sink its teeth into her, but she still couldn't see anything. Whatever it was remained completely hidden in that dense grass. And it wasn't all that surprising, she supposed. She could barely tell that *she'd* been through there. She wasn't even trampling it down as she went. It was as if it were swallowing her up.

As she looked forward again, something tall and dark darted across her path, startling her.

She clasped her hands over her mouth, barely holding in the scream that came bubbling up her throat.

How was it able to move so fast through the grass? And so *silently*? It was unreal. *Unnatural.* And how had it not caught her yet if it could move like that? Were these things just playing with her? Was this just some kind of cat and mouse game?

It went left, so she turned right and hurried onward, stumbling with every step, practically clawing her way through the overwhelming vegetation.

Somewhere in the distance, something let out an inhuman howl that chilled her blood in spite of the suffocating heat.

What the hell were these things? Why were they here? Were they *always* here? Did she somehow find herself in *their* territory?

Again, something caught her foot and she fell. This time, it yanked her remaining shoe off. She didn't dare go back for it. It wasn't worth it. She scrambled back to her feet and kept going.

She wasn't sure how much more of this she could take. Her body was aching. She was hot and itchy. How long had it been since she had a proper rest? How long before her body just simply gave out on her? Was that the witch's plan? To kill her with exhaustion? Make her run herself to death in this heat?

She wiped at her eyes and nose and pushed onward, struggling.

Again, something growled, this time somewhere to her left.

Did she just glimpse something peeking up over the grass from the corner of her eye? Or was that only the endless tears blurring her vision?

"Fucking witch," she grumbled.

"What witch?" whispered a voice in her ear.

She couldn't hold back the scream this time. It belched from her mouth, shrill and terrified. She twirled around, trying to push the unseen speaker away, but no one was there. All she managed to do was tangle up her feet and fall again.

What the fuck was that? Who said that? Was it Dolly again?

"Sorry," whispered a voice that seemed to creep through the grass around her, "but Dolly's not here."

"Who said that?" she demanded, her voice cracking with fear. What was going on? Now someone was talking to her?

"She's busy playing with her new toy."

Her new toy? Albert? Was she hurting him? And if this wasn't Dolly, then who the fuck was it? "Who's there?" she gasped. "What do you want?"

An awful sensation crept through her body. She felt hands on her sweaty skin, but there was nothing there when she went to push them away. "I want to watch you squirm in agony," said a voice so close to her ear that she could feel the breath on her skin.

She screamed again and tried to crawl away, but almost immediately a burning pain blossomed in her palm.

She snatched her hand back, confused. What was that? What did she touch? There was only a single bead of blood, as if she'd pricked herself with a needle.

Then she saw it. Something was moving in the grass, something small and brown, barely visible, gone before she could get a good look at it.

"What the fuck?" she gasped, scrambling to her feet.

Now that she was looking, there were a number of things moving around under the grass. They were all around her, surrounding her.

Were they always there? Had she been running past those things this whole time? Had she only been lucky until now?

No. Somehow she just knew that the owner of that voice had summoned them. Who was that? *What* was that? Was that what she saw moving in the grass? The towering shape that blocked her path before?

"Let's have some *fun*," hissed the awful voice in her ear again, wrenching another scream from her.

She twirled around, her arms raised to defend herself, but there was no one there. Instead, another of those sharp pains exploded on the side of her foot, making her jump back and lose her balance again.

As she rolled over, she saw one of them scurrying out of sight. It was only about three inches long, but thorny all over. It looked a little like a crab, wider than it was long, scurrying on several stubby legs, but without any pincers. Instead, it had a strange tail that curled under its belly and protruded from under its blunt head, where it ended in a long, sharp stinger.

Again, she scrambled to her feet, her eyes wide open.

What the fuck were these things? Were they venomous? Were they aggressive?

Again, she looked down at the sting on her hand. It was swollen now, looking more like a wasp sting than a pinprick. And the pain was getting worse.

Her heart pounding, she turned around, scanning the ground at her feet. There were even more of them now.

"Oh fuck…" she gasped, her voice cracking again.

"So much fun," purred the mystery voice from the grass all around her.

Chapter 25

Erin was dragged under so quickly that she never had the chance to draw a breath. Even worse, she was startled so badly in that terrifying moment that she lost what breath was in her lungs to a useless, drowned-out scream, leaving her aching for air as soon as she was beneath the frigid surface.

And whatever had her was unnaturally strong. No amount of kicking and struggling would wrench her ankle free. It felt for all the world like a human hand, but when she reached down to pry it away, her own hands found nothing to grab onto. Yet *something* was pulling her down. She wasn't simply *imagining* it. Imaginary things didn't *drown* people!

Unable to find whatever it was, she gave up trying to pry it off her and stretched out her body, straining against it, reaching for the surface, desperate for a breath. But it was no use. She couldn't reach it.

She didn't want this dreadful dark place to be the last thing she ever saw!

And yet she managed enough rational thought to realize that drowning might very well be the *best* outcome in this situation. With no idea what was holding her like that, she couldn't imagine what awful fate might claim her if the water didn't.

Perhaps she'd live long enough to know what it felt like to be *eaten alive.*

But no teeth sank into her flesh. No claws ripped her open. Just as quickly as the mysterious hand grabbed her, it simply let go.

She didn't waste time wondering why. She swam upward, propelling herself back to the surface, her chest aching for air. It seemed to take entirely too long, as if she'd been dragged to an impossible depth. A desperate panic was welling up in her. She couldn't hold her breath much longer!

Then, at last, she broke the surface and took in a great gulp of air.

Gasping, half-sobbing and half-screaming, she turned and shined her light around, searching for her mysterious attacker.

But there was nothing there.

Had it retreated back into the water, out of sight? Was it watching her from the darkness right now, waiting for her to drop her guard again?

There was no way that was a human being. What was it? Where did it go? Where did it come from? She didn't understand what was happening! It made no sense!

Stranger still, as she struggled to tread water, her bare foot struck the stone floor beneath her, revealing the water to still be shallow enough to stand in.

Why, then, did it take so long for her to reach the surface? Was she not actually swimming *up*? Frightened and disoriented, had she swam *forward* instead? That would probably make the most sense. And yet somehow she was sure it was nothing so straightforward.

Not that it mattered. Terrified that the thing might come back to finish the job, she turned and splashed the last few yards to the raised platform, then climbed up onto the dry stone and crawled away from the water's edge before finally pausing to catch her breath.

She lingered there, still down on her hands and knees, shivering, her teeth chattering, fighting back tears, willing her heart to stop pounding.

Why was this happening? What did that antlered monster do to her that day?

What kind of horror movie nonsense had she gotten herself into?

Her legs were trembling, but she managed somehow to stand and shine her light around. She saw no sign of the mysterious figure lurking in the gloom. Nor was there anything to be seen of the shadow that dragged her under the water. Yet she knew without a doubt that she wasn't alone here. She could feel eyes on her, watching her from some shadowy hiding place somewhere in that surrounding darkness.

And yet…how was that possible? She was supposed to be alone here. She *remembered* being alone.

She blinked into the darkness, confused, one hand pressed to the wall, the other clutching at the fabric of her silvery dress. What was this memory swirling around inside her head? It made no sense. She recalled descending those steps in search of the thorn's vault. She recalled crossing the frigid flooded chamber. And she recalled something attacking her, dragging her under the water, frightening her out of her mind. But she also recalled nothing of the sort happening. She swam across that water, cold and miserable and frightened, but unimpeded, and climbed up onto that raised platform without incident. How could she remember both of those things? That made no sense.

Was she alone down there or wasn't she?

How could there be two different *pasts*?

She didn't understand it. And she didn't *like* it.

Another vague memory tickled the back of her mind. A voice in the darkness that shouldn't have been there.

(*I'll see you again.*)

She shivered as if still enveloped in the cold of those mysterious waters. Broken or not, she didn't have time to ponder the past. She had to keep moving. There was precious little time here in the present.

But she stood there a moment longer, looking down at her phone, confused. What was that just now? That weirdly familiar sensation of being somewhere else entirely…

Or perhaps…some*when* else? Was that a thing?

Then she blinked into the darkness, distracted. Wait. *What was she doing*? She literally *just* escaped something trying to *drown* her! Why was she just standing here, staring off into space? What was wrong with her head?

All around her, nothing was moving. Everything was silent. It was as if she'd only imagined being attacked back there.

It made no sense.

She crossed her arms over her bare chest, half for warm and half for modesty, and trudged forward, following the raised walkway deeper into this eerie darkness toward whatever terrifying experience awaited her next.

She stared down at the floor as she walked, at the smooth, seamless stone. Horatio made her feel as if the thorn had been hidden away in some distant, ancient time, and yet this place didn't look ancient. That wasn't a natural cavern floor. It wasn't cobbled stones or bricks. And they certainly weren't concrete. It had the texture of polished granite, but with none of the distinct colorization. It was a perfectly uniform shade of dark gray. Did someone carve this entire place out of a single, giant slab of that stuff? She didn't understand what she was even looking at, much less why it would be here under a hill deep in the wilderness of Kentucky.

And it was so immaculately clean. There was no dust or mold. There weren't any cobwebs. There weren't even any water stains. Was someone actively coming down here and tending to it?

The more she thought about it, the more uneasy she felt. Nothing made sense. It was like she'd stepped into a space human beings were never meant to see, a space that refused to fit into the framework of the world she knew.

Was this stone? Or was it something else? She suddenly found herself imagining that she'd stumbled into some kind of long-buried alien spacecraft, a place that belonged to a time both far advanced and long lost to the past.

But that was ridiculous. She didn't believe in that sort of thing. There were no aliens or UFOs or…

"…or freaky men with antlers and burning orange eyes…" she muttered to herself.

On second thought, maybe she shouldn't get ahead of herself.

She shined her light behind her. There was still no one back there. Where did her mysterious attacker go? Why did they stop chasing her? Why just let her go like that?

She swept it across the water on either side of her. Nothing was moving there, either. Not as far as she could see, anyway, which wasn't far.

She seemed to be alone again, at least for the moment. And being alone had never bothered her. She'd learned long ago that she needed to look out for herself. She couldn't rely on others. But this was much harder than anything she'd ever faced before. She was so cold. She was shivering so hard it was difficult to catch her breath. And that encounter with the grabby thing in the water had unnerved her worse than any of the freaky things she'd seen these past months.

No… This was an entirely different kind of alone. She glanced at her phone screen, at the not-at-all-surprising complete lack of a signal. This wasn't watching her own back because she'd never grown close enough to anyone to truly trust them. This wasn't having no one to go to when life became too stressful. This was "stranded in the middle of nowhere" alone. This was "lost in the woods when no one knew you were there" alone. She was literally inside a cave that nobody knew existed, where no one would ever think to look for her. She had no family to report her missing. She had no idea how far she was from her car or how long it would take for someone to notice it.

No matter how she looked at it, this was one of those situations where, if something terrible happened, no one would ever even find her *body*.

And why wouldn't something terrible happen? Wouldn't that be exactly what she deserved for being stupid enough to find herself in such a vulnerable situation? What was she thinking? Why would she crawl into that cave? Why did she keep going after what happened in that cemetery? Why did she ever get out of her car?

The second she saw the name Breastbroke on that old map hanging on the wall of that quaint little diner she should've driven away and never looked back.

"Kids like us have to look out for ourselves," a girl named Jade told her once not long after she found herself in her first foster home. "Because no one else will. We'll always be the least important people in the room."

She remembered thinking at the time that the girl was being rather dramatic. The people there had been very kind to her, after all. And that remained true as the years passed. The people at *all* the foster homes she lived in were kind. No one ever harmed her. No one ever even yelled at her. She certainly wasn't abused in any way. And yet for some reason she never forgot those words. They became the model on which she'd eventually built her adult life. The fact was that she never saw any reason *not* to follow that advice. Why shouldn't she look out for herself? With no family, she was going to need to be self-sufficient. She couldn't be afraid. She couldn't run away just because she was uncomfortable. It was this mindset that allowed her to do what she did for a living, meager as it may have been. And what she did made her happy. That was all there was to it.

But look where it had landed her now.

Soaking wet, shivering and naked. Alone and terrified. Phantom eyes crawling over her in the dark.

She was a strong woman. Independent. Self-sufficient. Capable. That was the identity she clung to in order to live the life she loved living. But was she strong enough for this?

The path ahead of her began to widen. It happened gradually at first, but then more quickly. It should have been a relief to see the frigid water receding into the darkness along with whatever frightful things were hiding in it, but somehow she didn't care for the thought of losing sight of it. She wouldn't be able to see if something dreadful crawled out of it.

She swept her light back and forth, uneasy. Then she turned and shined it behind her. Nothing there.

Nothing she could see, anyway.

But she stared back into that darkness for a moment, imagining something standing just beyond the reach of her light.

That feeling of being watched wouldn't go away.

And why would it? That definitely wasn't her imagination back there in the water. That was clearly a hand that seized her ankle.

No matter how much she wanted otherwise, she wasn't alone down here.

Chapter 26

Wayne's head was spinning. This was a lot to take in. He was still trying to wrap his head around *coming back from the dead multiple times*. And now he suddenly had a daughter? This was… Well, it was *a lot*! How was he supposed to process something like that at a time like this? How long had it been since he slept or ate? Was it still the same day? Was it even the same *week*? So much had happened since they stepped off Max's mysterious pale train. And it just *kept* happening! His friends were in danger? Keith had *died*? What happened? It couldn't have been that many hours since they saw him… He didn't understand any of this!

He just wanted to go home and lock himself in his bedroom. He couldn't take any more. His poor brain was at its limit.

Olivia must have noticed how overwhelmed he was feeling because she pressed herself closer to him and started doing the thing with her nails on his back that always made him feel calmer.

"I know it's hard," said the little girl. "Sometimes things have to happen a certain way. There's just no getting around it." She reached out and patted his hand. "Sometimes bad things happen because it's the only way to keep *more* bad things from happening."

Wayne wanted to tell her that sounded like bullshit, but that was no way to talk to a child. Any child, much less his own. (God, this was weird!) She expected him to believe that Keith's death was just a necessary evil? An acceptable casualty? Nothing more than collateral damage in the Keeper's convoluted schemes?

"It's important to remember that the dead aren't gone," she

added. "Especially not here. That Erin woman is dead, but *she's* here. I know it's confusing, but she's really nice. And she's here to help you."

"She literally *killed* me," he grumbled.

She giggled a little at that. It sounded just like the way Wendy used to giggle. It was still so surreal to keep glimpsing his baby sister in there.

"You already know you're special when it comes to death."

He nodded. "Special," he muttered. That was one way to put it.

"Almost everyone's special in some small way or another. Some more than others." She was still clinging to his hand, still smiling that joyful smile, still staring through him with those pretty, haunting eyes.

It was so surreal, looking down at her there.

"For example, there are people out there who possess an innate ability to affect the mood and thoughts of the people they interact with on a subconscious level. They're almost never aware that they have this power. It's completely subliminal. But they can effectively override your brain's ability to make its own decisions without you ever realizing that they did anything."

"That sounds terrifying," gasped Olivia.

"It could be, but it generally isn't something that gets used to hurt people. More often, this ability manifests as positive emotions. Your friend, Albert, for example."

"Albert?" asked Wayne, surprised.

She nodded. "He's a good guy. Really nice. Kind. And he really loves you guys. He cherishes your friendship and wants so badly for you to like him back that you can't help but do just that."

"That doesn't make any sense," he grumbled. Why would he need some kind of mind manipulation to like Albert? He was a good friend. He risked his life to protect everyone last time.

"It's not overwhelming, really. It's just a sort of subliminal push. If there were something about him that you really didn't like, he wouldn't be able to overwrite that. The fact that he's already a likeable person is probably the only reason it works at all, which kind of makes the entire ability irrelevant, ironically. But it does come in useful at times. Like six years ago, when he and Brandy first followed the map my mother sent them. It was part of the reason she was compelled to go with him. That, and her own subtle psychic abilities."

"How do you know so much about our friends?" he asked.

"I know them as well as you do. We share a special psychic bond as father and daughter. And with the psychic abilities I inherited from my mother, I can see below the surface of people, even through your eyes. And some things I understand because the Keeper wants me to understand them."

This was all so strange. He was having trouble keeping up with it all. Albert and Brandy's psychic abilities? He remembered the Sentinel Queen telling them they were psychic, but she never really explained it. Albert was able to…*manipulate people's minds*? That sounded terrifying, if he were being honest. It reminded him of what Andrea told them about the man she called "Hotdog," and how he got inside her head, making her agree to all sorts of unsavory things. He was admittedly grouchy toward Everett while they were traveling together, exasperated by that reckless enthusiasm, but he really didn't wish the kid any harm. But when Andrea told them about *that* creep, he very much wanted to find him and beat the living shit out of him.

"There are a lot of people who have those kinds of psychic abilities," the girl went on. He wasn't sure if she was merely going on with what she was already saying or if she was responding to the thoughts in his head, but he was fairly convinced it was the latter. She kept telling him that she was intimately familiar with his mind, after all. "Some of them *do* use it for bad things. A lot of them subconsciously take advantage of other people. People like Claire Witler."

Wayne sat up straight at this. "What?"

Olivia's jaw dropped at the sound of that name on the girl's lips. Her pretty eyes widened. "Claire?" she gasped. She knew the story. He'd told her everything. He never kept secrets from her. It was the reason he was initially afraid to get close to her.

Claire Witler… The girlfriend—and later the wife—of an

old friend from his days growing up in Dunnen… A pretty young redhaired thing. And the very person who wrecked his relationship with his first love, his high school sweetheart, Gail.

"She's *not* nice," said the little Sentinel Princess. She scrunched up her adorable face as if she'd just tasted something foul. "She does really bad things. She has dirty thoughts about people and makes them feel the same way, sometimes in really *overwhelming* ways."

Olivia was looking at him now. "It wasn't your fault," she whispered.

Not his fault…? He felt numb. Was it possible? All he put himself through? All that guilt? All that self-loathing?

"She doesn't know she can do it," the little girl went on. "She just thinks she's hot stuff. *Super* narcissistic. She actually thinks men give themselves to her because she's irresistible. And her poor husband probably won't ever figure it out. She has him under her spell. He'll believe anything she says just because she's so conceited that she simply expects him to."

Harvey… His best friend once upon a time… A part of him wanted to immediately go and find him, to tell him the truth, to let him know what kind of monster he really married. But he hadn't spoken to him in years now… Even if she didn't have some kind of control over his mind, why would he believe him over his own wife? And really…wouldn't it be better to let him go on living in his happy delusion?

He felt sick. That woman…that awful summer day… If not for her, what would his life look like right now?

But the question had barely crossed his mind when he felt Olivia's head on his shoulder and he immediately asked it again.

If not for her…what would his life look like right now…?

What a strange and complex and heartbreaking and frightening and wonderful world he'd found himself in…

The little girl was still smiling up at him. "It's a lot to process, I know. But I think you needed to understand the truth about that. You're not a bad person. And you never were. Not even for that one moment."

He opened his mouth, but he wasn't sure what to say. It *was* a lot to process. It was like a weight off his shoulders, but at the same time it was frightening in its own way. What *other* people were out there, capable of the same sort of manipulation? How was he supposed to protect himself against things like that? How was he supposed to protect *Olivia* from things like that?

"It's doubtful anyone could ever do something like that to you again," she explained, making him again wonder if she were reading the thoughts that were churning inside his head. "Claire Witler affected you so intensely that you've built a mental wall against it. Only a very powerful psychic mind would be able to force you into another situation against your will. It would take someone like my mother."

He could almost feel those freakishly long fingers closing around him again at the mere mention of the Sentinel Queen.

But something seemed different about the memory now. For the past five years, he'd been reliving that awful memory inside his head, making him feel dirty, *violated*. It had felt like irrefutable proof that it was all *his* fault, that the he couldn't be trusted. That he'd continue doing those disgusting things on some kind of sick impulse. But this little girl was telling him that it never had anything to do with him… And now he was staring into the eyes of a strangely *wonderful* product of that frightful experience…

"You shouldn't be afraid of messing up," she informed him. "You're a good person all the way to your core and you always will be. That's why I love you, Daddy."

He stared back at her, surprised.

Daddy…

What a strange word to hear spoken to him…

What a strange storm of emotions churning and swirling through his mind…

Chapter 27

Had everyone else ended up naked here, too, Andrea wondered, like in the first temple? Or was it only her this time? She really didn't want to be alone in this place, but she couldn't stand the thought of turning a corner and finding herself caught like this in someone's flashlight beam, with all her private bits and pieces on display for anyone and everyone to see.

It wouldn't be one of the girls if it happened, she was sure. She didn't have that kind of luck. It probably wouldn't even be Albert or Wayne, who'd at least already seen her naked. It'd be someone she didn't know nearly as well. Or didn't know at all. The very idea was mortifying. The idea of being stared at by Corey or Everett or Keith…

But then she remembered what Tia told her back there.

(*That cute boat captain you set sail with.*)

She'd forgotten…

(*He's dead. Sorry to say.*)

No… She couldn't believe anything that monster told her. She was a liar and a psychopath. She probably made it up just to screw with her head.

(*Died right in Nikki's arms.* So *tragic.*)

Her chest hitched and she felt fresh tears welling up in her eyes. If she *was* telling the truth back there…

No. She'd done nothing but lie to her since the day they met. Everything about her was made up, even her name. She wasn't even *human*. Why would she be telling the truth about that?

But then again, it made a certain sort of sense that she'd delight in being the one to break the news to her. She sounded almost giddy to be talking about it.

(*I'll spare you the gory details, let you pretend that he went painlessly.*)

The Stella she thought she knew was a lot like that, too, after all. She loved to spread rumors and gossip, upsetting as many people as possible in the process. But that was always about petty stuff. Someone flirting with another girl's boyfriend. Someone else talking trash behind a friend's back. If she learned about it, she'd make sure the news made its way back to whoever needed to hear it to create the most havoc. She once found out that some guy was sneaking around with his best friend's little sister and started a full-blown fistfight that ended in both guys getting arrested, which seemed more than a little extreme, and yet delighted Stella to no end. Andrea never understood her fascination with drama. Not just watching it unfold—lots of people liked that sort of stuff, she'd found—but actively stirring it up, strategically interfering in order to make the situation worse. She was just sort of…*peculiar*, she supposed. But knowing that there was something sinister lurking behind that obnoxious laugh placed everything in a new and very chilling light.

And now that she was thinking about it…hadn't Stella always had a strange sort of talent for *finding* people's dirty little secrets? Everyone had always simply assumed that she was just nosy, always poking around where she had no business poking around, always eavesdropping on conversations, always asking questions about things that were none of her business. But that wasn't it at all, she realized. She had her own private peephole into everyone's personal affairs.

She was a rotten *cheater* on top of everything else!

She felt so stupid, falling for that woman's lies.

But that was the thing, wasn't it? She wasn't a woman at all. She wasn't even human. She was…something else. Something dreadful. She thought back on all the times she was alone with Stella, completely unaware of the abomination lurking under that fake smile. It was enough to make her feel sick.

She thought "Sneaky Stella" was her dark side, but now she understood that she was playing nice that whole time, hiding the true depth of her depravity. It made sense, even. She wouldn't have been able to get so close if she'd seen what a monster she really was. The *real* Stella—no, the real *Tia*, because there was no Stella, there never had been—was cruel enough to laugh right in the face of someone's grief.

Her hand slipped off the stone, into an unseen void, and she froze, startled.

She'd reached the end of the passage. Was she in a mere intersection, or had she found another chamber? She stood there a moment, holding her breath, listening, all too aware of the countless dangers she could have stumbled across while she was distracted. She needed to get her head in the game. It was too dangerous to be unfocused.

When nothing made itself known, she reached out a little farther with her foot, prodding at the floor, looking for any ledges. Images of vertical drops and spike pits danced through her head, but it would be just as dangerous to stumble across an unseen set of steps in this blind darkness.

She shuddered at the memory of falling down those dusty stairs back in Tia's red-skied nightmare playground. For something that wasn't real, she could still feel the agony of bouncing down those steps, her bones snapping.

She *really* didn't want to do that again.

The floor seemed normal enough. She took a cautious step forward and felt around the corner. The wall continued on to the right. She wasn't sure if it mattered, but it felt safer to keep close to the wall, so she turned and followed it, one hand sliding along the cool, smooth surface, the other sweeping the space in front of her, wary of any unseen obstacles.

After a few steps, she stopped. She dared to let go of the wall and stepped away from it, reaching into the inky blackness across from her. There was nothing at first. She crept out another small step, then another, then leaned into the darkness, reaching. Her hand brushed more stone. Another wall.

Another passage.

Quickly, she stepped back and crowded closer to the first wall. She wasn't sure why. The other one would have been just as safe. It was doubtful there was any difference between the two.

This was just another empty corridor among millions of others just like it. But it felt a little like she could trust this one more. It was silly, she knew, but she'd been following it since Tia stranded her here.

She turned her blind gaze back the way she came. Where did Tia go, anyway? Was she still lurking around back there, watching her every move, waiting for a chance to hurt her again? Or did she mean what she said about going out and tormenting her friends?

(*I'm still going to make sure no one opens that door.*)

She *really* hoped she didn't hurt anyone else.

Although, she supposed it was too late for that. She admitted to causing all the trouble that plagued them just getting to The Lady of the Stage in Cedric's Cove. Glum and his barely-there. Hotdog and his creepy god. She even sent the horsemen to run them off the road. And that didn't even include all the ways she interfered with her friends on *their* journeys here. Also, didn't she say something about capturing someone else in the Ruin and tormenting them like she did her? Someone who managed somehow to slip away before she'd finished having her fun?

She scrunched up her forehead as a new thought occurred to her. Did Tia have something to do with Keith's death? She didn't tell her *how* he died.

Did *she* kill him?

And if so, would she hesitate to kill anyone else?

(*I'm going to keep fucking up the Keeper's plans as long as possible.*)

This was so frustrating. She couldn't even warn anybody that there was a literal chaos goddess sabotaging them all.

She focused her attention forward. She couldn't just stand around like this. She needed to find her way to the bottom. She needed to finish whatever it was she was meant to do here so she could get back to her friends.

She needed to protect them.

She started forward with renewed vigor, forgetting the whole reason why she was moving so slowly to begin with.

The floor disappeared from under her feet and she fell with a deafening scream.

Chapter 28

Gina wondered how long she'd been sitting here, watching over Nicole's motionless form in this unnatural darkness. Her legs had gone numb a while ago, but she didn't dare to move. The things in the surrounding tangle of passages were creeping closer. She could sense them out there, grotesque and terrible presences drifting toward them, then slipping away, back and forth, in and out, but gradually drawing nearer, like the ebb and flow of an incoming tide. It was only a matter of time before one finally noticed them. And she had no idea what she was going to do when that happened.

She sniffled and wiped at the tears that wouldn't stop welling up in her eyes. "Please wake up," she whispered. She'd lost count of how many times she'd begged her, but still she hadn't so much as stirred.

She was becoming more and more convinced that she'd made a terrible error in judgment dragging her into this glass nightmare. If she'd left her behind back there, she probably wouldn't be lost in this unnatural sleep right now. She'd probably have found her way to someone else, someone who could do a far better job of keeping her safe.

Was it those mirrors? Were they too dangerous for a normal person to interact with? Had they somehow fractured her delicate psyche? Or was it the glass labyrinth as a whole that was doing this to her? Either way, it was all her fault.

She wiped at her nose and forced herself to take a deep breath. This sort of thinking wasn't going to help anyone. It was difficult, but she needed to stay alert and focused on her surroundings. Nothing was set in stone. They were both still alive.

She had time to find a way out. If she let that dreadfully familiar despair overwhelm her, she'd miss any chance that might present itself to her. And *that* would be her fault.

She closed her useless eyes and once again cast out her psychic gaze. It was harder to make it all out than it was before they passed through the mirror room. This part of the glass labyrinth was even more complex. There were more passages here, first of all, crowded into tight little knots that overlapped in strange ways, making them difficult to tell apart. The very geometry of it all didn't make sense to her human brain, even accounting for that bizarre crinkling. Most of it seemed to double back on itself in impossible ways, preventing her from piecing together any kind of map leading away from this spot. There were intersections that went nowhere and corridors that twisted back on themselves, but not in ways that made any sense. It was like looking at not one labyrinth, but *hundreds* of them all laid over each other until the lines between them were blurred. And there were more of those drifting voids that seemed to creep through the walls, moving around of their own will, displacing everything almost as quickly as she could sense them.

She leaned her head against the wall behind her as the complexity of it all caused a pain to blossom somewhere in her weary brain. She couldn't understand it, of course, but she found herself thinking that she was trying to comprehend passages that traveled in directions that didn't exist…

Again, she forced herself to relax. Panic and despair were her enemies here. She needed to clear her head and think. Of course she couldn't understand it all. This was the world of the unnatural. There were dimensions at play right from the start that her human mind simply couldn't comprehend.

"Dimensions…" she muttered under her breath. That sounded right. It was like when she was trying to wrap her head around the cracks in the glass. A three-dimensional girl trying to pass through a one-dimensional crack into a world of unknown dimensions. She was on the other side of the crack now. She needed to stop thinking of the glass labyrinth in the context of the same three dimensions that framed the stone labyrinth on the other side.

She opened her eyes, useless as they were, and stared blindly up at those strange, squiggly patterns carved into the surface of the ceiling above her. There was something about those patterns. She couldn't possibly understand what they were, but some part of her was aware that those were related to whatever it was she was searching for down here.

Without thinking about it, she began tracing her finger along one of those grooves in the floor next to her, following the pattern of it. Nicole said they looked sort of like brains. But a brain was just neurons and electrical impulses. Neither stone *nor* glass conducted electricity. And yet something about the analogy struck her as profoundly true.

(The streams flow, one atop another, collecting, combining, and leading the way.)

She frowned at herself in the darkness. What did that mean? Streams? Leading to where? Where did that thought even come from? Was it something the goddess told her in one of her dreams? Or was it just more nonsense from her stupid, broken brain?

Again, she closed her eyes, frustrated. "Goddess help me," she whispered, knowing all too well that even the goddess couldn't reach her here in this black and unnatural place.

But her eyes flashed open again as she realized that something dreadful was looming over her.

She never sensed it approaching. It wasn't there a moment ago. It was as if it simply blossomed out of the darkness directly in front of her.

Did she attract this thing to her when she spoke her pointless prayer to the goddess? Did it hear her?

Terror gripped every cell in her body, numbing her. She sat there, frozen, too afraid to even risk drawing a breath.

She was completely trapped. She couldn't flee. Even if it wasn't right in front of her blind eyes, Nicole was still asleep and helpless on her lap. She couldn't abandon her. She *wouldn't.* No matter what happened.

She couldn't even wrap her psychic mind around what the

thing was. Even for something unnatural, it was too strange and terrible to comprehend. It was somehow both tiny and enormous, both solid and immaterial, both soft and hard. It filled the entire passage, and yet it was taking up no space at all.

The air here was stale and still, yet that awful part of her brain that showed her the unnatural things in the world revealed something hovering over her that was like hair caught in a shower drain, wafting and wavering in a current that didn't exist.

They were both going to die here. Nothing she could do would stop it.

She felt tears streak down her face. It wasn't fair. Why did Nicole have to pay for her mistakes?

Why was the world so unkind?

But somehow, that strange vision of floating, wafting hair was drifting away from them again. Her inner eye watched as it slid past her, not following the contours of the physical passage, but rather in impossible directions, through the walls and ceiling and floor all at once.

A moment later, it was gone.

They were alone again.

She'd endured another terrible fright. She'd remained still and silent in spite of her sheer terror. She'd protected Nicole for a little while longer.

But a great, bubbling sob forced its way up her throat, choking her. The dam broke on her tears. They flowed freely down her cheeks.

She couldn't do this.

She wasn't strong enough.

Chapter 29

Nicole screamed on and on and yet the sound of her screams never reached her own agonized ears. The shrieks and wails of the nightmare hellscape around her were impenetrable, stabbing like poisoned daggers through her eardrums and into her very brain.

She'd been here before, she knew. This was the Depths Beneath Everything. The torturous prison realm of the Patient One, Goar Nangup, beneath the crushing weight of not just the world or even the universe, but of all existence. It was a place of unfathomable suffering, of agonies no living person should be able to experience. The air was freezing against her skin yet searing within her lungs. The wind cut like carving knives through her body. Her eyes throbbed as if they might burst from her skull. The very ground beneath her was corrosive and toxic, eating away at her as foul and noxious things slithered beneath her skin, devouring her bit by bit. It felt as if something inside her were alive and struggling to escape, clawing and biting and tearing at her insides. And that hideous, maddening contradiction of everything and nothing all at once was ripping her very mind in half.

She didn't understand how she could still exist like this. It felt like every part of her, all the way to her very soul, should have shattered by now, scattering her in that violent, carving wind until there was nothing left of her.

And all the while that horrible, undulating thing was writhing through the broken sky above, a fractured and withered shape beyond anything she was capable of imagining. It was a living mass of intangible concepts and broken emotions, a thing older than all other things. And far, far stranger and more terrible.

Anun amum ut mu. Anun gan sutol um go.

She wanted it to stop. She didn't care how. She didn't even care if her soul was torn to pieces. She just wanted it all to stop.

But it wouldn't.

Anun gan tezul um shog.

Somebody, please… She couldn't stand it… It hurt too much…

Anun Goar Nangup.

Chapter 30

Albert didn't know how long he'd been here. Days? Weeks? *Years*? Or had it only been hours? Perhaps even *minutes*? The horrors wouldn't end. He was subjected to one despicable act of violence after another until they all began to blend together into a sort of crimson blur, leaving him feeling unsettlingly numb.

Was that what was going to become of him? Was she going to torture him with her deranged fetishes until she scrubbed away his very essence? Until these horrors held no meaning and he was stripped of any sense of sympathy or compassion, incapable of feeling *anything*? The thought was even more terrifying than the brutal events playing out before him. He didn't want to become someone like that. He'd rather be one of the witch's butchered victims than be stripped of his humanity.

"Why'd you stop?" asked Dolly. "You were just getting to the good part."

He blinked down at the bloody sewing shears clutched in his hand. The stench of blood was overpowering. The woman lying on the floor under him was so young and pretty, with strawberry blonde hair and dimples. And such lovely eyes.

He'd seen this one before. More than once this tragedy played out before him. It must have been one of the witch's favorites. And he thought he could see why. She took a *long time* to die.

"Don't tell me you're broken already."

Perhaps he *was* broken. He wasn't sure how he'd be able to tell. *Everything* felt broken here. This place defied logic, after all, and logic had always served as his greatest tool. Logic solved puzzles. Logic unraveled mysteries. Logic made sense of the world. But this wasn't the world he knew. This wasn't *any* world he knew. This was like that room Shanzer locked him in back in the psychic predator's lair, the very place where she managed to plant this evil seed inside his brain.

(*It's a mental construct, not very different from the dream state you and your lovely bride fell into recently.*)

A dream…

That was what all these horrible shifting visions reminded him of. They all ran together, their edges blurring into one another, with no beginnings or endings.

Dreams weren't just random images concocted by the slumbering brain. They were so much more than that. The creepy cat lady told them as much in her strange, wandering voice.

(*In dreams…human mind is capable of creating temporary realities…entire universes, complete with their own physical laws…unique flow of time. Everything that happens in a dream is real…but only for duration of dream. The moment it ends, it not only ceases to be real…it ceases to ever have* been.)

Everything had changed again. Gone was the unfortunate strawberry blonde woman. He was standing in that endless hallway full of mismatched doors.

"How cute," purred Dolly. She was behind him again, her arms wrapped around him, teasing those black nails across his chest. She stretched up onto her toes and whispered into his ear, "I'll bet you think you're the first one who's ever resisted me, don't you?"

Resisted her? Was that what he did? Did *he* break away from that awful memory of the pretty blonde woman? Did he hit some kind of reset button on her mind control?

"Everybody gets through at least once," she informed him. "It only means I'm that much closer to breaking your spirit. Soon you'll be mine completely." He felt her tongue flick the back of his ear. "And *forever*."

She wasn't bluffing. He knew this somehow. She was in control here. And he felt very much as if he only shrugged off those horrible visions because he'd grown weary. He lost focus, as if he were back in college, sitting through a lecture that had droned on too long. He'd become distracted, begun to daydream.

But why *was* she the one in control? This was *his* brain, wasn't it?

"I see," she whispered. "You want a turn, don't you? You want to visit one of *your* most precious memories."

One of *his*? What was she playing at?

"Okay," she chirped, sounding positively delighted with herself. "Let's do it."

He felt a strange shifting in his body. His muscles abruptly relaxed. He staggered forward a few steps, disoriented. He could move again. His paralysis was broken! Immediately, he twirled around, his arms raised to defend himself against the witch.

But everything was different again. He was no longer standing in the endless hallway of mismatched doors.

He was somewhere far worse.

Statues surrounded him, life-sized and three-dimensional and perfect in every miniscule detail. Men and women, each one a unique individual, and each one engaged in some manner of sexual intercourse.

Not *this* again! He couldn't be here. He had no resistance to this place's bizarre emotional magic.

He needed to close his eyes, but his brain and body seemed to be disconnected somehow. His eyes remained wide open. They were drawn upward, above the statues directly in front of him, to a far too familiar pile of stone bodies. Each one was clawing and tearing at the others, a violent and sexual brawl—frozen in time both in the past and in the present—where even in stone he could see scratches and bruises as perhaps fifty of these men and women fought with crazed desperation for something he couldn't see, something above them, much higher than the ceiling would allow him to gaze upon.

Atop it all, a single woman rose up, buried to her hips in clawing, groping arms, covered in scratches and bleeding from her lip and nose. Even one of her fingers seemed to have been broken in the scuffle. She was reaching up to the ceiling, her face contorted into such a deep yearning that he could hardly comprehend it in his own mind. Her eyes shined with want, her mouth open, silently crying out for whatever it was that lured her upward.

"Albert…"

That voice! Brandy?

He twirled around, his heart leaping with excitement to see her again.

But the person standing there… What was happening?

It *was* Brandy. She was standing just behind him, her eyes locked on that same, violent orgy. She was breathing in quick, shallow pants, her breasts rising and falling beneath her sweatshirt. Her knees were slightly bent as though she urgently needed to pee. With her free hand she rubbed at the crotch of her jeans as though coaxing a dull pain. The flashlight trembled, ready to fall.

(When did she change clothes? Why was she wearing her old glasses? Why did she look so *young*? And why was it so difficult to think?)

He went to her, meaning to steady her, but she flung her arms around him and kissed him with such ferocity that he was shoved backward against the motionless-yet-flailing stone foot of a woman who might have been choking to death on a man's entire, swollen penis and loving every agonizing second of it. He heard something strike the floor and was barely aware through his confusion that it was Brandy's flashlight.

(*You want a turn, don't you? You want to visit one of* your *most precious memories.*)

This wasn't real… This was another of the witch's illusions. Only this time, the memory was his own. This wasn't his Brandy. She was somewhere in the Temple of the Three Whispers right now, alone and vulnerable, probably worried out of her mind for him. This was the Brandy from six years ago, from the night the two of them ventured deep beneath Briar Hills and discovered the Temple of the Blind.

But understanding this didn't make it any less overwhelming. He seemed to be trapped in the events of that night, unable to veer from the script they wrote themselves down there. Everything looked and sounded and felt exactly as it did back then. Even the pain from backing into that statue was identical to the way it happened the first time.

But the pain in his back was no match for the one in his head. It was as if his brain were rotating inside his skull. The things he saw in this perverted chamber made his eyes ache and his genitals throb. His yearnings were more than he could bear. In moments he and Brandy stripped each other bare and were writhing on the floor, caught in the same sort of furious sex that the statues depicted all around them. The world spun and the statues twirled with it, the pornographic images bombarding them as they did what no one on earth could possibly describe as making love, for it was pure animal lust without romance or even a preference for who their partner was, as long as that partner could satisfy that endless burning within.

They did it not just once, but continuously. With each orgasm, he was maddeningly unsatisfied and bursting with fierce wanting for the next. He kept thrusting, willing his softening body to respond, forcing himself to do it over and over again, long after his muscles began to ache with the exertion. He was barely aware of the object of his lust.

She cried out with her own hungry wanting and met his violent thrusting, clawing at him, begging him not to stop, even when each heavy thrust began to drive nails of pain deep into her body. Their voices rose into the echoing darkness as they were both raped by the strange, overwhelming lust that somehow emanated from this gray room of stone perversions.

"What a perverted boy you are," teased Dolly.

Albert blinked hard at the woman lying beneath him, her long, black pigtails spread out on the stone floor around her. What was he doing? When did they both get naked? Why was he on top of *her* instead of Brandy? *Why was his body still moving*?

"Forcing yourself on a weak and innocent little thing like me? You disgusting monster."

He was no such thing! Putting aside the blatant abuse of the words "weak" and "innocent," he'd *never* do anything like that!

Except that he was doing *exactly* that right now. His body

was still moving on its own.

But this *wasn't* him. It was *her*. She was forcing him, using his body just like a doll.

He wanted to stop. He wanted to run away. He wanted to *scream*, but it was hard to even *think*. The statues of the sex room loomed around him, worming their seductive emotions into his brain, overwhelming him, washing away everything that wasn't carnal desire.

He couldn't stop himself.

"And you called *me* sick."

Chapter 31

The room on the ninth floor was as empty as everything else in the city. There was no furniture. No decorations. No sign of life whatsoever. Just like the streets outside, it was empty, devoid of any kind of sound or smell. But at least there was the wind out there. Here, inside, there wasn't even that. The space was unsettlingly silent. Even the sounds of his own body were absent. There was no ringing in his ears, no rush of blood, no faint rhythm of his pulse. He could hear himself breathing, but for some reason he found himself thinking that was different somehow. He didn't understand what that meant, exactly, but it felt strangely true.

But he wasn't here to ponder the sound of his breath. He was here to fix that flickering light.

There were no switches in the room. There were no vents or outlets or thermostat, either. The only features were the door, the one big window and the light fixture in the center of the ceiling. It was little more than an oversized closet. He could think of no logical purpose for this room to even exist.

But then again, this room *didn't* exist. He had to remind himself that this was all perception and metaphor. This was just a means for his brain to comprehend an utterly alien environment for the purpose of interacting with it.

The light, big guy.

Right. The light. That was the only difference between this room and all the others on this floor. It was the reason he was here.

He looked up at the fixture. He was tall enough to reach it, which was good because there was nothing in this building for him to stand on.

Was that a coincidence? He doubted it. The whole idea was for him to be able to do something here. If he couldn't handle the job in front of him, he might as well be lost in space again.

Don't think too much about it.

Right. He couldn't understand most of it anyway. And what he *did* understand was largely rewritten and dumbed down by his primitive human brain into something that merely functioned as an explanation but very likely came laughably short of anything resembling the grand truth of the matter. He needed to stop trying to understand it all and just do what needed done. That was the important thing.

He reached up and unfastened the fixture's cover. It swung down on a convenient hinge, revealing the inner workings.

But that wasn't what the inside of a light fixture was supposed to look like.

He frowned up at it. There was a single bulb, long and thin like a fluorescent light, but also not entirely right. There was no ballast. There were no wires. There was only a single black knob at one end. He reached up and twisted the knob, curious, only to find that it wasn't a knob, but a screw?

He gave it a twist and the flickering light went dark.

No. Not a screw. He removed it and looked closer at it, holding it up to catch what little light was shining through the window from the buildings across the street. It appeared to be an old-fashioned fuse. The kind that always blew at inappropriate times in old horror movies set in spooky old mansions.

Why would something like this be in a modern light fixture? Did that even make sense?

Why would anything here make sense?

He glanced back at the door. Violet's words rang so clearly in his head that he half-expected her to be standing there, watching him as he inspected the fuse.

He supposed he was simply so used to her being around that he could imagine exactly what she'd say if she were there. His voice of reason. The foil for all his wild theories and fantastic imagination.

Or maybe it was just the nature of this bizarre place he was in. Everything was already so weird, why wouldn't there be some ghostly version of his best friend following him around? It wouldn't even be the strangest thing he'd seen today.

Either way, she wasn't here. She was back there in that fascinating labyrinth somewhere, probably discovering all sorts of amazing things.

He hoped she remained safe, wherever she was.

He turned his attention back down to the fuse. *Why would anything here make sense?* he thought, replaying Violet's imagined words. It was a good question. Nothing else made sense. A city without people. Without *any* sort of life. Without any *smells*. It was like when he was floating out in space. It wasn't real. It *couldn't* be real. So why would this thing in his hand be real?

Again, he looked up at the strange interior of the light fixture. There was only the bulb and this fuse-like thing. If he were in his own world, a light like this would be fluorescent. To fix it, he'd need to replace the ballast, which would require tools. And time. And a way to shut off the power so he didn't electrocute himself.

This would be simpler. And why should he go to any extra trouble to repair a light that was just a made-up thing his subconscious mind dreamt up because he had no idea how to repair a whole *star*.

But even if this was all he had to do, he was still missing one important component. He needed a new one to replace it with.

There was nothing in the room. Besides the missing furniture, there were no shelves or closets or cabinets or drawers of any sort. No storage whatsoever. There weren't even any surfaces. No tables or counters. There was only the floor and the windowsill, neither of which had a black fuse sitting there, waiting for him to pick it up.

The only thing in this room was the fixture above him. He turned and scanned the rim running around the edge of the cover. That was the only place in this whole room where something could be. And sure enough, he found it there, half-hidden behind one of the hinges.

He grabbed it and quickly screwed it into the socket. Immediately, the light blinked on, blindingly bright, and stayed on.

"Did it," he announced to no one, proud of himself.

That was simple enough.

He closed the cover and stepped back from it, admiring his work.

"One down," he muttered under his breath.

Then he turned around and frowned. Simple enough…

He stepped up to the window and looked out at the city spread out beyond. The buildings seemed to go on forever into the night, the lights growing smaller and more distant with each city block. He could see so much more from here than he could from the street. And there were so many flickering, malfunctioning lights out there.

Hundreds.

Thousands.

More and more the farther away he looked.

"This's gonna take a while," he realized.

Chapter 32

Everett told her to keep going, but Violet had no intention of listening to that kind of bullshit. Or at least, that was how it was supposed to be. He was so quick. He jumped down to that lower area and told her to keep going and then he was gone, down through a small hole on the right and out of sight. She stepped up to the ledge and crouched down, intending to follow him, but she froze.

Everything in front of her turned a strange and horrid nightmare shade of a color she couldn't name. Or at least that was as close as she could come to describing it. She wasn't entirely sure *what* she saw, or if she even *saw* anything at all. It was like the things she perceived in those dreams of the distant past from inside the alien body of the other one. It was outside the range of her human understanding.

But it was *terrible.*

She didn't move. She *couldn't* move. She was too frightened of the unimaginable thing in front of her. It filled her head with dreadful sensations and bombarded her brain with that awful murmuring and whispering and shrieking sound that she now understood was none of those things at all, but some kind of hideous vibration in the air that rattled her insides and filled her *own* head with those perceived noises.

Then it passed. The entity—or whatever sort of horror the graymother was—funneled into the hole Everett scurried down, chasing after him, just as he intended, and everything went deathly silent.

The space below her was now *filled* with those deadly, razor-sharp threads. They were stretched across every surface, glinting and gleaming in the beam of her flashlight. Thousands and thousands of them.

There was no way she was going to be able to follow him.

Tears began to well up in her eyes. But the emotion behind them was difficult to define. She was scared for him, of course. What was going to happen now? What would become of him now that the monster had caught sight of him and given chase? The idea of anything happening to him was heartbreaking. But she also felt so *angry*. That was so *stupid*. Why didn't they both just run *forward?* He said they were getting close to the top.

But of course the answer to that was in how quickly the thing showed up. If she hadn't dropped her flashlight, if it hadn't hit one of those strands, they might have had a chance. But he knew how quickly it was going to be on them. Maybe he sensed it. Maybe Alice told him. But the fact was that he knew what to do. Down was faster than up. He could jump *down* to that lower section and scurry *down* that hole before it arrived, but they wouldn't have been able to reach the next wall and climb *up* it.

Her heart aching, she stood up and backed away from the ledge. Her legs felt unsteady. She didn't trust herself not to fall.

This sucked. She didn't want to leave here without him. But she sure as hell couldn't try to follow him. The graymother had made certain of that. All she'd accomplish was dicing herself to pieces and summoning it right back to her. Then what would be the point in any of it? He meant for her to make it. He might as well have pushed her over the edge and let it have her if all she did was throw that heroic gesture away.

Stupid kid…

She wiped at her eyes. Now she was crying… She really hated that.

There were a few of those gossamer strands clinging to the walls here and there, but the path forward was clear. It curved farther to the right, then back to the left. The floor was extra rough here, hard to walk on, painful on her stockinged feet. Two more openings appeared, both of them leading down, both of them crisscrossed with that deadly webbing.

The farther she ventured, the more she understood that

they never would've outrun it.

The path before her was tilting steeply downward now. Ahead of her, it turned sharply upward again. There were webs glistening along the bottom, forcing her to carefully reach across the gap and find a grip before she could start climbing.

Stopping to double and triple check for hidden strands was slowing her down, too, but even with Alice's help pointing them out, they never would have made it this far without being caught.

Everett knew exactly what he was doing. That was twice now he'd rescued her.

The stone surface leveled out and she was able to stand again. There was a narrow space ahead of her, the walls bulging inward, making it tight. On the other side of that was a gap in the floor that she was going to have to step over. But beyond that was another wall and another opening above it.

(*Get to the top!*)

She wiped at her eyes again. She couldn't get emotional now. She needed to see clearly. There were shimmering strands above her, too high to be of any concern, but there could be more that her light wasn't catching, hidden in the darkness, so easy to miss.

Slowly, her eyes peeled, studying her every step, scanning every surface multiple times, she squeezed between the crowding walls and shined her light into the hole in the floor beyond. It was no small crack. It went *way* down into the depths of the next, and there were hundreds of shimmering iridescent streaks criss-crossing that darkness.

She didn't want to do this alone. She was so tired. Physically and emotionally. She just wanted to crawl in a hole and cry for a while. And she *hated* feeling like that.

Bracing herself, she jumped across the gap, wincing at the impact on her unprotected foot. She was going to have so many blisters and calluses when this was over.

Assuming she lived that long, she supposed…

She turned and shined her light back the way she came, yearning to see Everett walking out of the darkness, that goofy grin on his face. But of course there was no one there.

By now the kid was probably…

No. She wouldn't let herself think that. She couldn't. She wiped at her eyes and turned her attention to the wall in front of her.

She shouldn't be taking this long. He gave her this chance so she could get out of this place. The longer she took, the more likely she was to throw away his sacrifice.

But as she started climbing, the tears welled up in her eyes again.

Sacrifice… What a terrible word. She didn't want to think about such things.

She blinked hard. She needed to see. There could be more of those strands just waiting to cut her and summon their monstrous maker.

She reached the top and shined her light into the space above. There were several strands of graymother webbing stretched across the path, but nothing she shouldn't be able to crawl under or step over.

But first, she was going to need a minute. It was hard to see clearly through these damned tears.

Her emotions were a mess.

Why did it have to be this way? Did the Keeper intend this as well? Did he *plan* all this?

"Shit!" she spat, frustrated. First Gina and her friends. Then Albert and Brandy. Then Corey. Andrea. Everett. And now Everett *again*. She just kept losing the people she was supposed to be watching out for! She sank to her knees there on the coarse stone, a great, defeated sob bubbling up from inside her.

She should never be trusted with children, she decided. She couldn't even keep track of adults. She'd make a *terrible* babysitter…

Chapter 33

Brandy cried out and stumbled backward again. How many times had she been stung now? She'd lost count. Her feet felt like they were on fire. And there was still no end to these damned things.

There wasn't even anything here in this endless grass to defend herself with. There still wasn't a tree to be seen, so there weren't any sticks to pick up. She hadn't seen any rocks, either. She didn't even have her one shoe anymore.

She cursed. But the word didn't carry much bite. It bubbled up in a pitiful sort of blubber instead. Between that and the tears that wouldn't stop streaming down her face, she wasn't fooling anyone. She was at her limit.

She prodded at the grass with her burning toes, searching for the little hiding monsters. At least she'd solved the mystery of what was *growling* at her. It was these things. They made the most awful sound just before they struck. They sounded nothing at all like tiny little crab-scorpion things. Not that she knew what tiny little crap-scorpion things sounded like, but she was fairly sure it wasn't this. They sounded more like hungry wolves. *Big* ones. It was terrifying.

Her stomach was a steaming, knotted mess and she couldn't even vomit because there was nothing in her belly to bring up.

And every second she spent trapped in *this* hell, Albert was out there in an entirely different kind of hell.

(*Dolly's not here. She's busy playing with her new toy.*)

She hated this. She'd never felt so fucking helpless in her life.

There was another growl from right behind her and she

lurched forward, terrified.

Why was she being put through this? Did the Keeper intend for this to happen, too? Was this a part of his "great plan" that everyone kept telling her about? Was all this pain, all this worry, all this *fear* just another device in his twisted script? Did it serve a purpose she couldn't possibly comprehend with her feeble, human mind or did he simply enjoy watching people suffer?

What *was* the Keeper's goal in all this, anyway? What was the point in any of this?

She remembered that strange confrontation between Albert and Kneede back in the hotel's quiet bar.

(*Aren't you going to tell us the truth? You told Warner to tell us the truth. If he didn't, you would.*)

A truth kept from them from the very beginning… Some kind of profound secret the Keeper and Warner were keeping to themselves…

(*I will if I have to. But there's still time for the parasite to do the right thing. It should at least come from* him, *if not the Keeper, himself.*)

And why would the Keeper reveal his secrets now? The horrid little monster hadn't even shown himself this time around. He was nowhere to be seen. He sent Warner and the pervert instead.

Maybe he knew just how much she wanted to punch him in his saggy jowls. The freaky little bastard.

Another growl. Another explosion of pain. Another scream and more blubbering curses.

God that hurt! It was at least as painful as a wasp sting! She couldn't take much more of this. She was nearing her limit. And she still had no idea if the foul little crustations were venomous or not. Were they slowly poisoning her in addition to this unbearable pain?

"Are we having fun yet?" whispered the awful voice in her ear, startling yet another scream from her while the last was still fresh in her ears.

She twirled around, swinging her fists at nothing at all.

"Fun, fun, fun…" chanted the sadistic voice. It seemed to circle all the way around her, floating through the grass as if it were fog. Was it only her imagination, or did the voice sound sort of familiar? It reminded her of someone, though she couldn't remember who.

"So much fun…"

"Let me go, you fucking psycho!"

"You mean you're not having fun?" asked the voice, sounding positively bemused that she wasn't tickled to death about being tortured by freaky, growling, grass-inhabiting crabs with fucking *stingers* under a blazing hot sun in the middle of literal fucking nowhere.

She turned and scanned the grass around her, only to feel another explosion of pain in her ankle as another of those tiny monsters sank its stinger into her.

"Let's change the game then."

All around her, those monstrous crabs began growling. The sound was terrifying. She turned, eyes wide, searching the ground for them.

When she turned forward again, the towering figure from the path was right there, reaching out from the tall grass. Even this close, it had no features she could make out. It looked almost as if it were entirely wrapped up in slick black tape, its skin little more than a patchwork of fleshy darkness that defied the blazing sunshine and its face a nightmarish cavity filled with crooked teeth and strange, wriggling things that looked like worms but reached toward her like the tentacles of some monstrous deep-sea predator.

Before she could do more than scream at the dreadful sight, one gnarled hand closed around her leg and yanked it out from under her. In a single, terrifying instant, she was being dragged through the grass at an impossible speed, the tangled vegetation tearing at her exposed skin.

"We'll play together *forever*," the horrible voice breathed into her ear in a voice as cold and dangerous as the hiss of a snake.

Brandy couldn't stop screaming. It poured out of her in an uncontrollable gush. It felt as if she were being dragged across jagged rocks. Thorns gouged her. Weeds tore at her flesh. Stiff leaves slashed at her like knife blades. She was being cut to pieces, bit by bit. And of course there were the stings of those growling monstrosities, like glowing hot irons pressing up and down her back.

The pain was excruciating. She couldn't stand it, but she couldn't stop it. The only thing to grab onto was the grass itself and it only tore itself from her grip, bloodying her bare hands.

"Fun, fun, fun, fun, fun," laughed the sinister voice in her ear as she shrieked and wailed.

As she felt her consciousness waver and darkness began to close around her, she found herself remembering the first temple and that awful tower at the heart of the labyrinth where the Caggo got its foul hands on her. It was strong like this, too. She still vividly recalled the surreal sensation of being picked up by that thing as if she weighed nothing at all, then hurled through the darkness. Just like back then, she found herself convinced that she was about to die.

But then the disfigured hand holding her leg was gone.

Just like back then, she found herself falling.

Death seemed inevitable.

She cried out for Albert. Or perhaps she didn't… She wasn't entirely sure. Perhaps she only kept screaming.

Then she hit the ground. The wind was knocked out of her, silencing her in an agonizing instant. And in the absence of the sound she heard the growls of the crab things all around her.

Gasping for breath, she tried to push herself off the ground, tried to stop her head from spinning. Everything hurt. At some point, she lost Albert's shirt, but somehow she still had her glasses. If she could only blink away the tears so she could see something…

Why had the sky turned red?

"Funnnnnn…" hissed that awful voice once more.

Then the monsters were swarming her. Dozens of them. Hundreds. *Thousands.* All of them scurrying from the grass and crawling over her body, each one sinking its agonizing stinger into her flesh again and again.

Helpless, all she could do was scream and writhe in agony as the world faded to black around her.

Chapter 34

Erin crept down the steps, careful not to slip on the smooth stone.

At the far end of the previous chamber, she found a towering wall with a small, square passage leading through it. There was something oddly *familiar* about that passage, despite the fact that she'd definitely never been there before. She kept imagining herself creeping through a tunnel just like it in the dark. Had she seen it in one of the strange dreams she'd been haunted by these past few months? Was that it?

Anything was possible at this point, she supposed…

At the end of that passage awaited a vast, natural cavern plunging straight down into the depths of the earth. These steps she descended were carved into the very rock face of that cavern's walls, zigzagging down the steep surface, carrying her ever deeper into this cold, dank nightmare.

Water drizzled down the coarse walls and dripped like rain from unseen stalactites somewhere high above her, creating a cold mist that did nothing to ease the chill from crossing that dark pool.

But far worse than the cold was the voices.

She kept trying to tell herself it was only the sound of the water trickling and dripping down the walls, nothing more than a trick of the mind, echoes off the stone. And yet she could swear she heard distinct words.

Could this place be haunted?

She didn't think she'd ever been this frightened in her life. She couldn't stop shaking and it wasn't merely from the cold.

For the sixth or seventh time now, she stopped, her head

tilted to one side, trying to hear over the dripping and burbling of the water all around her. It didn't just sound like a voice. It sounded like *several different* voices. *Distinct* voices. Sometimes male. Sometimes female. But she couldn't make out the words. It was nothing more than a murmur.

"Just water," she whispered to herself. It just sounded like that sometimes. That was all. She needed to get ahold of herself.

But on the other hand, she was certain that what she experienced in that last room wasn't "just water." There was someone—or some*thing*—standing in that darkness. And she absolutely didn't imagine something grabbing her and trying to drown her. It would be foolish to assume she *wasn't* hearing ghostly voices.

She pushed onward, her teeth still chattering against the cold, terrified of slipping and falling into that infernal darkness looming below her. There were no railings, no handholds, no safety features of any kind. There was only a terrifying drop straight down into darkness.

No one knew where she was. No one would even know she was missing. Even her landlady wouldn't figure it out anytime soon. Although she had a little apartment of her own, it served mostly as a base of operations, an address to place on her tax forms and a place to keep some of her stuff. She sometimes traveled for months at a time and frequently spent only a night or two at a time there. She arranged automatic payments for her rent, so she wouldn't forget about it. It could literally take *years* for someone to realize she was missing!

The worst-case scenario wouldn't even be dying. It would be finding herself at the bottom of this cavern, broken and in agony, unable to climb back out, forced to wait hours or days or even weeks for merciful death to claim her, probably in the form of an excruciating infection.

But she was only going to freak herself out letting things like that fill her head. She pushed the awful thoughts from her mind and focused on not slipping on the wet stone and manifesting that exact horrible fate.

Below her, something began to emerge from the darkness.

A stone platform. A bridge stretching to the far side of the chamber. Again, there were no railings or other safety features, but at least it was *flat.* Anything was better than these steep, slick steps.

She realized that the sound of dripping water was getting louder, more resembling the steady drone of a light rain, and cast her light out across the darkness below her, revealing the twinkle of reflected light on the surface of a pool some distance beneath the walkway.

More water. What was it with all the water, anyway? It didn't go unnoticed to her that there were some eerie similarities between this place and the Elysium Fog's curious aesthetic. That place was made to look like a cave, too.

The underworld, she thought, feeling a fresh shiver at the thought. Like all those old myths in almost every culture about the spirit world being somewhere deep underground. She especially found herself thinking about the River Styx as she descended toward that shadowy pool. She could almost imagine an eerie robed figure steering an old boat in that gloom.

It was in the very name, after all. The Elysium Fog. Clearly named for the Elysian Fields of Greek Mythology, which was basically an exclusive version of heaven reserved for the gods' favorite people and all their illegitimate children.

But she pushed the thought away. Now wasn't a particularly good time to be thinking about that sort of thing.

She stepped onto the wet walkway and hugged herself against the cold. Even the workout those steep stairs gave her wasn't enough to combat the chill. She wanted nothing more than to be back out in that sweltering Kentucky heat again.

Why did she ever set foot in that creepy club? It had brought her nothing but trouble. And for what? She already knew what the outcome was going to be.

She made her way onward through the dark, cringing at every drop of cold water that landed on her naked skin.

The upper part of the cavern had been fairly small. She could see the other side. But it had grown larger as it went down, expanding beyond the reach of her light. Now, as she walked forward, she realized that it opened into a large horizontal chamber.

Unlike the previous passage, most everything down here was natural stone. Only the steps and the walkway were noticeably manmade. It reminded her of something, but she couldn't remember what.

She shivered again at an image that flashed through her mind—endless roads of gray stone winding through a black forest beneath an empty sky and littered with the scattered debris of dead universes—but it was gone again as quickly as it came to her.

A brief recollection of yet another dream, perhaps. She'd had no shortage of unsettling nightmares since she first looked into Horatio's burning eyes.

Ahead of her, something new emerged from the gloom, distracting her.

Pale shapes floated into view overhead, long and twisted, like ghostly fingers reaching down through the darkness.

Roots of some kind?

No. That wasn't right. They weren't hanging down from the ceiling. They seemed to be jutting up from below.

More and more of them appeared as she crept forward. And when she leaned closer to the edge and shined her light down, there were more down there. Many more.

Not roots...but perhaps some kind of strange, underground tree? *Were* there such things? She didn't think she'd ever heard of anything like that before. She was hardly an expert on cave flora, but she thought that the whole point of a tree was to compete for the most sunlight out under the open sky. It was what the leaves were for. And didn't a tree technically need leaves to be a tree? Wasn't that sort of a defining feature?

So probably not a tree.

Some kind of giant fungus, then? That would make more sense, she supposed. Mushrooms could be that color. Yellowish white and smooth.

She stopped walking and shined her light at the nearest one, at the flared shape.

Wait…

She felt her stomach tighten as a new and much more dreadful thought occurred to her.

Was that…*bone*?

Were those *skeletons*?

She turned and shined her light the other way. It was no wonder the thought didn't occur to her immediately. If these were bones, they belonged to creatures unlike anything she'd ever seen before. Long and twisted and branched, flared in strange ways, like some titanic alien megafauna. No creature this size had ever existed in her world. Not as far as she knew, anyway. Not as far as *anyone* knew. She'd been to museums. She'd seen dinosaur fossils. They looked nothing like this. These belonged to something much bigger and much, *much* stranger.

She couldn't even tell what part of the body she was looking at. Were those ribs? Legs? *Horns*? She could see no spinal columns or distinct joints. Where was the skull? There was no *shape* to it. It was just a forest of bones, some as big around as hundred-year-old oaks, many far too long to see either end.

And with no way to know how deep the water was or how much mud and silt might be settled beneath it, it was impossible to guess how much of the thing was hidden beneath the surface.

They'd been there for a very long time, though. Some of them looked almost frozen, with thin, white icicles dangling down from their undersides. But that wasn't ice. Those were minerals from the dripping water, she realized. They were stalactites, some of them stretching thirty feet or more to the water's surface.

She turned and shined her light farther out into the darkness. Now that she was looking, she could see the ghostly outlines of more of these strange bones jutting up on either side of her. Did this all belong to a single creature? Or were there hundreds of them piled up here, like some ancient alien boneyard?

Could any of these monstrosities still be alive?

Or worse…was there something *even bigger* lurking down here? Something that had killed all these things and dragged them back here to feast?

The thought made her feel sick to her stomach.

She hurried onward, eager to be out of this cavern before she could find any unwanted answers to all these questions.

But she stopped again as her light uncovered a new shape looming in the oppressive darkness. At first, she thought it was a *wall* of bone. It was simply too big to be anything else. But that didn't make any sense. *Walls* didn't have bones.

Was that a single bone? A gargantuan shoulder blade, perhaps?

No. Nothing so recognizable, she realized as she approached it. The "wall" was only one side of it. It curved around, even bigger than it looked. A skull, perhaps? But if so, it belonged to something truly massive. It was at least the size of a two-car garage!

She crept closer to it, revealing more and more from the cover of darkness. She couldn't wrap her head around it. It was tapered and bulbous, with great, gaping holes at the bottom of one side, but nothing that resembled eyes or ears or a nose. She could discern no teeth.

What had she stumbled onto?

She continued past it, still shining her light on it, still trying to make sense of it right up until it was swallowed by the darkness again.

She shined her light forward, searching for any more clues about what these things used to be, but the rest of the bones were farther out in the sprawling cavern, little more than ghostly shapes in the gloom.

She peered over the edge again, down into the water below her where several long, twisted bones crossed beneath the platform in a sort of tangled pile, as if woven together.

She found herself imagining some kind of strange, gargantuan thing lumbering between great, towering stone structures…

Just her imagination? Or another fragment of a forgotten dream?

She swept her light back and forth, curious, then froze as it fell on something new.

Something was standing in the water down there. Something not made of ancient bones. Something dark and vaguely human-shaped.

Was it the thing she glimpsed in that flooded passage? What may or may not have been the same thing that grabbed her and dragged her under the water? Like then, it was just standing there. But this time she could see clearly that it wasn't merely her imagination. She could see the ripples from the dripping water bouncing off it.

She had no idea what it was, but she was immediately certain that it was no human standing down there.

She stepped away from the edge and hurried onward, her heart pounding with fresh fright.

But as she swept her light back and forth, she realized that there wasn't just one shadowy figure down there. There were several of them, each one just…standing there…not moving…not reacting to her light…

Were they statues? Like that freaky faceless guy back at the beginning of this place?

No. Somehow she knew these were nothing so harmless.

More and more of them appeared as she hurried forward.

Dozens of them.

A dreadful feeling was settling into her belly. She didn't understand any of this strangeness, and yet she couldn't shake the feeling that she was in danger here.

She slowed and shined her light down at one standing closer than the rest. It looked like a roughly man-shaped clump of black clay. It was lumpy and asymmetrical, swollen in places and oddly melted in others. And its lowered head was curiously shaped, *pointed*, as if its face tapered into a freakish beak, not entirely unlike those old creepy plague doctor masks.

Did they all look like that?

When she turned and shined her light back the other way, however, she discovered something terrible.

All the ones she'd walked past, regardless of how they were standing when she passed them, were all facing her now. Those drooping plague-mask beaks were all pointed in her direction.

She didn't linger to investigate further. She rushed forward, an icy panic welling up inside her.

What the hell was this place?

Chapter 35

Olivia felt a strange mix of emotions. For five years, she'd been telling Wayne that she refused to believe he was capable of ever betraying her the way he believed he betrayed Gail. And she wasn't merely trying to make him feel better. Someone who looked at her the way he did just simply couldn't do that. She wouldn't be convinced otherwise. And now this peculiar little girl was telling him that she was right all along, that it was never his fault in the first place. She felt so relieved for him. He *needed* someone to tell him that. It was something that had haunted him since that day. He felt *terrible* about what he'd done. It broke his heart. It left scars that would never heal. She knew it sometimes kept him up at night, terrified that he couldn't trust himself, that he was doomed to keep making terrible mistakes and destroying the things most precious to him. And what happened with the Sentinel Queen five years ago, in his mind, was only further proof of that. *Twice* he'd allowed a woman he didn't love to seduce him, without so much as a word of protest, as if he couldn't trust his own body. But now he knew it was never his fault. Those women cheated. They used powerful psychic powers to manipulate him, to *force* themselves on him. It even made a certain amount of sense. It explained why he always described it as happening without any warning, how he never even imagined doing that with his best friend's girlfriend until after it was over. It was because it was all *her. Claire. She* was the one with the betraying intentions. *She* was the one who plotted to cheat on her partner, who had impure thoughts about his best friend.

(*She has dirty thoughts about people and makes them feel the same way, sometimes in really* overwhelming *ways.*)

She felt a hot anger flooding her belly at the thought of that woman taking advantage of Wayne. And not *merely* Wayne.

(*She just thinks she's hot stuff.* Super *narcissistic. She actually thinks men give themselves to her because she's irresistible.*)

What a *bitch*! She wanted to find that woman and slap her. Or maybe *punch* her. She definitely wanted to hurt the nasty little slut. Not just for what she did to Wayne, but for what she was *still* doing to *her own husband*. What kind of woman could do that sort of thing? She was giving a bad name to women everywhere!

But she also felt a strange sense of unease as it occurred to her that without that woman's psychic sluttiness, Wayne may never have broken up with Gail. He may never have attended Briar Hills University, which he chose specifically in order to move away from Dunnen. He may never have entered Gilbert House that night and found her. He may have never entered her life at all.

She felt profoundly *afraid* at the thought of how fragile the present was, at how easily life could have taken a completely different turn, at how close she may have come to never finding her happiness.

And of course there was still the lingering horror and regret at the news that poor Keith had perished somewhere in this gray labyrinth… That thought lingered behind all the others, weighing on her heart, making her feel as if she were perpetually on the verge of tears.

And as all these conflicting emotions swirled around inside her head, she found herself distracted by the fact that every time this child called Wayne "Daddy," she felt a strange pang of *jealousy*.

She was a beautiful little girl. She seemed very sweet. The way she looked up at him with those big, blind eyes, the joy on her face that she was physically with him at long last… She didn't want to compete with that. How *could* she? She was his *daughter*. But she didn't want to share him. She didn't want someone taking away his attention.

It wasn't an angry or spiteful sort of jealousy. She didn't find herself glaring at this little girl, hating her, wishing she'd just go away and leave him alone. It was more of a hopeless sort of *sadness*. As if these past five years she'd only been a placeholder in his life, just waiting for someone else to come along and replace her.

She caught herself clinging tightly to his arm and had to force herself to relax before he noticed and asked her what was wrong. Because she absolutely didn't want to try explaining it to him. A sharp guilty feeling stabbed her at the very idea.

It felt as if she were *drowning* in feelings.

"So what happens now?" asked Wayne. "Why did you bring us here? You said something before about a…spirit terminal, was it?"

The little girl's smile softened a bit, but didn't disappear completely. "It's a place deep inside the Murk passages of the gatehouse, an anomaly, reachable only by the dead, but only the living can activate it."

"That doesn't make sense," he said, confused.

"How can you be both dead *and* alive?" asked Olivia.

But she only smiled that sweet smile and stared with those blind eyes at Wayne. "By being someone who walks both worlds at once," she replied.

Wayne's expression was strained as he struggled to understand. "But I'm *not* both. I'm either alive or I'm dead. I can't be both at the same time."

"Of course you can," she giggled. "It's precisely why you're here."

Olivia was confused as well. She was on Wayne's side on this one. She just said that the spirit terminal thingy could only be reached by the dead, but if he had to die and travel there, then he couldn't be alive when he reached it. He'd have to come back to his body to do that.

"And I can't exactly just *drop dead* on command, either," he added. "I had to use those killing vines to fight off the scarecrow man in the bone chamber."

She couldn't help glancing around, making sure none of those awful plants were growing up any of the walls in this room. She didn't see any, but she wasn't entirely comforted. For all she knew, there were hundreds of inconspicuous little things out there that were as frightfully deadly as those killing vines.

"That's not true," the little girl informed him. "Your soul is special. It's not tethered to your physical body. You can come and go as you please. And when you're on the other side, everything is different. The rules of the living don't apply."

What did that mean? She didn't understand. How could his soul not be tethered to his body? It sounded like he could simply slip away from her at any moment without warning. The idea made her grip his arm tighter again.

Wayne didn't understand it either. He looked bemused. "I'm…not sure I'm smart enough to understand all this, to be honest."

Again, the little girl giggled. "It's okay." She pressed herself against him, hugging him. The gesture was adorable, but sent another of those guilty jealous feelings pulsing through Olivia's heart. "That's why I'm here. I'm going to show you."

A fresh wave of dread passed through her at this. What did that mean? What was she going to do? She wasn't sure how much more of this she could take!

Chapter 36

Andrea hit the ground hard. Pain flashed through her already aching body. She let out a second cry, this one of pain rather than surprise, and rolled onto her back, clutching at her leg.

She thought for sure she was going to die for a second there. After all that careful creeping around, it only took a moment to forget herself and fall into a trap. She had no idea how far she was going to fall or what was waiting for her at the bottom, but her mind flashed so vividly back to the sight of Beverly Bridger's lifeless body lying in that blood-soaked pit in the first temple, all those wicked stone spikes driven through her flesh...

But she only fell for a second or two. She hit the bottom so quickly, in fact, that she didn't have time to brace herself. Almost before she knew she was falling, she hit the ground. Her toes and her injured knee were screaming in pain, as were her hands and elbow. It was overwhelming, washing every other thought from her mind. Fresh tears were streaming down her face.

Had she finally broken something for real? Would she even be able to stand once the pain eased? Or would she spend the rest of this horrid journey dragging herself along the floor, helpless and afraid?

She supposed it was too soon to be thinking things like that, but she couldn't help it. There seemed to be something wrong with her brain. It delighted in jumping to the very worst scenarios right from the start.

Albert used to say that they never really did anything in the first temple, that they were little more than rats the Keeper made run through his convoluted maze. They might as well have been puppets at the ends of strings for all the difference they made.

Everything happened exactly as he planned it from the very beginning. But even so, they didn't get through unscathed. Albert broke his arm. Brandy broke her tailbone. Nicole had a spike go through her hand. And Wayne *died.* (For a while, anyway.) If that was what happened when everything went according to the Keeper's plan, then what would happen with that crazy floozy, Tia, running around sabotaging everything?

She groaned and sniffed back more tears. This sucked.

Did Tia do this, too? Did she get inside her head somehow, distracting her at just the right moment? It wasn't that hard to imagine a god-powered Stella doing something exactly like that. But it was also, unfortunately, just as easy to imagine her doing this sort of thing to herself…

Grunting with pain, she rolled over onto her hands and knees.

No. She definitely didn't think she'd broken any bones. Despite how much it hurt, she doubted she had any serious injuries. Just a lot of bruises.

She rose to her feet and took a shaky step.

Something sharp dug into the bottom of her foot, causing her to let out another painful cry and stumble forward, where she banged her forehead against something hard.

Clutching at her head, her eyes squeezed shut and her teeth clenched, she stumbled backward, only to again step on something sharp and fall hard onto her butt.

"Owie…" she moaned. What was happening? Where was she? Why was the floor so angry? It felt like she was sitting on *gravel.*

She reached out and dragged her fingers across the floor. It was all cracked and broken here. Had she stumbled into some sort of even older area?

Or somewhere even worse?

Her mind flashed back to that horrible version of her and Nicole's apartment in ruins. Had she stumbled back into *that* world? If she could see through all that foul murk, would there be another eerie red sky hanging over her?

Again, she rose to her feet, her heart racing with fresh fear.

Was it all just a cruel trick? Did Tia tell her she was going to let her go only to plunge her back into that nightmare of endless deaths?

She reached out and ran her hands along the wall next to her, trying to wrap her head around the layout of the space around her. There was a wall here... She turned and tiptoed through the gravel and pressed her hands against another wall. That was what she hit her head on. She was in another passage.

But where did she come from?

She reached up higher and found a ledge. Another space about six feet up.

She ran her hand along it and found a corner. An offset passage?

Wait...

A fresh and far more gripping dread spread through her gut.

The floor of the upper passage was smooth. As were the walls. Only the floor beneath her feet felt damaged.

This wasn't the Ruin.

It was a *hound passage.*

How did she not realize that immediately? Those things had scared the hell out of her five years ago. They were walking nightmares with chainsaw skin and anger issues! And yet with all that nasty Tia business, she'd forgotten all about them!

She had to get out of here.

She reached up and grasped the ledge of the upper passage, but froze as a sound touched her ears. It was subtle, but unmistakable, something heavy stepping down on the crumbled stone.

Something was moving in the darkness.

Something *close.*

Did it always smell so foul here? Did she just not notice it because of the pain? Or was the stench getting closer, too?

Terrified, she gripped the ledge and jumped, her bare feet pawing at the stone, trying to heave herself upward. But she was tired after all she'd been through. It felt as if she were weighted down. She couldn't climb high enough to get her knee over it.

She groaned and strained, but she couldn't do it. She dropped back down, the broken stones jabbing at her poor, bare soles.

"Oh no, no, no, no, no," she panted. This wasn't good.

Again, she heard the crunch of broken stones in the darkness. A soft scrape. A huff of breath. The stench was definitely getting stronger. It was almost overwhelming. Like something dead and rotting on the side of the road.

She gripped the ledge and tried again, her toes slapping at the stone, trying to get a grip. Her hands were sweaty. She didn't know how long she could hold on. But if she couldn't climb up…

The very thought made her feel faint.

Again, she dropped down. Again, the broken stones jabbed her.

Was that a *growl* she heard?

She tried again. She jumped, ignoring the pain in her feet and knee. She kicked at the stone, pushing against it, struggling for traction. She strained and pulled.

This time, she managed to lock her elbows. She was above the upper floor. If she could see, she'd be looking down the safe passage. But she still had to get her weight up and over the ledge. And she could already feel her sweaty palms slipping.

The stone was too smooth. There was no grip, no friction. And she was quickly becoming tired. Her breath was growing ragged. It was going to be harder to hear whatever was moving in the darkness.

She lifted her leg and tried to hook it over the edge, but she couldn't quite reach. She wasn't as strong *or* as flexible as Nicole.

She couldn't do it. She dropped her leg and dangled there, her teeth clenched, struggling to hold on. But panic was quickly seeping in. How much longer did she have? She didn't know how much longer she could hold on, but if she dropped down again, she wasn't confident she'd have the strength to get up this far again.

She hiked her leg up, struggling to stretch up to the edge, but still couldn't reach it.

Then there was a great huff of a breath from somewhere in the lower passage, almost a snort. A dreadfully familiar noise roared to life, like the screaming of a chainsaw in some intense horror movie scene, chilling her blood.

Terrified, she thrust her leg up again, kicking at it, straining with all her strength, searching for the ledge.

She could hear the noise growing louder. The hound was coming, rushing down the passage toward her. She couldn't see it, but she remembered clearly what they looked like from last time. The image had burned itself into her brain, able to haunt her nightmares for months afterward. It was a massive thing, low to the ground, stocky and solid, built for sheer strength and power. The noise was its countless upright scales slashing back and forth, rubbing together, a blur of motion promising to shred flesh and bone alike.

And it was about to tear off her dangling foot!

With a terrified cry, she thrust her leg up again.

This time she made it! She dug her heel against the stone and heaved herself up as a disturbing gust of putrid wind puffed against her bare thigh and butt.

Then the noise was receding.

It had just rushed below her, she understood, barely missing her.

That was *way* too close!

And yet, she wasn't out of trouble yet. She was still dangling dangerously over the edge, one leg still flailing.

There was a great snort and the distinct sound of kicked gravel from the direction the hound went. Realizing it had missed her, it was turning around for another pass.

She let out another panicked cry and forced herself up into the safety of the upper passage.

But her balance was off.

She tried to roll onto her belly, but too much of her weight was leaning back. She was going to fall!

The hound was rushing toward her again, the sound of its scales deafening in the eerie darkness.

With a great, desperate sob, she thrust all her weight forward.

Below her, the hound shot past again, snarling and snapping

its powerful jaws, its blades screaming through the darkness.

She rolled into the passage and immediately crawled away from the ledge, half-convinced that it would find a way to climb up after her.

Crying and screaming, she scurried across the floor, then scrambled to her feet and ran, her arms thrust blindly in front of her.

Chapter 37

Gina sat motionless as something indescribable wafted through the space around her, tears wet on her cheeks, her heart aching. She'd always felt small and helpless, but this was an altogether different sort of small. She was literally little more than a speck in the vastness of this great, glass abyss. The twisted dimensions of this unnatural plane had warped such concepts as size and distance. It was probably the only reason these things hadn't already devoured her. But she couldn't hope to hide here forever. Already the unnatural things were circling closer, sweeping, searching, *hunting*.

It was only a matter of time.

She didn't belong in such a place. *No* human being was ever meant to be in a place such as this. This was the realm of monsters. Not *beasts*. Not *phantoms*. Not *abominations*. These were true *monsters*. Indescribable things beyond the most horrifying nightmares, things that would never fit into any sort of classification. They were beyond *definition*. They were outside of the meager range of human understanding.

She didn't dare move. Not a muscle. She didn't even risk a breath until the dreadful wafting thing had moved well beyond this empty chamber. But she followed it with her psychic gaze, watching its every movement, ensuring that it wasn't going to swing back again.

How much longer could she last in such a place?

But even as she watched that shadowy form vanish into the queer refractions of those unnatural glass walls, she felt a hand close around her own and she gasped, her heart leaping. "Nicole?" she whispered.

"Where are we?"

A great, wet sob bubbled up from deep inside her. She felt nearly dizzy with relief. Thank the goddess. Thank *all* the gods. *Any* gods. Thank *the* God. Whoever it was that brought Nicole back to her. She didn't *care* who it was. She'd never been so happy to hear someone's voice in all her life.

Nicole sat up, her hands groping at her, confused by the darkness still enveloping her. "What happened?"

"Don't worry about it," she gasped, already rising to her feet. "Get up. Hurry. We need to move."

"What's going on?" She was disoriented, but she stood up without protest.

"This way."

She'd lost count of how many times she'd mapped out the glass walls around her, plotting the fastest route away from the circling monstrosities closing in around them. There was little else *to* do but sketch out in her head what she should do in case Nicole miraculously returned to her.

And she'd done just that!

"Are we okay?" whispered Nicole. She sounded scared. Disoriented. And it was no wonder. She'd been asleep for a while.

"We will be," she promised. Was it possible she was only exhausted from all that had happened? She'd been through a lot, after all. Physically *and* emotionally. She'd have to ask her about it when they were a safe distance from the circling monstrosities. But right now it was more important to move from that spot they'd been stuck in for so long.

She turned left. Then right. Then *up*.

Again, Nicole stumbled as everything rotated. "I'm sorry…"

"It's fine. Not your fault. Just a little farther."

"Okay…" She sounded so meek and wounded. It was like speaking with another version of herself. And that felt so utterly *wrong*. She *hated* that she sounded like that! This was Nicole. She was strong, not weak. Confident, not cowering. She was nothing at all like her.

Again, she wondered if this was all her fault. Had she

messed everything up? Was she the reason it all went wrong?

She wiped away another wave of tears and turned down again, stumbling a little as the layout around her shifted, forcing her to change direction to avoid colliding with a wall.

There was a split in the path ahead of her. Right was a dead end. She needed to go left, but something was moving toward them from the right, about to cut them off. She didn't dare get to close to anything moving in this darkness, but going back would take too long. Things back there had noticed the movement. There was a swirling of those wafting, hairlike entities sweeping through the glass passageways, crowding closer with each passing second.

Her heart pounding, frightened out of her mind, she held her breath and rushed forward, darting into the left passage even as something wispy and electric danced through the air around her.

But then the two of them were past it, the path ahead clear.

That was entirely *too* close for comfort.

She turned left again. Then up. Then right.

Those awful unnatural presences dimmed into distant shadows and she finally stopped running.

She clutched at the thin fabric of her blouse over her pounding heart and leaned against the wall. "We should be safe here for a minute," she gasped. Long enough, hopefully, to at least catch their breath.

In the darkness, she felt Nicole lean against her.

"You okay?" she asked.

Nicole nodded. She seemed weary. And it was no wonder. The second she awoke from that strange, stubborn sleep, she grabbed her and dragged her through those glass corridors as fast as their legs would carry them.

"Sorry about that," she sighed, wiping again at her eyes. "Let's sit."

She slid down the wall and closed her eyes. She needed to rest. She wasn't used to all this physical activity. She was a homebody. And an artist. She spent most of her time sitting in front of a drawing pad. She should probably buy a treadmill or something…

Nicole knelt down beside her. Again, she pressed herself close, leaning against her.

"I'm sorry," she said again. The poor woman was probably exhausted and disoriented.

But having her this close to her was…well, *distracting.*

Her emotions were all jumbled up and it was no wonder. Fear and sadness, over and over again, fake and real, inward and outward. It was all so much. It must be weighing on Nicole, too.

But then something very unexpected happened. She felt Nicole's cheek pressed against her own. She felt her breath on her skin. She felt her lips brush against her skin.

Then a small kiss, gentle and soft.

"What're you doing?" she asked, her voice cracking a little. Again, her heart was pounding.

"You saved me," whispered Nicole.

"That's okay," she said, leaning back, uncomfortable.

But those strong arms reached around her, encircling her, holding her. She was pressing closer, her lips tracing a path down her cheek, to her lower jaw, along her chin, kissing her again and again. So softly…

It felt so…*alien.*

"You don't have to do that…" she said, her voice trembling.

"Relax," she whispered. "Let it happen. Trust me."

Relax? How could she just "let it happen"? What *was* even happening? Why was she doing this? She was so confused!

"It's dangerous here… We shouldn't…"

But then Nicole was kissing her lips and every thought inside her head seemed to melt away.

This wasn't anything like when that monstrous entity kissed her before shattering the glass labyrinth and setting the thing with too many mouths loose to wreak havoc. That was strange and sinister and frightful. It felt like the owner of that mysterious voice was making fun of her. This was different. This was so much warmer…so much…nicer…

Nicole was so beautiful. A woman like her should want

nothing to do with a meaningless little nobody. She never would have dreamed that something like this could ever happen to her. It was so wonderfully tender and beautiful… It was like an unobtainable dream… She wanted so badly to just let it happen…

Then those sweet lips pulled away. She gasped, breathless.

She felt as if she might pass out.

Again, Nicole's body pressed against hers, those firm, beautiful breasts soft against her own modest chest. She kissed her neck. Then again, a little higher this time.

Why did she feel so dizzy? Was it this intimate feeling that she never thought she'd ever experience? Or was it the woman pressed against her, so mesmerizingly beautiful? Or was it this place, toying with her mind, muddling up her feelings.

She felt Nicole bite down on her earlobe, firm but gentle, nibbling at her, sending an intense tingle through her body. The sensation was like nothing she'd ever felt before. It made her feel sort of lightheaded.

Then Nicole whispered into her ear, "Anun amum ut mu."

Gina froze, an icy terror instantly gripping her entire body. All at once, that tingly sensation didn't feel so nice. Suddenly, her skin was *crawling*. "What?" she squeaked.

Nicole let go of her earlobe and pulled away. In the same instant, her hands closed around her throat. "Anun Goar Nangup," she hissed in a voice that was like something out of her nightmares.

Chapter 38

Albert couldn't remember what happened. He was caught in the sex room again, stripped of his senses, reenacting the events of that night six years ago with the woman who would someday become his wife. Except it wasn't Brandy. At some point that witch took her place, forcing him to do those things to *her* even though he would sooner have gouged out his own eyes.

It wasn't that she desired him, he knew. It was precisely because he didn't want to do it that she forced him onto her. It was that sick obsession of treating people as dolls, the twisted power trip she must have felt forcing people to do things they'd never do on their own and watching their minds unravel in the process.

But what really turned her on was violence. It didn't take long for the illusion to descend into bloodshed. He couldn't remember precisely how it happened, or when, but at some point he realized he was choking her. Then he was hitting her. Over and over again. There was blood everywhere. Everything descended into madness.

He was back in *her* memories now, playing the part of another of her unfortunate slaves under her complete control. He was naked. He wasn't sure if he was still naked from that fucked-up nostalgia tour back to the sex room or if it was only because the people in this memory were naked. And he was covered in blood, though he wasn't sure whose. He couldn't even remember standing up. What happened to the sex room? He was stalking a limping, sobbing woman down a dark hallway with a pair of kitchen shears.

(Dolly was fond of scissors, it seemed.)

This couldn't go on. He wouldn't last much longer. She'd

drive him insane. He had to get out from under her thumb and regain control.

He had to get back to Brandy.

But it wasn't like he could just run away. All of this was taking place inside his head, wasn't it? What happened to his body? Was he lying unconscious in the temple somewhere, dreaming all of this?

No matter how he looked at it, there was no way out. He was trapped in this place with her. He might as well be locked in a cage with this monster.

(*Remember, magic can open doors that can't be unlocked.*)

Shanzer's cryptic words crept back to him. Was it only a coincidence that he remembered those words just when he thought of this situation as being "locked up"? Or did the clever old pervert's advice have more meaning than he ever expected?

He stopped walking and stood there in the darkness, distracted.

Magic…

Dolly was right in front of him now, her face almost touching his, those deceptively pretty blue eyes searching him, suspicious. "What's going on in there?" she wondered.

What indeed? He found that he wasn't exactly *thinking* anything. He didn't dare to let the thoughts form into words. She was right here, after all, not really standing in front of him, but *inside him*, aware of every passing thought in his brain.

He let his mind stay blank while some deeper, far more hidden part of his subconscious pondered this mess.

The shaman's book might hold the answer.

He didn't have it. Not here in this Dolly-controlled nightmare. He didn't even have the shorts it was in. But that wasn't really a problem. He'd found that he could read it in the dark. He'd found that he could read it without even taking it from his pocket. Why would he need to even know where it was to read it?

He could almost see the pages turning in the far back of his mind. Words and phrases floated through his consciousness like shadows across the surface of a trickling stream. They possessed no substance, but they were there. He was aware of them. They filled his head in a strange and subtle way that he couldn't describe.

But he found that he liked it. This was easier than studying the old-fashioned way.

Dolly leaned closer, those piercing eyes boring into him. "You think you're clever, don't you?"

He did, actually. He'd always been good at figuring things out. And right now, something felt very *right* for a change.

(*Psychic abilities and magic make a surprisingly natural combination. One enhances the other. Magic can be used to boost psychic strength and likewise those same mysterious powers of the mind can increase the effectiveness of magic. I can't say with any certainty whether there was a connection between the two from the start or if they came about separately and it was merely by chance that they paired so well. The origins of both predate this universe, after all.*)

Somehow, he understood that the book itself was the key to this trick. He wouldn't be able to do the same with just any book. It needed to be a spellbook.

Dolly smirked at him. "Doesn't matter," she decided. He felt her hand close around his scrotum, a sadistic gleam in her eyes. "You know the phrase, right?"

Of course he did. How could he miss it? She had him by the balls. Both literally and figuratively. She was in control here. These were her memories. This was *her* twisted brain at work.

She had her own psychic powers, after all, frightful powers that turned anyone she set her sociopathic attention on into a helpless puppet.

Somewhere in the spellbook, deep within the passages that were once locked away beneath that magical code but was now revealed to him, Shanzer wrote about the burning mountain, about the four women who all began as strangers but would each and every one become like family to him, and how they all worked together, helping him to eventually reach the blazing summit even with a broken arm.

He wrote about the Keeper and about Lucas Kneede, the pretend devil, about lies and deceit…and about a secret he still couldn't see…

The Shaman of Wevenwert knew an awful lot about things, it seemed. He even wrote about that frightful confrontation between him and Kneede, his attempt to stall him so that the girls could reach the door and end it. But Kneede was a step ahead of him. Unbeknownst to Albert, he was barring the way forward the entire time, preventing them from reaching the door.

If not for those carrion eaters…

A sharp pain tore through his groin, scattering his thoughts and wrenching him back to Dolly's nightmare prison. That deceptively dainty hand clasped around his scrotum. Those sharp, black nails.

He cried out and grasped at her wrist, trying to pull her hand away.

How was she so strong? She was so *tiny*.

"I don't like being ignored," she informed him as she dug her nails in deeper.

She was going to rip them off!

As he struggled to release himself from her cruel grip, she reached up with her other hand and closed it around his chin. Her nails sank into the flesh of his cheeks like syringes. There was pain. Lots of it. But the worst part was feeling those nails emerge inside his mouth, sliding across his teeth, cutting into his gums. There was so much blood. It filled up his mouth, coating his tongue. He cried out and watched it spray from his lips, spattering her face, making her look even more deranged.

"Somebody's getting a little too cocky for their own good, I think." That evil smirk was back on her face again, those deceptive eyes twinkling with renewed delight. "Pervy little playthings like yourself need to be put in their places."

With a searing pain, she snatched the hand cutting into his face back, neatly slicing through the flesh, opening him up.

His blood-filled screams echoed down the endless hallway.

He let go of her other wrist and reached up to cover his face, meaning to stop the bleeding, but what his hands found wasn't neat cuts but gaping wounds.

"Not so cute anymore," she informed him in that sadistic

giggle.

He couldn't see what she'd done to him, but he could feel it. His face was in tatters. He could feel his teeth showing.

"No girl in her right mind is gonna let you fuck her now." She crowded closer to him, a wicked gleam in her eyes, and whispered, "so you're not gonna need *this* anymore."

Before he could process what she'd just said, she did the same with her other hand. There was a terrible sort of ripping sound and a great, wet splatter of blood. But most of all, there was *pain.*

Chapter 39

Corey didn't know how long he'd been at it. He'd long ago lost count of how many fuses he'd changed. But it seemed to him that entirely *too much* time had passed, far longer than he should've been able to spend at this work.

It was as if time were as empty as everything else in this bizarre city devoid of substance, like that strange lack of any kind of smell, making it impossible for him to feel the passing of it. It felt like a strange thing to think, as if he were letting his imagination run wild and Violet should be telling him any moment to stop talking nonsense and focus on what he was supposed to be doing. (She used to do that all the time when they were in school and he couldn't focus on his studies.) But at the same time, he found that he simply knew it to be true. Even time was hollow in this place.

He located the next malfunctioning fixture and went to work. It was no wonder his mind simplified the process of fixing the lights from replacing the electrical hardware to merely changing a quick fuse. He wouldn't have had a fraction of this many done if that were the case. This was far easier. And he'd managed to fall into a rhythm. He could practically do it blindfolded. He didn't have to think about it. Which meant he could let his mind wander. He could ponder the strange, living metaphor his consciousness was immersed in.

It was no coincidence that he'd imagined the Keeper's machine—which was shaped like a great, sprawling city—as an actual *modern* city. It made sense that this version would be deserted and silent and devoid of so many of the things that defined a city when the City Beyond Memory had none of those things. It even made a certain sort of sense that he'd imagine the damage caused by the mystery saboteur as an electrical problem, since that was about as close as his human brain could probably get to whatever was really going on.

He closed the cover and immediately made his way back to the elevator. There were three damaged lights in this building and that was the last one. He could return to the street now and move on to the next.

As he descended, his thoughts drifted back to the conversation he had with Austin about all the things the human mind couldn't comprehend, and how Austin, himself, was one of those things.

(*I can't explain something to you that you have no way of understanding. There are components of my body that exist outside the range of your human senses and beyond your ability to understand.*)

It wasn't just something he dreamed up. It was a scientific fact that there was a lot more going on in the universe than human beings were capable of perceiving. The universe they existed in could only be defined by their senses, what they could see and hear and smell and taste and feel. Not to mention all the other senses the human body possessed that didn't tend to get mentioned, like one's sense of balance or temperature and all the senses the body used for everything from body awareness to deciding when to stop eating or drinking to when and how deeply to breathe. That was a lot of information the body collected, and yet it was also so very limited. He'd always been intrigued by the fact that the visible spectrum was only zero point zero zero three five percent of the total electromagnetic spectrum, meaning that there could be a great deal happening everywhere that people simply couldn't see. The same was true of human hearing and smell, which was far more limited than most other animals on the planet. And when confronted with something it couldn't comprehend, the mind simply made stuff up to compensate. It filled in the blanks with false data to make sense of the chaos.

(*Human brains are foolish. You never know what nonsense they'll choose to believe over the truth when it's outside their narrow field of understanding.*)

He wondered just what that meant for him here in this place. If he tried hard enough, could he change something? Could he conjure himself up a limousine to shuttle him from one infected building to the next? Even better, what about a taco truck? He could really go for a bite. How long had it been since he ate? *Could* he eat in this place? Or would it only be like *dreaming* about eating?

Thinking with your stomach again.

"Can't help bein' hungry," he replied. Then he frowned at the realization that he'd just spoken aloud to Violet's voice inside his head. Why would he do that? What *was* this voice in his head? Was it another part of the illusion? A splash of familiarity in an otherwise alien world? Or was it only in his mind? Some sort of subconscious manifestation, perhaps having to do with knowing that there could be a very real possibility of him never seeing her again?

The elevator arrived at the ground floor and the doors slid open. He followed the empty hallway back to the front entrance and stepped out onto the gloomy street again.

How many buildings had he set right? He'd lost count. And yet had he even made a difference? Lights flickered up and down the street ahead of him. Some had dimmed to a faint glow. Others had taken on strange and sickly hues, as if shining through some foul and noxious mold.

Again, he was reminded of floating helpless in the depths of space, unable to do anything, unable to even move. How many buildings would he have to climb? How many lights would he have to repair? How many thousands of buildings could be standing in a city this size? How easy would it be to miss one?

He began to realize that the problem was much bigger than he anticipated. It wasn't merely the terminal that was infected. Whatever this thing was, it had wormed its way through the entire machine, across the entire City Beyond Memory, spreading its malicious programing throughout the temple. Was this even possible for just one man?

Time, Violet reminded him.

Right. That sense of empty time, the feeling like he'd been

combing these deserted streets for an impossible number of hours. Or days. Or even *years*, for all he knew.

A failsafe, perhaps? A clever feature coded into the program long ago to ensure he could complete the task? Or was it merely the nature of a virtual existence that time would be rendered meaningless?

It might feel like forever, but somehow he understood that at some point he'd just simply find himself standing in front of the final building, feeling simultaneously as if he'd spent an eternity in this place and as if no time had passed at all.

He just had to keep going.

He set his sights on the nearest of those tainted windows as he approached and made a mental note of where those rooms were.

But a strange feeling passed over him, making him freeze in his tracks.

Something wasn't right. Something in the air had changed.

No, that didn't feel right. *Was* there air in this place? Was he breathing? He *felt* like he was breathing, he could feel the sensation of taking in air and expelling it again, and he certainly wasn't suffocating, but he felt strangely as if whatever was filling his lungs was as empty as everything else, as if it were merely a habit. This place was so bizarre. He felt simultaneously as if he did and didn't exist.

"Digital world," he muttered to himself, thoughtful. "Like virtual reality." And yet it was nothing so mundane as a VR headset. Again, he was trying to fit it all into his narrow, human perception of the universe, applying the logic of things he understood in an attempt to understand what he was experiencing when in reality, none of this had nothing at all to do with computers or video games or viruses or anything else he could possibly comprehend. And yet he wasn't entirely wrong, either. Whatever this place was, it was closer to a virtual world than anything else that existed in his universe. But those similarities were little more than coincidences.

He was caught in a paradox. He couldn't possibly understand what was really happening here. He didn't possess the tools to comprehend the basic workings of beings as complex as the sentinels. And so he was forced to apply logic that he *could* comprehend in order to navigate it. As such, that logic was deeply flawed. And yet he needed that flawed logic in order to operate within this alien environment.

The blueprints embedded in his genetic memory were satisfactory for working within the physical temple. He was able to do what needed done almost on an instinctual level, practically without thinking, like using muscle memory. But in here, he was at the mercy of a framework of logic that contradicted his very reality.

It was like walking through an alien world.

And just like in some grand space odyssey, there were unknown dangers.

Something caught his eye and he looked out across the city skyline. Something seemed to ripple through the air, invisible but for brief shimmers, like glints of light on the surface of flowing water in the dark. It seemed to rise up from behind the distant structures, an amorphous shape that was much less seen than felt.

As he watched, it crawled over the walls, blotting out the glowing windows of those distant buildings.

The infection…

It didn't merely sabotage Austin and the machine and then move on. It was *still here*. A malicious virus worming its way through the system, wreaking havoc.

It sloughed across the skyline and out of view.

Corey hurried forward to the next intersection so he could see which way it was going, only to find that it was even bigger than he expected.

Rolling blackouts crawled across the skyline, blotting out the lights in the windows one by one. And when the darkness passed and the lights winked back into existence, many of them were dim or sickly colored or flickering.

It was like watching some invisible titan crawl through the city, spreading destruction everywhere it touched.

So many damaged fuses…

It was moving far faster than he could possibly fix them. He never stood a chance against it.

Chapter 40

There were a lot of filaments now. Violet had to creep through the space, ducking under some, stepping over others. More than once, she'd had to crawl. It was excruciatingly slow. And deeply unpleasant. But by some stroke of uncharacteristic luck, she managed not to cut herself on any of them and bring that *thing* rushing after her again.

She hadn't heard any of those monstrous murmurs or felt any shudders in the stone since Everett lured it away. Had his ballsy sacrifice actually allowed her to slip away unnoticed? Once again, it seemed she owed him her life.

The little shit had better not be dead…

She wiped at her eyes and forced herself to concentrate. It wouldn't matter what he'd done if she let herself make another stupid mistake.

She turned sideways and slipped past two more threads stretched across her path—one vertical, one diagonal—then paused to scan the space ahead of her. For the first time in a while, she found the way clear.

But she didn't dare let her guard down.

That raw, porous stone stretched up into the darkness ahead of her, less a wall than a steep slope. She didn't want to keep going. Her hands were burning. Her feet felt raw. Her knees were scraped up and bleeding. And it felt like every muscle in her body was aching. But staying here wasn't an option. She needed to keep going. If she stopped, she might miss Everett. And she wanted so much to see him again.

So she could kick his scrawny little ass for scaring her so bad!

She started up the slope, her weary body protesting, her eyes wide open for any hidden threads waiting to ambush her in the dark.

She *really* didn't want to do this anymore.

But when she paused to shine her light up into that darkness, still searching for more of those dangerous webs, she saw that there was an opening at the top. Not just another hole in the stone to crawl through, but a complete shift in texture. Smooth and polished, with perfect ninety-degree angles, in stark contrast to the raw, coarse stone around it.

The labyrinth.

She was almost there!

She never thought she'd be so happy to see those dull gray corridors again. Her heart leaped with relief at the idea of being free of the graymother's strange nest. But at the same time, it seemed to sink into her stomach as she realized that she'd found her way here without Everett…

She wiped at her eyes again and began to climb. The sooner she reached that passage up there, the sooner she'd at least have a little less to worry about. No more razor-sharp webs to stumble across. No more rough stone butchering her poor feet. No more *graymother.*

No more Everett…

She clenched her teeth and growled at herself. She didn't know that. He could still be safe. He was resilient. That much was abundantly clear by now. If *anyone* could find a way out of that mess, she was sure it was him.

And he had that creepy-ass doll with him. That had to be worth *something*, right?

She continued up the final slope, wincing at the pain in her poor, unprotected toes against the rough, punishing stone.

Thinking wasn't doing her any favors right now. Her mind wouldn't stop going back to him, wouldn't stop prodding at the worst possible scenarios. She was so worried, so afraid she'd never see him again. She needed to focus on climbing. She needed to focus on getting out of this dangerous nest. And she needed to focus on watching out for those invisible filaments. If she wasn't careful—

Something bit into her little toe, startling a painful yelp from her.

She closed her eyes and hissed through her teeth. That hurt! How deep did it cut her? She was afraid to look. She still didn't know just *how* sharp those strands could be.

But she didn't have time to worry about the pain or the severity of the injury.

Another of those dreadful shudders swept through the stone all around her, freezing her insides and filling her head with those awful not-voices that made her want to scream.

Now she'd done it. She was so close to the exit, and she let herself miss one of those damned webs. Now the graymother knew where she was. It was speeding toward her already.

She ignored the pain in her toe and climbed as fast as she could go.

The exit was only about twenty feet away, but it was twenty feet roughly *up*. Her foot ached with every step she took. She could feel a hot and unpleasant wet feeling spreading in the bottom of her sock. Blood. Yet she had no choice but to keep climbing, regardless of the pain. The air around her was heavy, like a foul, wafting miasma. And it was *screaming*. Her ears pounded with the intensity of it, in painful contrast to the eerie silence that surrounded her. It felt as if her bones were turning to ice. And a tightness was gripping her heart, making it hard to catch her breath.

How close was it? How quickly would it catch up and swallow her in that horrible, nameless color?

She glanced up. Fifteen feet remaining, give or take. She was moving far too slow. She'd never make it in time. Already the darting light from her flashlight was changing colors, tinting toward the unknowable.

Everett's sacrifice was for nothing after all.

It's not like anything else that ever was. An anomaly, alien to every world, a consciousness from somewhere beyond.

Beyond *what*? Violet didn't understand. What was "beyond"?

Something never created, never born, never evolved. Something that was already there. Something from far away that came here long ago.

She stared down into the gaping earth at the rough, porous stone the faceless monstrosities had unearthed. It sounded as if this…*thing*…had come from beyond…well, *everything*. Like an alien lifeform from the farthest reaches of whatever was beyond the boundaries of the entire known *universe*. A literal extra-terrestrial, but not one from anywhere as close by as Mars or even the most distant galaxy. Did that make that rough stone she'd been climbing through some kind of massive *meteorite*?

And the Keeper's faceless worker bees just…built their city *around* it?

It is a thing beyond our comprehension, monstrous even to us, yet even it *has a place in the Keeper's unfathomable design.*

This was too much. Her thoughts were reeling. *What* place could a thing like that possibly have except to instill terror and to kill? Who *was* the Keeper? *What* was he? That was what she wanted to know. Because he sounded crazier than that psychotic Priestess of Ruin!

And for that matter, what was she even doing back here in this distant, long-dead dream world? Wasn't she in dire peril at the moment? Wasn't the alien entity lurking inside that massive tangle of stone on the very verge of *devouring* her in her own time and place?

There's nothing to fret about, the other one assured her. This body had no face. It had no mouth, no lips, and yet somehow she clearly felt the other one smile. It was as if she'd reached down inside herself with those long, freaky fingers and pulled up the corners of her own human mouth. *I was able to help again.*

Violet gasped and sat up. Where was she? What happened?

The world had been painted in that awful nonexistent color again. The graymother's silent-yet-shrieking voice filled her head. She clutched at her ears, though it did no good. There was no sound. There was only an intense sensation of that deafening noise *inside* her.

Then it was all just simply gone.

She was sitting on the smooth stone floor of one of the

temple's many labyrinth corridors, her flashlight lying beside her, illuminating the doorway leading back into the graymother's nest.

It was filled with countless shimmering webs, barring the way back.

The other one had taken the wheel again and helped her to escape, just like she did from the Not-Everett so many hours ago…

A terrified sob escaped her before she could stop it and she lay back on the hard floor, clutching at her face.

She couldn't handle much more of this.

Chapter 41

(Wake up.)

Everett groaned and opened his eyes.

He was lying on the ground in the dark. His head was pounding. Where was he?

Slowly, it all came back to him. He had to save Violet. He left her in that space and hurried *down*, hoping to draw it away from her. But even with Alice showing him the way, he wasn't able to navigate the rough path. It was narrow and uneven. His ankle turned.

He fell.

He must've hit his head when he landed. That would explain the terrible headache. But what happened after that? How did the graymother not…well, he wasn't entirely sure *what* the graymother did to people it caught. But somehow he didn't think it just sniffed his motionless body, kicked some dust at him, then wandered off like a satisfied bear having made its point.

(Carried you.)

He frowned at this thought. Alice carried him? That didn't make sense. He must've misunderstood her strange language. Because Alice was only a doll. She couldn't move on her own, much less lift the weight of a person. And she hadn't moved, he didn't think. He could feel her, still clutched against him, as if even unconscious he hadn't dared let her go.

Or maybe it was *she* who was actually clinging to *him*.

He sat up and rubbed at the knot on the back of his head. That really hurt.

He blinked into the darkness for a moment, processing everything. Where was he? The floor under him wasn't rough like the graymother's nest. It was smooth and flat, more like…

(Labyrinth.)

"I'm back in there?" he asked aloud. The sound of his voice startled him. It sounded so loud in the silence that surrounded him.

(Not where we need to be.)

He frowned. No, he supposed they wouldn't be. She told him they needed to go *up*. To the top of the nest. But he went down to lure the graymother away. If she *did* somehow "carry him" out of there, it wasn't through the exit she meant for him to take. She must've found a different opening back into the labyrinth.

"Sorry," he said, whispering this time. Although he wasn't *really* sorry, he supposed. He hoped Violet was safe, wherever she ended up. That was the most important thing.

He rose to his feet and felt at his surroundings. Walls on two sides. A ceiling above, low enough for him to reach. It felt like one of those many passageways, but he was completely blind without a light. Which way did they go from here?

He turned and looked to his left. That way.

It was so weird the way she did that. There were no words, no movements of any sort. He merely asked a question and then immediately knew the answer, as if he'd always known it.

But he didn't know the answer. That was why he asked the question.

This was so weird.

(Long way.)

"I know," he muttered. They were taking the long way. And she wasn't particularly happy about it. But there was no use fussing over it now.

He started walking. It was weird, making his way through this place in the dark. Kind of unsettling, if he were being honest. Last time he was left to wander in the dark, he was with Andrea. She held his hand through most of that.

It was still kind of funny that it turned out she had a flashlight in her pocket and he had fresh batteries in his that whole time. He smiled a little at the memory. The way she giggled when they figured it out was so endearing.

He hoped *she* was safe out there, too. And Olivia and Wayne. He hoped *everyone* was safe.

He was approaching a passage that branched off to the right. Alice wanted him to take it. He reached out and dragged his fingertips along the wall, confirming what she planted in his head. There was, indeed, a passage there. Not that he doubted her. He was past that. He simply didn't trust himself not to turn too soon or too late and run face-first into the wall.

The path before him flickered through his mind like broken images on a movie projector. Passage after passage. Intersection after intersection. They seemed to stretch on forever, with no destination in sight.

He scowled down at her. "No, it would *not* have been better to leave her for the graymother and escape. That's terrible. Keep talking like that and I'll leave you here."

It wasn't an idle threat. He brought her back from the dollhouse because she helped him. He felt like he owed her that much. But if she became a danger to others, he wouldn't hesitate to abandon her in this darkness.

She seemed to understand this, because the selfish notion vanished from his mind as if it had never been there at all.

He pushed onward, saying no more about it. But he wouldn't forget it. It was concerning, the idea that she could put awful notions like that into his head so easily. He had to remind himself that she wasn't human. Alice was a spirit that slumbered alone for eons in the upside-down place beyond the void. Given that, it was probably a matter of simple logic. Even a human being wouldn't know about things like friendship and kindness and selflessness if they grew up all alone, without any social contact. Survival would probably be the primary motivation for everything they did. It wasn't malice that made her suggest that course of action. She didn't want to hurt anyone. She only wanted to protect herself in this strange new world she'd stumbled into. And she wanted to protect him, too. He felt this deep down. She wasn't merely clinging to him because he rescued her from the burning dollhouse. She didn't *have* to stay with him. She was choosing it as much as he was.

The fact was that he felt responsible for Alice. He was the reason she was in this form, a product of his imagination made physical by the weird properties of that inverted world. He remade her. He captured her. He *imprisoned* her. He gave her no choice but to help him escape that paper dollhouse, but she *did* help. And he owed her for that.

He *really* hoped he didn't make a mistake by bringing her back with him.

Chapter 42

Brandy screamed and sat up, slapping at the monstrous little crab things.

But they were gone.

She was no longer surrounded by towering grass beneath a blistering sun. She was somewhere dark and cold and wet, filled with the smell of earthy, underground places.

Was she back in the temple again? Everything was pitch black. Where was the flashlight? Did she lose it?

No… She remembered now. It was in her pocket. She put it there to save the battery when she found herself outside in the sun.

She fumbled for it with one hand while running the other over her body. This was so confusing. The excruciating pain from all those stings had vanished as completely as that field, as did all the scratches and gouges from being dragged through that rough grass.

Was none of that real? Was it all some sort of vivid nightmare?

No. It was nothing as simple as that. She was still damp with sweat. Her skin felt hot, as if she'd taken too much sun. And her shoes and Albert's shirt were gone. She was down to only her shorts and socks. The bottom of her foot even felt a little sore from limping around in just one shoe. But it was as if everything after she ducked off that path never happened.

"What the fuck was that?" she breathed.

"Just having some fun."

She cried out in surprise and scrambled away from the voice. She was still here? Was she just sitting there in the dark, waiting for her to wake up so she could start torturing her again?

She finished fumbling the flashlight out of her pocket and switched it on, then jabbed it at the darkness where the voice came from.

No one was there.

She swung it back and forth, scanning the space in front of her, then turned and looked the other way.

What the fuck was going on? Where'd she go? What was she even dealing with?

Somewhere in the darkness, however, someone was giggling.

"Who's there?" she demanded.

"Me?" asked the unseen presence, mocking coyness.

"No, the *other* spooky bitch hiding in the dark," she snapped.

The voice laughed at this. Again, she felt as if she'd heard that laugh somewhere before. Who did this remind her of? This wasn't how that creepy cat lady talked. Or either of the Luciannas…

"I'm just your ordinary, everyday Goddess of Ruin."

Ruin? That nightmare apocalypse dimension with the blood red sky where everything turned ancient and rotten?

(Beware the Ruin.)

Warner warned them of that place. And Lucianna said someone was interfering with things. Someone *powerful*. Someone capable of sending the mysterious infection that killed the original gatekeeper.

(*Only a god could've conspired to bring the infection here. No one else possesses that kind of power.*)

It was all an excruciating blur, but didn't the sky back in that blistering field start to turn red as those stinging monsters swarmed her?

And now this woman was introducing herself as a goddess?

"Get away from me," she growled.

"Don't be afraid," cooed the self-proclaimed goddess. "I'm friendly. *Very* friendly."

Someone grabbed her from behind, startling her, making

her drop the flashlight. It rolled away, leaving her bathed in gloom while arms that were soft and slender but frightfully strong held her, preventing her from moving. One hand closed around her breast and began kneading it.

"Hey!" she shouted, trying to pry the offending limb off her. "Hands off!"

"What?" purred that awful voice in her ear again. "You don't want to play with me?"

"Get off me!" She tried to pull away, but she couldn't move. This woman—if she were any such thing—was far too strong. She couldn't budge her. She couldn't even turn her head to see who was there. All she could see was long, dark curls of hair in the gloom.

"But I thought you were a sex witch," she whispered, her lips brushing her earlobe, her breath tickling her. "Don't nasty little sluts like you *enjoy* being used like filthy playthings?"

"Excuse *you*!" snapped Brandy. "Get your whore hands off me!"

But she didn't take her hands off her. Instead, she inserted her tongue into her ear.

She screamed. The sensation was both ticklish and revolting. She couldn't stand it, yet she couldn't pull away. She was trapped under her weight. "*Get off me*!" she shrieked.

"Come on," she cooed, though Brandy couldn't figure out how she was able to talk without withdrawing her foul tongue from her ear. How long *was* that tongue? It felt like it was burrowing into her skull! "I can make you feel things that'll make the sex room feel like Sunday school."

"Fuck off!"

The tongue vanished. In an instant, there was no one there. She was alone again.

Was that all in her head?

She didn't waste time trying to understand it. She lurched forward and snatched her flashlight off the floor.

"Girls not your thing?"

"Fucking *psycho* girls with *god complexes* sure aren't!" She turned and shined her light behind her, revealing not a woman standing there, but the towering form of an actual, living sentinel, its huge, ungodly penis dangling right in front of her face.

"Is this more to your liking?" asked the voice as two freakishly long hands grasped her head, holding her in place.

She screamed and tried to pull away, revolted at the very idea of what might happen next, only to fall onto her back when the sentinel, too, vanished without a trace.

Immature laughter echoed throughout the dark chamber.

"*What the fuck is wrong with you?*" shrieked Brandy, swinging her light back and forth, trying to pinpoint the origin of the voice. "*Come out where I can see you! Fucking bitch!*"

Then she was right in front of her, a flesh-and-blood woman. And little *else.*

"Wait…" she stammered. She knew this woman. That high forehead. Those freckles. The slight overbite. Immediately, she realized that this was exactly where she recognized that laugh from. "Stella?"

Something hit her, knocking her onto her back again. In an instant, she found herself pinned to the floor with Stella Umbertain, of all the people in the world, perched atop her. "Surprise!"

Andrea's friend from college? *She* was the all-powerful god wreaking havoc everywhere?

Brandy couldn't move. Stella held both her wrists with one hand, pinning her in place as if she were a helpless child instead of a grown woman. She wasn't even sure how she managed to do that. It happened so fast! "Get off me!"

"What? You'd rather I send you back out into the grass?"

She cried out, frustrated. Was that a threat? Could she do that? *Would* she do that? So much was happening so quickly. She could barely keep up.

With her free hand, Stella reached up and caressed her cheek. "Just be a good girl and relax. I promise I'll be gentle."

"Fuck you!" she spat. "I said get off me! Why are you here?"

"I'm always here. I'm *everywhere.*"

"What the fuck does *that* mean?"

She leaned close to her, grinning an unsettling, salacious

sort of grin. "I've always been just out of sight, watching, listening. I've seen every dirty thing you've ever done. You naughty little whore."

"Oh my god! Go to hell, bitch!" What was with everybody spying on her? And why *her* of all people? "*You're* the one fucking everything up?"

Stella reached up and swept her hair out of her face, letting those obscene, heavy breasts sway just inches above her. "I keep telling people I'm a chaos goddess. It's not my fault if you think I'm just being facetious."

"And you look like *that*?"

Her expression soured. "Really? You too?"

"What?"

She plopped down on top of her, forcing a startled "oof" out of her. "Forget all that. Let's have some *real* girl talk."

"Get your gross tits off me!"

But Stella ignored her. "Tell the truth. You're sick and tired of the Keeper's shit, right? You're done. You don't want to play his fucking game anymore. So here's an idea. What if you just…*didn't*?"

"What are you talking about?" What was wrong with this woman? Was this *really* Andrea's friend? The same one that sometimes came to parties with her? Had she been letting an actual evil goddess into her home these past four years? That made no sense!

"I'm talking about breaking his precious machine."

"Why would I do that?"

Stella's eyes sparkled with mischievous delight. "Come on. I'll let ya fuck me."

"In your dreams!"

Stella's laughter echoed through the darkness. She was clearly enjoying this.

"Why are you so determined to fuck up the Keeper's plans?"

"Because if I leave it all to *him*, I know the next world will be fucking *boring*."

"Better boring than non-existent!"

"Are you sure about that?" she countered.

"Pretty fucking sure, yeah!"

"No, not the boring versus non-existent thing. I mean the part about the next world not existing if you don't follow the Keeper's script."

"What?"

Stella was leaning over her, so close that their noses brushed together. "Wanna hear a secret?"

Chapter 43

Erin made her way across the stone walkway suspended over those dark, half-submerged figures and surrounded by those enormous alien bones, desperate to cross this space before something terrible could happen. And why *wouldn't* something terrible happen in a place like this? But she didn't dare run. Her foot had already slipped once, threatening to send her plunging into whatever nightmare was waiting below for her, a heart-stopping reminder that she couldn't afford to be careless.

Every time she shined her light down there, she saw more of those figures. They were everywhere. Hundreds of them. And every time she dared to look back, they were always facing her, regardless of how they were standing when she passed over them.

Were they *always* there? Had they been down there since she first reached the bottom of the steps and she simply didn't notice them? They were somewhat hard to see. They were little more than shadows against the black water. But there were so many of them. It was hard to imagine that she didn't see them at first.

Were they *gathering* down there?

That bad feeling in her gut was getting worse.

Whatever those things were, she was convinced that they weren't just curious about her. They were *dangerous.* The more she saw of them, the more convinced she was that they were perfectly capable of harming her.

But *why* were they there? The question nagged at her. Were they *supposed* to be standing down there? Were they a part of this place? Were they guarding the thorn from would-be thieves? And did that include *her*?

Horatio sent her here. He told her this was the task she was meant to complete. Didn't that mean that she was *supposed* to be here? And if so, would they ignore her? Or would they protect their treasure indiscriminately, even from the one person the thorn had been waiting all this time for?

But on the heels of that came another unpleasant thought. What if she'd been lied to? What if she *wasn't* the one who was supposed to retrieve the thorn? What if Horatio wasn't who he claimed to be and she was instead the very intruder these things were guarding it from?

After all, what did she really know about any of this? Everything she'd been told, every gut feeling she'd had, every thought in her head could have been a part of some convoluted scheme since the very beginning and she'd never know the difference.

She wanted to look back to see what those creepy black figures were doing, but she didn't dare. She was afraid of what she might see. What if they were climbing up onto the walkway?

Or reaching out from right behind her?

A terrified sob escaped her at the thought and she hated it. She didn't cry easily. Crying never solved anything. It only made people think you weren't strong enough to take care of yourself. She learned that early in life.

But she supposed nothing in her life could ever have prepared her for this.

It felt as if the whole world had gone mad.

More of those enormous bones emerged from the darkness ahead of her. She still couldn't make heads or tails out of what manner of creature it was or even what sort of body part those particular bones would have supported. Nor did she have time to contemplate it. Twisted and gnarled and half-woven together, they stretched up and over the walkway like groping fingers. She ducked under the first of them easily enough, but the next were lower, forcing her to drop to her hands and knees and crawl under.

Her naked butt brushed against the underside of one as she scurried beneath it. It was cold and wet and both rough and slimy. The feel of it against her skin filled her with a revulsion that, even in her heightened state of panic, felt disproportionate to the situation. They were only bones, after all.

She crawled on for another several feet to make sure she wouldn't touch it again when she tried to stand, then stood and dared a look back.

The shadowy things were still gathering below her, each and every one of those creepy beak-like faces turned to follow her.

God, but they were creepy! Why were they only moving while her back was turned? They were like those freaky weeping angel statues from *Dr. Who* that she'd seen while surfing the web on her phone. She'd never even watched that show and those things were terrifying! Why would there be something like that here?

She hurried forward, her heart racing.

Why was she here? That was the real question. Thinking back on it, she couldn't fathom what the hell she was thinking. Why would she go to the location she saw on that map on the diner wall? Why would she get out of her car? Why would she wander alone into a strange forest in the middle of the Kentucky wilderness? She was just asking to get lost, if nothing else!

None of this made any sense. She'd convinced herself that it was because of those strange visions she kept having. Those shadowy things that no one else could see. Those bizarre, fungal-looking growths. The creeping shadows darting in and out of the corners of her eyes. And the nightmares, of course. Always those. She set out for Breastbroke to find some sort of relief from all those frightful things, but she had to have known she'd only find more to fear. At the very least, she should've ran away after escaping the things in that deserted cemetery. But no. She crawled into that cramped cave, risking spiders and snakes and bats and who knew what else.

And that freaky, faceless statue… Why did she hand over her clothes? It was a *statue*! What was it going to do if she didn't? But she just stripped right down. *What was wrong with her*? She remembered having this strange feeling, as if she simply *knew* it was going to be all right, that she was on the path she needed to be on. But how would she know any such thing? And how was *this* the right path?

What did Horatio do to her that day in the pitch-black backrooms of the Elysium Fog?

She didn't want this. She shouldn't be here!

And yet…

She blinked hard. This was all so confusing. She kept getting lost in this bizarre duality. She stared into the darkness, one hand still pressed to the wall next to her, the other still grasping at the dress she was wearing when she died.

"You're okay," she whispered to herself across the strange span of time connecting these two versions of her.

No one lied to her. She knew that now. Horatio didn't brainwash her that day. All he did was show her the truth about the world. The rest was her decision to make. It was just difficult to see the whole picture when she was alive. It didn't translate well. Even now, knowing what she knew, she couldn't begin to explain it all while in this manifested form. But there was one thing she knew very well: if that other her in the past should somehow break the pattern and flee the boneyard without the thorn, it would have unfathomable consequences in the present. She had to calm herself down.

"Don't stop," she urged herself. "Don't give in to fear. Everything will be okay."

Everything will be okay.

She stumbled to a stop and blinked hard again. Her head was suddenly spinning. For a moment there, she seemed to black out a little. It felt like she was somewhere else entirely.

She shined her light back and forth, half-expecting to see someone calling out to her, but she was alone.

More or less, she supposed.

Don't stop. Don't give in to fear.

She didn't understand where these words were coming from. But she *did* somehow understand that turning back wasn't an option. Something terrible would happen if she tried. She was already in too deep. The only way out was to keep moving forward. She had to find the thorn.

She continued walking, still wondering if Horatio had planted all these bizarre thoughts in her head in order to control her. It was a frightening concept, the idea that she might not be able to trust her own mind. But now wasn't the time to stop and think about it. For better or worse, she was already in this mess.

Ahead of her, the end of the cavern finally came into view. There was another passage carved through the wall, square and smooth, in stark contrast to the dripping natural stone all around her.

She hurried into it, eager to be away from the creepy black figures, and found another set of stairs leading even deeper into the darkness.

How much farther was she going to have to descend through this nightmare?

And how long would her cell phone battery hold out? She shuddered to think about trying to find her way out of this mess in perfect darkness. Especially with those *things* back there.

More water waited at the bottom of the steps. It splashed up her legs as she plowed forward, making her draw a hard hiss of a breath. She didn't dare waste any time. She wanted to be done with this stupid job. She wanted to go back and collect her clothes and leave this place forever.

But she froze as she entered the next chamber.

One of those creepy black figures was standing in front of her.

She stood there, naked and shivering, the cold water numbing her feet, staring at the black monstrosity blocking the way. Up close, it looked even less like a person and much more like a person-shaped glob of black mud. There was no anatomy to it, no visible joints, no eyes or mouth. There was only the rough, humanoid outline and that strange, drooping plague mask beak.

And yet somehow these things were able to move on their own.

At least the others were down below that stone walkway. This one, however, was standing right in her path, with nothing between them.

She didn't dare take her eyes off it.

Her heart pounding in her breast, she tried to think through the numbing terror. This chamber was much smaller than the last, barely twenty feet across and a little smaller than that in width. There was a narrow opening on the other side of the room, behind the thing, the only way out besides the way she came. Every other surface was rough stone.

Cautiously, without taking her eyes off the freaky black figure, she pressed her back against the wall and began circling around it, her light fixed on it.

It didn't move. It didn't turn that freaky head to follow her. It still looked like some ugly, lifeless clump of clay. And yet she had no doubt in her mind that if she took her eyes off it, even for a moment, it would attack her.

She still didn't understand any of this. Why would *she* be the one who had to come to this awful place? What was it about her that made Horatio choose her of all people? She prided herself on being strong and self-sufficient, but this was *insanity*.

She crept along the wall, her eyes burning. She didn't dare blink. She kept picturing those dreadful angels from *Dr. Who*. If she so much as blinked, would it suddenly be right in her face? She could almost imagine that strange beak peeled open, revealing oozing fangs ready to tear into her flesh.

The thought sent a fierce shiver through her and she *did* blink. She couldn't help it. Her pounding heart seemed to stutter.

But nothing happened.

The thing still hadn't moved.

She was letting her imagination get the better of her. She needed to get control of herself.

She reached out with her free hand and felt the opening as she approached it. She was almost there. Just a little farther.

She crept closer and then backed into the opening. It was smaller than she first realized, forcing her to crouch in order to fit. But she'd done it. She was past the creepy figure.

And yet a terrible realization popped into her mind as she backed away from it.

There was another one behind her!

Startled by the thought, she turned and shined her light forward, cold water splashing up around her. But there was nothing there. The passage ahead was dark and cramped, but empty.

Only her imagination again.

But when she pointed her light back at the figure, she was horrified to see that it had turned around and was looking at her.

She stood there, a frozen scream painted on her face, her heart slamming against her ribs.

For a moment, she couldn't make herself move. Her feet seemed fixed in place, as if the water enveloping them had frozen solid in that single instant.

What were these things? And what were they going to do to her?

(*Everything will be okay.*)

Would it, though? This was seriously fucked up. Why the hell was she here? Why the hell was *any of this* here? None of this should exist!

And yet somehow her feet began to move. She took a step backward. Then another. And another. Slowly, the black figure faded back into the darkness.

(*Everything will be okay.*)

She didn't dare take her eyes off the passage. Not for a second. She waded backward through the frigid water, feeling her way along the floor.

Maybe she *could* do this. After all, she was almost there. She wasn't sure how she knew this, but she did. This cramped little tunnel was going to take her to where she needed to be.

It was almost as if she could *remember* it… But of course that still made no sense. How could she *remember* something that hadn't happened yet?

Still, she found that she was certain of it.

All she had to do was make it a little farther.

Then something grabbed her from behind and dragged her backward through the passage.

She screamed. It was all she *could* do. She didn't understand what was happening. What had her? She couldn't feel anything holding her, and yet she was definitely in the grip of *something.* She kicked and flailed, but all she managed to do was batter her hands and feet against the unforgiving stone.

At some point, she dropped her phone. Everything had gone dark. She couldn't see!

Then the floor vanished from beneath her and she found herself plunged fully into the frigid water.

Again, she was being pulled down into the suffocating black depths.

She was going to drown!

Chapter 44

Wayne was having a hard time with all this. And he didn't think anyone would blame him. He was sitting here on a cushy bed in the middle of a white palace inside something called the "Keeper's Compendium" (which was inside the second temple which was, itself, inside an impassible wall at the center of the Denselands, deep in the heart of the Wood) with a little blind girl who claimed to be his *dead daughter*, trying to wrap his head around the idea that his soul had its own private hall pass and could come and go as it pleased, making him the only person able to reach some kind of magic *ghost terminal* that had to be activated in order for his friends to reach the Oblivion Door so they could all go home. Or…all but one of them, he supposed, because Keith was dead. (Can't forget that cheerful little detail…)

And he thought Gutler's Weep was confounding.

He closed his eyes and tried to relax. His muscles were tense. An anxious tightness had gripped his chest, making it feel hard to breathe. His stomach felt as if it had become permanently clenched. He just wanted to walk outside and take a minute, but there was no outside here. There were only those empty white corridors beyond that door.

But he wasn't alone. Olivia was right there by his side, still clinging to his arm, still pressing herself against him, still gently tracing her nails down the back of his tattered shirt, reminding him that she was there for him.

God, he loved her!

And clinging to his other hand was the little girl who looked like Wendy and talked like a wise old woman and looked at him like he was something far more special than he was. He was having trouble understanding any of this—he could barely keep up with all the information that was coming at him—but he was finding that he didn't *distrust* this adorable girl. He believed her. Somehow, he could just feel it in his heart. This wasn't some mysterious creature deceiving him. This was his own flesh-and-blood daughter. This was his little girl. And something about the thought of it filled him with a surprising warmth inside.

It was still possible, he knew, that this was all some kind of elaborate trick. In a world filled with Gilbert Houses and Gutler's Weeps and Temples of the Blind, where trolls and Caggos and zombies and ghosts and gods and fester vermin roamed freely in unnatural darkness, there was always a chance that this feeling was a clever lie. Could he really trust his own instincts in a world as weird as this?

But the fact was that the Keeper sent them here for a reason. Sandy told them so. Maeve told them so. Nadia told them so. And this little girl was telling them so. He had no reason to doubt her yet.

And wasn't this exactly what he wanted?

He remembered walking away from the City of the Blind that night five years ago, the Sentinel Queen's words heavy in his mind, an unwanted sadness weighing him down at that idea of her taking a child from him only to carry it to the grave with her…

The idea that the child could have survived, that the Keeper would spare her, care for her, give her a home, would always have given him joy. It was simply the weirdness of this place that made him hesitant to accept her. This entire journey had been filled with frightening and dangerous things, after all. Secrets and deceptions, traps and trials. And the Keeper kept so many secrets, let them know so little. It made it too easy to distrust.

But he sat there, taking in this quiet moment…his fiancée on one side and his daughter on the other…

The air wasn't all that heavy after all, he supposed.

"Okay…" he sighed. "What am I supposed to do?"

The little girl beamed at him with Wendy's smile. He couldn't get used to that. If this really were some kind of deceitful trick, it was an unfair one. How could he ignore something so familiar? Something so *personal*?

He'd always liked Wendy best. She was the only one of his siblings who never started anything with him. She wasn't competitive like Wade, or always picking fights like Whitney, or always whining and crying and tattling like Winter.

"Why does he have to keep *dying*?" whimpered Olivia. "I *hate* it. It's *terrifying*. What if he doesn't come back?"

Wayne leaned toward her and kissed her forehead. She was having a harder time with this, of course. She didn't see Wendy in this little girl's face, after all. She didn't grow up with her. She didn't have those same memories. She saw something different. She saw *his* face. To him, that felt like further proof that this was real, details that never would have crossed his mind. But she was still hesitant. She didn't want to gamble his safety on the word of a strange child they'd known for only a few minutes, much less one they found in the literal middle of nowhere.

"He *will* come back," the little girl assured her. "My mother's psychic genetics allows me to bond with his physical form, keeping his body functioning. He can stay gone for hours if he needs to."

"I don't want him to be gone for *hours*! I don't want him to go away *at all*! Why does *he* have to do it?"

"It's okay," he insisted. "There's a reason we're all here, right? If this is *my* reason, then I'm ready."

"Well *I'm* not!"

"I know. But if this is why I'm here, I want to do it. Because the sooner we do it, the sooner we can finally go home."

She pouted up at him. That face was always adorable. He wanted to kiss those lips, but he couldn't quite reach them from this angle. He was still wedged between the two of them, each one clinging to one of his hands.

"The terminal you need to activate is located deep in the Murk passages," explained the little girl.

(It was weird that she didn't have a name, Wayne decided. Was he supposed to give her one? She told them that sentinels didn't have names, that they possessed no such concept in their strange, psychic states of being. As her human father, was giving her a name his responsibility? He didn't feel qualified. They only just met, after all. And it wasn't like she was an infant. This was all so confusing.)

"But Andrea's the only one who can see those," said Olivia. "And we lost her. She disappeared." Then she leaned toward her, her pretty face brightening with hope. "Can you tell if she's okay?"

"She's fine now. She was in a pretty scary situation for a while there, but things have changed now. Something happened. I'm not entirely sure what. There are still dangers in her path, but nothing she can't handle. She's doing what she came here to do."

Olivia's relief was palpable, but she wasn't completely convinced. She was still gripping his arm, still reflexively digging her nails into him.

"In your spirit form, you won't have any trouble following the Murk," she went on, that pretty smile never softening. She looked so happy to be explaining these things. "That'll be the easy part."

"Easy…" he muttered. Just a simple matter of dropping dead and looking for the scary tunnels that were so filled with dead stuff that it rendered poor Andrea completely blind. A walk in the park, he was sure. Probably absolutely no chance that actually *being dead* would make those locations any scarier or more dangerous than they were for her.

"What's the *hard* part?" asked Olivia, a twinge of understandable distrust edging her usually sweet voice.

"The hardest part for him will probably be learning to let go of his physical form and step through the veil. Human beings are hardwired for survival, so he'll have to override his most primal instincts in order to do it."

"That sounds *horrible*."

"Not really," she countered. Those beautiful eyes were still fixed on some distant point, but that bright smile was aimed at Olivia now, fixed on the source of her voice and her psychic presence, Wayne supposed. "It's not like he has to hurt himself or anything. For him, it'll be like standing on a high dive and having to force himself to jump into the water. It's more about finding the courage to take that step."

He raised an eyebrow at this. Somehow he didn't think it was a coincidence that she chose to use that particular analogy. She was as clever as she was mysterious. Like Nadia, she was far too knowledgeable for the age she appeared to be. It was sort of distracting. There was something sort of *wrong* about the unnaturalness of it. It made it hard to fully let his guard down, but he still didn't think she was deceiving them. Some part of him seemed to be determined to accept her. Fatherly instincts, he wondered, or psychic intrusion?

But Olivia didn't want to listen. She clung tighter to his arm and pressed herself closer to him. She wasn't going to let him go without a fight, it seemed.

Again, he kissed her forehead. He hated making her worry like this. But the fact was that they were trapped here until they did what the Keeper wanted them to do.

"You don't have to be afraid," promised the little girl. "I saw it when the Keeper first brought me here. A glimpse of his cosmic blueprints. You're not just temporary parts in his designs. You're both a crucial element in the greater machine. He may test you, but he won't let anything really bad happen to either of you."

They both stared at her for a moment, letting that information sink in.

That pretty smile widened and she giggled. Looking positively delighted with herself, she said, "He wouldn't want me telling you that. It's breaking his rules. But I don't care. I appreciate that he saved my life, but I'm on my daddy's team first."

Olivia wiped at her shimmering eyes and looked up at Wayne.

"Does that mean what I think it means?" he asked.

"It's not entirely *impossible* for something bad to happen to you," she replied. "There's always a chance for things to go wrong. Especially when other forces are at work. And there's always a chance that the Keeper could have known I'd glimpse that information and fed me lies to keep me from knowing too much. But I doubt it. You're both way too rare to be disposable. And your deaths wouldn't accomplish anything. Your abilities would be wasted."

She had a point, he supposed. If all he could do was come back to life when he died, then wouldn't permanently dying just make him…permanently dead? Like, just plain old *regular* dead? And would Olivia's ability to see the future do anyone any good from beyond the grave?

"Everything you've been through has been a part of the Keeper's plans from the start," she informed them. "He's been molding you since long before you were both born. He intended for you to find each other. He intended for you to fall in love. He intends for you to get married and live happily together."

Again, Olivia looked up at him, her gorgeous eyes shimmering with hope.

"But he also intends for you to do scary things. It's up to you to trust him of your own free will, but I've seen a little of what he has planned and it goes on well past what you'll both do here in this gatehouse."

Wayne nodded. "Okay then." He kissed Olivia's forehead once more, then sighed. "Tell me what I'm supposed to do."

Chapter 45

Somehow, Andrea managed to regain control of herself before she could dash her brains out against a wall or fall into another hound passage or some even more gruesome fate.

She was slumped on the floor in the dark, sobbing and gasping for breath, her heart still racing from the fright.

She could still hear the hound back there, its slashing scales still screaming that awful power-saw-like shriek. But it was distant now. And it wasn't going to get any closer. The whole reason the hound passages were designed like that was to keep them corralled in their own areas. They could neither climb nor jump. Albert told her so. And Albert was smart. She believed him. And she *trusted* him.

But that experience was *beyond* terrifying. She really thought she was going to die back there.

She was *so* ready to go home.

She sniffled and wiped at her eyes. The worst part was that with the exception of the horrible hound passage, she still hadn't found any way to go *down* in this stupid labyrinth. All these passages were level. There were no stairs, no ramps. She was pretty confident she wasn't going to happen across an elevator down here.

She didn't want to do this anymore. She just wanted to sit here and wallow for a while. But she couldn't even do that.

That stupid hound scared her so bad, she was going to need to find somewhere to pee.

In fact, she might have peed a little while trying to climb up that wall. She wasn't sure. She was definitely frightened enough. But she'd never admit it to anyone. She was still embarrassed about stupid Tia calling her out about peeing herself back in her ruined apartment. But in her defense, she was caught a freaking *bear trap* when that happened. Or whatever manner of horrible device that was…

Frustrated, she stood up and leaned against the wall. She just needed to find somewhere private and she could…

She frowned at herself in the dark. Private? Really? She was hopelessly lost in a gargantuan labyrinth in the pitch-black darkness. How much privacy did she need?

She didn't bother taking another step. She squatted down and let nature take its course.

Tia was probably watching, she knew. That freak. She could almost feel those familiar brown eyes on her. She'd probably make fun of her the next time she showed herself. But at this point she didn't care what some older-than-dirt cosmic troublemaker thought about her needing to take a potty break.

It felt wrong, doing it here in this open passage, almost obscene, but what other choice did she have? It wasn't like there were any restrooms down here.

Did the sentinels not have toilets? Did they even *use* the bathroom? Did their unnatural, alien anatomy allow for such a thing? They didn't have mouths to eat or drink with… She'd never been able to wrap her head around how those things existed. They made no biological sense.

She lingered there a moment after she was done, feeling dirty, wishing she had something to use for paper, but finally simply stood up and continued forward again.

She could still hear the hound carrying on back the way she came. One thing was certain, at least: there was no question about which way she should go from here.

As long as it wasn't a dead end, she supposed.

She crinkled her nose at the thought. Why would her awful mind let her think something like that? It was utterly unhelpful!

But now that the idea had been planted, she couldn't help wondering what she'd do if she found her way blocked. Would she have to just sit down somewhere and wait for the monstrous thing to wander off again? How long would that take? And what if all the noise it was making attracted the rest of the monstrous pack?

Was it possible to end up stranded like that until she died of thirst?

She pushed the awful thought from her brain and continued onward.

She needed to focus on what she was doing, not on all the ways she could die down here. Ada told them this was all part of the Keeper's plan. Why would he bring her all this way just to let her die?

Why would he bring Keith *all this way just to let* him *die?*

She scowled at herself in the dark. Was that her own brain up to its nasty tricks again? Or was that Tia invading her thoughts and trying to make her doubt herself?

But what would be the point in sparing her back in that red-skied nightmare only to sabotage her now? That didn't make any sense.

Then again…she did say something about the Keeper protecting her. If that were true, if the Keeper was out there somewhere looking out for her, then Tia might be able to play all the cruel games she wanted.

She couldn't decide if that would be a relief or only make this whole ordeal a thousand times worse.

She needed to push the whole idea out of her head and just keep walking. There was no point in trying to understand the reasonings of goddesses and Keepers. She was only human. And a fairly average human at that, she thought. She didn't even understand how the Wood worked, much less these crazy temples.

But it was difficult to get control of her thoughts sometimes. They had a way of wandering off on their own a lot.

She'd been keeping to the right again, like before the hound passage. She wasn't sure why. Perhaps it felt a little less like she was going to get lost if she kept her hand on the same side. (Although that didn't make any sense when she thought about it. Wouldn't that just mean she was going in circles?) But now she stepped to the other side.

She wasn't sure if it was another of those grabby hand

things, but there was some sort of blob on the ceiling on that side that she didn't care for. It wasn't moving, thankfully, but that didn't mean it wouldn't wake up if she tried to walk under it.

She was almost past it when she realized what she'd done and she stopped, confused.

It was dark. She was completely blind. Why did she think she saw something up there?

She stood in the passage, staring at the spot where she imagined the blob was. She could picture it perfectly. Just a glob of murk clumped together, hanging down just a little farther than the shadowy streamers around it.

But she could *see* no such thing.

"What the heck?" she muttered under her breath. Why was it so clear in her head like that?

A part of her wanted to reach out and try to touch it, to see if it was really there, but of course the much greater part of her wanted to do no such thing. She didn't want to touch that stuff. Best case scenario, she wouldn't be able to feel it anyway. It was murk, after all. If it *was* one of those grabby things, she *really* didn't want to be grabbed by it. That was always freaky. And what if it turned out to be one of those *nasty* ones with the impossibly endless, spiraling abyss of teeth?

The thought sent a shudder through her bare body.

She turned and kept walking.

Maybe it was only her overactive imagination playing tricks on her. It did that sometimes. She'd always been an imaginative girl. As a child, she could entertain herself for hours with only the stories she made up in her head.

She pushed on into the darkness, eager to be out of earshot of that monstrous droning behind her.

Chapter 46

Gina could see it now. She wasn't sure how she missed it before. It was still pitch black, but her eyesight had never had much to do with anything. Only her *inner* eye saw the truth. And the truth was that there was a dreadful emptiness behind Nicole's eyes, as if she were nothing more than a hollow shell. She might as well have been a corpse. There was nothing left of the woman she used to be.

All that remained was Goar Nangup.

Tears streaming down her face, she drew her knees up between their bodies and thrust her legs outward, knocking her off balance and then wrenching herself free of those monstrously strong hands.

When the thing that was no longer Nicole groped for her again, she thrust her head forward, connecting with her mouth and knocking her backward.

"I'm so sorry!" she cried as she scrambled to her feet and fled.

"Gina!" cried a voice that sounded like Nicole, but wasn't. It was only a heartbreaking lie. "Come back! I'm okay now!"

No. She most certainly wasn't okay. She knew this without a shadow of doubt. The monster was already chasing her. If she hesitated for even a moment, it would get Nicole's hands around her again. And this time she wouldn't get away.

Was she just like Hochog now? Was that how he turned into that monster?

She felt so *stupid*. Of course that wasn't really Nicole. Why would she think for even a moment that someone like Nicole would have any kind of feelings for someone like her? She didn't even *like* girls. She had a *boyfriend.* Sort of, she supposed… A *complicated* boyfriend. A boyfriend who *literally just died.* Even if there wasn't some evil ancient god possessing her, she wasn't in an emotionally sound state.

How could she let herself get so distracted? How could she be such an *idiot*?

She turned a corner and doubled back the way she came before. It was no good. The monster was able to follow her every move. But when she turned *up*, it staggered in the wrong direction, widening her lead.

That was her way out.

Again, she turned the labyrinth upward. Then left. Then right. Then up again. This time, she kept going, spiraling over and over as she ran, tiptoeing through the strangeness like she did when she escaped the thing with too many mouths.

But this wasn't the same kind of predator. Whatever had possessed Nicole's body was able to move in ways the other thing couldn't. She sensed it coming, not on her heels, but *through the spiral*, passing just behind her, snatching at her trailing hair. She felt several strands yanked from her scalp.

Far too close.

Her heart thundering, she stepped out of the spinning corridors and raced ahead.

"There's nowhere you can go that I can't follow you," Nicole's voice called out through the eerie silence.

She clasped her hands over her ears and turned another corner.

There were things in the next passageway, but they didn't seem to notice her yet. She hurried past them and took the next passage leading away from that area. It was only a matter of time, she knew, before her luck finally ran out.

"I'll find you. It's inevitable."

She was running out of room. This part of the labyrinth was filled with dead ends and those strange voids. At this rate, it would have her cornered in no time.

She needed something more drastic.

An idea occurred to her. Not a good idea. She didn't like it at all. But it might be the only chance she had.

The intersection coming up… That was the answer.

Desperate, she clenched her teeth and turned the labyrinth again, sideways this time, like turning a cartwheel. The labyrinth spun. The corridor rotated. And the long, empty passage stretching away from her was turned *down*.

She fell, her terrified screams following her down and down and down.

It was working, she realized. She was definitely getting farther away from Goar's Nicole-puppet. But that was always going to be the easy part. Now she had to worry about the literal dead end waiting far below her. A wall that looked like glass but was solid and unyielding stone was speeding up at her at a terrifying rate.

She was going to have to time this right or she was going to hit that glass wall like a bug on a windshield.

Her stomach feeling as if it were trying to crawl up her throat, she twisted herself around. Gravity shifted. The wall beside her came crashing into her, jarring her shoulder, sending her rolling.

She was out of control!

But that glass floor was still speeding toward her much too fast.

With a terrified scream she twisted everything around again, pulling with all her strength.

She hit the other wall hard enough to daze her, but gravity was pulling her the other way now. She was sliding *up* the hill.

She gave another desperate pull and felt herself floating, her momentum carrying her toward the same glass surface, but now *upward*, like hitting the top of the bounce on a bungee cord. There was a single moment of pure weightlessness as gravity and velocity equaled out. Then she began falling again.

She turned once more, flipping the whole thing back on its head again, and with a great yelp of pain, she landed hard against the stone.

She lay there for a bit, dizzy and nauseous, her body aching, her heart pounding with fright. She was going to be covered in bruises tomorrow. Assuming she lived that long…

Fighting the urge to throw up, she pushed herself up onto her hands and knees, then somehow managed to get her feet under her.

She wasn't done yet. She'd only given herself a little breathing room. It wouldn't take long for that thing to find where she went. But her whole body was shaking so badly right now. She needed a moment.

She leaned against the cool stone, her eyes closed, struggling to catch her breath.

That was probably the most terrifying thing she'd ever done. And she absolutely would *not* recommend it.

She took a deep breath and tried to stop her legs from shaking. It was time to move.

Something slammed against the other side of the glass, startling a fresh scream from her.

"I can still see you!" shouted Nicole.

Gina backed away, clutching at her hammering heart. "Leave me alone!" she screamed.

"Anywhere you go, I'll still see you!"

That wasn't Nicole. Not anymore. Maybe not ever again.

She turned and fled into the deepest depths of the glass labyrinth, her tears overflowing, leaving Nicole behind in the unnatural darkness.

"I'm sorry!" she wept. "I'm so sorry!"

Chapter 47

Albert staggered forward. Each step was agony. All he wanted to do was sink to the floor and lie there until he bled to death. But the witch seemed to be in control of his legs. And she wasn't through torturing him yet.

He could barely even see what was in front of him. The pain was wrenching an endless stream of tears from him, blurring his surroundings. But he could see that the hallway of mismatched doors was gone. He was back inside one of them, stumbling through somebody's silent home, no doubt stalking another helpless victim.

He was leaving a trail of blood everywhere he went. How had he not passed out by now? It streamed down his neck and chest from his butchered face. He could feel it flowing, hot and sticky, down his legs.

"There's a good boy," purred Dolly from somewhere behind him. "No more pervy distractions for you. Now we can focus on finding some new toys to play with."

He didn't try to respond. He didn't think he could if he wanted to. Between the pain and the shock, his brain seemed to have gone out for a much-needed breath of fresh air and left him alone with her. It was like being in a drunken stupor, except he'd give anything to not be stone sober right now.

"You didn't need those things anyway," she informed him. "That filthy pig wastes his time on *sex magic* of all things."

Shanzer… The Shaman of Wevenwert…

"If he really wanted you to succeed, he would have taught you about *real* magic."

Real magic? What was she going on about? He couldn't focus. He couldn't think straight. Every time he tried to gather a thought, another wave of excruciating agony swept through his groin and up into his belly.

Maybe it really *was* true that men thought with their dicks…

He'd stopped walking, but he couldn't remember when. Again, he felt her foul hands on him. They crept up his back and curled around his shoulders. Those dangerous nails pricked at his skin.

"*Blood magic*," she hissed.

She brought her hands down again, cutting into him again, tracing lines of fire across his skin. Warm blood trickled down his back.

He wanted to scream, but he was again paralyzed.

He really was powerless here, he supposed. He never stood a chance from the beginning.

"Sex is an excuse for lecherous pigs like Lyle Shanzer to use magic for his own perverted desires. But *blood* infuses magic with *actual* power."

(*A man's coursing blood powers both his heart and his cock, but while his heart defines him as alive, his cock allows him to experience life.*)

He glimpsed this line in the shaman's book, somewhere in the back of his mind where it seemed to still be open somehow. But he also remembered Brandy reading that line to him back in the anxiety room, when she was desperately trying to find a way to save his life.

He couldn't decide if Shanzer's words were arguing her point or supporting it. But then again, he wasn't exactly firing on all six cylinders at the moment.

"I'll let you see for yourself," decided Dolly.

He pushed open a door he didn't remember walking up to. It was a bathroom. A nice one. Very spacious. Very clean and shiny. Except of course for the blood pooled on the marble tiles beneath the naked, trembling woman cowering on the floor. The light was turned off, making it impossible for him to see her face, but he could hear her sobbing. She was terrified. And it was no wonder. Dolly had turned him into a monster, after all.

"I think I'll choose this one," she decided, nudging him

closer to her. "What do you think?"

He blinked back those stubborn tears and took a step toward the woman.

He knew that figure…

"Isn't she pretty?"

Brandy was staring back at him with horrified eyes. There was a large, bloody gash in her forehead and a stab wound in the side of her belly. She was shaking her head, begging him. "Leave me alone," she gasped between sobs.

She'd never looked at him like that before. Not even that first night after what happened in the sex room, when she had every reason to blame him for what happened in there. He remembered the suspicion on her face. There was accusation. Disgust. And there was fear. In that moment of mortified confusion, her mind struggling to understand what happened, she stared at him as if he might be a monster. And she had every right to be suspicious. It was a suspicious situation. Either he'd done something to make her lose control like that or he'd intentionally led her to that place. Why else would something so strange have happened? If not for her ability to see the truth in people, she probably would've taken the flashlight and abandoned him to that darkness. But this was nothing like the look on her face that night. That look was full of fear but also determination, the look of a woman prepared to fight for her life if it came to that. This was a look of sheer terror. There was no fight left in her. She was helpless. She was sobbing and pleading and gasping for breath.

The sight broke his heart.

And somewhere deep in his gut, like a squirming parasite feeding on his very sanity, the sight *excited* him.

Those dangerous, dainty hands slipped around his waist again. "I want to see you peel off her face," she whispered. "Make her as ugly as you."

He stood there, staring down at his battered wife, his mind a trainwreck of broken emotions.

This wasn't real. He knew that. He'd already established it back when these nightmares began. But it was so hard to look at her this way. He wanted to save her, not hurt her. His heart ached to hold her again.

Those other feelings…the evil feelings…the thrill of it…the foul, carnal *hunger* for more…weren't real. Those were *her* emotions. They belonged to the real monster.

"Go on," Dolly urged. "I'm going to make you do it anyway. You might as well enjoy it."

He took another step toward the woman.

Did she know it was him? Could she recognize him like this? With his face shredded and his teeth exposed like some freshly risen Hollywood zombie?

For some reason, he again remembered the carrion eaters.

Something about them… A swarm of them filling that black sky, circling the inferno belching up from the depths of the temple, drawn by the flames…and ultimately consumed by them…

"Take your time. Make it last."

He took another step. He was standing over her now, his blood dripping into hers. He was holding those kitchen shears again, even though he was sure his hands were empty a moment ago.

"Make her *suffer*."

"That's not Brandy," he said.

He couldn't see her, but he found that he knew Dolly's expression soured when he said this. "What?"

"I said, that's not Brandy." He bent over the figure lying there, the pain dissipating like morning fog. "That's *you*."

Dolly let out a strangled gasp. *She* was the one sprawled out on the floor now, blood coursing down her face, a gaping wound in her side.

The carrion eaters were the key. Five years ago, he stood atop that burning mountain, staring down Lucas Kneede as those headless monstrosities with the backward wings circled above, gathering together.

After it was all over, he remembered having difficulty understanding that part of it all. It was kind of a haze. He was exhausted and dazed, his arm broken, terrified for the girls inside the final chamber.

He wasn't even able to describe the experience. He kept telling himself that he only imagined that part, that something about those things had drawn his attention. He was watching their unnatural movements, so random before but becoming more and more purposeful as he stood there.

The Keeper's doing, he decided long ago.

But it wasn't the Keeper. *He* was the one who controlled those monsters. He was the one who lined them up, swept them through that hellish fire and then piled their flaming carcasses atop Kneede, burning him to a crisp.

Because in the end, *he* was in control.

And he was in control here, too.

"What's happening?" gasped Dolly. Gone was the cocky smirk, the delighted shine in those bright blue eyes, the energetic enthusiasm in her expression. Now that pretty little face was full of pain. It was full of fear. "What did you do?"

But he didn't do anything really. He just finally remembered that he had control. "Don't worry," he told her. "I heard every word you said."

"What…?"

"'Peel her face off,'" he repeated. "'Make her as ugly as you.'" He lifted the shears and watched those eyes follow their movement. "You said, 'Make it last,'" he reminded her.

She was shaking her head now, her gaze glued to the blade. "You said, 'Make her *suffer*.'"

"Stop it! Let me go!"

He bent a little closer. "Shhh… Don't worry. I'm a good boy. A good listener. I'll show you what a good job I can do."

Dolly tried to scoot backward, but she didn't have the strength. She'd lost too much blood.

And she had no control here.

"Stop it…" The strength had left her voice. The words came out as little more than a pitiful whimper.

"You should've left my wife out of this," he told her. "Nothing in this world is strong enough to make me hurt her."

A great, wet sob escaped her. "Get away from me… Please…"

She looked so pitiful there, so *vulnerable*. But he'd seen too much of the monster she really was. He felt no pity for her. He might even enjoy what was about to happen. "Now you're going to watch every one of those 'precious memories' of yours play out one by one. And you're going to have the best seat in the house for each and every one of them."

Dolly screamed. And she was going to keep screaming. Over and over again, for a *very* long time.

These might be her memories, but this was *his* mind.

Chapter 48

Corey made his way to the roof of the next building and looked out over the city.

The infection was spreading at an incredible pace, washing over multiple buildings at once, rapidly darkening those gloomy streets.

What was already an admittedly monumental task had just become nigh impossible. There was no way he could repair the damage faster than that *thing* was causing it. He was only one man. That thing was literally infecting an entire block of the city in the time it was going to take him to ride the elevator back down to the ground level.

So much for having a plan, he supposed.

And what, exactly, would happen to him if he were inside one of those buildings when the infection crawled over it? Would the damage be limited to the fuses? Or would it infect *him* as well? The way it took over the Lucianna Mysteria's caretakers?

Albert described the scene they found in the lock chamber. A mutated skeleton still clinging to the mechanism, shielding it from intruders even in death. How excruciating must that have been?

He still wasn't entirely sure what was going on back there. For him and Violet, it was only a matter of that black-eyed Warner-thing meeting them at the main entrance and pointing the way for them. Violet's glass shard revealed a hidden staircase and they simply waited for the door to be opened. But for Albert and Brandy, it was a much more grand ordeal. There were monsters. Parallel dimensions. Time displacement. And even actual *magic*. He was sort of jealous, if he were being totally honest. But from what he was able to understand, the carriage house had always been a site of great importance, built into the very fabric of the universe from the beginning and guarded by a supernatural caretaker chosen by the Keeper himself. And yet *something* out there was dangerous enough to actually infect that caretaker. And now it was *here*, wreaking havoc in the machine.

Did it stow away on the carriage somehow? Did it infect one of them and travel all this way with them?

No… That didn't feel right.

He watched the shadowy shape as it oozed through those distant buildings. Maybe it was because he and it were both inside the machine at the same time, but he found that he knew a few things about it. He knew that it was old. *Very* old. Ancient even in times already ancient. And it was *alien*. Not merely from some previous universe, but from somewhere *outside* a previous universe. From somewhere far out in the distant depths of the Wood, somewhere so dreadful that even he didn't care to think too much about it.

Someone—or more precisely, he supposed, some*thing*—brought it from there long ago, long before his world was ever born. And that same someone/something was the one who brought it *here*. The *real* saboteur.

(Beware the Ruin.)

He felt a shiver pass through his body, which was a little weird, since he didn't think he actually *had* a body here. But at this point that was the *least* of all the weird things he could allow himself to be distracted by.

He pushed the thoughts from his head and scanned the skyline on either side of him. So many buildings. So many broken lights.

"It's a matter of perspective," said Violet.

He gave a grunt of a response. Perspective. Like the way his brain's initial reaction was to imagine himself as an insignificant speck afloat in the vastness of the cosmos. Somehow he shrank the whole thing down so that it encompassed a single city, and yet he was still nothing more than that same speck in comparison.

She pointed out over the city, toward the area with the greatest number of affected windows. "The amount of damage that thing can do before you can even get over there…"

"Ain't no way," he agreed, nodding. He was in way over his head. This wasn't going to work.

"So change your perspective."

He frowned. She said that like it was easy. Like he had any way of understanding how he was able to do it the first time.

"Make the big problem small enough to handle," she pressed.

Could it really be that easy? Could he just keep shrinking it down until it became something he could manage?

He looked down at her again, his mouth open, ready to say something, but he forgot the words before he could utter them.

Violet wasn't there. She hadn't been there this whole time. He was alone in this place.

So why was he just talking to her? Was he hallucinating? Was someone messing with his head?

Pay attention.

He blinked, confused. That wasn't a voice so much as a thought. He was merely imagining her speaking. And yet there was a certain urgency that wasn't his own.

He turned and looked back out over the city.

That ominous crawling darkness had changed directions. It was moving toward him now, as if it had just caught his scent and was coming to investigate.

"That ain't good…" he breathed.

Chapter 49

It wasn't as bad as Violet feared. The cut on her toe was deep and painful. It was bleeding a lot. The filament sliced through the sock, the toe and even some of the toenail. But she still *had* a toe. That was what really mattered.

If only she had a proper bandage for it…

She shredded one of her socks and used it instead. They were ruined anyway. All that climbing had basically turned them into Swiss cheese. And the tender bottoms of her feet had fared little better, unfortunately. Her skin was scuffed and scraped. She was bleeding in places. She wasn't sure she would've made it through there if her feet weren't already somewhat callused from all the summers she spent growing up with Corey and running around barefoot in their backyards.

Her hands had fared much better, but her fingertips were red and raw. She really hoped she wouldn't have to do any more climbing for a while.

She knotted the tattered remains of her sock around her foot. Hopefully that would do the trick. She doubted she was anywhere near done walking on it, after all. But it was the best she was going to do under the circumstances.

She leaned back against the labyrinth wall and shined her light back and forth. She kept doing that. Part of her was paranoid, still expecting some horror or another to come bounding out of the darkness at her. Another part couldn't stop hoping to look up and see Everett's dorky grin again.

She couldn't stop worrying about him. That was twice now he'd saved her from a terrible fate. And this time she very well might never see him again. She kept telling herself that he was quick. He was an energetic ball of optimism and curiosity. If anyone could slip through the graymother's nest and get away, it was probably him. But it was hard not to fear the worst.

The thing that moved around in there and left those dangerous webs in its wake was quick, too, after all. *Frightfully* quick…

She didn't like being alone. Being alone made it too easy to focus on all the bad possibilities. Plus, last time she was alone the Priestess of Ruin spirited her away to that awful world with the bloody sky and all those horrid monsters…

She let her light linger on the passage to her left a little longer. The graymother's nest was that way, around the next corner and at the end of the passage. She hadn't dared turn her attention to her injury until she was out of sight of anything that might be watching from behind those webs.

(*It's not like anything else that ever was. An anomaly, alien to every world, a consciousness from somewhere* beyond.)

The memory of those words sent a fresh shiver through her body.

What the hell did that even mean? Alien to every world? Wasn't literally *everything* supposed to be a part of the Keeper's cycle? Wasn't that what all those weirdos kept telling them? Every crumbling ruins and piece of strewn trash in that black forest was a remnant of some entirely different *universe* that died and fell apart. So how was it possible for anything to come from *beyond all of that?*

She wished Corey were here. He might have an idea how something like that might work. Or maybe Albert. He was like that too, she recalled.

You there? she thought, casting her voice into whatever inner place the other one slumbered in when she wasn't chatting with her or taking over her body.

But the other one didn't answer. Maybe she'd exhausted herself again. She was older than shit, after all. She probably nodded off every time she stopped moving for a few seconds.

You're funny.

She frowned. Was that an actual reply, or only something

she imagined the other one saying to such a rude thought. It was difficult to tell for sure. It was so faint, so *brief.*

She decided it didn't matter. Somehow she knew she was still in there somewhere, whether she was conserving her strength or hiding from freaky, psycho priestesses or just deciding she didn't feel like chatting right now, she could feel her in there somewhere. And that was enough. It was a tiny bit of a comfort to believe that she wasn't really as alone as she felt.

She reached up and wiped at her eyes. She hated to cry, but these stupid tears wouldn't stop. It was as if all the times she'd held back the waterworks had built up somewhere inside her and now it was all overflowing.

She sniffled and wiped at her nose. "Dammit." She didn't have time for this. So she was on her own. *Again.* It didn't matter. She needed to be on her feet and moving, not sitting here feeling sorry for herself.

She stood up, wincing a little at the aching in her poor toe.

She might as well keep going this way. It wasn't like there was a *right* way, after all. She was hopelessly lost in a labyrinth the size of a major city. Realistically, it would be a miracle if she ever found *anything* down here, much less the way out.

Limping a little, leaning on the wall to take some of the weight off her right foot, she ventured on through the endless darkness, wondering what else the Keeper of the Cycle was going to put her through before he was satisfied.

Chapter 50

Everett crept through the darkness, letting Alice be his eyes.

He was getting better at understanding her strange, mental language. Right now, she was simply making him aware of the walls around him, mapping out a sort of general floor plan in his head that was strangely subtle. The harder he tried to focus on it, the more difficult it was to perceive. It was easier to just keep walking and not think too much about it.

There wasn't much to perceive anyway. Walls on either side of him. Stone above and below. A long, empty corridor. There was an intersection ahead of him. Another passageway branched off this one and curved to the right. Beyond that there was another. This passage ended, merging with another that was running diagonal to this one. It was quite boring. He could sense nothing of interest in any of the surrounding passages. For a while there, he was aware of the graymother's nest somewhere to the left, the passages twisting and winding their way around it, but even that had vanished into the unknown darkness again.

He would have liked a distraction. With nothing interesting to occupy his thoughts, he kept finding himself thinking about Alice's intentions back there in that nest. It was disturbing to think that she could be some wicked little voice inside his head, urging him to betray his friends, like some cartoon devil sitting on his shoulder.

She wanted to protect him.

He frowned to himself as he walked, pondering this. That wasn't just an idle thought, he knew. It was her excuse. Her reasoning. She just told him that she wanted to protect him. She didn't understand what was wrong with that. And he supposed she had a point. He took her from that lonely place on the flip-side of existence, rescued her from the Priestess of Ruin and the burning dollhouse. But wasn't he also the reason she was in that mess in the first place? If he hadn't let himself get snatched away from Violet and dumped into the void, she could have continued her peaceful existence in that quiet place forever.

Lonely.

Yes, it would have been lonely there. But without him, she never would have known the difference.

But she *did* know the difference. He showed her things she never knew. Whole worlds filled with things *other* than silence and darkness and empty time. It was like someone turned on a light for the very first time. Everything was new and exciting. It was as if she'd finally been *born*.

He could most certainly understand that. She was like him. Alive, but not living. Merely *existing*. Unaware that there was so much more than those prison walls revealed. Until the day an angel descended and reached out a hand…

She didn't want to go back. And she didn't want to stay here, either. She wanted to remain with him, to go wherever he went, for as long as she was able.

He smiled a little in the darkness. He was right about her from the start. She wasn't a bad spirit. She was a child, experiencing everything for the first time. He couldn't expect her to understand everything. She could collect a great amount of information about the world just by connecting with his mind, but she wasn't going to be able to instantly grasp complex concepts like morality and friendship in an instant.

"Okay," he said aloud, surprised by how loud his voice sounded in this silent passage. "But we're setting some ground rules."

He didn't even have to list them. She already understood him. Friends were important. They couldn't just save themselves when things got dicey. The only way they were going to be able to stay together and keep seeing all the wonderful things the universe had to offer was to look out for each other. That was non-negotiable.

Life was important. It was precious. It was all too often fleeting. That was the lesson he wanted her to take in.

It was ironic, really, when he thought about all the risks he'd taken, all the times he'd put the thrill of adventure and discovery above his own safety. He didn't have much right to lecture her, he supposed. But he felt as if he'd changed since he last left home. He'd become someone new again, someone who realized that the answers weren't always worth any cost. There were always *more* answers out there, answers he might miss if he ended his journey for the sake of just one. And those other answers might even lead him back to any he'd missed, too.

He wondered if Wayne would think he'd grown up a little?

Probably not. But *he* thought he was improving.

He stared into the darkness ahead of him, distracted. That subtle floorplan inside his head was finally revealing something new for a change. A much larger space wedged between all the cramped corridors.

Excited by the prospect of discovering something new, he fixed his sights on it, mapping the path that would lead him there the quickest, and picked up his pace.

Chapter 51

"Wanna hear a secret?" whispered Stella.

"I want you to get the fuck off me," growled Brandy. She had her head turned all the way to the side, her cheek pressed against the cold stone. It was as much as she was able to do to get away from her. Why did she have to be so close? Why was she rubbing her naked tits all over her? This was gross. She barely knew the woman she was *pretending* to be, much less the *monster* she turned out to be.

And how was she so *strong*? She couldn't budge. It was like being back in the psychic predator's lair, bound to whatever that thing was that was holding her in that place. She still didn't know what she was caught in. She never saw it. It was dark the whole time. But it was weirdly unyielding while also not being hard or cold like wood or metal. This was like that. She could feel Stella's hands and thighs gripping her, but she wasn't crushing her. She wasn't even straining. She barely seemed to be using any effort at all, and yet those hands might as well have been iron shackles. Somehow, she was utterly inescapable.

Stella's free hand grasped her chin and twisted her face toward her as if she weren't struggling at all, as if she were nothing more than a limp doll to be posed any way she liked. "The truth is…" she whispered so close to her face that she could feel her lips brushing against her own, "…that none of it fucking matters."

"Get out of my face!"

Her eyes sparkling with childish delight, she grinned down at her. Then, bewilderingly, she flicked her tongue out and *licked* her. She felt the tip of it brush across both her lips.

Brandy let out a squeal of disgust as she wrenched her face free and turned away. She found herself certain that she was only able to do it because this monstrous woman let her. She wasn't able to free herself before. "Ew! Get off me! Fucking *weirdo*!"

"It doesn't, though," whispered Stella. She nuzzled closer, pressing her cheek against hers. "Nothing you do here means shit. It never did. Whether you live or die in this hole, the result is going to be the same."

"Why should I believe anything you say?"

"Why should you believe anything *anyone* says?" she countered. "Why trust literal monsters like Warner Harr and Lucianna Estrane? Or remnants of dead worlds like Lucas Kneede and the so-called 'goddess' of Cedric's Cove? Or wielders of perverse magic like Lyle Shanzer and the enslaved blood witch? And why the fuck would you believe anything you heard slither from the lips of the *Keeper of Lies*?"

Brandy hated to admit it, but she kind of had a point there…

On the other hand, however, none of *them* had ever *sexually assaulted her.*

"*Fucking get off me*!"

Again, Stella grasped her chin and forcefully turned her head to face her. "What has playing by the Keeper's rules gotten you? Hm? Exhausted and sweaty. Naked and filthy. Separated from your handsome groom. Worried sick for all your friends. Tormented and humiliated." She leaned closer, her lips nearly brushing hers again. "So why do it?"

She struggled to turn away. Why did she have to be this close? Did she really think she could concentrate on any of the madness spilling out of her mouth while they were practically kissing? This was disgusting. This woman was a complete stranger. Everything she thought she knew about her was a lie. She wasn't even human.

But she wouldn't let her up. She kept creeping closer, her breath washing over her, hot and nauseating. "You heard what his broken puppet said. He has a near-infinite number of backup plans. He's already accounted for the possibility that you might fail. He's *prepared* for it." She slid her hand downward and closed it around her throat, cutting off her breath with as little effort as she used to pin her down. "If I were to murder you right now, he'd just move on to the next step. So why keep putting yourself through it all?"

For a moment, she didn't let go. Brandy felt a panic swelling in her chest as she struggled for a breath. But then she released her grip and caressed her cheek again.

God, this was uncomfortable!

"So, what? I'm just supposed to sit down and refuse to play his game?"

"Sure. If you want. Or…" Brandy felt her hand slide down her shoulder and grasp her naked breast. "…we could kill a few hours playing together."

"In your dreams," she growled. "Go fuck one of those sentinel statues if you're that hard up."

For some reason, this made Stella laugh.

Why the fuck did she keep having to deal with all these *perverts*?

The worst part was that this wasn't even entirely out of character for the Stella she knew. She hadn't spent much time around her, but she knew that she loved making people uncomfortable for some reason. She was always blurting out something inappropriate or obscene and laughing at people's reactions. She couldn't count the times poor Andrea had to apologize for her behavior.

Andrea…

"Where's Andrea?" she demanded. "Does she know about you?"

Stella sat up a little at this. "Oh yeah, we had a chat just a little while ago. She got naked, too. We had a little fun. She was all kinds of worked up. It was *hot*."

"You better not have laid a finger on her!"

"Oh if you only knew…" she purred.

"Where *is* she?"

"She's fine," she replied, sounding bored with the topic. "Wandering around out there somewhere." She gestured at the darkness all around them.

That was a relief. She was worried this weirdo had done something nasty to her.

"I mean, I *was* going to murder her," she added.

"*What?*"

"You know, for shits and giggles. Just to fuck with the Keeper."

"Stay away from her!"

"But I changed my mind," she went on, ignoring her. "Turns out he has something interesting planned for her. So I let her go."

It was an unsettling thought. Was Andrea really alive right now because of nothing more than a whim? Or was she lying about having seen her at all? Or was she lying about not killing her? Her stomach twisted with fresh worry. She didn't know what to believe. This woman was insane. She was more of a monster than anything she'd encountered in the labyrinths or the Wood.

"But *you*…" She shook her head. "Like I said, you're not going to make any difference at all. I could gut you right here and now…" She ran her fingers down her side, dragging her nails along her skin. (Why did they feel so sharp? They were like knife blades!) "…and tomorrow wouldn't be any different than if I let you go."

Again, Brandy struggled to free herself, but it was hopeless. Those hands were fairly dainty, but they were like steel. She was trapped here. And she was in terrible danger.

Stella leaned close to her again, so close that their lips brushed together. "I wonder… What would you do to convince me to let you live?"

Her stomach twisted at the thought of being blackmailed into doing something foul with this evil woman. "Where's Albert?" she shouted, changing the subject.

"Him?" she asked, as if the question should surprise her. "He's probably dead by now, sorry to say. The blood witch is *very* hard on her toys."

Her stomach sank at the very suggestion. "No… You're lying!"

Stella made a face at this. "Sorry, but no. I *really* doubt your little boy toy is still in one piece."

Brandy yanked at her hands, trying once more to free herself. But this self-proclaimed goddess possessed impossible strength. Nothing she did would even budge her. "Let me go! I have to save him!"

"You're not listening to me. He's totally dead by now. I mean, you should've seen the messes she made with some of her other playthings. It was pretty gruesome."

"Liar!" She tried to kick the woman, but the way she was straddling her left her feet and legs useless. "Why the fuck is she even here? She's not supposed to be able to hurt us! It's in her contract!"

"*I* sent her, of course. Just like I sent the infection that killed the gatekeepers of the carriage station and Goar Nangup's yummy cultist to occupy your little friends on the lake road."

"*Bitch*!"

"The *biggest* bitch," she replied with a wicked grin.

"*Let me go*!"

"What will you give me if I do?"

"What?"

"If I let you live, will you be my plaything?"

"Gross! Fucking *weirdo*."

"I'll show you some *really* good sex magic."

"No! Leave me alone! Freak!"

"Come on. I promise I'll let you come up for air once in a while."

"Ew! Get away!"

But instead of letting her go, she licked her again, this time running her foul tongue all the way from her chin to her forehead.

Brandy screamed. The feeling was revolting.

Then Stella whispered into her ear. "In that case, what would you be willing to do to get your precious husband back?"

Brandy stared up into the darkness, her heart racing. Albert? Was it possible that she'd actually bring him back to her? Could she do that? Even if it were true, could she trust the lying slut? And what sorts of foul things would she be forced to endure?

"See?" she whispered. "Everyone has a price. Some whores are just cheaper than others, that's all."

"Give him back," she said. She tried to sound demanding. Forceful. *Intimidating*. But her voice gave her away. Even to her own ears she sounded desperate and terrified.

Stella was hovering just above her, those lips just above her own, creeping closer, eager, *hungry*. The sight was repulsive. It made her stomach turn just to look at this woman. To suggest that she basically *sell herself* to this monster…

But if it was for Albert… For her husband… If this turned out to be her one chance to get him back…

She really didn't think she could believe this woman. Didn't she just finish claiming that he was already dead? She was the whole reason he was gone in the first place! And yet if she ever found her way home and he wasn't there… If he was gone forever and she had this one chance…

Would she spend the rest of her life hating herself if she didn't try *everything* to bring him home?

Then she was free. Stella was gone. She was no longer pinned down. She was lying on the floor, alone. The weight was gone from her hips. She was free to move.

Confused, she sat up.

"No," said Stella, her voice drifting around the room again. "I've changed my mind."

"What…?" Brandy grabbed the flashlight off the floor and stood up. She was trembling, she realized. Her stomach was twisted into knots. Several emotions were swirling around inside her. Fear. Anger. Loneliness. An aching yearning for her husband's familiar arms.

And a dwindling glimmer of hope…

"What can I say?" sighed Stella from her shroud of darkness. "The mood passed."

"Bitch…" she breathed. She knew it. She never had any intention of letting her have Albert back.

"Remember what I said, though. The Keeper's a meticulous

little shit. He doesn't need you. He never did."

She turned around, following the voice as it drifted through the gloom. Where did she go? What was happening now? She felt so disoriented after all that.

Then Stella was in front of her again, her hands grasping her naked breasts.

"Bye now."

"Wha…?"

Stella shoved her backward. But at the same time, she found herself being shoved *down*. Before she could take a breath, she was plunged beneath the cold, slimy surface of the ichor, kicking and flailing and struggling, only to find herself sinking once again into that foul darkness.

This time, however, her lungs were empty. She couldn't hold her breath.

She was going to drown in this stuff.

That fucking bitch!

Her chest aching, she fought to swim back to the surface, but she was again caught in that strange current. It was sucking her to the bottom.

She wasn't going to make it.

Ichor filled her mouth.

She convulsed.

She began to black out.

Albert… She could almost see him…

As everything faded to black around her, she reached out and imagined that he was catching her, that he was wrapping her in his strong arms again.

Chapter 52

Erin coughed and sputtered. She was on her hands and knees, struggling to catch her breath. She wasn't sure what happened. It seemed to her that she was about to die. She couldn't escape whatever was holding her and she could feel the pressure building in her ears as she was pulled deeper into those black depths.

She had no recollection of being let go. Nor could she recall swimming back up to the surface. There wasn't even any sense of lost time. She simply seemed to jump from then to now.

She supposed it didn't matter. She *didn't* drown. She was still alive. And she was free of whatever the thing was that grabbed her. But what was she supposed to do now? She had no idea where she was. She didn't even have her cell phone anymore. How would she ever get out of here without a light?

And yet, even as she despaired at the thought, she realized that it wasn't entirely dark.

The space around her was illuminated by a faint glow.

She turned and looked behind her.

Something was shining in the water. Her dropped phone, perhaps? A desperate hope welled up inside her. She stood up and splashed toward it on trembling legs.

What was this space? She could see no walls or ceiling. Whatever kind of chamber this was, it was far bigger than this meager halo of light. And the water here wasn't murky like the water elsewhere. It didn't have that unpleasant slimy dirty feel beneath her feet. The stone was rough, like the cavern floor, but the water was clear. And it was only a few inches deep. There was no sign of the bottomless pool she nearly drowned in.

What was going on? Nothing made any sense.

For now, she focused on the light. She needed her cell phone.

But as she approached the glow, she realized that it wasn't her cell phone. Something *else* was in the water. Something with a bright *golden* color.

She knelt next to it and peered down into the water. There was a small depression in the stone here, almost as if whatever this thing was had come crashing to earth from the stars ages ago and lay resting in the crater it left. Although that seemed like a rather random sort of thing to think…

And yet…was it? After all, wasn't she here to retrieve some kind of ancient, mysterious key?

Yggdrasil's thorn, she thought as she stared into that golden glow. That *was* what she came here looking for. The whole purpose of this dreadful experience. The job Horatio sent her here to complete. What else could she be looking at right now?

So…all she had to do was take it?

She didn't understand anything. It was as if the entire world had gone crazy these past thirteen months.

But if collecting this thing was what allowed her to be done with this nightmare…

She reached down, her fingers dipping into the water.

"You sure you wanna do that?" asked an echoing voice from the silence.

Startled, Erin snatched her hand back and sat up, automatically covering herself.

Was it her imagination, or did it suddenly get much colder in here?

"You already know what'll happen."

Where was this voice coming from? It bounced around her, echoing off the unseen walls. But whoever was there remained beyond the light, unseen, mysterious. All she could discern was that it was a woman's voice.

"Who's there?" she demanded.

Strangely, her own voice *didn't* echo… Her stomach twisted with dread. What sort of weirdness was *this*? What was she talking to?

But the voice didn't answer her. Instead, it asked, "Do you really intend to die for it?"

She looked down into the water. It was a fair question, one she'd asked herself many times since her visit to the Elysium Fog. After all, why should she have to give up her life for this? And yet, every time she thought about it, something inside her always insisted this was how it was supposed to be.

(*Everything will be okay.*)

She frowned into that golden glow.

"Seems like such a waste to me," said the voice. It came from somewhere far away, and yet as it echoed back and forth across the room, it seemed to whisper directly into her ear. And at the same time, she felt someone caress her cheek.

She jumped to her feet, startled, and twirled around, but no one was there.

"Just another toy to be used and thrown away."

Seriously, where was this voice coming from? And what was this woman talking about?

"Such a pity…"

"Where are you? *Who* are you?" What the hell was going on? Was this some kind of test or something? Was she supposed to take the thorn or wasn't she?

"Want me to give you a little peek at where this path will lead you?"

She didn't get the chance to answer her. In an instant, she found herself hurtling through space and time, witnessing fantastic and terrible things. A pale train speeding through a vast forest filled with strange, black trees with bark that glistened like flesh and long-dead things that refused to stay that way. An empty and silent city, slowly sinking into a lake, where strange creatures lurked in flooded basements. An ancient, old-growth forest where vile creatures pretended to be children. A raging storm over the towering skyline of a city that wasn't a city at all. There were endless stone corridors like the ones that led her here and stone walls that stretched forever into the sky and nightmarish things that prowled dark chambers never before seen by human eyes.

What were all these places? Were they real?

And why did they all seem so strangely *familiar*?

"You already know there's nothing ahead of you but pain and suffering."

Something inside her seemed to open up. The sensation was indescribable. And it was *painful*. She forgot about covering herself and instead grasped at her head. It felt like something was being physically inserted into her very brain. She saw another world stretched out before her, one without physical properties, beyond her simple, human understanding. She witnessed time unraveling, revealing things so ancient and so alien that they felt like impossible dreams. She stood at the feet of things so immense and so terrible that she felt her sanity unravel for a moment.

"Everything's so much bigger than you ever knew possible."

Erin crouched down, still clutching at her head, trying to force away these strange, agonizing visions.

Could all this be real? Was this the true scope of reality? Entire worlds hidden just beyond human reach? Unspeakable monsters? Maddening histories lost to time? Gods and devils and every nightmare in between?

That's what this was, she somehow realized. The voice speaking to her right now, toying with her. It belonged to a god.

And she was nothing more than a speck of dust in comparison.

(*Everything will be okay.*)

Would it? How could *anything* be okay in a world like this?

She never should have come to this place. She never should have listened to that antlered monstrosity.

Except…

(*Everything will be okay.*)

She turned around and plunged her hand into the water. Her fingers closed around the thing resting there.

"Don't say I didn't warn you," sighed the voice as she stood up and stared at the pretty little charm.

It looked like a golden locket, small and dainty, hanging from a delicate chain. But as she stared at it, the light emanating from it faded. Slowly, darkness swallowed her again.

Then the voice spoke directly into her ear, close enough to feel the phantom breath on her skin: "I'll see you again."

Startled, she jumped and swatted at the unseen speaker, but all she managed was to smack her knuckles against the stone wall.

She twirled around, confused. What was that just now? For a moment there, she thought she was back in that mysterious vault.

This was all so strange. Why was she bouncing back and forth between then and now?

That voice back then… She didn't know what she was dealing with at the time. And she didn't fully understand it now. Not in *this* form, anyway. She didn't think it was possible for a mortal to fully understand the concept of a real god. And the Priestess of Ruin was a *very old* god.

She didn't remember what happened next down in that pitch-black chamber. Everything was a confusing blur. She remembered being terrified of something. She remembered screaming. She remembered running at one point. Then falling.

Something profound happened, she thought. Something that changed her in ways her living brain couldn't comprehend. Something to do with her *soul*, she thought. But it was like so many fleeting dreams, forgotten almost as quickly as it happened.

The next thing she knew, she was lying in the tall grass, squinting up into a blinding blue sky, the sun pounding down on her bare skin.

She sat up, confused, and realized that she was back outside the overgrown ruins of the Breastbroke sawmill, right where this nightmare began. Her clothes were still gone. And so was her cell phone. She was naked and sweating in the sun, as if she'd been lying there a while.

But when she looked down at her hand, she was still clutching the little golden charm.

Yggdrasil's thorn…

(I'll see you again.)

A fresh shiver passed through her in spite of the sweltering heat at the memory of that voice.

She stood up, eager to get the hell out of these woods. She was going to have to streak back to her Corolla. Her bag was in the trunk. She had clothes there. Luckily she kept an extra set of keys hidden on the vehicle or she'd really be screwed. She just hoped no one chose this moment to happen to drive down this otherwise deserted road.

Now, months later, she stood in the dark passage deep within the labyrinth below the storm-ravaged streets of the City Beyond Memory, her eyes wide with mounting understanding.

Those spare keys.

She wasn't sure why, but that one detail was like a spark in this otherwise endless darkness. The keys to something extraordinary…

That was what she needed to remember!

This was more than a mere passage. It was a physical portal between key points in the city's spiritual layers. And at the same time, it was a psychic portal between the past and the present within her own mind.

It was a *key* to her true role in the Keeper's plan.

More importantly, she found that she remembered now. The thing she was supposed to be doing. The thing she was searching for. The reason she was in this form, creeping through the gatehouse's dangerous murk.

She had a *soul to collect.*

Chapter 53

Olivia sat on one side of the bed, clinging to Wayne's hand, a sour expression on her face. "I don't approve," she grumbled, pouting down at him.

"I know," he said, giving her hand a reassuring squeeze. He was lying between her and the mysterious little girl who looked so much like him that it was unnerving.

She wasn't helping anything, she knew. But she hated this so much. Was she really supposed to just sit here and let her fiancé *die*? What did it matter if he had some kind of bizarre ability to come back to life? What if he *didn't* come back this time? It only took *once*! This whole ordeal was absolutely *terrifying*!

"If it's on his own terms," explained the Sentinel Princess, "he'll always be able to return. I'll be able to keep his body functioning until he comes back, no matter how long it takes, but even if he didn't have me, he wouldn't be in any real danger. He'll remain aware of his physical form no matter where he goes and be able to return to it in an instant. It's probably safe to say that if his body approaches the brink of failing, he'd have no choice but to snap back to it. It'd be like a reflex, impossible to resist."

Olivia didn't stop pouting. Was she supposed to take her word for that? This was *death* they were talking about! And she was treating it like a game! She stared at the girl, measuring her, trying to get some sense of what she was dealing with. Her psychic alarm wasn't going off. If anything, that part of her brain only gave her positive sensations. But the fact was that she was trying to take Wayne away from her. She was trying to *kill* him. Even if it *was* only temporary.

And she didn't care for the way she kept responding to things she was thinking. That was kind of creepy. Invasive. *Unnatural.*

But it *was* something the Sentinel Queen did that night, she recalled.

"The technique for letting yourself go is similar to how some people achieve astral projection and lucid dreaming."

"Lucid dreaming?" he asked, frowning. "That's a thing, too?"

"Of course it is. In fact, dreams are more significant than most people know."

His eyes still closed, he nodded. "Right…" he muttered. "Keith said something like that…" But he trailed off, his face twisting a little as he remembered that Keith wasn't out there anymore…

"They have the potential to take tangible forms," the girl went on. "And most importantly for you, they can be a gateway between the living and the dead. Crossing over isn't about pulling some imaginary plug and shutting down your body. It's about finding a state of mind closest to death without getting lost and letting the dreams control *you.* People who master lucid dreaming can enter a dream world, mold it into whatever they want it to be and live any fantasy they want. But you're even more rare than that. In your case, you'll be able to step away from yourself altogether, completely unattached to the natural world and fully immersed in the supernatural one."

That was a lot of big words for such a small child. It was almost spooky to listen to her speak. She wondered how long she'd been locked away here in this room, all alone, waiting for her father to arrive.

Time works differently here, she remembered her telling them. *And so does the aging process of the Faceless Ones. Even I don't know exactly how old I am.*

Her gaze drifted up to the white stone walls and ceiling above them.

(*There's no concept of time inside the Keeper's Compendium.*)

What *was* this place? And just what in the world was the

Keeper? How could he make something like this? And how did he know all the things he knew? He sounded like some kind of god, and yet no one called him that, even though they spoke of *other* gods. Andrea told them of *several.*

She watched the little girl lean over Wayne, still smiling. "Relax," she told him. "Loosen your muscles. Imagine yourself sinking into a comfortable cloud."

"Sure," he replied. "Just relax and drop dead. No problem."

She giggled at this. It was such a sweet and delightful sound, so out of place in the depths of that frightful labyrinth. It was the sound of a happy child, far too young to be talking about grand, cosmic designs and lucid dreams and the art of dying.

Olivia gripped his hand in both of hers. "You'd better come back," she warned him again.

"Yes, ma'am," he sighed.

"You already know he will," giggled the girl. "You can sense the amber threads. You can already see that he'll make it back to you. Otherwise, you'd be gripped by dread."

Olivia blinked at her for a moment, surprised. She was right, she realized. If Wayne were about to die for real, wouldn't her psychic alarm be going haywire? She was fairly sure she'd be in an absolute panic if he were going to sign off for good. That was how her ability worked, wasn't it? She could sense the possible futures laid out before her. And when something frightening or dreadful was about to happen, her brain reacted to it. Between the way Sandy explained it to her and her own experiences, she was fairly sure that was how it happened.

"She's got a point," said Wayne.

She pursed her lips at him, but he didn't see it. His eyes were still closed.

"Go ahead and try it," the girl went on. "Close your eyes and focus on him, on your future together. You'll be able to see it better than anyone. He'll still be there, as far as you can see."

She didn't want to close her eyes. A part of her didn't trust this mysterious child. But it was mostly stubbornness. She was still feeling weirdly jealous of the idea of sharing her big strong hero with his long-lost daughter. It was silly, she knew. Selfish.

Immature. She was a better person than that. But this whole situation was just weird! She was having trouble accepting it. She needed time.

Finally, however, she closed her eyes and focused on Wayne's hand clenched in her own.

No feeling of dread or impending sadness filled her. There was no panic, no anxiety. All she felt was a sort of uneasy impatience, like when he was working late and she wanted him to come home.

She was right. It didn't feel like she was going to lose him. She only felt a lonely sort of longing looming over her, not unlike what she felt back in that awful forest when the never-children spirited her away and wouldn't let her go back to him. It didn't feel like he was going to die. It felt like he was stepping out to run an errand. He was going to leave her for a little while. She was feeling that. But he wasn't going to stay gone. He'd come back to her. She found herself increasingly sure of this.

She felt nothing ominous about this girl at all. But was it really her psychic mind telling her this, or could this girl be *placing* these feelings inside her head, the way her mother whispered into her mind five years ago, subtly guiding her, urging her to stay calm and quiet and not move, assuring her that help would come. If this truly was her daughter, with the same psychic power, then she could easily do such a thing.

But was that a good thing? The Sentinel Queen claimed to have kept her safe that night. But she also lied about things. Albert told them so. She still didn't understand what really happened that night. There seemed to be a feud of some sort going on between her and that old man who helped Wayne rescue her from the Wood. Both claimed that the other was trying to get rid of them. It was all so confusing. Who was the real bad guy? *Was* there a good guy? Could she trust *anyone*?

She sat there, staring at the girl, watching as she smiled down at her father, still clinging to his hand. If she was really able to sense those amber threads Sandy told her about, then they were telling her that Wayne was safe with her. The question remained, however: how much could she really trust her psychic alarm? She still didn't know if it had any weaknesses or blind spots.

"Clear your mind," she urged Wayne. "Empty your thoughts and focus on the darkness behind your eyelids. Imagine yourself floating away in a gentle current."

"I'm not sure how this is going to do anything more than make me fall asleep," observed Wayne.

Again, the girl giggled. "That part's tricky," she agreed.

Olivia kept staring at her, kept trying to sort all those feelings inside her, trying to pick out the ones that were telling her what she needed to know.

Instead, she became aware of something else, something lurking deeper down in those swirling emotions. Something darker. Something that settled into her belly like a hot weight.

It wasn't about Wayne, she realized. This was something else, something farther away. Something to do with these mysterious amber threads.

Something she didn't care for…

"My nose itches," grumbled Wayne.

"You have to ignore that," giggled the girl. She never stopped squeezing his hand. She never stopped smiling, but those pretty, blind eyes had turned toward her. They remained distant, but suddenly they were staring right into her own, as if she weren't talking to Wayne at all… "You can worry about that later."

A strange certainty crept through her.

Something unsettling loomed in her near future. Something that had nothing to do with why Wayne was brought here. Something about *her*…

Something…*else*…

Chapter 54

Maybe it wasn't her imagination after all.

Andrea stood in the dark passage, unable to see her hand in front of her face, and yet she found that she could see shadowy shapes against the endless darkness all around her.

She didn't understand it. How could she see and not see at the same time? How did that make any sense?

And yet, what had sense ever had to do with anything in this messed-up nightmare world? What sense did it make that she could see the murk *with* her flashlight? Or that she could see it when Olivia and Wayne couldn't?

She thought back to her conversation with Erin after she was separated from Everett and Violet, when she showed her the murk for the first time and explained that they weren't what they appeared to be.

(*Your living brain is constrained by the senses you use to perceive the world around you. Whatever it is you think you're seeing and hearing is just your mind doing its best to tell you what's there.*)

Did that mean that she was never actually *seeing* them to begin with? Was that why she couldn't feel them when she passed through them? Because her brain was manifesting them as visible shadows when they were something utterly different?

If that were the case, then would it really matter whether she could see the physical world around her?

This was hard. It sort of hurt her head to think too much about.

She crept forward, squinting into the darkness, trying to make some semblance of sense out of what her brain was showing her.

It was a lot like she was just *imagining* what might be there. Except simply imagining things was sort of…*fluid*, she supposed? How would she describe it? Like those things were never fully anchored in the real world. You could imagine a giant spider crawling up the side of a building while riding along in the passenger seat of a car, staring out at the scenery, but that spider would just be wherever you happened to be looking when you thought of it. If you kept thinking about it after the building was out of sight, it would just jump to the next one. Or switch to a bridge or a water tower or whatever was there. And even if you were sitting in one place, something would change. Size. Perspective. The particular positioning of all those legs. At least, that's how it was for her. It was never some perfect, static image in her brain. This was a lot like that. She looked into that darkness ahead of her, knowing that she was walking through another empty passage, and she pictured that passage stretched out before her, its walls covered in those creeping black tendrils she saw back in those first passages. She pictured those dangling streamers of shadow. She pictured those strange, darkling specks floating in the air like little reverse fireflies. But unlike when she merely imagined something, she found that these images didn't change as she shifted her attention from one place to the next. They remained strangely fixed in place. They retained their shapes, their proportions, their relative distances.

They were altogether *too perfect* to only be a product of her imagination.

(*You've been given the ability to see the other side. That's your gift. And that's the role you've been given here. You can do this. You're the* only *one who can do this.*)

The reason she was here… The reason the Keeper chose her five years ago, when he arranged for the Sentinel Queen's messenger to paste Beverly Bridger's file on Gilbert House to her bedroom window instead of delivering it to Albert as she intended…

"You don't just hear ghosts," Ada informed her way back in Cedric's Cove. "You can see into the places where the realms of the living and the dead overlap. You can see the things that are hidden to others."

Her particular ability, unique from everyone else's, making her ideal for the Keeper's plans. She couldn't decide if she felt special or just unfortunate.

(*You'd be surprised how many spirit places you've walked right by without ever realizing it.*)

The ability to see what other people couldn't see. But not "see" at all. Because her eyes had nothing to do with it. She recalled marveling at the way the murk never cast any shadows when her flashlight beam passed over them. The way the light vanished when she dropped it, but its glow continued to illuminate the space not covered in murk.

Was she actually starting to understand some of this stuff?

(*It'll make sense after you're dead.*)

She shuddered a little at the memory of those words. Why did Erin have to say it like that? It made the whole thing so much creepier.

She continued onward through the empty corridor, distracted, staring at the twisting, creeping lines of imagined murk clinging to the stone surfaces, still trying to decide how she was able to see anything in perfect darkness.

Was there something there or wasn't there?

She looked back the way she came, at the same strange, half-there illusion of black-on-black patterns stretching away from her in the dark.

Her blind gaze drifted down to her hand. She was still dragging it along the wall, hesitant to stop for fear that when she reached for it again, she'd find it gone and herself utterly lost in some vast void. Her fingers were passing right through the murk that was clinging there, and yet she felt not so much as a cold spot inside that inky darker-than-darkness shape.

It was so strange, being able to see the murk, but not her own arm.

When she looked forward again, she was surprised to see that the murk was changing. Those imagined tendrils were spreading apart. The walls were parting.

The passage was forking.

A new wall had appeared before her, dividing the two new paths she was going to have to choose from, exactly like countless other such places she'd encountered. But those others she saw with her eyes and a flashlight, not with whatever part of her brain *this* was.

She reached out as she approached it and laid her hand on the new wall.

It was right there where she saw it, impossible for her eyes to have picked up.

She definitely wasn't imagining these things. The murk was real. And ironically, it was allowing her to see things even in this suffocating darkness.

The passage on the right was darker. The murk in that one covered almost every surface, even clumping in the corners in places.

She didn't like it when they clumped like that… She didn't want to go that way. But she was starting to understand that her job here was tied to those black ribbons and streamers. She would never leave this place if she kept avoiding them.

And as strange as it sounded, it looked like the only way she was going to be able to see anything without a flashlight was to keep following the darkness.

Begrudgingly, she turned right and set off down the murk-filled passage toward whatever next big fright was waiting for her.

Chapter 55

Gina couldn't stop crying. She'd made such a mess out of everything. She promised she wouldn't let go of Nicole, that she'd protect her no matter what. But she'd failed her. Just like she failed Keith.

She turned down. The glass labyrinth rolled around her. Or perhaps it only seemed that way from her perspective. It was probably more likely that the labyrinth wasn't moving at all. It was possible that she was now walking *down* a vertical wall. Or up it. Or sideways. It was impossible to know just how many times she'd turned it. But it was even more likely that she wasn't really traveling in *any* direction. This wasn't a natural space, after all. The rules didn't apply here. Nothing worked as it should. If she tried to understand it using real-world logic, she'd only drive herself mad.

And yet, regardless of that, she was able to use those strange, perceived physics to escape the Not-Nicole. So perhaps that sensation of the labyrinth rotating around her was as real as she needed it to be.

It was all so very *weird*.

There wasn't even a proper transition between the horizontal surfaces and the vertical ones. It wasn't as if she walked up to a gaping hole in the floor. She could have continued walking without turning downward. Somehow, she simply knew that she had the option of turning *down* and she was able to do it.

She felt like she could almost understand it if she could only concentrate. Something about her psychic abilities being able to see multiple layers of the tangled glass walls at once. But she couldn't push past the suffocating sadness gripping her in this awful moment enough to think clearly. Her head was filled with thoughts of Nicole taken from her… Keith dead… Andrea lost… Brandy and Albert left behind without a word of warning… So many mistakes. So many regrets. So many *failures*.

She stopped, her thoughts scattering. Something wispy and shadowy and vile was wafting through the nearby space. It wasn't coming straight at her, but it was close. It had sensed her here while she trudged along, distracted by her troubled thoughts. She needed to be more careful. It could easily have swept right over her in this state.

But then again, maybe that would've been better… She wasn't good for anything. Look at how badly she'd messed everything up.

And yet, even if that were true, she wasn't brave enough to risk it. She stood frozen in place, her heart thudding with terror, too afraid of the things in this glass labyrinth to dare face one, no matter how desperately broken she felt.

Tears just kept slipping down her cheeks. She didn't want to be here anymore. She didn't want to do this. She just wanted to walk away. The goddess never should've trusted her with something like this.

The wispy thing in the darkness wafted away, leaving her alone again. Her knees trembled and she leaned against the wall. She couldn't take this much longer. She just wanted to crawl into a hole and stay there.

She couldn't find her way through this awful labyrinth anyway. What was she even looking for? She thought she was making progress, but she was as lost as she was when she first stepped through the crack and entered this glass nightmare.

The cracks…

There was one ahead of her, she realized. Her psychic eye glimpsed that familiar refraction. In her mind, she imagined seeing it like the prism of light distorted through a crack in a window, but it had nothing to do with light. It was *space* that was breaking and refracting. It was *reality*. And the reality that was the stone labyrinth was bleeding through in that one spot.

She could leave this place. She could escape these wafting

horrors and Hochog's insane god. The other labyrinth was a confusing knot of corridors, too, but it was at least bound more tightly to the reality she understood. She could easily find a dead-end passage and curl up on the floor. She could stay there forever if she wanted.

And right now, that sounded like the best thing a screw-up like her could do.

She stepped forward, eager to escape this glass hell. She didn't care about the Keeper's plan anymore. Just look where all her trust in her goddess had gotten her. Keith was dead and Nicole might as well be. She might never escape Goar Nangup's monstrous grasp. And who knew what had become of the others in this awful place. It wasn't worth it. She couldn't do this. She pressed her hands against the wall, her mind made up. She only wanted to step through the crack once more and never look back.

But she stopped herself.

That was it. That was what she was missing!

The *cracks*. That distorted, refracted space her psychic eye glimpsed whenever she approached one. Countless potential destinations, and yet she'd been looking at it as if there were only *two* sides of the glass.

She stood there, frozen in place as the greater reality of the complex space around her finally clicked inside her head. "Mirrors…" she whispered. She kept calling them that, even though they had nothing to do with reflecting light. It was some kind of misdirection. A trick. An illusion. But she was thinking far too complex. It was *literally* like looking in a mirror.

The farther forward you looked, the farther *backward* you saw…

Everything was turned around.

She closed her eyes and focused on those cracks, on the multitude of spaces they opened onto. There was so much more the closer she looked. Each path diverged into more paths, each of which diverged even more. And each and every one of them had a *reflection*. A *forward* and a *backward*. Two ways. Two sides. Over and over again.

The way forward was back.

She wasn't sure how she missed it before. But then again, wasn't that exactly what she was just thinking? She was a complete failure, after all. Why wouldn't she only finally see it once it was too late?

More tears streaking down her face, she closed her eyes and focused on the crack in front of her.

The goddess promised she'd find the thing she was looking for, the thing she yearned for most in her life. But how could that be possible? As many mistakes as she'd made… She was, as poor Nicole would have called it, a colossal fuck-up.

But maybe if she just pushed forward once more…just *one more time*… Then just maybe she'd finally reach the end of this terrible journey.

Maybe she could just *disappear*. Maybe that was what she'd really wanted all along. To stop existing. To stop thinking. To stop suffering. To find *peace*.

She stepped into the crack, into the great multitude of spaces spread out before her. There were so many, now that she was *really* looking at them. Far too many for her to fully grasp. Any destination she chose would be random because it would have been impossible to map a way forward.

But she didn't want to go forward.

She cast her gaze at all the broken paths ahead of her. Then she stepped *backward.*

Chapter 56

Albert fell onto the stone floor, coughing and choking, dazed and confused. His body was cold and wet and slick and his head was filled with terrible images of bloodshed and violence.

The pain she inflicted on him, at least, had vanished. His mouth didn't taste like blood. He felt no gashes, no scabs, no scars. That unbearable pain in his groin was gone. He seemed to still be blissfully intact down there. Instead, he was gagging and gasping for breath, as if he'd very nearly drowned.

The ichor chamber… That was where he was when the witch dragged him into that nightmare. He was back in his real body now, free from her insane clutches. But the memories had followed him back, vivid and disturbing.

Especially at the end there…

Dolly…the shaman's petite little slave girl whose dainty little form concealed her monstrous truth… How long was he trapped in that reality with her? How long did she spend torturing him? And how long did *he* spend torturing *her*?

Somehow, he found the strength to break free of her morbid control and fight back. But something went dreadfully wrong at the end there. All that horror she funneled into his brain, all those nightmares she forced him to endure, all of her "precious memories" had poisoned him somehow. That was the only reason he could think of to explain what came over him.

Because that wasn't him. It *couldn't* have been him doing all those things.

She tried to use Brandy against him, inserted her into one of her sick fantasies and tried to make him hurt her. It made him mad. He didn't often get mad. And he *never* let his anger take over. But something possessed him in there. Something *awful.* He didn't just expel her wicked presence from his mind. He made her *pay* for what she'd done. He turned the horrors back on her, forced her to play the victim for a change. And not just once. He made her experience every last act of cruelty she'd ever committed.

Dolly's screams were still echoing through his head. He never knew a woman's screams could be so incredibly *satisfying.*

He pushed himself up onto his hands and knees and vomited.

It wasn't just the horrible things he remembered doing to her. She'd already shown him all of that stuff. She made him witness her every evil deed. And she made him play a leading role in most of those blood-soaked scenarios. The blood and the screams and the senseless violence were terrible, but it was that feeling of morbid satisfaction that truly disturbed him.

He *enjoyed* it. When she screamed…when she *shrieked* in agony…but especially when she begged and pleaded for him to stop, when she *sobbed and wailed like a helpless child…* It filled him with an almost euphoric pleasure.

Again, he vomited.

What the hell was wrong with him?

It could only be that the witch's deranged game had poisoned his mind somehow, seeping into his consciousness. She kept saying those awful things about how everyone was secretly like her, that everyone *enjoyed* playing her sick games. Was she somehow feeding that grotesque mindset into him that whole time, trying to turn him into a monster like her?

The problem with creating monsters was always the same. They had a way of turning on their makers.

All that time he spent, caught in her deranged trip down Murder Memory Lane, experiencing all the atrocities she'd committed over the years. Something like that could cause anyone to snap. The things he remembered doing to that woman… No one deserved it more than her. It was a taste of her own medicine, the very same torture she delivered and watched with sadistic delight, but even so, the very memory made him violently sick.

How could he bring himself to do something like that? Even to someone as evil as her?

He retched a third time, but there was nothing left in him to expel.

He crawled across the floor, away from the mess he'd made, only to bang the top of his head against an unyielding stone surface. He let out a painful grunt and collapsed onto the floor, clutching at it. That hurt like hell. There were stars dancing in the darkness in front of his eyes.

Where did his flashlight go? It wasn't in his pocket Did he drop it somewhere? Did the witch take it?

He curled himself up on the floor and waited for the pain to subside.

That was going to leave a knot…

He didn't have the strength for this right now. He was so exhausted. He still hadn't caught his breath.

A little rest was what he needed. He was too disoriented to fumble his way out of here in the dark.

What he needed was to shake off those nightmares. Because that was all it really was. Just a bad dream. Only in his head. It would fade. Then he'd be better. Then he could focus on important things like where he was or how to find his way back to Brandy.

A minute or two. That was all.

But it would be longer than that. Exhausted, he closed his eyes and immediately fell asleep.

Chapter 57

Corey retreated back into the safety of the building.

At least, he *hoped* it was safer inside, out of the thing's line of sight. But for all he knew, the thing had already spotted him. Or it was perfectly capable of seeing him right through these walls. *Could* it see? Did it have eyes? Maybe it *smelled* him, instead. Or perhaps it had some kind of psychic power that could sense him no matter where he tried to hide.

What *was* that thing, anyway? From his perspective it was nothing more than a gigantic, amorphous darkness crawling across the walls of those buildings, infecting the infrastructure of the sprawling city wherever it touched. He'd imagined that he could see some sort of shape oozing between him and those windows, blotting them out, but it was only visible in the way the lights winked out as it passed through the power grid. It was enormous, and yet that was very likely only a fraction of its whole.

If it really was some kind of sentient virus corrupting the temple's ancient coding, then perhaps it needed no senses to spot him. Maybe it had known he was here all along and the very idea of fleeing or hiding was laughable.

He made his way back toward the elevator, his mind churning with questions no one was going to answer for him. Even if someone *could* tell him what was out there, he wouldn't be able to comprehend it.

He felt so vulnerable. And that wasn't a feeling he was used to. He was usually the biggest person around, after all.

(*It's a matter of perspective.*)

That imaginary Violet seemed to be telling him that he

needed to do what he did when he found himself out in space again, but this time go even smaller.

If he were to compress it all down into a single building, perhaps…

But could he shrink it down so small? And would that be enough? What about the virus? Would it keep shrinking down with the world, too? He wasn't sure that made sense. If it were only a matter of size, then why not simply shrink the virus down until it was too small to affect anything? Or until it simply disappeared from existence entirely?

No, size had nothing to do with it. Like Violet kept saying, it was a matter of *perspective.* And perception had a way of cheating concepts like size. He just needed to find the right angle to view it from.

He pressed the button on the elevator and watched the doors slide open.

Perspective…

How much control did he have in this place? He knew that he had *something* to do with shrinking the job down from all of deep space to a single city, but he didn't think he did it all on his own. After all, he was trapped within the confines of the machine, wasn't he? He shouldn't be able to do anything that could compromise the coding. He doubted he'd be able to change anything in any way that the sentinels didn't intend. That seemed like a good way to *break* a machine.

An ominous tremble seemed to pass through the building. He felt it in the soles of his feet. Above him, the lights began to dim, as if something were draining the energy from them.

He stepped into the elevator and let the doors slide closed behind him, eager to be out of sight before the infection swept through the building. But as the car began to descend, he realized that he was now trapped in a metal box suspended seven stories in the air while some kind of giant monster bore down on the building.

Not his brightest moment, he realized. You never took the elevator in an emergency. Everyone knew that. But it was too late now. He was already canned.

The lights flickered. The car shuddered. The hum of the mechanics slowed. And there was a strange sensation of the space around him getting *smaller*, as if the very proximity of the monster were compressing the walls of the car like a submarine in the crushing depths of the ocean.

Better think of something, he heard Violet say somewhere inside his head.

"I'm tryin'," he huffed.

Chapter 58

What the hell was *this*?

Violet crept into the enormous chamber she'd found, her flashlight sweeping back and forth, from one faceless statue to the next. She hadn't seen very many of these guys up until now. There was the one in the terminal beneath the Lucianna Mysteria and another in that room where Everett pulled her out of that wormy grave. The only others she'd found were the six in that underwater chamber where she damned-near drowned.

But here, they were lined up along the wall on either side, one pair after another emerging from the gloom, mirroring each other as she crept between them, a mounting uneasiness swelling inside her.

And they were changing. Each pair was slightly different from the one before it, their poses shifting, their bodies in transition like frames in an animation.

What was happening here? Albert said these guys often served as some kind of hint or warning, but if that were so, then she had no idea what *these* freaks were trying to say.

This place was so weird. God, she wished she didn't have to figure this shit out all on her own.

She turned and shined her light backward, but the doorway she entered through had already been swallowed by the gloom again. She couldn't even see the first pair of sentinels.

It still felt strange just carrying on like this. What happened to Everett? She felt sick about leaving him behind, but there was no way for her follow him. That graymother thing swept through the space as soon as he was out of sight and filled it with those razor-sharp webs. And it did the same thing at the exit, after she cut her toe on one of them. Going back wasn't an option and she doubted she'd be able to circle around to one of the nest's other entrances, either.

"Get your shit together," she grumbled at herself. They were only statues. She couldn't let them freak her out. She turned her attention instead to their changing poses. They started in that same basic pose, like some naked, faceless, stretched out perversions of those famous Buckingham Palace guards, but each pair after seemed to be getting more agitated somehow. It started in the extremities. Those long fingers stiffening, then curling, then clenching into fists, those featureless heads turning, tilting, shoulders hunching, heels lifting.

Did they need to pee?

She lifted the glass shard and peered through it, but still nothing changed. She supposed that was probably a good thing. This place was freaky enough without worrying about hidden things.

This was all so bizarre. The farther she crept, the more statues her light unveiled, the more *unwound* they seemed to become. Now their feet were shifted, their knees slightly bent, their fists raised, their necks stretched and strained, their chests puffed out.

Then they stepped away from the wall, their elbows flared as if ready to swing those fists.

The next pair were raising their hands toward each other, their fingers unclenched, but still tightened. She couldn't tell if they were supposed to be *reaching* for each other or *pointing* at each other, but the gesture struck her as unsettlingly aggressive. Something was happening here that she didn't understand. And she was literally in the middle of it.

She squinted into the darkness ahead of her. There was something there, a shape she couldn't identify…different from the statues. And bigger.

Then an enormous face materialized before her eyes, startling her.

It was as big as a subway tunnel, and strikingly detailed. The stretched and strained features of a woman appeared to have been painstakingly carved directly from the temple stone. She had wrinkles and pores and creases and individual strands of hair. She even had *eyelashes*.

What the hell was *that* about?

She tried her glass shard, but once again, it refused to show her anything she couldn't see with her naked eyes, so she crept closer, slightly more curious than afraid, taking in all those intricate details. It was such a bizarre expression to immortalize someone in. She couldn't decide what she was looking at. Was the woman angry or frightened? There was some kind of panic there, but she couldn't say what kind from the face alone. The very *intensity* of it made it difficult to identify. The eyes were open wide, practically bulging, her skin stretched taught. Her mouth was open in a silent but unnerving scream, revealing teeth and gums and a tongue and even tonsils and a uvula. But beyond those was more darkness.

A door?

This seemed familiar somehow…

A giant face framing a door…not entirely unlike that giant statue the carriage passed through as it entered the Denselands…

"Oh shit…" she breathed. She remembered it now. Albert and Brandy warned them about this. They didn't go into a lot of detail, but they described three statue-filled chambers of increasing size that overwhelmed anyone who entered them with fear, hate or—absurdly enough—*lust*. Albert described doorways just like this, in the form of a hyper-realistic human face, so lifelike it was eerie. And that was certainly how she'd describe this one.

She turned and shined her light back at the sentinels. He described them, too, now that she remembered. She'd forgotten that detail. They were acting out the emotion in the room ahead.

But…what emotion *was* this, exactly?

They didn't precisely appear to be suffering crippling fear. They weren't *cowering*. They looked like they were prepared to *fight*. But at the same time there was something oddly *reserved* about their posture. Those last two seemed to be threatening each other, but she didn't get an "I'm going to kill you" vibe so much as an "I'm warning you" sort of feeling?

She supposed it didn't matter. If this was one of Albert and

Brandy's emotion rooms, then stepping through that woman's mouth and looking at what was on the other side would fill her head with whatever this was. She'd *become* one of those guys. Emotionally, at least.

It was still such a bizarre concept to her. It was no wonder she didn't remember it immediately. She wasn't sure she believed it. It sounded so utterly *ludicrous*. A room filled with pornographic statues that made people so uncontrollably horny that they just started screwing whoever was there with them on the floor like crazed animals? That was the stupidest thing she'd ever heard! It was like the plot for a shitty smut novel. And there were other rooms out there that would affect people differently? Statues that filled people with rage and made them turn on each other? Visions in stone so frightening they could scare you to death?

It was utterly ridiculous.

And yet here she was, literally staring it in the eye…

Her heart was already beating faster in anticipation of what awaited her in there. Was she afraid of what Albert described? Or was it a hint of whatever emotion was saturating the space ahead?

She aimed her light between those gaping teeth, at the shadowy gray shapes beyond.

The truth was that her curiosity was killing her. A part of her wanted to step into that gaping mouth and look at what was there, to see the rumored emotion-imbuing statues for herself, but she wasn't brave enough to dare it. Albert and Brandy both warned her how dangerous these chambers were.

(*Those rooms get deep inside your head. They can change a person. Permanently.*)

She took a step back at the memory of Albert's unsettling warning.

She looked back the way she came, contemplating retracing her steps, finding a way around.

There isn't another way.

She tipped her head to one side, curious. Was that the other one? Or was it only her own voice again? Because somehow she found that she knew this was true. She wasn't going to find a way around. Why would there be one? Why would the sentinels create a chamber like this and then make it possible to just circle around it? But also, she could almost remember being told something about that in that weird dream world beneath the too-colorful sky. Something about the Keeper's design and certain things that had to be completed before the path to the doorway could be unlocked.

"Unlocking the way," she muttered under her breath. That also sounded familiar.

Albert and Brandy said something about that, too, didn't they? Something about places like this potentially being connected to *locks* of some sort, using the very emotions those statues generated to open the way forward. Something to do with emotional energy and their weird sex magic. That sounded even *more* like bullshit if you asked her, and yet she was standing at an emotion room's front door…

But what did that mean, exactly? Using the emotions to unlock the way forward? Was she *supposed* to experience whatever overwhelming emotion was waiting for her inside? The very emotions Albert warned her were dangerous and could potentially change who she was?

She turned back and faced the door, taking in that crazed expression, those wild eyes, that silent scream.

She didn't think it was her imagination. Looking at it like this was doing something. Her heart was beating faster again. She felt uneasy. Unsettled. Anxious and spooked. Some primal part of her was itching to run away in spite of the fact that she knew it would do no good.

Forward was the only way.

She looked down at her flashlight. She knew the trick. Albert said the rooms were based on *vision*. No light, no invasive emotions. But he also said there were sometimes traps. Deadly pitfalls filled with stone spikes. Or sometimes just jutting out from among the statues themselves.

"Damned if you do, damned if you don't," she sighed. She switched off the light, plunging herself into perfect darkness. "This is going to suck *so* bad."

Chapter 59

Everett crept through the darkness, blind, his hand stretched out in front of him. Alice told him in her strange, wordless language that he'd entered a large chamber of some sort and that he was supposed to keep going straight. But that was all the information she gave him. What kind of chamber was it? Was it just a huge, empty room? Or were there interesting things all around him that he was missing? Was there only the one way out or were there many and she was merely pointing him in the direction she wanted him to go? He didn't like being in the dark, not because he was afraid of it. He wasn't. He didn't like the idea of missing something. What was the point in doing all this if he didn't get to see all the amazing things along the way?

But he didn't care to ask her about it, either. He was still feeling somewhat shaken by the fact that she was perfectly willing to sacrifice Violet to save their own butts. That didn't sit right with him. Not at all.

He continued onward, his thoughts churning. So much had happened in such a short amount of time. How many days had it been since he set off for Gutler's Weep? He'd gone *way* beyond proving that there was more to the world than he'd been led to believe his whole life. Never mind the lies his mother told him about there being no afterlife other than hell. He'd found whole other worlds. He'd found zombies. *Fairies* of all things. An entire *spirit world* filled with not just the souls of the dead but with countless spirits of all fantastic sorts. Gateways to other worlds. Mystic keys. A vast, black forest filled with dangerous, man-eating trees. An ancient cycle of birth and decay stretching unfathomable eons into a past no one remembered. And remnants of those fantastic, lost universes scattered across the Denselands.

And yet all of that paled in comparison to his desire to simply know if his friends out there were still safe.

Had Violet managed to escape the graymother's nest? Where did Andrea go when they crossed into the city? And was she still safe? Whatever happened to Wayne and Olivia? He hoped they were still together. They really didn't like being separated.

This would all be so much more fun if they could all just stay together.

How big was this room? It just kept going. He was about to ask Alice how much farther it was when there was a sound from somewhere behind him.

Two sounds, really, one after another. A sort of muted "thunk-thunk" sound.

He turned around, confused, and discovered that there was now a dim light glowing in the darkness there.

Curious, he walked toward it. Why would there be a light? Nothing else had made any light on this long journey. There hadn't been any lights beyond the flashlights they carried with them since they stepped off Max's train.

And indeed, as he drew closer, he saw that it *was* a flashlight. But where did it come from? Why was it just lying there on the floor? And how did it get there? It wasn't there a moment ago, he was certain. He would've seen it.

This was kind of eerie. This was the sort of scene they liked to use in horror movies. When the dumb victim went to investigate, he'd get a really bad scare.

But Alice had always warned him of danger before. They might have disagreed about the decision to protect Violet over himself, but she wanted to keep the guy who was actually willing to take her with him safe, didn't she?

Maybe it was foolish of him to trust her, but he did. He made her what she was, after all. She might not understand the concept of friendship very well, but he very firmly felt that he could trust her.

He knelt down and picked up the flashlight, his lip curled

with mild revulsion. What was it covered in? It was all goopy. He wiped the lens clean with his thumb and it brightened. Whose flashlight was this? It wasn't his.

He became aware of another sound. Faint. Like…dripping?

There was more of that oily goo on the floor. He reached out with the light and shined it farther into the gloom. It was spattered on the floor all around him.

A fresh glob of it dripped onto his outstretched arm.

Confused, he aimed it up.

A pale figure was hovering above him.

He let out a startled yelp as it dropped onto him, knocking him onto his back. He dropped the flashlight *and* Alice.

He scooted backward and sat up, but already he realized that it wasn't a monster. It was a *woman.* But where did she come from? What was this gross goo she was covered in? And why was she *half-naked*? She was wearing only a pair of shorts and a single sock.

He tried to lift her up so he could try to help her, but she was too slimy to get a grip on, so he hooked his elbows under her armpits and tried to prop her up.

The flashlight was pointed the other way now, making it too dim to see very clearly, but she definitely wasn't someone he recognized. She had very fair blonde hair that was unlike anyone else he'd met.

But who she was didn't matter much. She was unconscious. Was she *breathing*? He didn't know what to do. He wasn't trained to perform CPR. Was this one of those artificial resuscitation situations?

Then, suddenly, she convulsed and coughed a great spout of that gross, brownish goo directly into his face.

That was…unexpected…

He wasn't sure what else to do, so he simply held onto her as she coughed and gagged and struggled for air.

Her arms groped at him, clinging to him like a drowning victim (which he supposed she technically was) and continued coughing and sputtering.

Now that she was holding onto him, though, he was able to

reach up and wipe the foul goo from his face. It felt hideous. Cold and slick and viscous. But it didn't smell gross. It didn't burn his skin or anything, which was good.

And coughing was also good. If she could cough, she could breathe. And if she was breathing then she should be okay.

Whoever she was…

She seemed disoriented. She was still coughing, but now she was pulling at him, grasping at his shoulders, practically climbing up his shirt.

She managed a great, desperate gasp and then, weirdly, she kissed him!

He froze, his eyes wide open in the dark.

Was this like what happened with Violet? That thing about if you saved a girl from being buried alive she was apt to kiss you?

Another coughing fit came over the woman again. It seemed to hit her suddenly, because she was still kissing him when it started. (Not exactly a romantic moment, he decided.) She turned her head and finished coughing. Then she laid her head against him, weary.

This was a really weird first meeting.

She coughed again, then turned and blinked up at him. She had really pretty light blue eyes.

She scrunched her face up at him, confused. "Who the fuck're you?" she asked him.

"Um…?"

Then those pretty eyes went really wide. Her chest hitched. Her cheeks puffed.

Then she vomited up a huge quantity of that foul goop all over him.

Chapter 60

Keith stood alone at the end of a dark corridor, trying to remember how he arrived at this place or what this place was or even just what happened before he found himself here. It was all so confusing. This wasn't that stone labyrinth. These walls were stone, but they were black, not gray. Raw. Cobbled together. The floor was bare, black earth. And there was no ceiling that he could see. It stretched upward into that heavy darkness, seemingly forever.

How long had he been standing here, staring up into that black nothing above, trying to remember things?

"There you are," said a familiar voice from somewhere behind him.

He turned around. Erin was standing there, still wearing that same sleek and silvery dress, still barefoot, still hauntingly beautiful with her long, black curls and sunflower tattoos. "It's you…" he said.

She scowled at him. "Good to see you again, too," she chided.

He gave her a half-hearted shrug. "Sorry. Just…if it's you, then I guess that means…"

"Yeah. You're like me now."

"Dead." The word felt so strange on his tongue. He didn't think a word had ever felt so heavy before.

"Real bummer, isn't it?"

He let out a weary huff of a laugh at this. That seemed like the understatement of a lifetime.

He looked down at the earth beneath his feet, then up into the darkness hanging overhead. He still couldn't remember much. "How long have I been here?"

"Hard to say. Time is different when you're dead. And it gets broken so many times when you travel as far as you have. Even more so in the Denselands and inside the wall."

Everything about this place is broken, he remembered Gina telling them when they first disembarked into that strange land. *The ground and the air. Gravity and pressure. Space and time. It's all crinkled up here.* The memory gave him a shiver, though he wasn't sure why he could still shiver if he was dead…

"Not long, though," Erin added. "A few hours, I'd say."

"That's all?"

"Comparatively, I suppose. The passage of time fluctuates depending on where you are inside the gatehouse. All of us here, living *and* dead, passed through the city wall at the same time, but not everyone's been here the same *amount* of time."

"That's…an odd thing to think about."

"Isn't it? There's no knowing how much their inner clocks might be out of sync by the time they get home. Some of them might be as much as a few days closer or farther apart in age."

"So weird…" he muttered. And he didn't fail to notice that she said "they" and not "you." Because *they* could all still go home, but he was… Well, he wasn't sure exactly. What was *supposed* to happen next?

Again, he looked around at those towering, black walls. "Is this what death is supposed to be like?" he asked. "Just…darkness and dead ends?"

"No. You're still in the twilight stage. Confused and conflicted. Maybe a little in denial. Everybody's different. Some never make it out of this stage, sadly. They remain stuck in this dreary limbo forever. Especially when they die suddenly or with severe emotional trauma. In your case, you're really clinging to your physical form."

He looked down at himself, confused. He was still wearing his shirt as a bandage. His feet were still wrapped in the tatters of Nicole's tank top. He was even still bloody where that bone monster jabbed him in the side. Looking at that wound, he realized that it still hurt, even. "Am I supposed to be transparent or something?"

She laughed at this. "Not necessarily. You can be anything you want to be. But you're dead now. You're much more than just that body."

He stared at his own hand for a moment, uncertain. "Okay," he said. "If you say so." He turned and looked around. "Where *is* my body?"

"You got yourself kind of caught up in the spiritual currents flowing through the Murk passages. Sort of like falling in a river and getting washed downstream. You wouldn't believe what I had to go through just to find you here."

He blinked at her, confused. "I'm sorry. Didn't mean to cause you trouble."

Again, she laughed. "It's okay. I'm here now. That's what's important. We'll go together."

"Go where?"

"We have a job to do. The reason the Keeper brought us here."

Slowly, he nodded. He wasn't sure why, but that sounded right. A job. A very important task. He couldn't remember what it was, but he was immediately convinced that this wasn't the first he'd heard of it.

Something from one of his many dreams, perhaps? Something about…golden strands…or something? And intruders in the walls? "Yeah… That cat lady said something about that once. A long time ago, feels like…"

"That's right."

He frowned. "But there's something else I have to do first, isn't there?"

She smiled and held out her hand for him to take. "Let's go find her."

"Nik…" he breathed. That name should've tasted bitter on his lips, and yet something had happened. Something changed before he died. She needed him again, but far from filling his belly with unpleasant feelings, he found himself eager to see her.

(*I don't want to lose you again. Not before I get a chance to take it all back.*)

Once upon a time, in a dream that wasn't real, she was his whole life. A gift from the spirits of the sentinels who watched over the obsidian pool, waiting for the day he arrived. An entire lifetime that he'd never get to live. A life as beautiful as he could ever imagine.

"I'll show you the way," Erin promised, still holding out her hand.

He nodded. He reached out and took it. "I'm ready."

Chapter 61

"I don't think this is working," grumbled Wayne.

"It won't if you keep talking," giggled the little girl who claimed to be his daughter.

She kept telling him to relax, to empty his thoughts, to let himself drift away, but how was he supposed to relax in this strange, white room? Between being told that he was a father and learning what happened to Keith, his head was filling up faster than he could empty it. And then there was the fact that Olivia was clearly—and understandably—unhappy with what he was trying to do here.

The Sentinel Queen's child… He still couldn't quite accept it. He'd never been able to come to terms with the fact that she seduced him and conceived a child with him against his will. That the child had actually been born…that she'd grown into this eerily intelligent but absolutely *beautiful* little girl… A part of him didn't *want* to accept it. What was he supposed to do about it? If he was truly this girl's father, wasn't it his responsibility to take care of her? But he didn't know she was alive until right now. And she was *here* of all ungodly places. This white palace inside the Keeper's Compendium, whatever the hell that was. Inside the second temple in the heart of the Denselands. How did she even get here? He'd struggled just to keep his fiancée safe throughout all this madness. How was he supposed to care for a *child*? And yet…in spite of all that…didn't he *want* this to be his child? Hadn't it always filled him with an unfair sense of sadness and regret that the Sentinel Queen took something so precious from him only to let it die?

He was so confused.

It was so much easier to just do as he was told and follow her directions. It was so much easier to just…well, lie down and die…

What a world it was turning out to be…

"Death isn't what people think it is," explained the sweet girl. "It's not floating up into a blinding light."

He cracked one eye open and peered up at Olivia. "You guys said you literally walked through the 'tunnel of light' five years ago."

"I mean, that's what *Andrea* called it," said Olivia. "*I* don't know anything about it. But there definitely wasn't any light. It was pitch black in there."

The girl giggled again. "That was a spirit highway." She reached out and placed her hands over his eyes, urging him to keep them both closed. "They're complicated. They *do* exist. And they exist exactly for the purpose of ferrying spirits from the living world to the Murk. Most people, the moment they die, their soul is swept away by them. Like rainwater down a storm drain. And for the rare soul who makes that trip and comes back, they *do* sometimes recall the experience as a bright light. But only because they can't comprehend the same things they could when they were free of the restricted senses the human body is restrained to."

"Sounds strange when you talk," he informed her. "Not like a kid…"

"I told you, time works different in this place and in this body. I'm not as young as I look. Not by human standards."

"Makes sense," he lied.

He felt the bed move, then heard her voice speaking from very close. "Focus," she directed him. She was practically right in his face, close enough to feel her breath with every word. "You've been there before. Somewhere in there, you remember it. It's not warm and bright. It's not clouds and angels. It's dark and it's cold and it's *big*."

Wayne frowned at this. Big? Something in the far back of his memory stirred at this word. A big, dark, cold place…

"Dying is like falling overboard in a storm in the middle of the ocean. It's numbing. It's chaotic. It's scary. But it's silent. And you're powerless to do anything but go where the current carries you."

Dark and cold…

Numbing…

Like the freezing sea swallowing him up in the aftermath of a shipwreck…

Silent like the depths…

Drifting…

He felt the hairs on his arms stand up as an eerie sense of déjà vu washed over him at these forgotten sensations.

"Not all souls are the same," said the girl. She'd leaned back again. She was still bent over him but her face wasn't hovering so close now. "Most are weak. The spirit highways exist mostly for them, to make sure they don't get trapped or lost. Stronger spirits can resist the flow, but most let it take them anyway. They know it's time to go. Or they're eager to find someone they've lost. For the rest, there are lots of destinations they can choose. Spirits who remain earthbound are complicated. They change from what they were in life. Some are slaves to their emotions, others imprisoned by their environments. A lot of them end up turning into something monstrous. So many of them simply get lost."

"You make it sound so scary," said Olivia.

"It *is* scary," she replied. "Dying isn't a straight road up or down depending on how good a person you were in life. It's more like the maze outside these walls. There are more destinations than you can imagine and more dangers than in the entire living world. But *you* don't have to be scared. Daddy's soul is special. It's stronger than most. And it's *unique*. It's literally impossible for him to get lost. He'll be back. You'll see."

Wayne supposed that was all there was to it. They'd simply *have* to wait and see, because they only had her word to take for it. And he knew Olivia well enough to know that she wasn't liking this one bit. She didn't understand any of it, after all. *He* didn't understand any of it. But he didn't know what else to do but follow this child's directions.

The bed moved again and he felt the girl leaning close to

him.

"Imagine yourself floating in the darkness," she instructed, "the waves tossing you back and forth, out of your control. You can't move. You can't talk. You can't feel. You can't breathe. But you don't need to. You're not in this world anymore. None of that stuff matters."

Olivia's grip tightened on his hand. He wanted to squeeze her back, reassuring her, but he wasn't supposed to be moving. He was supposed to be relaxing his muscles and emptying his mind.

He was…pretending to be dead…he guessed?

Sure. He was just…playing make-believe with his daughter. That was all. Just a happy little game of Daddy's Deathbed. Followed by a cheerful game of Daddy's Funeral followed by a tea party with the stuffies and dollies.

What was he doing? This was madness!

"Everything's dark and cold and empty," the girl went on. "You feel like you're being carried away."

But these things she was saying… It was all so *familiar*… Hadn't he felt something like that before? Hadn't he experienced somewhere like that?

He could almost remember it…

"There's nothing above you but empty black sky. There's nothing below you but endless, black depths."

He could feel the waves pushing and pulling him, tossing his helpless body…

Except…did he even *have* a body here?

"Death is an ocean," she whispered. "Let yourself sink into it. Let its currents carry you away."

Lost in an endless ocean…cold and alone…helpless…

He felt the blankets disappear from beneath him. The hands holding his faded like dreams.

He knew this place entirely too well. A creeping fear gripped him.

This was death. This was the churning nothing that haunted his dreams every night and vanished from his memory every morning.

A sudden and overwhelming terror gripped him as it all came flooding back to him. He didn't want to be here again. He wanted to wake up. He wanted to cry out. But it was too late.

Swallowed in a freezing darkness, he felt himself being swept out to sea.

Chapter 62

It didn't take long for the murk to envelope every surface of the passage, plunging Andrea once again into perfect darkness, depriving her of even the strange illusion of sight that she'd discovered back in that last corridor. And yet, even now she found that she could tell there was a difference. It made no sense, even to her, that she should be able to distinguish between murk darkness and regular darkness, but she found that it was true. The farther she walked in this blind state, the more apparent it became.

Did Tia know this would happen? Could she have taken away her flashlight specifically *because* she knew that she'd discover this strange quirk of her ghostly abilities faster this way? That didn't sound right. That made it sound like she was in on the Keeper's convoluted scheme the whole time. But both Erin and Ada warned her that she was the enemy of the cycle. Tia said as much herself! And she really didn't think that was an elaborate show she was putting on back there. She felt very certain that she had every intention of murdering her right up until she glimpsed that snake she was imagining.

And by the way, what was up with *that*?

That strange and frightening image of the giant snake popped up in her head just before Tia could plunge those deadly blades into her throat…except *was* it only in her head? Because Tia saw it, too. It surprised her. It baffled her. But most of all, it delighted her. She called it "the Murk Serpent" and jumped around and laughed like a hyperactive child. (Except for those obscene naked boobs bouncing around, she supposed. There was nothing childlike about those.)

(If he's waking the guardians…)

What did that mean? What were the guardians? What was the Murk Serpent? And what did any of it have to do with her?

Everything about that whole ordeal was just *weird.*

And whatever happened to Erin? She just stopped talking to her. Did Tia send her away like she did Ghost Girl? She did warn her that she was no match for the so-called "Priestess of Ruin." (Of course *Stella* would come up with a pretentious title like that.) She couldn't even remember the last time she spoke to her. Wasn't it when she was still walking with Olivia and Wayne? Then Tia butted in and snatched her off into that tortuous nightmare with the blood-red sky.

There was more going on than she could keep up with. She'd practically *forgotten* about Erin after all those horrible fake deaths she experienced. And she could really use someone to give her some advice right now. She had no idea what to do. She was just wandering around, *literally blind*, with instructions to just "go down." And the only *down* she found was that hound passage that nearly did her in.

She stared into the darkness ahead of her. It was strange. Nothing really *looked* any different. Her eyes were useless here, of course. And yet she found that she simply understood that there were *two* darknesses in this place. One that her natural eyes perceived and one that her *inner* eye perceived. And in that latter darkness, she found that she could see something on the wall ahead of her. It wasn't a *darker* darkness, exactly. It was more like…a *denser* darkness? Did that make sense? Like, if darkness had mass, then that small space she was staring at was more compacted? Maybe she should've paid more attention in science class. Maybe then she'd be able to get it. But she doubted it. Murk wasn't something they taught in schools. And neither was how to understand psychic powers.

She sort of wished Albert were here with her. Not that she wanted to be naked in front of him, of course. That'd be weird. But she liked it when he explained some of this stuff. He always had really interesting thoughts about it. Listening to him made it all feel just a little bit less freaky, like it wasn't all just some kind of unexplainable nightmare.

She crowded closer to the opposite wall, her blind gaze fixed on that strange ball of "denser darkness," and crept past it.

It had something to do with those grabby things, she knew. Something was telling her it wasn't one of the ones that would snatch at her, startling her, then hold on for a moment before just letting go. But it was the same sort of idea. The murk was clumped together there, as if trying to take a different form.

She still had no idea how she knew this without being able to see it, but there it was, undeniable.

She hurried on past it, eager to be out of reach in case it should suddenly wake up and growl and start chasing her.

She wished she understood this stuff.

Again, she thought of Albert. Naked or not, she'd welcome the chance to travel with him. He was a nice guy besides being smart and having interesting theories about this stuff. She'd always felt extra close to both him and Wayne. She supposed spending hours naked together and surviving something like the Temple of the Blind would do that to anyone. She even *kissed* Albert once. After she opened that portal thing and saved them all from the collapsing temple, she was so happy and excited to have them all back that she just sort of planted one on him. She didn't even think about it. She never felt embarrassed about it, either. In that moment, it was just simply the most natural thing in the world.

She wasn't like Nicole, though. She didn't strip off her clothes and lounge around his and Brandy's apartment naked. But like her, she wasn't exactly shy around Albert and Wayne. She'd changed clothes in front of them. Just this summer, she'd sunbathed topless in front of them a few times. She almost understood what Nicole found so appealing about it. That feeling of comfort and closeness, of friends so dear you could let yourself relax completely without any doubts or fears.

She could use a little of that right about now. More than anything, she wanted someone who would tell her it was okay, that she was doing what she was supposed to be doing, who would just be there by her side while she figured all this madness out.

But she didn't have anyone right now. She was alone in these darknesses. And that wasn't going to change. Because she wasn't going somewhere anyone else could go. She was venturing deeper and deeper into the murk, all the way to the bottom of this dark and frightful labyrinth.

She wasn't sure how it was that she knew this, but she did. This was somewhere no one could follow her. So she might as well get used to being alone.

Ahead of her, another of those denser clumps of darkness appeared, this one much bigger. It was on the floor, taking up almost half the passage.

She stopped walking and studied it. She didn't like it when the clumps were that big. That was the size of the clumps that moved and growled and yawned open to reveal giant mouths filled with endless spirals of deadly teeth.

But this one wasn't moving. It was just sitting there, motionless.

Going back wasn't really an option. She could go back and try the left side of the fork in the path, but she doubted that would take her anywhere good. The more she tried to avoid the dangers in the murk, the longer this ordeal was going to take.

Holding back a frightened whimper, she pressed herself against the wall and crept past it.

Still, it didn't move.

As soon as she was clear, she hurried onward, tiptoeing away from it, eager to be out of sight in case it should suddenly wake up.

It was only a matter of time, she was sure, until she ran out of luck.

Chapter 63

Gina stood in the darkness, disoriented, tears still wet upon her cheeks. This was somewhere new, somewhere *deep* within the glass labyrinth, all the way at the very bottom of whatever spiraling abyss lay beneath all the tangled passageways.

There was order in the chaos here, she realized. The passages around her were no longer knotted and twisted in impossible geometries. There was an organization to them. They were all funning toward the same destination, a space somewhere just ahead of her and at the same time just beneath her feet.

Every surface was still etched with those strange, swirling patterns that Nicole described as looking like brains. The longer she was here, the more she understood that she wasn't so far off. There were strange, yet distinct energies flowing along those lines, coursing through the curves and squiggles, not entirely unlike the electrical impulses by which a biological brain functioned, even though these energies had nothing to do with electricity. It was too faint to notice before, but now it was clear. They might as well be glowing like heating elements.

More importantly, there were none of those unnatural entities blocking her way. It seemed to her that something about the intensity of that energy—or whatever that flowing sensation she felt coursing through the grooves in the stone might have been—somehow repelled them, like wild animals retreating from an approaching wildfire.

Nothing was left to keep her from accomplishing the task the goddess gave her. It was literally right in front of her.

And yet…

She looked back. There was nothing to see. Her eyes remained useless in this pitch-black darkness. Even the crack she passed through to get here was no longer there. She couldn't go back if she wanted to. And the realization of that broke her heart.

She'd left Nicole behind.

She'd broken her promises. The one she made to Keith (*She's a handful, this one. A real pain in the ass sometimes. But do me a favor and look after her will you? She's really important to me.) and* the one she made to Nicole (*We started this together and we're finishing it together. I won't leave without you*).

What had she done? Terrified and aching with regret, she'd attempted to flee the glass labyrinth entirely, ready to give up. Then she became distracted by the realization that she could move backward through the cracks. She didn't think it through.

She knew what could happen if they were separated. How many times did she warn Nicole not to let go of her hand? She was so careful, so desperately afraid of losing her in the maddening glass corridors, *knowing* she'd likely never be able to find her again.

(*Don't let go of me. I don't know what might happen. We can't risk getting separated.*)

And Nicole's response…

(*I trust you.*)

A wave of such agonizing emotion rushed through her that she dropped to her knees, her face contorted with the force of unbearable sobs. She cried out in the eerie silence, a terrible, painful wail. She couldn't remember the last time she broke down this hard. She'd worked so diligently to maintain her composure over the years, struggled to train herself to keep it all held inside, to bottle it up tightly, to never let anyone see the pain she was in. But this was too much. She couldn't stand it. She wasn't strong enough.

Wherever Nicole was now—the *real* Nicole, not Goar Nangup's monstrous puppet—she desperately hoped she'd forgive her for being so weak.

Chapter 64

Her flashlight tucked safely away in her pocket, Violet felt her way through the screaming woman's mouth, careful not to bang her head.

Brandy told her that she was significantly nearsighted, allowing her to simply remove her glasses in order to proceed through some of these rooms without much trouble. And by putting on her glasses, Albert was able to reduce his own eyesight enough that he was able to navigate some of the fear room, as well. Violet, however, had perfect eyesight and therefore no glasses of her own *or* anyone else's to borrow. The safest route forward for her was to do so *literally* blind. She'd just take her time and feel her way through whatever statues were here.

The biggest danger was those spikes Albert mentioned. (Or whatever other horrible trap might be waiting for her in here.) She was going to have to take it slow and test every single step she took, meaning this was going to be an agonizingly slow process.

And she still hadn't cleared the door yet.

She ducked into the space beyond, her hands sliding along the stone, feeling the smooth walls on either side. She reached up to make sure nothing was there to bang her head on as she straightened up and prodded the floor ahead of her with her bare toes.

Satisfied that there was nothing dangerous right in front of her, she crept forward, venturing a little farther into the darkness, her hands groping blindly in front of her, her feet shuffling along the floor.

It was a deeply unpleasant feeling, not being able to see

what might be in front of her and knowing that she couldn't let herself see any of it. It was almost as bad as her raging curiosity. What did an emotion room's statues look like? How did they work? What would they force her to feel? A part of her wanted to take just a *little* peek. Just a glance couldn't hurt. But she knew better than to assume something like that. She pictured that last pair of sentinels in the previous room, the intense way they were staring each other down. (Or so she assumed, she supposed, seeing as how they had no eyes to actually stare with.) She still didn't understand what it was they were depicting, but it clearly wasn't a *calm* emotion. They certainly didn't look like two individuals who could calmly and methodically creep through a dark room filled with dangerous, emotion-instilling statues and probably deadly traps. They looked exactly like the sort of sentinels who would run straight into the nearest spike.

Her hand brushed against something in the dark. Cold and hard, smooth to the touch, but with a slight texture. It wasn't a wall. It felt like it could be one of those sentinels, but it wasn't freakishly tall. A person? She resisted the urge to run her hands all over it. As much as she was curious about it, she was afraid that even *feeling* what they looked like might be enough to poison her mind with whatever emotion it was enchanted with. She settled for checking for any outstretched limbs or held objects that she might smack her head on while creeping past it.

And spikes. She was *definitely* going to be watching out for those.

It still sounded so utterly…*fake*. Spike pits? What in the actual Indiana Jones stereotype was up with that? This place already had *hounds*. They weren't an adequate home security system on their own?

Her hands fell upon another statue in the dark. Most of these seemed to be human. She found herself groping at more than one very distinct face or hand, hard and unyielding, but easily definable even blind. This one had its arm raised. She traced the curves of its bicep, felt the knob of its elbow. A man, probably. She tried not to take in any more details than that. What these people looked like, what they were doing, what they were wearing, these things all remained a maddening mystery.

Who *were* these people? Albert said the emotion rooms weren't just random depictions, but actual events from the past, *infused* with the emotions they displayed. But how would that even work? How old would these people have to be?

Were these her ancestors from a world long dead and gone? What were they like? How did they speak? What was their culture like? What kinds of clothes did they wear?

For the first time, she was sort of glad that Corey wasn't here. She didn't think he'd be able to resist looking. He'd have all the same questions she did, and so many more. He'd come up with things she'd never think of. He always came up with the most *ridiculous* questions. And he always came up with the very *best* questions.

Again, her hand fell against stone. Again, she ignored any details, focusing only on any outstretched limbs or sharp things jutting out at her. But as she slid her hands over this statue, she found that something was off.

It was the same stone as all the others, the same cool, hard touch, but this wasn't a person. It was something else, something without those same intricate details. She felt no creases or wrinkles, no muscle tone. It was tall and weirdly thin. It had arms, but no hands. She reached up and felt its shoulders, strangely rounded and smooth, with a thin neck so long she couldn't reach its head…

"What the hell?"

Somewhere far back in the recesses of her mind, something stirred. An old memory? Something from her childhood? An icy prickle crept up her spine. Was that some long-forgotten childhood nightmare? Something frightening…

(…*hiding in plain sight*…)

Something dangerous… Something *predatory*…

(…*could be anywhere*…*any*one…)

Her hand still resting on the statue, she turned and looked behind her, forgetting that she was still blind. Did she hear something? Was someone there?

(…*don't trust your eyes*…)

She realized her other hand was reaching for the pocket holding her flashlight and she had to restrain herself from digging it out. That would definitely be a bad idea. Without the darkness to hide this stone menagerie, the emotions would overwhelm her.

In fact, it already had.

She snatched her hand from the statue and took a step back from it, startled. The shape she'd encountered was so strange, so *different* from the others, that she'd forgotten herself. She started trying to understand what she was feeling. But that was the *last* thing she wanted. These things were supposed to stay unseen. Otherwise, she'd be overwhelmed by…

(…*they're everywhere…they spread…like a disease…*)

She shivered hard and hugged herself in the darkness. Was that an actual memory from the distant past? Something terrifying that happened in a previous universe?

That was a deeply unpleasant sensation. And it wasn't going away. She turned around, eyes wide in the dark, her heart racing. One part of her was sure she heard something that time. Another part of her knew she didn't.

Forcing back the urge to reach for her light, she pushed onward, but those images lingered in her head. Horrible, revolting creatures lurking in the shadows, sneaky, pretending to be things they weren't.

Chapter 65

The elevator doors slid open and Corey stepped out into a cold, sterile corridor lined with symmetric rows of tall, black cabinets filled with boxes like stacks of neatly organized books. Each face was a starscape of blinking green, amber and blue lights. The unsettling silence inside those empty buildings had been replaced with a much more natural drone of cooling fans and hum of air conditioning. Huge bundles of cables were stretched overhead, connecting the countless machines like veins and arteries inside a living organism. It was a vision of perfect order and precision, a space that acted like a digital skull, encasing the very *brain* of the machine.

A server room. Not very unlike the one at his father's office building, though considerably larger. And darker, too. The real server rooms he'd been in had always been well illuminated by bright, fluorescent lighting that he thought always made the space feel like a hospital operating room. But the only lights here were the ones glowing on the servers, casting an eerie glow through the gloom.

He turned and looked behind him. The elevator was gone, replaced by only more cabinets stretching off into the distance. He wasn't surprised by the change. He found that he was entirely expecting it. It was the same as the shift from deep space to the deserted city streets. He hadn't moved. His perspective had changed. He'd shrunk the problem down again, this time to a single room.

Although it wasn't exactly a *small* room. He couldn't even see the far ends from here. *Did* it end?

He turned forward again and realized that there was a bag at his feet, similar to the one he lost back in the Denselands when the Not-Jeremy spirited Violet away into that black forest.

Tools. Naturally. It made sense when you understood what was happening.

He kept thinking of the temple as a machine. And he kept rationalizing Austin's bizarre existence as a component of that machine, what he likened to a bootup disk. Ancient, faceless alien races and the changing scientific and natural properties across countless generational lifecycles of universes were beyond him, but he understood modern technology, so he borrowed the analogy of a computer to help piece together something he could work with. Hardwiring a vital piece of hardware into the main system was simply a far easier concept for him to grasp than whatever was actually in front of him. As such, the idea of some kind of infectious saboteur attacking the ancient workings of the temple was far easier to conceptualize as a dangerous computer virus.

This was considerably more complex than simply changing a fuse in a light fixture, but at least it made more sense. It was a familiar setting. He knew what he was doing. And he wasn't going to have to scour multiple buildings to locate every malfunctioning component. Everything was right here in front of him.

And yet, it was easy to become distracted by the concept of the *true* machine. It had been called the City Beyond Memory, the second temple and the stoneworks, as if it were too vast and complex to fit under the label of just one or two names. But what was it, really? Staring out at all those blinking LED lights like the pulse of a mysterious heartbeat…the hum of flowing air like whispering voices…cables like nerves and veins, coursing with mysterious data… It felt less like technology than *biology*, as if he were standing inside a living being.

What was really going on inside these memory banks? He knew it wasn't data. Not as he knew it, anyway. He'd already grasped the notion that there was no electricity involved. Now he found himself certain that there was no concept here that resembled mathematics, either. There was no binary code. No zeros or ones. No numbers of any sort. This machine processed things far, *far* older than switches. These things more closely resembled *rituals* than logic. Those blinking lights pulsed with the heartbeats of forgotten life in distant dreams. The fans whispered in chants and incantations in a language too ancient to be spoken aloud. The cables didn't carry information, but raw memory entwined in time itself.

The longer he stared down that endless, shadowy corridor of cabinets, the more he found some deeply buried part of his mind understanding these things. And the more he understood, the more unsettled he felt. These weren't things a human mind was meant to understand, after all. These were concepts the human race had left behind countless eons ago, in a universe long dead and forgotten. These might have even been concepts *older* than mankind, belonging entirely to the sentinels, an existence wholly alien to human DNA. Either way, the more he imagined himself grasping, the closer he felt himself slipping toward something terrifying. Something *maddening*.

He picked up the bag and slipped the strap over his head and shoulder, then opened it and peered inside. Everything he needed was here, naturally. All the necessary tools to do the job he was given.

And yet, even as he looked down at these tools, he found that these were at the same time precisely what he was seeing and nothing of the sort. They were tools, yes. But they were also mystical apparatuses, designed to harness and manipulate ancient energies. They were powerful talismans able to peel back arcane barriers and tap into the lifeblood of existence itself. They were intricate surgical instruments crafted in the deepest and most ancient realms, able to pierce the flesh of gods. They were all of these things and, simultaneously, they were nothing at all. Just make-believe. A game of pretend. Because none of this was real. He wasn't here. It was all nothing more than a fantastic dream.

"Get to work," scolded Violet.

He nodded and gave a grunt of an apology. She was right. He needed to focus on the job he was doing. If he kept thinking about all the *other* things that were true of the bag and of these surroundings, then he'd inevitably confuse himself and whatever bizarre illusion this was might break apart. He understood how to repair servers. But if everything changed before he was done, he might find himself tasked with something he *didn't* understand.

"Start over there," she instructed.

"I see it," he replied, already making his way toward a malfunctioning server and slipping the anti-static strap around his wrist.

Then he glanced back, curious. He wasn't sure where Violet's voice was coming from. He was fairly sure it was no longer merely inside his head. But at the same time, she definitely wasn't here with him. Was it only his subconscious speaking to him on her behalf, keeping him focused the way she'd do if she were here with him?

Not that it mattered. He didn't have time to focus on that right now. A drive had failed. He opened the rack and set to work removing the screws. Already, he was taking note of the next problem. A faltering in the constant hum in the next row. A power supply unit had burned out.

And yet even as he set to work, he marveled at the idea that nothing he was doing was what it seemed to be. These weren't network components. He could just as easily be standing in some alien engine room, replacing glowing crystals or pulsating fuel cores. Or standing in an operating room, cutting open a body, revealing the failing heart of some ancient organism. Or deep in a mystical cave, chanting incantations into the void, coaxing life back into the corpses of slain gods. It was all the same. It was all just a matter of perspective.

But pondering these things, too, was a waste of precious time. Worse still, it might be dangerous. He could accidentally make changes to that perspective and find himself somewhere he couldn't understand.

"Head in the game," agreed Violet.

Yes. He had a job to do. And he'd already wasted too much time pondering all these impossible things.

Chapter 66

"I'm so sorry about that," groaned Brandy. "That was *so* gross."

"Don't worry about it," replied Everett. "No biggie."

No biggie? If someone vomited all over *her* it would *absolutely* be a "biggie." She'd be fucking *pissed*.

Besides, he didn't exactly *look* all that okay. He was just sitting there, looking kind of dazed.

God this was awkward. Who was this kid, anyway? She was so disoriented when she woke up that she thought he was Albert. She even *kissed* him. Plus, she'd lost Albert's shirt somewhere along the way, so she was kissing him *and* rubbing her naked tits all over him. While covered in slime, no less. How *mortifying*! It was no wonder he looked a little shaken up… He was basically molested by a filthy stranger with one sock. (She'd tossed that aside at least, so she looked marginally less crazy.) And it wasn't helping anything that she was now crawling around on the floor, propping herself up and holding the flashlight with one hand while covering her exposed breasts with the other, squinting at everything. She probably looked like a freak.

On the other hand, now she was sort of *glad* Albert got confused and laid one on Nicole when they sex-magicked themselves to her location. He wouldn't be able to get mad at her for doing the same thing.

She started coughing again. It wouldn't stop. That disgusting gunk was still tickling her windpipe. She couldn't seem to get it all out.

"Take it easy," advised the kid. "It's not like in the movies, you know. You don't just cough up the water and then you're fine in a few minutes. You're gonna feel pretty gross for a while. Believe me, I know. And if it wasn't totally impossible, I'd say we should take you to the emergency room just to be safe."

"Well, it *is* impossible, isn't it?" she grumbled.

"You want my shirt?" he offered. "I mean…it's kinda puked on, but…"

"That's…sweet of you," she replied. "Very chivalrous."

"Sorry."

She was only half being sarcastic. It really was sweet of him. And *she* was the one who puked on it, after all. Luckily, she didn't have much of anything left in her stomach after all this time, so all she did was heave up more of that revolting ichor.

(*So* gross!)

She shined the light back and forth, squinting into the gloom. Where were they?

"What're you looking for?"

"My glasses. I can't see without them." She hated saying that. She sounded like Velma from *Scooby Doo*.

"Oh."

"Yeah…"

"Let me help." He was already on his feet, looking around.

"Thanks." He seemed nice, at least. That was good. She sat up, still covering herself and swept her light slowly around the room, trying to catch a glimpse of a reflection off one of the lenses, but everything was a dull gray blur. She couldn't remember when she dropped them. Were they still back in that last room? Did Stella think it'd be funny to take them? If she lost them, she was fucked.

"So where did you come from? I mean it was like you just…dripped out of the ceiling."

"I did?"

"Yeah. I kind of caught you. That's why I was holding you when you woke up coughing."

"Gotcha…" That *did* explain why he was right there in her face. It was no wonder she simply assumed it was Albert. "It's kind of a long story."

"Right. Yeah. Mine too, I guess." He took a step to the

right, still searching the dark floor, and his foot slipped in a puddle of ichor. "Whoa. Careful when you stand up. This stuff's slick."

"I'm familiar with it," she huffed.

"Oh! Here you go!" He tiptoed through the goop, careful not to slip again, and stooped over. She shined her light after him and caught a glint of reflected light as he picked up her glasses. "They're covered in goo, but they don't look broken. I think this stuff might've actually protected them from the fall."

"Thank God," she sighed. She crossed her other arm over her chest and reached out with her empty hand, waggling her fingers at him in an impatient "gimme" gesture.

She wasn't entirely sure why she was bothering to cover up. He'd already seen her. But it was still embarrassing. It wasn't like when she and Albert ended up naked in the first temple six years ago. For one thing, she wasn't married to someone else back then. And for another, this kid seemed really young. Was he still a minor? That would be extra awkward. And illegal.

She wiped the ichor off her glasses and returned them to her face. They were still filthy of course, but at least she could see. Now if she could just find her shirt…

Except, didn't she lose that when Stella dragged her through that field? Was there any chance it could've followed her here? After all, she lost her other shoe back there, too.

She wanted to tell herself that none of it was real, that it was only some cruel illusion that hateful witch planted inside her head, but the proof was *sunburned* into her skin. She could feel the unpleasant warmth of it on her face and shoulders and arms. Whether or not that was really Andrea's troublemaking friend back there probably remained up for debate, but the *experience* was entirely real.

When she looked up, Everett was holding his shirt out for her and pointedly looking the other way. "I know it's kinda gross, but it'll be better than nothing."

She accepted it and covered herself with it. "Thanks."

"What's your name?"

"Um… I'm Brandy." Another tickle irritated her throat and

she coughed again. That was going to drive her nuts.

"Oh, *you're* Brandy. Cool."

She squinted up at him, confused. "You know who I am?"

"I mean, I know your name. *Oh*! Mine's Everett."

"Never heard of you."

"Right… Yeah. Makes sense. We all arrived on different roads. I came here with Wayne and Olivia."

"Oh…" Now that she was thinking about it, she supposed they never did figure out exactly who all was here. Corey said he ran into Olivia and Wayne, so she already knew they were here somewhere. And he said that weird robot guy arrived with them, too. There were supposed to be twelve of them, if that creepy cat lady was telling the truth. Everett must have been number twelve.

She stood up, still clinging to Everett's shirt, and shined her light around. Now that she could actually *see* where she was shining it, there still wasn't shit to be seen. But she was still hoping to find her shirt. It was Albert's and there was a silly sort of sentimentality about that. Especially since she still had no idea what happened to him or where he could be or if she'd ever even see him again…

"Are you okay, by the way?" he asked. "I mean, I wasn't *trying* to look at your, um…" He trailed off, not wanting to finish the sentence. "But I saw those scratches," he pushed on. "I have some bandages if you need some."

She peered down under the shirt she was holding there, at the claw marks that bitch left on her breast. "Thanks, but I'm not really bleeding anymore."

"It looked really uncomfortable."

"It doesn't really hurt that much anymore. I'll be okay."

"What kind of monster did *that*?"

"The skanky kind," she grumbled.

"What?"

"Nothing. Another long story." She turned away from him and swept her light across the floor behind her. Her shorts were all she had left now. What was the deal with this place trying to strip her naked? Every time she moved somewhere new, she was a little more naked than when she left. It was like a cheap plot device for a pervy movie.

It was probably the pervert's doing. That gross bastard.

She coughed again and shined her light back the other way. She didn't remember very much about that scary ordeal, only that she was convinced she was about to drown in the filthy stuff. And given even half of all the weird shit she'd been through, it definitely didn't sound all that farfetched that she just sort of "dripped from the ceiling," as he put it. She shined her light upward. She couldn't see the ceiling from here, but she could see several grotesque strands still dripping from up there.

Her light fell on something in the darkness beyond the spattered ichor, but it was the wrong color to be Albert's shirt. "What's that?"

"Oh, right," said Everett, hurrying toward it. "She's with me."

She blinked at him, confused. "She?"

He picked the object up off the floor and held it out for her to see. It was a little blonde-haired doll in a pretty yellow dress. "This is Alice. She's a spirit from the other side of, like, *everything*, I guess, that I kind of turned into a doll and she's been helping me."

She stood there, clutching his soiled shirt to her naked chest, trying to process the absolute weirdness that just came out of his mouth.

"Yeah, I know. I heard the way it sounded, too. I keep saying things that sound nuts. But it's not me, I promise. Everything here is just *nuts.*"

"Okay…" she said. Now it was *her* turn to feel dazed. "If you say so." Then she pointed at the doll. "But if that thing murders you in your sleep, don't come haunting *me.*"

"Fair enough," he replied.

Chapter 67

"He's gone," said the mysterious little Sentinel Princess.

Olivia sat up, her heart leaping in her chest. "What? He's…?" She tightened her grip on Wayne's hand and laid her other hand over his heart.

"Don't be scared. He'll be fine. I'm keeping his body functioning. I won't let him die for real."

She could feel his heartbeat. It was slow, but it was there. His chest was still rising and falling, slow, shallow breaths, as if he were in a deep sleep. But there was something oddly *wrong* about him. His hand was unsettlingly limp in hers, as if all that wonderful strength had left his body. For some reason, it was as if she couldn't feel his familiar presence…

Her breath caught in her throat. Tears welled up in her eyes. She felt sobs trying to boil up from inside her and had to fight them back.

This was awful. He had a pulse. He was taking breaths. And yet she was staring at her dead fiancé. She wanted him to come back *right now*. This was pure torture!

"Death is often just another part of the Keeper's design. Especially in places like the gatehouses, where the worlds of the natural, the supernatural and the unnatural are all mixed up and tangled together."

She blinked back tears. She wanted to scream at this girl to bring him back right now. She didn't want him to be gone.

"As long as his body remains alive, there's nowhere he can travel that he can't come back from. I promise."

She promised… But she was still a stranger, wasn't she? What proof did she have that this little girl was really what she claimed to be? There were bad things lurking in the temple. Not just the monsters the sentinels bred here, but intruders from outside, too. The scarecrow man was creeping around out there, searching for them. And there was Erin's ghost, who was helpful one moment and murderous the next. And then there was that Priestess of Ruin Andrea warned them about… She was supposed to be some kind of evil god. What if this sweet-looking little girl was *her* in disguise? What if they'd already fallen into her trap?

What if she'd already let that monster murder Wayne?

And yet, in spite of that awful wrongness she felt while sitting over him, she still found that she felt none of that looming dread gripping her over the fact that he was gone. It still felt as if he were there by her side, as if she only had to wait for him to wake up.

"More importantly," said the girl, turning those blind eyes away from Wayne and onto her. "We're alone now. We can talk about why *you're* here."

Olivia's heart sank. An ominous feeling began to swell deep in her belly. Her psychic alarm was beginning to ring. "What're you talking about?"

The little girl smiled that sweet smile, but her words were like a nest of venomous snakes. "I'm talking about the scarecrow man."

Chapter 68

Andrea stopped and looked back the way she came, confused. When did everything change? She was in another passage, exactly like hundreds of others she'd walked through before, focusing on the path at her feet, afraid of falling into another hound passage. Her hand never left the wall on this side, but there was now a wide-open space on the other side. It made her uneasy to think that everything could change so quickly, and without her noticing it. What kind of danger might she have wandered blindly into while her attention was directed downward?

But as she blinked into the darkness behind her, she felt disoriented. Something about the space back there didn't make sense.

And yet, it didn't make sense that looking back there didn't make any sense when it was still pitch black and she couldn't see anything to begin with…

She reached up with both her hands and rubbed at her face. She was probably just tired. It wasn't any wonder. How many hours had it been since she woke up in Keith's boat? And it wasn't like she slept all that well even then. She kept having bad dreams.

And she'd probably be having a lot more of those when this was all over.

At least she couldn't hear that hound anymore. That was one small relief.

She dropped her hands and blinked into the darkness again. That feeling of being in a larger space was gone. In fact, she felt almost claustrophobic, as if the walls were closing in on her, threatening to crush her.

She squeezed her eyes closed and forced herself to take a deep breath.

"Get a grip," she grumbled to herself under her breath. Even in a temple, the space around her couldn't change shape on its own. It wasn't *alive.*

And yet, the thought had barely crossed her mind when she recalled the story Olivia and Wayne shared with her when they reunited after her gross and exhausting trek through the mud chamber. Didn't they tell her that the labyrinth did just that? Something about the walls dropping, closing open passages and opening new ones?

Maybe these temples *could* change their layout. But it sounded like a very abrupt change, something that happened so fast they didn't really see it. It sounded almost *violent*, the way they described it. She would've noticed something like that.

Again, she opened her eyes and squinted into the darkness.

For a moment, that was all there was. Darkness. Empty and black and featureless. But slowly the images of murky shapes clinging to the walls began to take form in her head. Again, she saw the outline of a familiar passage. At the same time, however, she found herself staring across a great, black abyss. Not merely on the one side, either, but in every direction.

But the wall was right beside her only a moment ago. She hadn't moved. She thrust her hand out to feel for it again and racked her knuckles against the stone, wrenching a surprised yelp from her that felt as loud as a gunshot to her own ears.

That was strange…

She pressed her hands to the wall. Of course it was still there. Where else would it be?

Curious, she stepped away from the wall and reached out into that gaping emptiness on the other side.

Again, she found the wall.

This was the same passage from before. Nothing had changed.

So why did she keep feeling like she'd left the passage and entered a larger space?

She stared back the way she came for a moment, wondering if perhaps she should just sit down and rest for a while, but she wasn't going to be able to rest. Even as she stared into that darkness, she began to wonder if that was really still the way she came or if all this weirdness had caused her to get turned around.

The thought was like a punch in the gut. She pressed her back against the wall as if that might help keep her in place while she sorted this out and tried to remember how many times she'd turned around.

She really didn't want to go back toward that hound.

But she hadn't turned around. Not yet. She was only being paranoid. If she kept overthinking it, however, she was definitely going to end up going the wrong way.

She forced down her doubt and continued walking. It wasn't like she knew where she was going anyway. Stupid Tia just dumping her in the dark like an abandoned puppy…

She was dragging her hand along the wall again, keeping track of it. With each step, she prodded the floor with her naked toes, searching for any more unexpected pitfalls before they could catch her off guard again.

Still, however, that feeling of being in a much larger space persisted.

She stopped walking, distracted. Now that she was thinking about it, hadn't this happened before?

Back when she was still walking with Olivia and Wayne, in that last passage, the one so filled with murk that she was rendered blind. She felt the same weird sensation then, too. She started seeing things in the murk, even though that shouldn't have been possible because she couldn't see anything *for* all the murk.

After that red-sky nightmare, and then that frightful encounter with Tia, she'd forgotten all about it. But this was the same thing, she realized. She started to see things, even though it was already dark. As if there existed some kind of *even darker* darkness that could be seen in places like this. She remembered asking Olivia and Wayne if there was something on the ceiling. And there was something above them, wasn't there? And something tall and scary just sort of standing to one side as she crept past?

Tia was talking inside her head at the time, still letting her think she was only pretending to be Stella to get under her defenses, and she told her they were dangerous.

(*You've wandered off the map.*)

Again, she looked back the way she came, uneasy.

(*There are things hidden deeper in the murk. Things you can't imagine in your worst nightmares. Things that don't like being seen.*)

Did that mean this was another murk-filled passage? One of those that would render her blind even if she had a light? Or was it only the fact that she couldn't use her human eyesight that made it easier for her to see these things, regardless of the amount of murk surrounding her?

She couldn't decide if that would make it better or worse. On one hand, she didn't like being in the murk. It was scary in there. But on the other hand, she supposed if she was in an area of the temple that was completely filled with it, then it would've made her flashlight useless anyway.

She continued walking, letting her blind eyes wander across the black emptiness that enveloped her. She'd had this same sensation of glimpsing an area that was different from the dimensions of her physical surroundings, too. The darker-than-dark things she thought she saw weren't confined to the passage back there. Just like now, it seemed as if the murk had its *own* dimensions, fully independent of the three dimensions of the physical world.

Thinking too hard about this was going to make her head hurt. It was kind of exhausting. But on the other hand, she was sure Albert would *love* to hear all about it when she saw him again.

She really hoped she'd get to see him again. She really hoped she was able to see *everybody* again.

Chapter 69

There was so much pain. Nicole couldn't stand it. It was going to drive her mad. Goar Nangup's hellish prison was a place both freezing and burning, a place where the earth beneath her was a carpet of writhing, stinging, biting, burrowing nightmares and the sky above was as heavy as the whole of the ocean crushing down on the deepest trenches, a place of hopeless darkness that seared her eyeballs and deafening silence that made her ears bleed. It was a place where mere existence was pure torture. Her very mind threatened to unravel into agonizing madness.

And yet… Why had the pain stopped?

Everything had stopped. It was as if time had suddenly stood still around her.

"Why are you so much trouble, Nik?"

She blinked up through the tears, confused, and stared into Keith's handsome face again.

Why was *he* here? He shouldn't be here. He was dead.

Was *she* dead? Had that vile god finally killed her?

He was cradling her in his arms, carrying her through this strange darkness, nothing in every direction but the two of them, utterly alone, and impossibly together.

Tears welled up in her eyes and she blinked them away, desperate to keep looking at him, to keep taking him in, terrified that he'd only disappear again if she let them wash this happy vision away.

"Keith…" But what could she possibly say? Where did she begin? How did you put an entire universe of feelings into words?

But she didn't have to. "I know," he assured her. "It's okay.

But you have to listen to me. We don't have much time."

Somewhere in the distance, she heard the faint roar of that hellish nightmare world reaching out for her again, trying to drag her back in.

She clutched at him, pressing herself closer. She didn't want to go back there. She didn't want to leave these strong arms. She wanted to stay here forever.

"You've gotten yourself into a real mess this time," he said. "You're not just dealing with an undead psychopath. That's an actual *god* with its hands around your neck. A literal eldritch abomination kind of deity."

She wanted to say, "No shit, I hadn't noticed," but the words didn't make it out of her mouth. She felt too weak and exhausted. All she could do was nod, her cheek rubbing against his shoulder in the process. The feel of his skin against hers was calming.

He felt so…*real*…

But he wasn't.

He couldn't be.

He was nothing more than a fragment of a dream… A memory. A delusion, perhaps, brought on by the snapping of her sanity.

She didn't want it to be this way. Couldn't they just forget about the scary-as-fuck evil god and go home together? She wanted to start over. She wanted to go to bed with him and show him how sorry she was, how much she missed him. She wanted to prove to him, to everyone, to *herself*, that she could do something right for a change, that she didn't *always* have to be such a colossal fuckup.

But of course that wasn't possible anymore…was it?

Some mistakes couldn't be undone.

Some things you couldn't apologize for.

"Are you listening to me, Nik? This is important."

She squeezed her eyes tighter against a fresh wave of tears. She felt like a naughty child being scolded. The guilt. The regret. The overwhelming fear of it all. But she nodded. She was listening. She could hear every word he spoke.

"You're only going to get one chance at this. Next time he won't let me in. I won't be able to help."

She didn't know what he expected her to do. She'd already pretty much proven that she was useless. Against that awful god. As a friend. As a girlfriend.

"I can interrupt Goar's connection only once. And only temporarily. you're the one who's going to have to shut him out for good."

She shook her head. That couldn't be right. She couldn't do something like that. She couldn't do *anything* right. He should know that better than anyone.

"We don't have time for you to feel sorry for yourself." He spoke slowly and calmly. He didn't raise his voice. He was perfectly patient, and yet she felt those words as clearly as a slap in the face, as if he'd punctuated them with a sense of desperate urgency that he somehow drove right into her brain. She felt a part of herself snapping to attention, those other, unhelpful thoughts driven away. "Gina's almost reached the terminal. When she activates it, the glass labyrinth will be inverted."

Inverted? What the hell did *that* mean? She tried to tell him that she didn't understand, but she was still pressing her face against him and her words were muffled.

"Everything on this side of the glass will be crushed into streams of unnatural energy and redirected into the mechanism that opens the Oblivion Door," he explained. "If you're still in here when it happens, your physical body will cease to exist and Goar Nangup's private hell will swallow you forever."

An eternity of suffering in that awful, screaming realm of agony and despair?

"I'm taking you back to where the mirrors brought you. That's as far back as I can rewind the dream."

What the fuck did *that* mean? She was so confused.

"He'll come to take you back. When he does, you're going to face him head on."

She shook her head, her heart filling with terror at the mere thought.

"You *can* do it. You have the strength inside you. It's why he chose you. He knows you're the only one who can challenge him."

"How am *I* the only one?" she cried into his shoulder.

"I guess you're just that stubborn, Nik."

Was that supposed to be a joke? Stubbornness wasn't going to make her strong enough to defeat a literal *god.* She was fucked if that was all he was going to give her. And if the glass labyrinth was going to *invert* or *implode* or *whatever…* Finally, she lifted her head a little. "Gina…?" Her voice was little more than a timid squeak. She was still paralyzed with fear, still trembling from her time in that agonizing hell. "What'll happen to her?"

"Gina will be safe in the terminal. She'll be returned to the stone labyrinth, as the sentinels designed it. You don't have to worry about her. She's way stronger than even she knows. Focus on yourself. If you hesitate, no one will be able to save you. And then Goar wins."

This was all so frustratingly maddening! She didn't understand anything! She didn't even understand enough to know what questions to ask!

And even if she *could* think of one, there wasn't time. Her feet landed on the floor. She stumbled forward, disoriented.

Keith was gone. She was alone in the pitch darkness of the labyrinth, one hand pressed against the stone wall to steady herself.

(I'm taking you back to where the mirrors brought you.)

Did he mean that room Gina said was filled with mirrors even though there was clearly nothing in there?

(There are so many ways we can go from here. So many places we could end up. One wrong step and we could go somewhere impossible to come back from.)

She remembered closing her eyes and letting her lead the way…

(Don't let go of me. I don't know what might happen.)

But there was nothing after that. Then everything was nightmares and living hell. Did she let go of Gina's hand like she warned her not to? Or had that foul god simply swept in and dragged her away in some moment of weakness?

She turned around and reached out into the darkness. "Keith?" Where did he go? Had he vanished again? She didn't want to be alone!

But his arms were suddenly around her, holding her close, making her gasp. "You've got this, Nik. I know you do." Then he kissed her.

The world and all its horrors melted away for a moment and she was back in the blissful past, before her idiot brain sabotaged her, convincing her for some unfathomable reason that she needed to push him away.

It was all so confusing! Why was she like this? What was wrong with her?

Then he was gone again. She was alone in the dark corridor, blind and vulnerable and afraid.

"Keith?" Her heart was pounding again. He couldn't leave her alone. Not now. He said she could do this, but he was wrong. There was no way! She was only one woman. Not even a particularly *special* woman! Gina and her goddess told her so! She was only a pathetic tagalong standing against a *fucking god*!

And there was no time to prepare.

A terrible certainty made itself known within her, driving all the other thoughts from her mind. She twirled around, her fists clenched, a crippling dread filling her every cell.

He was coming.

Chapter 70

Keith stood staring into the darkness as Nicole's face faded back into the haze of the dream, a great and painful regret gripping his heart. "Will she be okay?"

"You've given her everything she needs," Erin assured her. "The rest is up to her."

That didn't really answer his question. She didn't *have* an answer, of course. She didn't know if Nicole would be okay. It was all in the hands of the Keeper's will now. But she wasn't lying. He'd done what he could do for her.

"Come on," she urged. "We have more to do."

He nodded, but he stood there a moment longer, worried.

Erin said no more, but he felt her hand on his shoulder. Her fingers were warm. She felt so *real.*

Again, he nodded. *Stay safe, Nik*, he thought as the two of them faded into the gloom.

Chapter 71

This was taking *forever*. How long had she been creeping through this darkness? An hour? Two? Even more? Time was wonky in other worlds, but Violet was sure she wasn't just bored. She'd lost count of how many statues she'd felt her way past. Was she even still heading the right way? Twice, she'd found herself up against the chamber's wall with nowhere to go. And three times she'd found her path blocked by statues and had to go back. She kept expecting to stumble across a doorway only to find the inside of that giant woman's gaping mouth again, forcing her to start all over.

She wanted nothing more than to take out her flashlight and turn it on for just an instant—just a *flash*—enough to see if she could get eyes on the exit. But she didn't dare. She didn't know what even that brief peek might do to her. It had *already* affected her, even without a light. That dreadful, half-memory of those inhuman, too-tall beings pretending to be things they weren't… It felt like something she watched in a movie years ago, and yet it left her feeling jumpy and uneasy. She kept stopping and listening, convinced she was hearing something behind her. It was taking a lot of extra effort just to keep herself moving at a safe pace. If there really were deadly traps in here, it would probably only take a little bit of that invasive emotion to distract her and make her careless.

Again, her hand brushed against stone. Another statue. She was careful not to touch too much of it. She swept her hand to the side, measuring out a clear path, then crept around it, her toes still testing every step for perils.

But almost immediately, she encountered another.

She prodded at the space around her. Another blocked path. The statues were crowded so close together that she couldn't squeeze between them. This was another maze. She was going to have to backtrack and find a way around. What were the odds that she was still facing the right direction? She lost track of which way she was going a long time ago.

Was this even something she could do? It felt like an awful lot to expect of someone. Especially *alone.*

She stopped moving and held her breath, listening to the eerie silence. Was it only her own movements echoing back at her? Not for the first time, it sounded like someone else was in here. It was becoming more difficult to convince herself she was alone.

Was it *her*? The Priestess of Ruin? Had she found her again now that she was separated from Everett and all on her own?

(*Bringer of Darkness. Harbinger of Ends. Goddess of Decay.*)

She *really* didn't want to go back to that dead world with its bloody sky and violent abominations lurking around every corner.

Grasping at what felt like a stone elbow, she continued onward, picking up her pace for a moment before catching herself and slowing down again. This was so difficult. Why would the sentinels make it so challenging? What was the point in all this, except to torture them?

She knocked her elbow against something hard and cursed at the sudden pain.

That was careless. She needed to slow down. She needed to focus on moving forward. *Without* focusing on the things she was weaving around. That was the trick, she managed to understand. These weren't dangerous, emotion-imbued statues. They were just stone. Just a maze of cold rocks. They didn't have faces or expressions or poses or *meanings.* They were a bunch of paperweights piled up in her way. That was all.

She crept forward, steadying herself on those hard, *unremarkable* surfaces.

But when she reached out again, one of the statues wasn't standing where it was before. Her hand found only empty darkness where it should've been.

Her heart leaping, she let out a terrified squeak and turned, thrusting her hands out to defend herself. She knew there was something off about these things! Something *was* in here! Something *right in front of her*! But the back of her flailing hand struck something hard and unyielding and she cried out in pain.

That *really* hurt! She clutched her hand to her chest, grimacing in the darkness.

Nothing there.

She didn't realize she was backing away until something hard jabbed her in the back, sending another jolt of pain through her.

Calm yourself.

Easy for you to say! she thought at the other one, her hand still throbbing. Did she break it? She hated this. She growled, frustrated. This whole goddamn place was bullshit! She was sick of it all!

But she forced herself to stop moving. She closed her eyes. She took a deep breath.

There *wasn't* anything there. It was dark. She was disoriented. She misjudged where she was placing her hand. The statue didn't move. She merely missed it and then panicked. That was probably it she smacked her hand against.

Why was she so on edge? Was it simply that she was alone and vulnerable again? Mixed with the extra stress of trying to navigate a potentially deadly maze of statues in the dark? Or was it that the emotions radiating from the statues were affecting her even without seeing them? A little of both, perhaps?

Or maybe a *lot* of both…

Whatever the reason, it was important that she get control over herself. It felt as if her emotions were all over the place. She couldn't decide if she was more frightened or angry. But at least the other one was talking to her again. That meant she wasn't really alone right now.

That made it a *little* better.

And yet, even as she stood there, trying to ease her nerves, she felt a sudden twinge of certainty race through her. Something was right behind her.

She twirled around, startled, and raised her arms to shield herself.

But again, there was nothing there.

"What the hell is wrong with me?" she muttered into the silence of the chamber. Her heart was pounding. She could feel tears welling up in her eyes again. She even realized she was trembling a little. She *really* hated that. She wasn't some weak little girl.

A fresh wave of anger swept over her. Anger at this room, at the sentinels who built it, at the Keeper whose orders they were following, at the injustice of having to do all this by herself, at *all the things she'd been through…* And anger at herself, for not being strong enough to handle it, for turning into a crybaby when things got hairy…

That way.

She blinked back those damned tears and turned toward her left. That way? She reached out into the darkness and found no statues blocking her path on that side. She crept forward, apprehensive, half expecting something to jump out and attack her, considerably *more* than half expecting to be jabbed by another statue, but there seemed to be a path here.

For some reason, she found herself frowning at this. As much as she wanted someone to show her the way out of this mess, why would she suddenly decide to help now?

I can show you your path, she remembered her saying once in one of those hazy dreams, *but I won't be able to help you with the trials you'll face along the way. The Keeper forbids it.*

So why would the other one suddenly point the way?

She hesitated. Unless that *wasn't* the other one. Was it something else? Something in this room, toying with her head, trying to lure her into a trap? Or perhaps the Priestess of Ruin again, eager to drag her back to her hellscape of a playground for another round of horrific torture?

And then a new and far more dreadful thought entered her mind: what if there never was an "other one" in the first place? What if she was *always* a cruel trick, leading her astray from the very beginning?

She squeezed her eyes closed and growled into the darkness, frustrated. Why did shit like that have to pop into her head at times like these?

Again, she took a deep, calming breath. She held it. She let it out slowly. She realized her fists were clenched and forced herself to relax them.

What else was she going to do? At this point, she didn't know forward from backward. And it wasn't like she could quit now. What was she going to do? Sit down on the floor and pout until someone came to get her? As if that were an option.

The only way out was to simply keep wandering around until she stumbled across the exit. That was literally the definition of solving a maze. The more she second guessed herself, the longer it was going to take. And this bullshit had already gone on far too long as it was.

She steeled her nerves and continued creeping forward, her toes testing each and every step, her hands in front of her, sweeping for obstacles.

She could do this. She just needed to ignore the messed-up things in her head and keep pressing onward.

Her toes struck something in the dark, making her stop. That wasn't stone.

What in the world was it?

She reached out with her foot and nudged it. Something soft. *Warm*. Was it something *alive*? A sharp pang of dread shot through her at the idea that she'd stumbled across something dangerous in this unnerving darkness.

Before she could step away and reach for her flashlight, however, something grabbed her ankle.

Her screams flooded the chamber and echoed through the surrounding corridors.

Chapter 72

Corey worked his way through the server room, replacing failed drives, swapping power supplies, resetting memory modules and tracing faulty wiring.

The work itself was easy. He knew his way around these things. But the scale of the job was still off. Why couldn't he see the end of the room? *Was* there an end to it? Or did it just go on forever? He thought he'd solved the perspective problem, but this was still too big for just one person. He felt like he'd already been at it for hours and yet there remained no end in sight. And the damage was getting worse. Each new cabinet he opened had more problems than the last.

He thought he'd succeeded in shrinking down his perspective enough to finally complete the task, but had he accomplished anything at all? Or was he only trading one flavor of infinity for another?

Would it even matter if he did it again?

He plugged a new hard drive into the slot.

(*As long as his body remains alive, there's nowhere he can travel that he can't come back from.*)

He stood there, his fingers still resting on the drive's casing, distracted.

(*We're alone now. We can talk about why* you're *here.*)

He could see Olivia's face in his mind. She was talking to someone, but he couldn't see who. She seemed upset, as if something had happened. He hoped she was okay.

He closed his eyes, trying to get a better grasp of the vision, but it was fading. In another few seconds, it was gone. There was nothing.

That had happened several times now. He glimpsed Albert and Brandy a little while ago. They were arguing about something. Not fighting, exactly, just disagreeing. They seemed tired and frustrated. And there was something unpleasant blocking their way, something he wanted to push past while she insisted on turning back. And before that he was fairly sure he caught a brief glimpse of Gina running from someone.

These weren't just random thoughts popping up in his head, he understood. Handling the server's memory devices occasionally allowed him access to the memories of the temple itself. Snapshots of things going on elsewhere in the labyrinth.

Somehow, he could even tell that some of the memories were less recent than others. That argument Albert and Brandy were having happened before he even entered the machine.

He wanted to know more. He dragged his fingers across the servers, touching each one in turn, feeling nothing. Then he ran them back the other direction.

There was a flicker of something. Just a flash of Violet bathed in an eerie, red glow, her face pinched with fright.

He lingered there, but no matter what he did, it wouldn't repeat itself and it wouldn't show him more.

He really hoped she was still safe out there.

He finished his work and closed the cabinet door, then moved on to the next row.

He'd determined that these machines didn't process and store data. Data was nothing more than information, after all. Binary code written on magnetic drives. But there was no code here, really. This was something much closer to *human* memory, less like hard drives than the literal *brain* inside his own head. It was a bizarre concept. And a somewhat distracting one, too. He kept trying to stop and ponder it. He wanted to know how such a thing worked, even if he knew he couldn't possibly understand the true scope of it.

He opened the next cabinet and went to work removing screws. But another flash passed through his head and he stopped.

That was Andrea.

And it was *much* more recent.

She'd returned from wherever she disappeared to and was back in the labyrinth. She was alone, but she was safe. And that was a tremendous relief.

But that meant that the one they lost was Keith…

That was deeply unfortunate. As much joy as he felt at the knowledge that Andrea was safe, there was a surprisingly deep sadness welling up in his chest despite the fact that he only knew the man for a very brief amount of time. The two of them had barely even spoken. They didn't have time to share a conversation. He didn't know anything about him. His interests. Where he was from. He didn't even know his last name, he realized. It felt wildly disproportionate. And yet, at the same time, it made perfect sense. Because regardless of how little he knew about Keith, they were the same. They both traveled all this way. They both came here with a job to do. They both did their best to protect their companions along the way. They shared something profound. A bond that didn't require them to know each other to feel an emptiness when one of them was suddenly gone.

This was probably what it was like for soldiers in the heat of battle, he decided. Even if they'd never spoken, he doubted you could fight side-by-side against a common enemy and not feel something when you watched a comrade fall. Not if you were ever human.

So many distractions…

He pushed it all out of his mind and forced himself to focus on the task before him again. There was a cable loose. He needed to reconnect it. Or perhaps replace it.

And yet as he reached into the bag for his multimeter, he realized that something had changed.

He stepped out from behind the cabinet and looked down the endless corridor.

It was there. The infection was crawling through the network, blotting out lights and sending up sparks and smoke.

"Too late," whispered Violet.

Too late? Had he blown his chance? Did he let himself get distracted too many times?

No. That wasn't it. Just like back in the city, he never stood a chance. It was too big. It was moving too fast. It was doing too much damage.

"We have to go."

"Where?" he asked. But who was he even talking to? There was no one here. Violet didn't come here with him. She was out in the labyrinth somewhere, probably with her own job to do. This voice he kept hearing couldn't be her.

"Run!"

Right. Run. Like there was anywhere to go.

But with the infection spreading toward him through those endless racks, he dropped the bag and fled in the opposite direction.

Maybe this was a battle he was never going to be able to win.

Chapter 73

"So Andrea and Violet both made it past the city wall," said Brandy, relieved. "Finally, some fucking *good* news. When Nicole and Corey told us they were separated, I was worried sick."

Everett remembered Andrea and Violet mentioning someone named Corey. If he should run across either of them again, he'd be sure to let them know. That would give them a few less things to worry about. "I don't know where they are now, though," he said. "Andrea disappeared as soon as we went through the gate and me and Violet ended up getting separated *twice*."

"It's like this place is *trying* to separate us all."

"It *does* feel like that, doesn't it?"

They were back in the confined walls of the labyrinth, following the map Alice was drawing in his head as he walked. She couldn't seem to tell him where he needed to go, but she could reveal the layout of their surroundings, letting him avoid dead ends and make decisions based on what was out there.

It felt a little weird walking around without a shirt on. He wasn't used to that. He felt a little self-conscious. But he was certain it would be a lot *more* uncomfortable if *she* was still topless. It was awkward enough having seen her bare chest. That felt wrong. Especially since he hadn't failed to notice that she was wearing a wedding ring…

"Poor Olivia…" said Brandy. "Sounds like she went through some shit."

"Yeah, those fairies sounded pretty nasty. It was kinda weird that they only seemed to be interested in her. I never even saw one. Neither did Wayne, as far as I know."

He told her all about Gutler's Weep and the fairy circle, the train ride through the Wood and getting lost in the Denselands. Meeting the Eeshee and then wandering into the gouging station. The potato men. Andrea. Violet. And all that before he even laid eyes on the wall. Then there was the whole thing with the void and the dollhouse and the Priestess of Ruin. And the graymother, of course. He tried to keep it brief, but a lot had happened. Even he wasn't sure how he'd been through so much in such a short amount of time. And it was a testament to everything *she'd* seen that she hadn't told him he was crazy and run away from him and his scary doll.

She told *him* a story just as weird, about a crazy hotel, actual magic, time travel, multidimensional doorways and psychic monsters that ate people's *minds*. She even mentioned the Ruin with its blood-red sky, just like Violet described it. Apparently, the Priestess was causing trouble for *everyone*.

He was trying to keep up with all the weirdness, but it was getting hard to even remember who told him what. Wayne and Olivia told him that story back on the train about all the crazy stuff they went through with the first of these places, something they called the "Temple of the Blind." They didn't talk much about the people who were with them, only mentioning that they went through it all with some friends. He'd met Andrea and now Brandy. That was four of the six who were there that night. And Brandy kept mentioning someone named Albert, which was a name he heard *all of them* mention. He was fairly sure he was Brandy's husband. She sounded as fussed about him as Wayne was over Olivia back in Gutler's Weep.

It didn't sound like Violet was a part of any of that, though.

He was going to have to start keeping a notebook.

He glanced over at her, at his soiled shirt she was wearing, curious. "So, what was with that goop you were covered in when I found you?"

"Fuck if I know," she grumbled. "Some pissy asshole we dealt with called it 'ichor.' Said it had 'pandimensional properties,' or some shit. I don't get it. But it has something to do with allowing people to move between worlds. Or even between places in the same world, I guess, since it brought me to *you.* There's a whole fucking *lake* of the shit in here somewhere." She shuddered at the memory. "*So* gross."

"Is that how you and Albert ended up separated?"

"Yeah."

Ahead of them, the path forked. Alice couldn't tell him where either passage led, but she showed him that the one on the right was a lot more complicated, with dead ends and spirals. The one on the left was better. Less choices to make. Less twisting and turning. Less walking in general. A *lot* less likely to get confused and double back. Plus, there was a place over there that he didn't understand. A small area that merely presented itself as "dangerous" in his mind. If he were on his own, he might have gone that way just out of curiosity to see what "dangerous" meant in Alicespeak, but it didn't seem like a good idea now that he was fortunate enough to not be alone anymore. It seemed like she'd been through enough already, so he kept to the left.

Brandy shined her light down the other passage as they moved past it. She didn't say anything, but he could tell she was wondering about the path they were taking. He already told her it was Alice who was leading the way, and she was having trouble trusting an inanimate object as a navigator, which was admittedly understandable. Besides the fact that dolls were a major horror movie trope, there was always the fact that she was an inhuman spirit from the flipside of the universe that he sort of trapped in that form, meaning there was no way for him to accurately describe exactly *what* she really was. She was literally an alien intelligence speaking into his head.

He was definitely going to keep it to himself that she tried to convince him to abandon Violet in the graymother's nest to save themselves. *That* wasn't going to win her any popularity points with *anyone.*

Brandy shined her light back the way they came, a curious expression on her pretty face. "Can Alice tell if there's anybody else near us?"

"Maybe. But they'd probably have to be pretty close. And this place is huge. Like, there's a whole city out there."

"I know."

"Oh." Right. She did say something about seeing the storm when she first arrived. He'd already forgotten. There was so much to process. "Well…I mean I found *you*, so you never know."

"Sure."

This felt awkward. She wasn't as warm and cheerful as Olivia and Andrea. She was kind of cold, even. Was she mad about him kissing her? Technically *she* kissed *him*, but he kind of let it happen, he guessed. Only because she caught him completely off guard, of course. He definitely *would've* stopped her if he'd seen it coming. Clearly, she was disoriented and confused. She looked like she'd nearly drowned in that slimy stuff she was covered in. He was so surprised, he didn't know how to react, was all. Plus, she was all *slippery*. It was all he could do not to drop her. It was remarkably difficult to avoid being kissed while trying to hold onto a slimy naked girl who dripped out of the ceiling and into your arms without any warning. He didn't want her to hit her head on the stone floor or anything.

But all that aside…she *was* a married woman. He wouldn't really blame her if she was mad about it. Also, she sort of gave him the same vibe Wayne did, like she was over him and his goofiness almost the second they met. It kind of seemed like she'd rather have left him and his spooky doll where she found them but just didn't want to be alone.

The silence was uncomfortable, but he couldn't think of anything to talk about, so he kept his mouth shut and focused on the map Alice was still drawing in his head.

Something was changing, he realized. There were several open spaces ahead of them. They stood out from the rest of the labyrinth, but he couldn't tell exactly how. Something about the shapes, he thought. Was that somewhere *outside*, perhaps? Out in the storm again?

Alice said no.

And he supposed it wouldn't be. These angles were all wrong. Most of the walls he saw when he and Violet were out in that storm were straight, ninety-degree shapes. Those "buildings" were all square and blocky. The surfaces she was showing him in his head were curved. They were more organic.

And they were *deep*. There was no floor in those places, he realized. Was it some kind of open pit? A chasm in the middle of the labyrinth?

Again, no… It was something else…

Then it finally dawned on him. "Water."

Brandy stopped walking and looked at him, confused. "What?"

He pointed in that direction. "There's water over there. Like, flooded chambers or something."

"Oh…"

"Sorry. That was kind of random. I was trying to figure out what Alice was showing me, but it was just water."

She looked in that direction, as if she could see through the walls. "There was water in the first temple," she recalled. "Places we had to swim. It might be the way we're supposed to go."

"You think?"

She was already walking again. "No idea. But I'd *love* to wash off. I don't care if it's fucking freezing."

Chapter 74

Wayne found himself adrift in the silent waves of that dark and churning ocean again, unable to move, his mind a muddled mess of distant emotions and broken memories.

Why was he here again? Had he fallen asleep? Or had something happened to him again? It was so difficult to pull his thoughts together when he was here.

And he was so tired… He just wanted to let the waves carry him away and sink into blissful nothingness. It did no good to fight it anyway.

It was always like this, his only company the broken remnants of past lives tossed in the waves and the frightful shadows cruising the depths far below. Helpless and lost until the waking world reclaimed him.

Except…*was* it always the same?

Sometimes it was different. Sometimes there was a current. Sometimes he felt himself swept away to…somewhere else…

And the thought had barely crossed his mind when he realized that he was caught in one now. No longer was he simply being tossed back and forth. He was moving in a straight line, picking up speed, less like an ocean than a river.

The second temple…

He remembered. He was in the City Beyond Memory. With Olivia. And with…that little girl…his daughter…the same daughter he thought he lost the night the Sentinel Queen died…

She told him there was something he had to do…somewhere he was supposed to go… Somewhere Olivia couldn't follow him.

He opened his eyes. Or perhaps he didn't. Did he *have* eyes?

He didn't have a *body*. He wasn't alive. And it was still so dark. Perhaps it wasn't his eyes that he opened, but instead his *mind*. Because the things he saw weren't in front of him. They were all around him in a strange, everywhere-at-once sort of way. And it felt as if he could see practically *forever*.

And what he saw with this strange, everywhere sight was the temple. The stone labyrinth was spread out all around him, stretching away in every direction. Darkness upon darkness, dotted with life here and there. Some of them human, friends, companions. But most were something else. Monsters. Creatures. Mysteries that should probably remain mysteries.

And he could see something else, too. Corridors within corridors…passageways wound around passageways…

The Murk passages that Andrea described… It wasn't merely a handful of hidden hallways. It was an entire labyrinth unto itself.

It was interwoven throughout the entirety of the sprawling temple, from its deepest depths to the top of its highest tower, like some kind of massive root system. But as for *what it was*, he couldn't describe it. It was something and nothing and everything all at once and also none of those things. Simply beholding it felt as if it should drive him mad, and yet there was something perfectly ordinary about it at the same time. It was the difference, he realized, between being alive and being dead.

It was the Murk.

Andrea was right, he realized. Even if he could remember this when he next awoke, he wouldn't be able to explain it to anyone. Whatever that was, there existed no words to describe it in the living world. Not in English. Not in any other language, either. Not in all the languages of all the people in all the worlds that ever lived, probably. Attempting to describe it would only result in a myriad of contradictions and an incomprehensible sort of conceptualization that would circle around and around what it was without ever really touching on it.

And he was speeding both toward it and through it, as if he were far away from it and yet somehow already inside it at the same time.

The current was taking him deep inside that murky labyrinth.

There was something in there, something he was speeding toward. He felt as if he could almost picture it. And something about it frightened him.

He threw one last look backward, though it did no good. He couldn't really see anything.

Olivia… Where was she? Was she okay? He hoped he hadn't frightened her too much. But this was something he had to do. He understood that now. His daughter was right. It was clear on this side. She was telling the truth. About everything.

Chapter 75

"What does that lunatic have to do with anything?" gasped Olivia. She slid off the bed and onto her feet, uneasy. Why would she bring up the scarecrow man like that? And what was this awful feeling spreading through her belly?

"He's a problem," replied the little girl. "He's an intruder, sent by the Goddess of Ruin to sabotage the cycle."

"Why are you telling *me*?" She wanted to back away from the little girl, but she didn't dare let go of Wayne's hand.

"Because you're the only one who can defeat him."

Olivia actually laughed at this. It was a hard and humorless laugh. Practically a bark. Not cute at all. But it was a laugh. And why not? It was a laughable concept. *Her*? She was just a helpless girl lost in a huge, dangerous world. And she was terrified out of her mind of that monster.

The little girl didn't seem fazed by the laugh. She only sat there, smiling her patient smile, letting her process the information, as if she'd simply realize that she was right, that it was obviously the most logical solution to the problem.

"Why did we have to wait until Wayne was…?" Her voice caught in her throat. She didn't want to say "dead." She couldn't bear the feel of the word on her lips. She didn't want to say "gone," either. Because he wasn't gone. He was coming back. She'd see him again. She felt it. She *believed* it. She *had* to believe it or she wouldn't be able to stand it. She'd had so many scares on this frightful journey that she wasn't sure her heart could take much more. She'd go mad if she really lost him!

"Isn't it obvious?" the girl asked. "He wouldn't allow it. Daddy loves you so much. You're the most important thing in the world to him. He'd insist on facing the scarecrow man himself. He'd argue that it was *his* fight, that it was his ability to return from the dead that fascinated him. He'd say it was his fault that monster was out there now. No one would be able to convince him otherwise."

That *did* sound like Wayne. He was so protective of her. He had been since he first found her hiding in that awful restroom. He even grabbed that killing vine in a desperate attempt to defeat that dead crow and its awful bone monsters back on the stone road. She knew him well enough to be certain that he wouldn't have done something like that just to save himself. Or anyone else in the world. He did it because *she* was in danger.

"But read the amber threads," the little girl went on. "You can see the truth, if you look closely enough. If *Daddy* faces the scarecrow man, he'll die. And he won't ever come back."

She tightened her grip on Wayne's hand, her heart sinking. *Was* that something she could see? She couldn't even think clearly right now. She could barely focus on the room around her.

"You have to go while he's out there in the Murk," the girl explained. "If you wait until he comes back, he won't let you go. And if he goes in your place, or even if he goes with you, we'll lose him forever."

"No… I can't do something like that on my own."

"You can. You have to."

She shook her head. It wasn't possible. She wasn't brave enough to do something like that. She'd freeze up. She'd panic. What chance would she stand? That maniac was walking around in the rotting carcass of a razor-skinned hound with a swarm of razor-winged bugs at his command. He was a twisted psychopath. He wasn't even *human*. She didn't know *what* he was, but that wasn't a *man* who stalked them across the endless Wood. It was some kind of possessed *bird carcass*. She was no match for a bunch of nasty *children*, much less some kind of zombie puppet master monster!

"The Keeper plans for everything," the girl said. "The good *and* the bad. Not everybody gets the happy ending. But our best chance of coming out the other side is always to play the game he sets in front of us. I'm not asking you to go out there and face the scarecrow man because he says so. I'm asking you to do what you have to do to save my daddy's life."

Olivia's face crumpled at this. How was she supposed to say no to that? Tears were welling up in her eyes again. She stared down at Wayne, her heart aching, her belly filled with burning dread. But no matter how she looked at it, she wasn't strong enough to take on that monster. If Wayne was no match for it, then she *certainly* wasn't.

This child kept telling her that she already knew these things, that she could feel them, that she could see the amber threads laid out before her like Sandy told her way back in Dunnen. But she didn't know *anything*. She was too afraid to feel whatever her psychic alarm was telling her. She couldn't see anything through these tears. She couldn't hear anything over the pounding of her frightened heart.

Could she really trust this girl? How did she know the Sentinel Queen's child wasn't trying to get rid of her? The way she was clinging to Wayne's hand… Did she want him all to herself? Did she see her as nothing more than an obstacle standing between her and her daddy?

The Sentinel Princess turned her blind gaze back down to her father's face and squeezed his hand again. It was such an adoring look she gave him. And something inside her told her the look was honest. She wasn't putting on some kind of show while plotting against him. Somehow, she could tell. This little girl loved her daddy.

"If there was another way, I'd tell you," she said without looking up from Wayne's peaceful face. "I know how much you mean to him. If something happens to you, he'll be devastated."

Olivia was still leaning over the bed, still gripping his other hand, desperate to not let go, not even to wipe the tears from her cheeks.

"I wish it was as simple as sending you out some back way so you could avoid him until the Oblivion Door is opened. But that won't work. He has strange powers. He can move through the labyrinth in unique ways. He'll find you. He'll confront you.

And one way or another, he'll kill Daddy. And he'll probably kill you, too." Again, she turned her blind gaze toward her. "You know that if you lose him, you'll lose your will to fight, too."

That was a truth she felt deep inside her heart, all the way to her soul, as if all those amber threads had somehow just lit up somewhere inside her mind. If she watched her beloved Wayne murdered for real, it would break her.

"Protecting him is your strength. You'll find a way. The threads will guide you."

Again, she shook her head. She made it sound so simple, but she couldn't possibly believe that she could actually beat a monster like that. There was no way!

"I know you're afraid, but you beating the scarecrow man is the only outcome where the two of you go home together."

Olivia felt her tears welling up again. The only outcome… The only path to her happily ever after…

She squeezed her eyes shut and clenched her teeth against the sobs that wanted to bubble up from inside her. She hated this. She couldn't think of a more terrifying task. And yet how could she say no? This was her fiancé. Her future husband. She couldn't let anything happen to him. She *wouldn't.*

She sniffed hard and wiped at her face with one hand. "Fi-ne…" she grumbled.

The little girl didn't look pleased with herself. In fact, she looked surprisingly unhappy, as if she'd just done something very naughty. "Good," she replied. "I'm glad you understand."

"Not like you gave me any choice," she grumbled.

"That's true. But please be careful out there. You only save Daddy if you beat the scarecrow man. Only if you survive."

She shot the little girl a nasty look that she was fairly sure she noticed even though she was blind. "Yeah. I got it."

"He won't make it home without you," the little girl said, giving his hand a loving pat. "And even if he could, Daddy would never be happy again without Mommy."

Olivia's chest hitched at the word. Fresh tears sprang to her eyes. "That's not fair," she whimpered.

Chapter 76

Things were getting steadily stranger as Andrea felt her way through the lightless passageway. That other, larger space was growing more pronounced in her mind. It stretched out in every direction, a cavernous chamber that was both there and not there at the same time. And yet her hand never left the smooth stone of the wall beside her. She remained inside one of those simple, square passageways, completely enveloped in that same gray stone, unable to step outside of this confined space. What she felt didn't match what she saw, and yet she found that she simply knew that both of those things were true at once.

Was it like the pocket dimensions Gina described to them way back when all this started? Like the ones the barely-there created? And the ones Violet and Corey explored? Was that how it worked? She didn't know anything about any of this stuff, and yet for some reason, this felt different somehow. She found herself thinking that this was unique to the murk. Not a space within another space, but rather some kind of spirit world equivalent.

Like the Elysium Fog, then, she wondered? Or at least like the partial one Erin created in order to speak with her away from Tia's prying ears? As she recalled, she referred to that place as some kind of "spiritual construct" she made from her own memories.

(Why did she keep trying to understand this stuff? She wasn't smart enough to figure any of it out.)

Her blind eyes kept darting around, fixing on things they couldn't see, but her mind somehow could. Most of them were beyond the passage walls, out in that *other* space, clinging to the walls, dangling from the ceiling or simply jutting up from the floor, making her think for some reason of gross-looking fungal growths on sickly trees. They were nothing more than odd lumps of darkness. They weren't doing anything. They weren't moving or growling like those things with the impossible maws full of endlessly spiraling teeth. And yet somehow she sensed that they were dangerous. She didn't trust them to stay where they were. And she didn't trust these stone walls to protect her if one should suddenly charge her.

Fortunately, none did.

Every now and then, however, she glimpsed something out there in that all-encompassing darkness that *was* moving. Little things, mostly, no bigger than a cat, perhaps, and all of them so far a safe distance away, but still unsettling.

Her fingers reached the end of the wall and slipped off, distracting her. Another intersection? Or an open room? What she could "see" in this darkness had nothing to do with the physical layout around her. She reached out, prodding at the stone, feeling her way right, then left, then cautiously exploring the darkness in front of her.

Another crossroads between two intersecting corridors. She could continue going straight or she could turn left or right and try the new one. She could tell no difference between the three choices, not in this physical sense. But it seemed that the right passage was aimed directly at a couple of those worrisome clumps of darkness, so she immediately scratched that one from the list and focused on the other two.

The hair on her arms stood up and a strange chill seemed to trickle through her veins. She twirled around, startled, as something shadowy melted back into the darkness from which it came.

What the heck was that?

She didn't waste time wondering if she'd only imagined it. Somehow she was certain she didn't. Whatever it was, it was standing right behind her for a second there. She could almost see it reaching out for her with long, twisting fingers, like the creeping shadows of tree branches through a moonlit window.

Once again, her heart was pounding. She never sensed it

approaching. And she didn't think she was merely distracted by the choice she was attempting to make. It simply wasn't there…then *was* there…with no transition whatsoever.

There are things hidden deeper in the murk, she thought, recalling Tia's creepy words again.

Things that turned up behind you without having to creep up on you, apparently. Things that were tall and wispy and paper-thin but also nothing of the sort because there was no way to describe such a thing using only the senses possessed by a mere human being.

Things you can't imagine in your worst nightmares.

And she'd had some pretty bad nightmares these past five years…

She took a step backward, her blind eyes sweeping the darkness all around her. Where did it go? She didn't see which direction it went. It didn't seem to move at all, in fact. It just sort of…winked out like an extinguished candle, perhaps? Or was that a bad analogy since there was no light in this place? Everything in here seemed to be made from different layers of darkness. Whatever it was vanished seamlessly into the other darkness somehow.

And yet she found herself very sure that it hadn't vanished at all. It wasn't gone. It was still here somewhere, still watching her from the shadows of shadows.

(*Things that don't like being seen.*)

She shivered and took another step backward. She didn't like this. Something was very wrong about this new darkness she'd found.

Desperate to keep moving, she spent no time considering the better path. She chose the one in front of her and hurried on.

What the hell was that thing? And now that it had noticed her, would it continue to follow her? Was it stalking her *right now*?

And yet she couldn't afford to run in this darkness. She'd already learned that lesson once the hard way. All she wanted was to flee this space, to get as far from the mysterious shadow thing as possible, but she forced herself to slow down and feel for dangers with each step.

It felt torturously slow. And if this passage was anything like a million others just like it in this endless labyrinth, there was nothing here. She should be running as fast as her legs would carry her away from the danger that was literally right behind her a moment ago. But there were also plenty of dangers in temple labyrinths. There were countless places that intersected with the hounds' territory, like the one she fell into. She'd seen passages that simply opened onto nothing. There were deadly spike traps and dead ends to crash into and huge staircases to fall down. And there was no telling when one of those sentinel statues might just be standing in the middle of the passage with its obscene junk hanging there for oblivious blind girls to grab hold of like some creepy pervert. (She was still kind of mad about that.) And given all these things that might be in front of her, for all she knew the shadowy thing that crept up behind her was already gone and there was nothing to even run away from.

Again, her hand slipped off the wall, telling her that she'd exited the passage again. But where was she now?

That strange, imaginary layout of shadows inside her head was telling her that she was still in that larger space, but that had nothing to do with the confines of these passages. She reached out and felt around the corner, finding a wall leading away to the left. She turned around and checked the other side to find the same. Another perpendicular passage? But when she stepped out to feel for the wall on the other side, there was nothing there. She tiptoed several paces, her hands searching but finding no surfaces.

Not another passage. A chamber. A room. But how big? And containing what sort of nasty surprise for an unaware blind girl with no luck to speak of?

She retreated back to the wall and started following it to the right. There should be another passage leading back out somewhere around here.

She *hated* being stuck down here without a light. If she had her flashlight she could at least avoid hazards while running from the things in that murk.

But then again, would she even be able to see the murky

stuff if she had her light? It had already crossed her mind that perhaps it was only because it was dark that she was able to focus with her psychic sense.

Again, she wondered if it was intentional. Did Tia take her light to force her to use her special abilities? It still seemed to her that she wouldn't do such a thing. She really didn't think she was just pretending to be a bad guy back there. More than likely, she just thought it'd be funny to strip her naked and abandon her in the dark. So perhaps it was the Keeper who intended it to be this way. Maybe he knew she'd take her light and played her like he did everyone else.

But would even the Keeper be able to make use of a wild-card like Tia? She wished Erin would talk to her again. Maybe she could answer some of these questions. At the very least, she could use the company.

She stopped walking and frowned, her head tilted to one side, listening. What was that noise?

It was soft enough that she hadn't noticed it at first. It seemed to be coming from the other side of the room. If it was the hounds again, they were really far away. But it didn't sound quite like that. It was a more subtle, constant sort of soft…roar, maybe?

She stared blind into the darkness. In that strange, half-imagined way that she kept seeing the murk shapes, she was still standing in some kind of vast chamber. There was a giant column of some sort off to one side. A support beam, perhaps. Even imaginary rooms that size probably needed supports of some sort to hold them up, she supposed.

But she wasn't in that imagined place. She couldn't get to that column if she wanted to because there was a wall between her and it. If she was going to get out of here and find her way down to where she was supposed to go, then she was going to have to focus on what was here in the *physical* space.

And that probably meant investigating things like this sound…

She steeled her nerves and let go of the wall. Very slowly, one cautious step at a time, she made her way across the empty space, feeling out every inch along the stone floor.

Again, she thought of Gina's pocket dimensions. Overlapping spaces where two different things could exist in the same place at the same time. This was like that, she was increasingly certain. Except in this case, she was in the curious position to be blind to the one she was in and able to see the one lying underneath it.

Unfortunately, that came with the somewhat unsettling realization that she needed to find a way to get into that other space. And that other space looked a *lot* more frightening than this one.

The sound was getting louder. And it was getting louder faster as she went. She was getting closer to the source.

She tilted one ear toward it, trying to hear it more clearly.

Then her toe connected with hard stone.

"Ow!" she cried, her voice sharp with surprised pain. "Dammit!" She stepped back and stooped down, rubbing at it. That really hurt. What did she stub it on?

She reached forward, feeling at the floor in front of her. There was some kind of ten-inch vertical rise in the floor. Steps? That wasn't right. She was supposed to be going down, not up. But when she reached out, there wasn't a second step. Instead, the raised portion stretched away for just a couple feet and then dropped again. As she leaned closer, she could hear that roar much clearer.

She knelt down on the raised ledge and crawled forward, listening.

Rushing water.

And a very long drop down to it, from the sound of it.

Was this one of those chambers with the spiraling staircases, maybe? Was that how she was supposed to go "all the way to the bottom," as Tia instructed? Because that didn't sound like a safe thing to attempt in the dark.

"You should be careful," Tia's familiar voice spoke up in the darkness as if summoned by the very thought.

Andrea looked up, her eyes wide in the darkness. Why was *she* back? Hadn't she caused enough trouble for a while? And where was she? It sounded like she was standing directly in front of her, but there was nothing to stand on there. Was she on the other side of this hole?

For that matter, how long had she been following her? Was she there this whole time, just waiting for a chance to torment her again?

"You're just begging for someone to take advantage of you in that precarious position you're in," Tia warned her.

Precarious position? She realized she was down on her knees and forearms, her butt up in the air and her thighs spread apart. She was trying to ensure she wouldn't lose her balance while this close to the hole. Of course *Tia* would turn it into something pervy.

She started to scurry backward so she could stand up, but before she could go anywhere, she felt Tia's warm hands grab her naked butt.

"Hey!" How'd she get back there so fast?

"Too late!" she laughed.

"Get your hands off me!" The psycho bitch better not stick her nasty fingers somewhere inappropriate!

Then Tia pushed her. Hard.

Andrea never stood a chance against her strength.

Her screams followed her as she plunged through the darkness and into the raging waters below.

Chapter 77

Gina was stalling. She didn't want to stand up. She didn't want to move forward. She didn't want to find what she was looking for. Because when she did, she knew that there would be no going back. She didn't understand exactly what would happen when she reached the very bottom of the glass labyrinth, but she knew that this was a one-way trip. She'd be leaving Nicole behind, caught in Goar Nangup's clutches.

She felt awful. Her belly physically *ached* with regret. She was on the verge of throwing up. But there was simply nothing she could do. Regardless of how she looked at it, she wasn't strong enough to save her.

She'd failed her.

Nicole was probably the strongest woman she'd ever met, but she was still only a woman. They were *both* only human. They couldn't possibly resist the will of an actual god.

She didn't know what she could have done differently. Had they been doomed from the very start?

And if she didn't finish this now, she might yet fail everyone else who'd been so kind to her on this frightful journey.

That was the worst part of it all. She couldn't bear the thought of leaving Nicole behind, but if she did *nothing*, then she might as well have abandoned *everyone* to this awful darkness. Brandy and Albert. Violet and Corey. Andrea and Keith. All the people who'd been so kind to her. All of them *gone*.

Did the goddess know this would happen, too? Did she see, in all her vast wisdom as the Great Beholder, foresee the heartbreak she was going to suffer in this black nightmare? She'd seemed so kind, and yet this felt so cruel.

She lifted her face and blinked into the darkness looming before her.

She hated this more than anything…but she couldn't put it off any longer.

Her heart breaking, she stood up, her legs still trembling beneath her, and continued walking.

Chapter 78

He'd already found her.

Nicole stood terrified in the darkness as that awful and overwhelming presence sped toward her, a wicked and unclean aura like nothing else that ever was before and ever would be again, utterly alien, like something from the far side of the cosmos, filled with cruel, *evil* intent.

Goar Nangup. Older than all the universes. Older than time, itself. A *primordial* sentience from whatever nightmarish protoreality existed before anything pure and clean and *good* was ever dreamed into being.

She wasn't sure how she knew these things. Something about being trapped in that awful prison with it, probably. But she knew this horrifying truth absolutely. Just like she knew that this *thing* rushing toward her wasn't Goar Nangup. It wasn't even the equivalent of a single finger poking out into the surrounding universe. He was trapped so completely and fully in that torturous place beneath the weight of untold worlds that no part of him would ever be free from there as long as the three realms existed. Only by ending the cycle and letting it all crumble would he ever have even a chance to be free.

No… The thing speeding toward her right now in this dreadful darkness was less than a single *breath* from that horror's foul lips. A single whisper of a voice, spoken across the span of countless worlds and passed through the ears of Goar's deranged servant.

That was all this foul deity was able to infect the worlds with. And yet even this insignificant-sounding speck of a presence was enough to drive men to madness, possess a human body and subject a mind to his own tortured existence.

In comparison, it was *she* who was the speck. It was vast and overwhelming and dreadful beyond her worst nightmares and it was but the faintest sigh of its monstrous whole. If such a thing were to ever be set completely free…

The thought alone was enough to make her want to vomit with dread.

And yet Keith had left her here to stand against it all alone in the dark.

(He'll come to take you back. When he does, you're going to face him head on.)

"You've got to be fucking kidding me…" she uttered into the darkness in front of her.

(You can *do it. You have the strength inside you. It's why he chose you. He knows you're the only one who can challenge him.)*

No. There was no way. She was nothing compared to this thing. Literally *everyone else* in this fucking temple would stand a better chance than her.

This was Keith's revenge, wasn't it? He left her here to make her pay for how badly she treated him…for having to leave his life behind and ferry her across that black lake…for leaving him alone to be attacked and injured in the Wood…for making him run into that awful meadow…

For letting him die…

That was bullshit and she knew it. Keith didn't have a vindictive bone in his body. Even out in that forest when she was blatantly treating him like shit, the nastiest thing he did to her was ignore her.

No. He didn't pull her out of that hell just so this prick of a god could drag her right back again. He knew something she didn't. And when all was said and done, she trusted him.

That was the truth.

She clenched her fists and set her jaw. It was almost upon her. She wasn't sure how much time had passed since she first felt it approaching, but she knew somehow that it had been longer than it needed to be. It was toying with her, letting her hear it coming, frightening her as much as possible before snatching her up and subjecting her to that torture again.

That wasn't the behavior of something that had anything to fear from the likes of a terrified woman lost and alone in a vast labyrinth. That was the confident cat playing with its prey before devouring it.

Her every instinct was telling her that she was fucked.

But Keith said otherwise.

There was no running away. She couldn't escape the nightmare before her. She was going to have to choose whether to give up completely or trust the man who gave up everything for her.

Nicole stood her ground as the unfathomable evil reached from the darkness and enveloped her.

It felt as if a vast weight were suddenly crushing down on her. Everything seemed to grow distant. The deafening cacophony of that maddening prison made itself heard in the distance. And a terrible rumble of a cruel laugh rolled through her bones like thunder heralding a devastating storm.

She could feel her legs straining beneath her, struggling to hold up her weight. And the air had become so thick and heavy that she could barely catch her breath. She felt as if she were being smothered under a heavy blanket.

That awful voice was chanting inside her brain again. Uttering that foul, mysterious language.

Anun amum ut mu. Goltom untol mu.

Why did it keep talking at her like that? Did it think she could understand it? Was there some kind of power attached to those words? Some kind of horrible incantation? Or was it just showing off that it was bilingual?

She *hated* this thing! It was every bit as bad as that pervert cultist who wouldn't shut up about it!

Then something clicked.

She gasped. Fresh air filled her lungs.

Everything suddenly made much more sense.

This wasn't the god she was so afraid of. The realization was almost tangible. It was important. It was *significant.* A lifeline in this otherwise hopeless moment. This was, after all, only a *breath* puffed from that god's foul lips, nothing more than a whisper.

"Only his voice…" she sighed into the darkness.

That was it. She understood now.

She stood up straighter, pushing back against that terrible weight that had been trying to drag her down.

She *wasn't* a match for an ancient and all-powerful god. She never was. She never would be. Goar Nangup would crush her very soul out of existence in an instant. She was an insignificant insect compared to him.

But this wasn't Goar Nangup.

This was only the scant, tattered remains of a brutalized human spirit tainted by Goar's foul influence. The so-called "god" she was so afraid of was no such thing. It was nothing more than Hotdog Creep's crippled ghost, still groping for her even in this pitiful state.

And she'd already kicked *his* miserable ass *several* times.

The chanting died away. The sound of that awful prison dulled to a distant rumble.

She opened her eyes to perfect darkness, and yet she saw him there. Not the monstrous, broken thing that stalked her through these dark corridors when she was alone and terrified. Not the deceitful creep that tried to murder Andrea in that dark parking lot. It was the same gray eyes, the same handsome face—if you were into creepy assholes, she supposed—but this man was small and timid and weak. He trembled in her gaze, his breath escaping him in sickly wheezes.

Elias Hochog. The man who sold his soul to an ancient god and lost everything, even his humanity. It made sense, even, why someone would go so far to be reborn. She almost felt sorry for him.

Almost.

She reached out into that darkness and closed her hands around the pitiful man's scrawny neck. "You picked the wrong team, Weiner Boy."

She felt his flesh against her hands, as real as her own. She felt the cords in his neck. The pulse racing through him. She could almost believe that she was strangling a living person. But the living didn't crumple like paper beneath her fingers. Their bones didn't snap like toothpicks. And they didn't melt into nothing like cotton candy in the rain.

The last spectral trace of Elias Hochog broke and crumbled like sand through her fingers and Goar Nangup's awful voice at last went silent.

He was gone. Both body *and* soul. And with him any lingering links to his foul god.

It was over.

She was free.

(*I guess you're just that stubborn, Nik.*)

"You bet your sweet ass I am!" she shouted into the darkness at him.

Then she dropped to her hands and knees and retched.

Chapter 79

Terrified out of her mind, Violet wrenched her leg free of the unseen horror lurking in the dark and kicked it, driving the heel of her foot into it as hard as she could before it could grab her again. The thing, whatever it was, let out a satisfying cry and a muffled curse.

Wait…

Was that a *person*?

There was a painful groan that definitely did *not* sound like any monster she'd ever encountered.

She fumbled her flashlight from her pocket and turned it on, thrusting it out in front of her and into a face that was scrunched up from a combination of pain and the sudden blinding glare, but was otherwise a familiar one. "Albert?"

"What the fuck?" he moaned, clutching at his chest and trying to block out the light.

She knelt beside him, confused. "What're you doing here?"

He looked…well, not well. He was half-naked, wearing only a filthy pair of shorts. He was dirty and slick with sweat. His hair was matted and greasy. It looked like he had a black eye and there was a painful looking gouge in his lower chest that looked like it had been bleeding. What happened to him? How did he get here? Why was he lying on the floor? The more she saw of him, the more questions she had. She had to stop herself from bombarding him with them.

"That hurt…" he groaned, rolling onto his side.

"I'm sorry. You scared me."

"Understandable…"

She knelt down to help him up. "Are you okay?"

"I think you cracked a rib."

"Sorry."

"It's okay. Don't worry about it." He blinked up at her, squinting at her face. "You…" he realized. "Thank God. We were worried about you."

We… She sat up a little as she remembered that he was supposed to be with Brandy. Why was he alone? Was she here somewhere? She cast her light across the floor, looking for another body lying in the darkness.

"Wait…" He rolled over, his eyes widening at the sight of the statues looming over him. "Is this an *emotion room*?"

She blinked at him for a moment, then looked up at the statues surrounding them. "Oh shit!" She'd forgotten why she had her light turned off in the first place.

Albert had already squeezed his eyes shut and covered his face, shielding himself from any further exposure, but here *she* was just…*looking around*. She dropped her gaze and switched off the flashlight.

Was it too late? Distracted by her unexpected find, she'd forgotten all about the room. She was looking at *him*, not the statues. Even when she looked around for Brandy, her attention was fixed on the floor. But now she'd seen what was in here. And what she saw had already burned itself into her thoughts. There were dozens of statues. Ordinary people, just like her. Most of them were naked, but there was nothing particularly erotic about them to suggest that she was in any kind of sex room. They reminded her of those old Greek statues she'd seen in books. A few were wearing simple wraps or dresses. Some had sandals. There was nothing particularly remarkable about the way any of them looked, except for the exquisite level of detail. They were so perfectly carved that they looked like real people simply *painted* to look like stone. What struck her like a punch to the gut was their expressions. Each and every one of those faces was twisted and stretched into grimaces and howls. They were shouting and pointing, a strange, overwhelming mixture of anger and fear pouring off each and every one of them. Feelings and ideas and thoughts flooded her head that weren't her own. Deceit. Betrayal. Lies. Cheating. Desperation. Despair. Antagonization. Fear and hatred. The harder she tried to push them away, the more clearly she seemed to remember them!

She pressed the heels of her hands hard against her eyes, trying to drive back the images.

It wasn't real. They were only stone. They couldn't hurt her. They couldn't make her *feel* anything. No matter what freaky alien physics were at work here. She was her own damned person. *She* decided what she let affect her!

She took another deep breath and held it. She could do this. She just needed to stay calm. Slowly, the storm inside her head seemed to be easing.

"Okay…" sighed Albert. "That's good. That's better."

"Sorry."

"It's fine. But keep your light off. I've done this before. Just…tell me what we're dealing with."

"What?"

"What emotion is it?"

"I…" She blinked into the darkness. "I don't know. I couldn't tell, exactly."

"Okay." He didn't sound impatient or frustrated, which was good. His voice had a calming effect. "What did the *face* look like? The door you came through."

"Umm…"

"Was it a man or a woman?"

"A woman." She knew that one. That was good. She was being helpful.

"A woman," he repeated. "So it's not either of the ones I found before. That's probably a good sign. Means I haven't gone backward, at least."

She was having trouble keeping up. Was he saying he'd already found two more of these *here*? In addition to the three he described from the first temple? And did he not see the door himself? Was it because he didn't seem to have a flashlight? "How'd you get here?"

Questions were good. Questions took her mind off those invasive feelings.

"No idea. I just woke up here when you started kicking me."

Again, she cringed. "Yeah… My bad."

"It's fine. I get it. I don't blame you at all. This place puts you on edge. You couldn't help if I startled you. But this is the first I'm seeing of these statues. I don't know what might happen."

"It's weird. I can't describe it very well. It's like an odd mix of anger and fear?"

"Okay… That sounds dangerous, not gonna lie." She could hear him shifting in the dark, sitting up, perhaps, rubbing at his wounds. "Last time it was lust, hate and fear."

That still sounded like bullshit, even while she was literally *sitting on the floor of one of those rooms*. Seriously, why did something like this even exist?

"Here, we found sadness and anxiety."

Anxiety? Really? Wasn't that a little overly specific?

"Tell me what you've been feeling since you got here."

"It's kind of hard to describe. Jumpy. Kind of mad. Impulsive, maybe. Like, I hurt my hand lashing out at something that wasn't there. And really scared, too, like I said. But maybe that's just being in here by myself."

"Disgust, maybe?" he pondered.

Anger, fear, sadness and disgust? What was this? *Inside Out*? Except for that sex room part, she supposed. Maybe when they got around to the seventh or eighth movie, when Riley's a frustrated single working woman in her early thirties with a slight drinking problem and relationship issues.

"Or maybe it's more…*paranoia*?"

She frowned at the idea. That last pair of sentinels, not exactly attacking each other, but certainly threatening. All those people, agitated and yelling, as if throwing accusations. Those too-tall, featureless *things* spreading across the land, taking over.

(…*could be anywhere*…*any*one…)

(…*don't trust your eyes*…)

She shivered at the unwanted memory. "Yeah. Something like that, I think." Or something pretty close to it.

"That's…not the best scenario. At least when it comes to fear and sadness, you can kind of come together. This is the kind of emotion designed to drive people apart."

He was right, she realized. She was already at the point where she was losing the ability to trust a bunch of inanimate statues. What was going to happen when she started thinking that she couldn't trust *him*? "I really don't want to be alone again."

"Yeah. Me neither."

"So how do we deal with something like this?"

"We have to be careful not to let our feelings outweigh our senses. Otherwise we'll start feeling like we need to get away from each other. And we don't want to get separated. But worst-case scenario, we could panic and hurt each other."

"Again, I'm sorry for kicking you in the ribs. We're already starting off on the wrong foot for this."

Albert chuckled. "Like I said, forget about it. It wasn't your fault. If anything, I'm glad it was me and not someone else."

"I know you said you made it through the first three rooms by impairing your vision, but we don't have that here. We're gonna be stuck in the dark, aren't we?"

"I think that's best. Even though not being able to see won't help with any paranoid thoughts." Again, she heard him moving around. When next he spoke, she realized he was standing up and rose to her feet as well. "In the anxiety room, Brandy and I figured out that we can use a kind of emotional override when things get too hairy. We can literally overwhelm the invading emotion with a different one."

She wrinkled her nose in the dark. "Let me guess. *Sexual* ones?"

"I mean, we *were* on our honeymoon when this all started, so yeah. But it doesn't have to be sexual. I'm not suggesting that we do anything inappropriate. I'm not interested in any of *that* with anyone but *her*. So please don't think that's what I'm after."

"Yeah. I get it." And she found that she believed him. She'd never gotten any kind of creepy or leering sort of vibe from him. And she'd seen for herself the way he looked at Brandy all the way back in the carriage. He was a man in love, for sure.

"Any emotion will do. If you start to feel something from this room, try to shift your thinking, try to think of something happy or funny or calming. Anything *positive.* Nothing that can feed into the emotion that you're fighting."

"Piece of cake," she grumbled.

"Yeah, I know. But it's the best we have right now."

"Okay…" She reached out into the darkness and found his hand. "Don't let go of me, though."

"Sure."

"I'm sick and tired of *losing* all you people."

Chapter 80

Corey hurried down the gloomy corridor, past rack after rack of stacked servers, huffing and puffing.

He wasn't particularly good at running. It wasn't his thing. He tried not to do it very often.

And yet he certainly couldn't stop. The infection was closing in on him. He could feel it back there, like a wall of pure *wrongness* pushing against his back. And he could feel it pushing against the back of his *mind* as well. Strange thoughts drifted around back there. Images painted in shades of darkness and time flitted in and out of his consciousness. Wordless tales crawled through his brain like worms, stories spanning eons while saying nothing at all, like memories of maddening emptiness woven into a physical thing that threatened to entangle and strangle him. Half-memories not his own played at the fringe of his consciousness, tantalizing glimpses of worlds long gone that he wanted to see more of, but at the same time tainted with horrors and tragedies he couldn't bear to witness.

This was the mind of the infection, he understood. It wasn't a computer virus. It was never *any kind* of virus. It was something far more destructive. It was rot. It was decay. It was like someone had taken time itself and extracted whatever specific element was responsible for its ability to literally *end* everything that existed and then gave that dreadful element unnatural life. The more he understood of it, the smaller he felt in comparison.

One image kept surfacing among all the chaos invading his thoughts. A silhouette of a woman with long, curly hair and a wicked grin. A woman who was no woman at all, but something far greater, far older and far more dangerous.

Priestess of Ruin.

It was her. She was the enemy. She was the one who brought this thing here.

On either side of him, servers were crashing. Cooling systems were failing. Hardware was shorting out. Lights went dark. Sparks and smoke erupted from one of the cabinets.

Once again, he never had a chance. The problem was far too big for him alone. He wasn't sure if an entire *army* of him would have been enough to hold this thing back.

"So make it smaller," said Violet, as if it were that simple.

Hadn't he been *making* it smaller?

"Have you?"

He frowned at this. Had he? Or had he only been changing the *illusion* of size?

"You're overthinking it. If you need it to be smaller, just *make it smaller.*"

Ahead of him, he finally glimpsed the end of the corridor. A heavy, solid door stood there, exactly like the security door on the server room in his father's office complex. This was it.

(*…just make it smaller.*)

Something behind him exploded, sending a shower of sparks raining down around him.

He pushed himself to go faster.

Just make it smaller… Not just the space around him, but the *whole world.* A finite space. Surrounded by walls.

Somewhere in the back of his mind, he heard the curly haired woman laughing at him as he threw his weight against the door and shoved it open.

Chapter 81

This was new.

Brandy peered down into a deep, still expanse of dark water stretching well beyond the reach of her meager flashlight beam in every direction. Unlike in the first temple—or in the storm drains she ended up washed into with Albert and Gina—the water didn't come right up to the floor. There was a twenty-foot drop down to the surface. And there was no visible way back up if they fell in.

So much for washing the puke off this shirt, she supposed. She tugged at it. It wasn't as big as Albert's. It was a little tight. It felt like she was wrapped up in her own vomit. (So gross.) And then there was the fact that it was clinging to her like a second skin. She might as well still be wandering around with her tits out for all it was hiding.

But Everett wasn't being creepy about it, at least. She hadn't caught him staring at her. That was nice. He seemed like a good kid, keeping his attention on their surroundings, even if it *was* fairly obvious that he was distracted by her. It was kind of cute, even, how hard he was trying. She'd take it as a compliment.

Besides, it wasn't *his* fault she mistook him for her husband and gave him an R-rated hello.

He pointed into the darkness ahead of them. "It looks like it isn't very wide. A hundred feet or so, maybe? Just a little farther than we can see, I think."

"Your doll tell you that?" She couldn't entirely suppress the sarcastic edge in her voice. She couldn't help it. The whole *idea* of some sort of haunted doll guiding them through this place was creepy as hell, like something right out of a horror movie.

"She did. Although it's not like she really *tells* me anything. There's no words, really. She kind of speaks in *ideas.* I just sort of *know* what she wants me to know and picture it in my mind. It's not always accurate, though. Sometimes it gets garbled."

"Wow. That's even creepier than if you just said your doll talked to you."

He looked down at Alice and shrugged. "Yeah, Violet didn't seem to like her much, either."

"Smart girl." She turned and shined her light to the right. There was no continuing forward, but the passage didn't exactly end, either. There was an eight-foot-wide walkway leading both left and right, following the curving edge of the water below. A wall on one side and a sheer drop on the other. No handrails, naturally. The sentinels apparently had no concept of safety. It was clearly as pointless to them as pants.

Again, she tugged at the too-tight shirt. It wouldn't be nearly as uncomfortable if not for the sting of that sunburn…

"It goes on really far in either direction, though," Everett reported. "Kind of like a river running through the labyrinth. And there are other passages on the other side that we can't see from here."

"Any way across?"

He seemed to ponder the question for a moment. More likely, he was consulting his creepy miniature guide. Then, finally: "No. She's not showing me any bridges or anything."

So it was yet another pointless obstacle making everything harder than it needed to be. It was like a big, useless *crack* running through the middle of the labyrinth, separating the two areas. If the place they were supposed to go was on the other side of that water, how long would it take them to find a route that would circle around it?

She followed the walkway for a few yards and shined her light into another passage leading back the way they came. If Albert were here, what would he choose to do? Abandon this area and explore more of the space on this side? Maybe look for a way up or down? No. Something was telling her he'd be fixated on the water. He'd want to follow the path around. He'd say it was "something different" and want to explore it more before forgetting about it. And she supposed that made a certain amount of sense.

(God, she fucking missed him!)

"It's really deep," said Everett.

She had no doubt. The water in the first temple was really deep in places, too.

She glanced back at him, uncertain. What was up with that doll, anyway? It was just plain creepy. She didn't like it. But was it any different from when they followed the Sentinel Queen's directions? Or the Keeper's?

His story about how he found her was out of this world. She wouldn't have believed a word of it if her own story hadn't been just as insane. And that part about someone he called the "Priestess of Ruin"… Was he talking about Stella? Warner did tell them to "beware the Ruin" way back in Lucianna's hotel. And then there was the way she'd always referred to herself as a "chaos goddess" like it was some stupid private joke. (And looking back now, she supposed that was exactly what it was.)

"That's interesting," said Everett, distracting her from her thoughts.

"What is?"

"Alice says there's a passage down by the water on the other side."

She shined her light out across the darkness, but there was nothing to see.

"Farther that way a ways," he clarified, pointing. "We can't see it from this side. But she says it looks like it goes somewhere."

She turned and raised an eyebrow at him. He was kidding, right? And yet he just stood there, grinning that goofy grin at her. "So, your spooky, *Stephen King's wet dream of a toy* says we should just trust her and jump in that water without even being able to see a way back out?"

"Um…? Maybe?"

She rolled her eyes and pointed her light the other way. "Fucking…" She still hadn't stopped choking from the *first* time she nearly drowned.

"I mean…she didn't say to jump in," he amended. "She just told me it was there. A passage down close to the surface where we could climb up. She says it's different from the other passages in here. Like, it feels like a path that's meant to be followed, you know?"

If it was meant to be followed, why would it be positioned out of sight on the other side of a very deep pool of water that looked like an absolute death trap? Who in their right mind would blindly jump into something like that just to see what was over there? What if the passage was a lie? Best case scenario, they tread water until they exhausted themselves, then drowned. The only way to know they needed to cross would be to have something like Albert's psychic map. Or the thing that made Gina aware of every detail in her surroundings.

She glanced back at that strange little doll.

Or a creepy little helper, she supposed…

(No one truly knows the mind of the Keeper. His designs are beyond comprehension, even among those who can understand the secret workings of the universe. And his will is inescapable. If he intends something, it will be done.)

The Keeper… Lucianna spoke of him as if he were some sort of god, lurking behind the scenes, pulling all the strings. Wasn't he supposed to have all this shit planned out down to the most miniscule detail? Would he have planned exactly for this moment? Would he have meant for him to find her specifically to show her the way forward while she was separated from Albert and his psychic map?

(Placing trust in a being with so much power requires incredible courage and faith. But I can promise you that it is well-founded *courage and faith.)*

She walked on, following the walkway along the winding wall, her light sweeping the darkness beyond the edge, wondering what she should do.

What would *Albert* do? Would he have blind faith in the temple and jump right in? Or would he yield to caution like someone who *wasn't* a complete moron?

She aimed her light down at the water's surface. It looked perfectly still but looks could be deceiving when it came to still water. Even if she *could* trust that Alice the Doll was telling the truth, that there was a passage they could climb out of down there, this was a *temple.* There were deadly spike traps and bottomless pits hidden in here. There were emotion rooms and hounds and probably even more of those monstrous Caggo things lurking around somewhere. Why wouldn't there be a deadly current or undertow hidden in that water that swept them away the second they jumped in? Or maybe there were more of those stone spikes hidden just beneath the surface, waiting to impale anyone foolish enough to just jump blindly in. Worse still, what manner of horror might be *swimming around* down in those black depths? At the very least, she'd rather not risk encountering another of those nasty spider-squid things that nearly choked her to death with that foul fluid it squirted into her face last time.

"I mean, honestly," said Everett, sounding oddly timid for a change, "I'd much rather *not* do any swimming. I'm not great with water. So I'm not gonna argue if you refuse to go in there."

There was something about the way he said that that struck her as profoundly true. In fact, it probably had far less to do with the way he said it than with the way she heard him.

(*You can see the truth within people.*)

Right. She'd forgotten what the pervert told her about her psychic abilities. It didn't seem to make a lot of difference out here in the *literal middle of fucking nowhere*, after all, where there were a dozen living people in the whole of that eternal black forest. Tricks like she used with the lovey-dovey anniversary couple and Trixie didn't do her much good out here. But it was still working for her, because she understood without a shred of doubt that he wasn't just "not great with water," but rather that he couldn't swim very well. In fact, he struggled with a bit of a phobia when it came to water in general. Something had happened to him, something traumatic, something that left him afraid of deep water…especially of *lakes…*

(It's not like in the movies, you know. You don't just cough up the water and then you're fine in a few minutes. You're gonna feel pretty gross for a

while. Believe me, I know.)

The truth within people… It was still so weird to think about. Had she always been able to do this? Had she only just dismissed thoughts like these as her own silly imagination getting bored and making up little stories about people? Or was it more subtle up until the pervert decided to drag them through his own personal pornographic boot camp?

Either way, she found that she simply knew that Everett had a fear of water. And that could be problematic. Last time they had to swim across more than one body of water in order to pass through the labyrinth. If this turned out to be like those chambers, would he even be able to do it?

Again, she glanced back at him. She didn't want to ask him about it point blank. She felt like that might embarrass him. And she sensed that he would do his best no matter *what* they might end up having to deal with. He was a good kid. He was trustworthy.

The doll, on the other hand, she wasn't so sure about. She didn't think she could see the truth in…whatever *she* was… But she could see that *he* trusted her.

Ahead of her, the wall and walkway were both curving to the right. There was another opening there, another passage leading back the way they came.

"It's right there," reported Everett, pointing into the darkness across from the passage ahead of them. "I can picture it. It's like a small platform down by the water's edge and a passage leading off in that direction."

She shined her light down at the area where he was pointing. She couldn't see anything, but then again, he told her she wouldn't be able to see it from here.

She wished she knew what she was supposed to do.

Frustrated, she turned her light on the passage she was approaching, only to find someone standing there.

She let out a startled scream and stumbled backward, bumping into Everett. "Holy fucking shit!" she gasped. "What the fuck is *he* doing there?"

The passage wasn't a passage at all. It was merely a nook in the wall, just big enough for a sentinel—of all the fucking things—to stand in.

"That was scary," agreed Everett.

"Oh my god..." she gasped, clutching at her pounding heart. "I *hate* these guys!"

It was just standing there, its feet together, hands at its sides, back straight, dick limp, just like hundreds or thousands of others just like it out there somewhere.

She turned and leaned against the wall. That really startled her. And her quickened breathing was irritating her windpipe again. She cleared her throat and coughed.

"You okay?" he worried. "Sit down if you need to."

"I'm fine," she insisted. Although it *was* sweet that he was fussing over her like this. "I just need a second. That's all."

"Alice says you should be fine, at least. She says ichor isn't like water. It's something else. I can't really understand what she's trying to call it, but it seems like it's safer than water if you choke on it."

"She knows a lot for a doll."

"I know. I guess she just sort of takes things in from her surroundings, maybe."

"Does she know what we're supposed to do next?"

He looked down at her and frowned. "She says to ask the sentinel..." he translated. He turned and looked up at the statue, confused. "But I don't think he's talking."

Ask the sentinel. Wasn't that what Albert told her? Back in the ick chamber, when she was being a baby about wading through that shit—and look where *that* ended up getting her—he said they should listen to the sentinels, that they were there to point the way. She turned and shined her light at it again, taking it all in. Those long, stretched limbs, the lean muscles, the emotionless stance. And of course that smooth, empty face.

"He *is* talking," she realized. "He says we should cross the water."

He glanced back at her, then stared up at the sentinel. He didn't understand. "Why? Just because he's facing that way?"

"No." It was more subtle than that. It was in that blank

face. Or more precisely, in the *angle* of the face. He wasn't looking straight ahead like most of his brothers. His head was tilted. He was looking *downward* at an angle. "Because he's *looking directly at it*."

Chapter 82

Wayne was caught in the current, speeding through the cold, dark waters of this deathly ocean, farther and farther from his lifeless body. And yet at the same time, he realized somehow that he hadn't left the temple at all. He was still inside those walls, sliding deeper and deeper into the labyrinthine depths of the City Beyond Memory and the strangely tangled network of spirit passageways that twisted throughout those cold, stone corridors.

Somewhere in that confounding knot of interwoven strands was the passage so utterly infested with murk that Andrea had been rendered utterly blind. And where they'd lost her… Was it possible to find where she went from here? Could he catch even a glimpse of her, just enough to assure himself that she was still safe? It seemed doubtful. Those glimpses of life within the labyrinth were too fleeting and too numerous. He couldn't tell humans from monsters. And there was so much of it. The corridors went on and on, unending.

He couldn't even tell which direction he came from. Those passages seemed almost to be spinning around him as he was carried through it, spiraling and twisting, distorting in maddening pulses that he couldn't follow even with this bizarre, everywhere-at-once sight.

This wasn't the whole picture, he managed somehow to understand. This wasn't what the dead saw when they passed over. He was still partly connected to his physical form, still clinging to his earthly body even in the face of a purely spiritual existence.

He was caught *between* those two states of being.

He needed to let go completely. That was the only way to

fully embrace this side of things. But he wasn't sure how to do that. In fact, the more he struggled with the conundrum, the more aware he felt himself becoming, the more he could almost feel his living body again.

If he wasn't careful, he'd only snap himself back to where he started. He'd wake up in that bed between his daughter and his fiancée and have to start all over again.

Being alive, it seemed, was a difficult habit to break.

He needed a distraction. Something on this side to focus on.

He opened that eye that wasn't an eye that gazed out in every direction at once, scanning these bizarre surroundings. Almost immediately, he became aware of something deep in the labyrinth ahead of him. A strange and familiar sort of warmth in the otherwise cold nothingness enveloping him. A beacon in the darkness, like a lighthouse shining from a deadly fog.

And he was speeding straight toward it.

Chapter 83

Leaving Wayne behind and walking back through that door all by herself was one of the hardest things Olivia had ever found herself faced with.

"You're not really going to be alone," the Sentinel Princess assured her as she braced herself for the task ahead. "Not for a single second."

But having some psychic little girl nosing around inside her head wasn't exactly the kind of company she needed while facing a psychotic scarecrow man.

She felt sick to her stomach at the very thought of it. She couldn't even find the courage to let go of his hand.

And yet the girl wasn't wrong. If she were to still be here when Wayne woke up, he'd never let her leave without him. He'd insist on going with her, protecting her, perhaps with his last breath. And if death was all that awaited him if he accompanied her, she couldn't let him. As painful as the thought of leaving without him was, she couldn't risk losing him forever. As much as she didn't want to believe this child, she could feel the truth in her words. Her psychic alarm was telling her that she had to leave him. Imagining staying here with him filled her with an urgent dread that was only getting worse with each passing second.

It was possible that she was being lied to, that this child was using her psychic powers to fool that part of her brain. She still knew so little about how it worked, after all. But then again, almost every step she'd taken since leaving her future father-in-law's house had been a risk. They would've died that very night if she hadn't listened to her instincts and warned Wayne to turn around.

Sandy. Max. Maeve. Nadia. And now this girl. All of them had told them the same story. The Keeper's great plan. The cycle. A convoluted fairy tale full of nightmares and peril. Nothing had made sense throughout this mad journey. But nothing made sense last time, either. All she could do was trust that the Keeper intended for her to make it home.

And he did, in the end. She returned from that frightful experience in one piece. He even returned Wayne to her. And Andrea and Albert. Everyone he took away from her in that first temple, he gave back.

She looked down at Wayne. She was still holding his hand. Her psychic alarm was telling her that time was running short. The longer she put it off, the less likely she was to save him.

"Everything will be fine," promised the mysterious little girl. "I'll make sure he makes it back safe from his job in the Murk. And you'll make sure the scarecrow man never hurts him."

Yes… That plan felt right. She was terrified out of her mind, but that was definitely the course of action her psychic brain was urging her toward.

She wiped at her eyes once more, then bent over Wayne and kissed him.

It's not *a goodbye kiss*, she thought to herself, driving the words into the universe around her. They'd kiss again. As soon as she finished her job.

Her heart breaking, she let go of his hand and walked to the door, already pulling the flashlight out of her pocket and turning it on. "How do I know where to go after I leave?"

"Follow the threads," replied the Sentinel Princess. "They'll guide you wherever you need to go."

Right…because she'd done *such* a good job navigating with it so far.

She gripped the handle of the door and then stopped. She looked back at him one last time, a terrible, lonesome aching deep inside her. Then she forced herself to open it and step through before she could change her mind.

Immediately, however, she found herself not in the strange, white palace that was outside this door when she first entered, but back in the empty gray corridors of the labyrinth.

"Where did…?" she began, but when she looked back, the door and the Sentinel Princess' room were both gone. There was only another empty corridor back there.

A terrified squeak of a cry escaped her as she realized that there was no way back. She was trapped in the labyrinth again, but all alone this time.

I told you, you're not going to be alone.

She shined her light back and forth, surprised. "Hello?"

But the voice in her head didn't speak up again.

Was that only a passing bit of unwarranted optimism, or was her pretty little step-daughter-to-be keeping a close watch over her?

(*I know how much you mean to him. If something happens to you, he'll be devastated.*)

She took a breath and tried to calm her ragged breathing. Her heart felt like it was trying to burst from her chest. Her legs were trembling. Her belly was a boiling pit of acid, making her feel as if she might vomit any moment.

But this was what had to be done.

She couldn't let anything happen to Wayne. Not today. Not ever.

She was going to be his wife and that meant protecting him with every fiber of her being.

(*Protecting him is your strength. You'll find a way.*)

"Okay," she gasped. Her feet felt as heavy as lead, but she managed one step, then another. She had a job to do. And she was going to do it. No matter what.

Chapter 84

Andrea crawled out of the water, choking and gasping, her body shivering from the cold.

"Bitch actually pushed me!" she coughed.

That was *horrible*! She *really* thought she was going to drown for a minute there!

What kind of lunatic just grabbed someone's *butt* and shoved them headfirst into a *giant hole in the dark*? She had no time to brace herself, no chance to even try to grab onto something. She was just suddenly plummeting through the darkness, the wind whipping through her hair, screaming, with no idea what was below her. Was the water even deep enough to land safely in?

It felt like it knocked the wind out of her when she struck it, but there was no time to worry about that because the very next thing she knew she was being carried off by a strong, numbing current at what felt like breakneck speed, powerless to do anything but be washed away. It was like the world's most terrifying water slide!

Everything was utter chaos and sheer panic.

Then she was dumped in this room, where she probably would've drowned if she hadn't been washed up into shallow water like a piece of driftwood.

She crawled across the floor, her arms and legs trembling too much to stand, then rolled onto her back, still trying to catch her breath.

Her head was pounding. Her body ached. She could see stars dancing before her eyes.

Exhausted and frustrated, she balled up her fists and shouted into that empty darkness, "*What the hell is wrong with you*!"

Chapter 85

What an unusual chamber.

There were numerous passageways leading to this spot, none of them converging or intersecting for as far as Gina's psychic eye revealed, all of them spiraling and funneling directly to this one small room…and yet there was only one opening leading into the room. Dozens of ways to get here. Only one way in. And even stranger, she somehow understood that there was no way out. As soon as she stepped across that final threshold, there would be no turning back. The glass labyrinth…and everything and everyone in it…would be behind her forever.

It defied all natural logic. But then again, this wasn't a natural space. This was the unnatural. It was fundamentally different, all the way down to its primordial foundation.

There *was* a physical side, of course. She could see it. She could feel it. This space in front of her was extraordinarily close to the physical side of the city, separated by almost nothing, a whisper-thin boundary, fragile as a bubble, so that the two sides were fundamentally one and the same.

The room itself was small and oddly shaped, with strange, triangular columns surrounding a sort of hourglass-shaped obstruction at its center that she could tell somehow was a significant component of the greater structure. The walls were covered in those same curious, brain-shaped etchings and odd little blocks of stone that she could tell were only stone but for some reason reminded her of the little metal boxes found on large machinery, usually containing wiring or computer boards or fuses or whatever sorts of things were necessary to make them work. She had no way of understanding what she was looking at. Just like with everything else she'd encountered here, the logic behind it was beyond her ability to comprehend. But her psychic eye could see more than just the physical components. She could see ribbons that her brain perceived as glowing strands of various thickness streaming from those boxes and leading up to several narrow stone cylinders of various length protruding from the ceiling. She could see an odd, trickling fluid making its way down the grooves in the walls like some kind of ornate water feature. And there was something just behind the wall across from her that wasn't alive, exactly, but was oddly *aware*, like a lingering *consciousness* locked away within the stone.

She hesitated a moment longer, her heart breaking again at the thought of Nicole back there somewhere, possessed by that monstrous god, but then she stepped forward. There was no going back. If she tried, she knew deep down that Goar Nangup would win. So she forced the painful thoughts back out of her head and focused on the task in front of her.

She crossed the chamber, circling around the blocky shape at the center, her blind eyes glued to it in the darkness. It was some sort of terminal. Like all the other things she'd ever known to be true but shouldn't, she didn't understand where the knowledge came from. It was just there. She simply knew that it was a terminal. And she simply knew that activating it would open the way forward, allowing the others out there to accomplish what they came here to do as well. And if she didn't activate it, she'd doom them all to failure and almost certainly cost them any chance they might have of ever seeing their homes again, which seemed like an awful lot of pressure to place on a single person, but here she was.

How did she even go about activating it? There were no switches. No dials or knobs. No levers or buttons. She wasn't even sure why the word "terminal" popped into her mind. It was just...*stone.*

She stopped walking and turned to face it. This was the exact place, she could tell. This was precisely where she was meant to be, the very place she'd been trying to reach without understanding anything for all these painful and frightful and frustrating hours. But it wasn't entirely clear what she was supposed to do now that she was here. Was she supposed to put her hand somewhere? Was there a password she was supposed to know? A keycard someone forgot to give her? A magic word?

She felt so weary, both physically and emotionally. So much had happened. She'd shed so many tears. It was hard to think. She just wanted to find somewhere soft and curl up and sleep. But that wasn't going to happen anytime soon.

And the longer it took her to understand what she was supposed to do here, the more likely she was to lose more friends.

She found herself remembering the gate through which they entered the city, the key hanging around Brandy's neck. And Andrea's spear that was one of its two counterparts. Was she supposed to have something like that? Because neither Brandy nor Andrea were here. And Yggdrasil's seed vanished from the chain as soon as they arrived on this side of the wall. It was gone. If that was supposed to happen, then they *all* might be gone. Used up, perhaps, transporting them all across the impassible wall.

No… If a key were required here, she'd have one. That was the message everyone kept drilling into them. The Keeper and the sentinels and their infallible designs. This terminal was already hidden away in a place only she could reach. A key would be unnecessary.

She must have already had everything she needed when she arrived. She only had to figure out exactly what it was she was supposed to do next.

Uncertain, she reached out and touched the stone.

She knew that it was stone, just as she knew that the glass labyrinth was stone, identical in every way to the surfaces in the *physical* labyrinth. She could feel the cool, smooth texture against her fingertips every time she reached out and touched one of the walls. But what she saw with her psychic eye was a strange mix of stone and glass. It shimmered and shined, translucent, appearing almost *wet*. And somehow this odd perception of it gave her just a hint of a glimpse inside, to the mysterious flow of energy pulsing through it in a rhythmic sort of pattern that reminded her less of a machine than of a living *organ*. It was as if she'd found the labyrinth's *heart*.

That same energy pulsed through the very passages spreading out from this chamber, like arteries and veins carrying lifeblood to its many vital parts.

And yet, despite this very convincing similarity to a functioning, breathing *body*, she knew that the Temple of the Three Whispers wasn't really alive. This wasn't some complex, artificial life form whose enormous anatomy she'd been trudging through this whole time. It was more like the sentinels somehow based the technology they used to build it on biological functions, fusing the concepts in some highly advanced and complex way that she couldn't begin to understand. She wasn't smart enough, of course. No one alive was that smart, more than likely. But also there were components missing that were simply impossible to comprehend in her own reality, things that existed in prior universes but died with them.

It was actually quite humbling to think about.

But now wasn't the time to let such ideas distract her. The sooner she figured out how to activate this terminal, the sooner everyone could finish what they came here to do.

Except…she still didn't know what would become of Nicole. She was still out there in the glass labyrinth somewhere, still possessed by that foul deity… She hadn't been able to feel her since stepping backward through the crack and emerging here at the bottommost layer. Everything was so much…*denser* down here…so much harder to peer through, but she knew she was still here somewhere. The longer she hesitated, the more likely that thing was to find her and kill her before she could finish her job. But the moment she did what she came to do…

Her breath caught in her throat and tears welled up in her eyes at the very thought of it. She didn't think she could do it. How would she live with herself knowing she was the reason Nicole never made it home?

But the alternative, of course, was that she would fail everyone else. Andrea. Violet and Corey. Brandy and Albert. All of them out there right now, struggling to do whatever the Keeper sent them each here to do, all of them counting on each other…all of them counting on *her*…

Nicole wouldn't want her to hesitate because of her. She was sure of it. This was the same woman who kicked her through that portal back in Hochog's nightmare hospital, after all. She knew all-too-well what would happen to her if she were left behind. Her friends were more important to her then. They'd be more important now.

But that didn't make what she had to do any easier.

The longer she stood here, the more her psychic gaze was drawn to a specific part of the stone hourglass. A very subtle sort of pattern in the path of the flowing energy, closer to the surface than in the rest of the device.

She reached out and placed her palm against it.

The energy seemed to change. It reminded her of those plasma ball toys, the ones with the glass balls and the little arcs of electricity that concentrated wherever you were touching it… But it wasn't anything so flashy. It was subtle. And much more felt than seen. And it didn't stop at the surface of the glass. She could sense that energy passing through her body.

It felt oddly…*right*… She found herself thinking for some reason that it was calibrated specifically to *her* unique energy… But of course that made no sense.

Then again, since when had *anything* in her life ever made sense?

She understood what she needed to do now, at least. She needed to take her own energy and plunge it into the machine. And somehow, she was able to also understand how to do that.

But Nicole…

She closed her eyes. Fresh tears slipped down her cheeks.

The goddess sent her here. The goddess knew what was best. She had to believe that. Otherwise, what *could* she believe in?

"I'm so sorry," she whispered.

The energy flowing inside the stone reversed and everything around her turned inside out.

Chapter 86

Nicole groaned. She was lying on the stone floor, her stomach burning, her lips quivering, her body trembling. It felt as if she'd just stumbled off a crashed airplane in one piece. She could barely believe she was still alive.

It might have turned out that she was only fighting a feeble, damaged spirit, but there was still a very powerful entity anchored to it. She wasn't sure how she understood something like that, but she knew it to be true. Goar Nangup's power was terrifyingly *real*, even if it were being funneled through a proverbial pinhole. She comprehended completely that she was lucky to have escaped that monster with her soul still in one piece, much less her body and sanity.

She reached up and pressed her fingers to her mouth. Why did her lip hurt? Did she bite it at some point? It felt like it had been bleeding.

She supposed it didn't matter.

Slowly, she pushed herself off the ground and rose to her feet, her body still trembling.

Now what was she supposed to do? And where did Gina go? The last thing she remembered before she found herself in that monstrous prison realm was clinging to her hand.

(*Gina's almost reached the terminal. When she activates it, the glass labyrinth will be inverted.*)

A hard shiver raced up her spine as Keith's words rushed back to her.

How long had she been gone? Was Gina forced to go on without her? Was she trying to finish what she came here to do?

Strange slivers of fractured memories bubbled up from

somewhere deep inside her. Muddled recollections of chasing someone through the darkness. And…did she *kiss* someone?

She could almost recall the sound of Gina screaming.

Did she do something while her mind was trapped in that torturous place? Did Hotdog Creep take possession of her body and attack Gina?

A dreadful image flashed through her mind. Her own hands clasped around a slender neck, squeezing…

"Oh fuck…" She stumbled forward, panicked, but only collided with the wall in the dark. She reached out, feeling at the space around her. It all felt like the same cold, smooth stone she'd been trapped within since she woke up in this horrid temple, but she knew that these weren't the same walls. This was the *glass* labyrinth. The place Gina said would be too dangerous for her if she let go of her hand…

She clenched her empty fist, her heart sinking.

"Shit!" So much for following directions, she supposed. Yet another of her colossal fuckups.

Was that the reason that dead creep got into her head? Did he make her hurt Gina?

No… That pain in her lip…that subtle taste of blood… She fought back. She ran.

That was good.

And yet how long ago did that happen? Where was Gina now?

(*Everything on this side of the glass will be crushed into streams of unnatural energy and redirected into the mechanism that opens the Oblivion Door.*)

"Oh fuck…" she sighed. She stepped backward and bumped into another wall. "Oh fuck, oh fuck, oh fuck…"

Where was she? She couldn't see shit in this darkness! Did she still have her phone? Did it still work? She felt at her pockets and found something bulging in one of them that she didn't expect.

Her flashlight!

Or…*Keith's* flashlight, she recalled with a sharp stab of regret.

She pulled it out and shined it back and forth. She was in the corner of a small chamber with several passages leading out into the surrounding labyrinth. But although she could see, she had no idea where she was supposed to go from here. Which way was out? She didn't recognize this room. How was she supposed to know where she was if she couldn't remember where she'd been and was already lost before that?

(*If you're still in here when it happens, your physical body will cease to exist and Goar Nangup's private hell will swallow you forever.*)

She groaned, her stomach twisted into a knot. "What do I do?" she cried out, hoping that Keith could still answer her.

But no one replied. She was alone. Utterly and completely.

Hopelessly.

She felt her legs tremble beneath her. She might as well let them give out, might as well drop to her knees and just give up. What else could she do?

(*I'm taking you back to where the mirrors brought you. That's as far back as I can rewind the dream.*)

She frowned. What the fuck did he mean by that? She was so confused! The mirrors? That room Gina described as some kind of highway interchange of portals she couldn't see? Was that where she was? She shined the light around again. This wasn't the same room they were in when she closed her eyes. That was a dead end, with only the one passage leading into it. But was this where those portal things brought them? Was this the other side of those mirrors? And did that mean the mirrors were still here?

Was there a reason he brought her to this spot?

She turned and looked at the walls around her, the ceiling above. She couldn't see any mirrors. She was *never* able to see them. How could she use something she couldn't see?

Something was happening, she realized. She could feel it, like a rising vibration in the floor passing up through her feet, a rapidly swelling sort of trembling sensation.

She wasn't sure how she knew it, but Gina had reached the terminal. The inversion was happening *now*. She was out of time.

And she still didn't know what to do!
Blind panic overwhelmed her and she ran.

Chapter 87

Albert rubbed at the knot on his head. It still hurt. He banged it pretty hard crawling into what he thought was a wall but turned out to be one of these statues. He was lucky he didn't end up with a bloody gash. Or worse.

"Well, I'm glad to hear you found Gina and Nicole," said Violet, "even if it was only temporary."

"Same with Andrea," he replied. "We were all worried about her. Haven't met Everett, though." Talking was helpful. It kept his mind occupied as he crept through the darkness, feeling for spikes and pitfalls and whatever other perilous things might be lurking in one of these rooms. She was delighted, of course, to hear that they found Corey. She sounded understandably surprised that he was with a guy who turned out to be some kind of artificial humanoid construct from a previous incarnation of the universe…but not nearly as surprised for some reason to hear that he was rummaging around inside the guy's bisected body… ("That sounds like him, alright.") He even told her about the important job he had to do and that there was some small question of whether he'd have time to escape the labyrinth after he was done, but again she surprised him by simply insisting that, "He'll find a way."

Either Corey was far more formidable than he appeared, or she was in serious denial. He really hoped it was the first one.

Again, he rubbed at his head. It was strange feeling that pain lingering, but none of the pain Dolly subjected him to. It was as if none of that bloody nightmare ever happened. In fact, the whole experience had faded like the memories of a bad dream. It felt so distant, so *muted.* Most of those awful experiences were little more than fragmented memories, which was no small blessing. When he first stumbled out of that nightmare, he felt as if he were teetering on the edge of madness, but now he was perfectly fine.

His toe bumped against something in the dark, distracting him from his thoughts, and he paused to feel the space around him. He didn't care much for being barefoot in here. He kept thinking about the spiked floor on the far side of the fear room. The image made him cringe. But on the other hand, it was somewhat easier to feel what was down there with only his naked toes.

He wasn't sure when he lost his other sock. He had it when he first entered Dolly's twisted dreamworld. But then again, he still wasn't sure how much of any of that was real, so he might have lost it before that. He probably lost it around the same time he lost the first one, come to think of it.

Not that any of that mattered. He'd escaped. Dolly was gone. And he had no use for just one sock anyway. But he was running out of clothes to lose.

Violet was barefoot, too. She told him she lost her boots when she was pulled into one of those flooded storm tunnels. But at least she hadn't lost anything else. If she'd lost her shirt like Brandy did, he wouldn't have had anything to offer her. And that would've definitely made things awkward.

Another statue was blocking the path forward. And something blocky was to the left, preventing them from going that way, but it felt like there was a possible opening to the right. He swept the area in front of him with his arm, still searching for outstretched limbs and spikes, determined not to make the same mistake as last time. Once he was convinced that the path was clear, he continued onward.

It was odd holding a hand that wasn't Brandy's. It felt kind of wrong, even though he knew he wasn't doing anything improper. If anything, it would be considerably less gentlemanly to refuse to hold her hand. It was important that they stay together.

On the other hand, it was absolutely fascinating to hear her story. He now knew that, from her and Corey's perspective, he and Brandy had just slipped behind that ruined structure and then vanished without a trace, leaving their flashlights on the ground. It was a lot to process, but it also sounded like that same psychic predator tried to spirit *her* away, too, but something happened and she ended up somewhere, else. She woke up inside a "gouging station." Whatever the hell *that* was. And Andrea and someone named Everett was there.

A lot of her story was similar to his own. A lot of walking. A lot of darkness. Finding people and then losing them again. It sounded like they both ended up in some kind of nightmare reality where they were *tortured* for a time, even.

Corey did say that everything was according to the Keeper's plan, meaning it was all tied together.

He was curious about this so-called "other one" she spoke of. An actual, full-blooded female sentinel? From the actual universe when this temple was constructed? The idea was fascinating. *Thrilling.* He wanted to know more. As much as she could tell him. But he didn't want to overwhelm her with questions. It sounded like she'd been through a lot. He'd have to trust that they'd all have time to talk about things once this was finally over.

What was more important right now was the idea of the mysterious entity the other one called "Priestess of Ruin." He was definitely familiar with the word "Ruin." That was what Lucianna and the other weirdos back at the hotel told them to beware of. And the place she described being dragged into sure sounded like the same nightmare world with the same blood-tinged sky as the ruined version of the resort they ended up in every time they used the seed.

It was the first he'd heard that name, and yet there was something ominous about it, almost as if he already knew it from somewhere. Something about it sounded profoundly true for some reason. It sounded *significant.*

His hand brushed against more stone in the dark. Not smooth and flat. Not a wall. Another statue. He fumbled around for a moment, sweeping the area with his hands, searching for anything that could hurt them.

Were they in another dead end? This was getting frustrating.

"What's wrong?" asked Violet.

"Feels like we're going nowhere."

"No shit."

"How are you feeling? What's your emotional state?"

"Irritable, I guess. I'm *really* over being stuck in here. I keep feeling like there *isn't* a way out, like we're just wasting our time."

He nodded to himself in the dark. That was acceptable, given the potential of a possible *paranoia room*. He'd take, "This is pointless," over, "You're leading us in circles on purpose, aren't you!" any day.

"On a more irrational note," she added, lowering her voice as if afraid someone might overhear her, "I keep having these thoughts like the statues are moving around by themselves, purposefully changing the layout. It's stupid. They're only statues. But I can't stop thinking it."

He'd like to agree with her and say that it *was* a stupid idea, that it was impossible for a bunch of statues to play musical chairs in the dark, but was there any such thing as impossible anymore? For all he knew, she could be right and that was precisely why they hadn't found their way out yet.

And where were the traps? How could there be only *one spike* in all three of these chambers? And how was it that he managed to run right into it?

Gina told them the first room had no spikes, only that bottomless pit looming just beyond the door. Was there something like that in the anxiety room instead? Something they simply missed because he went and got himself run through like an idiot? And if so what was the big surprise going to be in here?

The Keeper and his sentinels were shrewd, after all. Sneaky. *Conniving.* They probably set the traps knowing exactly what he'd expect, luring him into something particularly nasty after all he'd been through.

The cat lady even told them that he'd kill people as part of his plan. Anything that suited him was fair game. The murderous little bastard…

He closed his eyes and pushed all these thoughts from his

head. He'd be the first to admit that he didn't know what the Keeper's ultimate goals were, but he knew well enough that *that* was the room talking. Distrust. Doubt. These were the seeds from which this emotion sprouted. If he kept wandering around blind long enough, it would eventually worm its way into his mind even without being able to see anything, just like the other two.

"You okay?" asked Violet. He'd just been standing there for a while now, his thoughts churning.

"Yeah. Something feels off, but I can't decide if it's something real or just the room."

"Kind of hard to tell the difference."

"I know. I feel like I need to get a glimpse of the surrounding space. But not with the light."

She was quiet for a moment as she processed this. "So…like, with your psychic thing, then?"

"Yeah."

"Didn't you guys say you needed to get all horny and shit to do that?"

"No," he replied quickly, embarrassed. "There's more to it than that. I don't have to get freaky, I promise."

"Okay…"

He closed his eyes and tried to relax. He did it back in Mysteria. He found a mindset that worked, that let him do what he needed to do, without having to get all pervy. He was able to focus on his romantic feelings for her, on how much he loved her, on how important she was to him. He could do that again. He was sure of it.

He just needed a moment.

Chapter 88

Corey burst through the doorway and stumbled into a brand-new space.

He stood there, gasping for breath, taking it all in.

Did he do this? He didn't recall making a decision. Just like with the city he was just…*suddenly there*. His only conscious thought was to get through that door before the infection enveloped him. And yet…this *did* seem like the sort of thing he might have come up with if he'd thought about it long enough.

It was definitely *smaller*.

He was standing in a single room with walls on all sides, completely closed in. And it carried on with the networking theme, too. It was an *internet café*, not very unlike the one he and Violet spent a great deal of time at when they were in college.

There were computer monitors and keyboards set up in front of comfortable chairs all around the room, some side-by-side, others partitioned for privacy. There was a counter at one end, with a register and a menu board offering a small selection of overpriced refreshments. The decorations were sparce, consisting of a handful of simple abstract paintings and some oversized photographs of famous city skylines. Everything else was bland and sterile. There were no people here, neither customers nor employees. The only sign of life was a single potted plant sitting on the counter next to the tip jar.

Windows dominated two walls, but there was nothing to see beyond them. Everything on the other side of the glass was darkness, without a streetlight to be seen.

He turned to face the door and checked it, half-expecting it to open back into that hopelessly sprawling city, proving that he hadn't shrunk anything down at all. But it wouldn't open.

It wasn't *locked*, he noticed. It simply didn't move. The latch didn't budge. It didn't rattle in its frame. Because it wasn't a door at all. It *looked* like a door, but it was only another part of the wall.

He cupped his hands to the glass and tried to peer out, but there was nothing out there at all. Even the darkness, he somehow understood, was a lie. There was nothing behind the glass because the glass wasn't real, either. Like the door, it was only an illusion.

He turned and looked across the café, eyes narrowed, suspicious.

If this was it…if everything had been shrunk down so that it fit into the confines of this one room…then where was the infection? Had it shrunk, too? Did his perception of the task assigned to him also affect the thing causing the problem?

No. Not *shrunk*, exactly… More like…*reevaluated*, perhaps?

He found his gaze drawn to the computers. If he perceived the infection as a sort of cosmic *computer* virus…

He sat down behind the nearest monitor and clicked the mouse. The startup screen vanished, revealing the desktop. A popup window appeared, flashing a message in a language he didn't recognize, then vanished again, replaced by an error message.

"There you are," he breathed.

Bringing it here had effectively turned it into an *actual* computer virus. And he had all the tools at his disposal to fight it.

For the first time since entering this bizarre virtual existence, he didn't feel small. This was it. This was how he was going to be a match for it.

He even felt a little smug as he scooted his chair forward and reached for the keyboard.

It was time to get to work. And this time, he'd finish what he came here to do.

Chapter 89

Everett didn't like the idea of jumping in. He kept flashing back to that awful night, his mother's car filling up with cold lake water… But he refused to let his mother's illness hold him back again. He wouldn't be afraid to live his life anymore. (And preferably, he wouldn't look like a coward in front of any of these pretty ladies he kept meeting, although that was admittedly a considerably more selfish motivation.) He stood at the edge of the walkway, the sentinel at his back, staring down into those dark depths, his heart pounding.

Brandy took his hand and squeezed it. "Trust the sentinels."

Easy for her to say. She was probably an amazing swimmer. She looked pretty fit.

But after that night, he made a promise to himself. He was never going to let fear control him again. He faced death and found not eternal hell but an actual *angel* standing before him. The lies that held him prisoner all his life crumbled and fell apart. The world opened up in front of him and it was *beautiful.* He wouldn't fear that world. He wouldn't fear the people in it. He wouldn't even fear the supernatural. He'd seek out the answers to all his questions. If he let something as dumb as *water* open him up to that fear again, he'd never forgive himself.

Brandy said to trust the sentinels.

Alice said there was a passage down there, just out of sight.

"I'm ready," he decided, trying to sound confident.

Brandy didn't hesitate. Still gripping his hand, she stepped forward, surprising him. He had to force himself to move with her instead of yanking his hand back. If not for the fear of getting separated again, he wasn't sure he would've made it. His body tried to resist him. He felt himself leaning back as he stepped forward, as if trying to topple himself over backward just to avoid the inevitable plunge, but she was still clinging to his hand, pulling him. And he'd never been all that strong.

In an instant, he was falling. He was aware of the air whooshing past him, of his hair and his belly lifting upward. He had a split second to wonder if the water beneath them was safe to jump into and another split second to realize that it was already too late to worry about such things. Then he hit the surface and the only thing he was aware of was the cold.

It hit him like an electric shock, paralyzing him. Before he knew what was happening, he let out a surprised cry, belching out most of his breath in a great flurry of escaping bubbles. And then he was sinking.

For a moment, he was right back in that dark lake, unable to lift his head above the water, terror gripping his heart. Somewhere above him, Brandy's flashlight was a hazy glow that looked just like the car's headlights through the windshield that awful night. Everything was muffled and silent.

It was happening again. He was going to die.

Somewhere inside his head, Alice's wordless voice was screaming at him, but he found that he didn't need her. This *wasn't* that night. He wasn't trapped inside a sinking car. And he absolutely wasn't the same terrified child he was back then. His feet were already kicking, his arms flailing.

He thrust himself upward, out of the water, and took a great gasp of lifegiving air.

He wasn't helpless anymore.

But he still wasn't a great swimmer. He splashed and kicked, struggling just to keep his head above water. Which way was he supposed to be going? He couldn't see anything. There was too much water in his eyes. Every time he managed to blink it away and glimpse the light, he bobbed back under. It was taking all his strength just to manage this pathetic sort of doggie paddle.

This was more difficult than he expected. His shoes and clothes felt like they were weighing him down. He was expending way too much energy, wearing himself out just trying to tread water.

He might be in trouble after all…

But then Brandy was there. She grabbed his arm and steadied him. Already, she was leading him across the water.

How embarrassing. He knew he was a weak swimmer. He'd never really learned. It wasn't as if his mother ever took him to the beach or the pool. She kept him well away from public places like that, telling him it was too dangerous, that there were too many wicked people out there, when in reality she simply didn't want him to see what kinds of lives other children had. He took a few lessons at school when he was in foster care. He was able to push past his fears enough to tread water. He thought he'd be able to cross something like this. But swimming in a warm, well-lit pool in trunks was a lot different. He wasn't prepared for the cold or the weight of his sneakers or the disorienting darkness. And he certainly wasn't prepared for just how much it would remind him of that night.

If not for Brandy, he might have been in real trouble. Just like Wayne warned him, he was going to bite off more than he could chew one of these days and get himself killed.

Ahead of them, the far wall emerged from the gloom in the flashlight's beam, a square passage yawning open, its floor even with the splashing water, just as Alice described it, and exactly where that sentinel statue's featureless face was turned.

Brandy helped him to the ledge, then let go and heaved herself up onto the floor. For a moment, she was perched there on her hands and knees in front of him, his shirt weighted down with the water, the modest swells of her breasts visible underneath, and he felt his face flash hot at the sight in spite of the cold.

As she rose to her feet, he took Alice from the crook of his arm where he'd been cradling her and placed her on the dry ledge, then climbed up out of the water, his teeth chattering.

Come to think of it, it was surprising he hadn't lost her back there. He was so panicked for a moment that he'd forgotten he was still clinging to her. He was starting to wonder if he was really holding onto her at all. Perhaps *she* was holding onto *him* this whole time.

"That never gets any fucking warmer," Brandy stuttered through trembling lips. "You okay?"

"Yeah." He pushed himself up onto his knees and wiped the water from his eyes. "Thanks for that. I guess I wasn't as ready as I thought I was."

"You're fine. Don't worry about it. We all have our strengths and weaknesses." She turned and pointed her flashlight down the passage ahead of them and he found his eyes drawn to the soaking wet tee shirt he gave her. It had gone mostly transparent on her. He could see the shadows of her areolas through it. And the chill had turned her nipples fully erect.

He set out in the beginning specifically to see all the wondrous things that were out there, but this wasn't what he was expecting…

He forced his eyes away, embarrassed, and picked Alice up off the floor. "This goes on for a long way, I guess," he reported, hoping he didn't sound exactly as if he were just ogling a married woman's breasts. "And I guess it goes *up* after a while, too. That's good, I think. We want to go up."

"If you say so."

"I mean, *I* don't really know. *She* says so."

"Right. Your little friend there." She turned the light on her, her quivering lips curled in a disapproving sort of expression.

"It's weird, I know. Believe me." He looked down at Alice. Again, he felt embarrassed. He felt like he kept having to defend her. And it was no wonder. He probably should've chose something a little less horror-movie-esque for her form. Then he noticed something odd. He held her up in front of him, bewildered. "Wait… How's she *dry*?" He literally just climbed out of the water with her!

He looked back, as if expecting that he'd only imagined crossing a body of water, in spite of the fact that *he* was still dripping wet. Even the hand he was holding her with was wet. How was it not soaking into the fabric of her dress?

"Yeah, that's a thing sometimes," said Brandy, turning her attention back to the path ahead of them.

He blinked at her, confused. "*That's* the normal part for you?"

She shrugged. "My husband has a book that did the same thing a while ago. Some things just don't like to get wet, I guess." She set off down the passage.

He looked down at Alice, distracted. How incredibly and wonderfully weird it all was…

"Come on," she called back to him. "We'll warm up faster walking."

Chapter 90

Wayne stood alone in the dark, confused. Where was he? What was he just doing? He couldn't remember. It felt like he missed something. Wasn't he just lying in that bed, between Olivia and his daughter?

(The very thought of having a daughter still made his head spin…)

She was teaching him how to slip into the spirit world without the need of one of those nasty killing vines.

He squinted into the darkness all around him. Did it work? Was he dead? He didn't *feel* dead. He felt perfectly fine. A little *too* fine, in fact. He reached up and pressed at the shallow wound in his shoulder, but there was nothing there.

That wasn't right. It wasn't *bad.* He wasn't going to complain about an injury disappearing, of all things. But it wasn't *right.*

And just where the hell was he? He recalled feeling as if he were floating in a vast, churning ocean for a moment…but that was already fading into a distant haze like the fleeting memories of a dream.

The girl told him he had a job to do. Something important. *Crucial.* Something he needed to do or none of his friends would be able to leave this place.

Something about a terminal of some sort?

He felt at his pockets, searching for his flashlight, but it wasn't there.

Because these weren't his pockets, he realized. These weren't his pants. This wasn't his body.

What *did* he have?

This way.

He turned and squinted into the darkness behind him. He wasn't entirely sure why. That voice he heard just now was more in his head than in his ears. He didn't hear which way it came from. And yet he found himself fixing his blind gaze on a very specific point somewhere out in that darkness.

"Who's there?" he asked. But no one answered him.

He cursed under his breath and started walking in that direction. Was that the girl again? His daughter? The Sentinel Princess he thought never had the chance to be born?

No. Somehow he sensed that he'd know if it were her. This was someone else. But someone *familiar*.

Where was he? This didn't feel like the temple. The ground beneath his feet was smooth and hard, like temple stone, but he sensed somehow that there were no walls in this place. There was no ceiling. He was walking through a vast *emptiness*.

Closer.

Where was he being led? If there was nothing here, why would he need to go to wherever this voice was calling out from? Why didn't she come to him?

She…? How did he know it was a woman? The voice was little more than a whisper inside his head. And yet he found himself certain of it.

She was calling him. It wasn't anything as simple or silly as laziness. This was something else. A sort of *homing* task. Like a game of Marco Polo. It was dark, after all. Not merely because there was no light, but in other ways as well. This was a blind zone where nothing worked the way he was used to. He wasn't trying to physically locate her. He was trying to *synchronize* with her. Whatever the hell *that* meant…

"Almost," she whispered.

The voice was becoming more real. It was no longer merely inside his head. That was an actual voice.

He reached out into the darkness in front of him, his hand groping for whoever might be waiting there.

"Just a little closer," she breathed. A slideshow of deeply buried memories began flickering through the back of his mind.

They did this the last time he was here, too. Back when she shoved him into the killing vine.

This was Erin. He knew it even before he felt her hand close around his, their fingers enlaced. She was waiting here for him. She *told* him she'd be waiting here for him.

Last time.

God, that felt like so long ago…

"Are you ready?" asked Erin.

"Do I have a choice?" he grumbled.

She laughed at this, though he wasn't joking. It was such a lovely laugh, so casual, so charming. So *familiar*, like he'd heard that laugh all his life. Like they were old friends. How long was he with her last time? Why did it feel like he'd known her for years?

He turned and looked back the way he came. He wasn't sure why. He couldn't see anything. And it wasn't like there was anything back there. It was more symbolic, he supposed. What he was really trying to look back at was Olivia. He'd left her alone in that room with that little girl. She was probably beside herself with worry over him right now. He felt guilty. But it wasn't like this was *his* idea. *He* didn't want to be here with this dead woman instead of back at his fiancée's side.

"She'll be fine," Erin assured him. "You can trust that girl. She's doing the Keeper's work. She wouldn't let anything bad happen to her dad."

"It's true then? She's really my daughter?"

"Of course she is. She won't lie to you. I think you already knew that, though."

"Yeah… I guess I did." He turned back and met her gaze. He wasn't sure how, but he could see her now. She was standing in front of him, dressed in that same silvery gown she was wearing last time they talked.

The same gown she died in…

There still wasn't any light. His eyes didn't work here. But somehow that didn't make any difference. He could see her as clearly as if they were standing in broad daylight. Those beautiful, cascading curls. Those lovely, expressive eyes. The striking yellow sunflowers tattooed on her shoulder.

It was so strange, all these memories floating back to him.

(*Don't be mad. I know how it all seems. Believe me, I wasn't thrilled about pushing you into that vine, either. But this was the only way. We have to talk. We have important work to do. And things have gotten dangerous in the gatehouse since you arrived.*)

They spoke for a long time. Much longer than he could have been away from Olivia. She told him about the intruders in the temple. She warned him about the scarecrow man's black eye. And she told him how to activate the thorn's next form so they'd be able to access the gate. She even told him that someone was waiting for him inside the labyrinth…someone special…though she never told him who.

He felt dizzy. Everything from that conversation suddenly felt like a vivid dream, even though he hadn't been able to remember any of it before now. And at the same time, his *real* life felt like an entirely *different* dream…

Again, he let his blind gaze sweep across that endless darkness all around him. "What is this place?"

"An in-between realm," she explained. "A fringe between the physical and the spiritual. There are lots of places like it. Some call places like these 'purgatory' or 'limbo' or 'Guinee' but they're really just…*fissures* between the two worlds."

"Gocha," he lied.

Again, she laughed. He liked her laugh. It was so warm. There was something rather special about this woman. She was oddly attractive. Not in a sexual way—he only had eyes for Olivia—but *emotionally*. She made him want to be near her. She made him feel safer somehow. It was sort of like the way he felt about Nicole and Andrea and Brandy. He loved them all, but in a different way than he loved his fiancée.

"Is it true that Keith didn't make it?" he asked.

Her smile disappeared completely at this. "It is. He's on this side with us. But like me," she added, "he was always a part of the design. He has a job to do, just like we do. Trust the Keeper's machine."

"If you say so," he grumbled. But he wasn't sure how he

was supposed to feel all that reassured when the creepy little goblin monster in charge of everything included *killing people* as part of his grand plan.

"You know what we're here to do," she said. It wasn't a question. She wasn't asking him if he knew. She was informing him. They'd already discussed this. Somewhere in that dreamy bunch of disjointed memories.

He nodded. "The terminal."

She smiled that wonderful smile again. But this time, it looked a little strained, as if even she felt a little apprehensive. "Let's get started then."

Chapter 91

Olivia uttered a terrified whimper and shined her light back the other way. Another dead end. Weren't those stupid threads supposed to point the way for her? Wasn't she supposed to be able to see the future? But it couldn't even warn her about dead ends?

This was awful. She hated being alone in these dreadful corridors. She was never alone inside the first temple. Not once. She was alone in Gilbert House. She was alone in the Wood. She was even alone in that awful fairy circle. But there was always someone beside her in those gray corridors. Until now.

Maybe she really couldn't do this after all. Maybe the Sentinel Princess underestimated her.

Or maybe she never intended for her to make it out at all. Maybe she really did want her father all to herself.

She retraced her steps to the previous intersection. She made a left here last time, so from this angle, right would take her back the way she came. Her choices were left or straight ahead. She shined her light one way, then the other, trying to feel the way, but just like the first time she was here, she felt nothing to tell her one way or the other.

Was she just too distracted to concentrate? It was frightening being in these passageways without Wayne at her side. Her body wouldn't stop trembling. She felt as if she might throw up. And it didn't help that she absolutely *hated* not being able to wait until he woke up. She just left him back there… If that little girl wasn't who she said she was, if she was somehow able to *turn off* her psychic warning alarm…

No. She couldn't think like that. It wouldn't solve anything.

She wiped at her eyes and nose and tried to compose herself. This was for Wayne's sake. He needed her. That was why she was doing this. It was the only reason she needed.

Steeling her nerves, she forced down those stubborn tears and focused on the task before her. Somewhere inside her head was a map. Sandy told her so, way back at the start of all this madness. She could see the paths leading to the future, the "amber threads" stretched between now and then. And not just *one* future. *All* of them. Every destination of every choice she made. That was how she described it. So why couldn't she tell which path would take her where she wanted to be? Was she trying too hard? Was she attempting to look too far ahead? Not far enough? Was she just not as capable as everyone expected her to be? She didn't understand!

She wasn't even sure what to focus on. Was she looking for the passage that would take her to safety? Or the one that would lead her straight into danger? Was she supposed to be looking for the scarecrow man? Was that the problem? Was she trying to go where her psychic alarm was trying to warn her away from?

Left or straight?

Or perhaps right. She came from that way, but maybe she made a mistake at a previous intersection. Maybe none of these were the correct way because she'd already messed up.

This was so *hard*!

She sniffled and wiped at her nose again. She needed help. She couldn't do this on her own. But there was no one else here. She was all alone. No one was going to help her.

She was so *useless*! She couldn't make one stupid decision on her own!

She shined the light left, frustrated. Nothing. Not a glimmer. Not a shiver. Not a single feeling of right or wrong or scary or dreadful or *anything*. What was she doing wrong? Was she even in the right part of the labyrinth? Had she been sent all the way to the far side of the temple?

She turned her light down the right passageway.

Someone was standing there.

She let out a startled scream and fled the opposite way.

Not yet! She couldn't possibly deal with that maniac right now! She wasn't ready! She wasn't in the right mindset!

The corridor turned right up ahead. She hurried around the corner, desperate to get out of sight, and then stumbled to a stop as the floor ahead of her dropped away.

A six-foot drop into a perpendicular passage running right and left. Her own passage continued on ahead, but she'd have to drop down and climb up the other side. And it only took an instant to see that the floor of that other passage was all scratched up .

A hound passage…

This was *not* the time for one of those!

She glanced back, her heart hammering in her chest. She couldn't go back. He'd be waiting for her. She was sure of it. Her choices were going to be to risk facing *live* hounds that may or may not be lurking just out of sight or the *dead* one that was definitely chasing her.

With a terrified whimper, she shined her light back and forth, squinting into the gloom. She couldn't hear anything, but between her labored breathing and her pounding pulse, it was difficult to hear very much.

And they didn't always make that noise, she recalled.

Fighting back tears, she sat down on the ledge and dropped into the lower passageway.

Was she even going to be able to get up that other side? The wall was higher than she was tall, after all. And there was no one to boost her up like Wayne always did. What if she was stuck down here?

It wasn't an easy task, by any means. She placed the flashlight on the floor above and gripped the wall. Then she sort of heaved herself up one side, hooking one leg over the edge with an unladylike sort of grunt.

For a moment, she wasn't sure she was going to be able to pull herself up. She was heavier than she was strong. Upper body strength had never exactly been her strong suit. But perhaps fear was her friend, because somehow she managed to crawl up and into the next passage.

But before she could catch her breath, she caught sight of a figure standing on the other side, where she just came from.

With a startled cry, she snatched up the flashlight, shot to her feet and fled.

That took a lot out of her. She wasn't sure how long she could keep running. Hopefully she could lose the maniac in the twisting corridors. Preferably without having to cross any more hound passages.

Another intersection appeared from the gloom ahead. Only two choices this time. Left or right. She didn't have time to feel them out. She chose right at random, hoping to be well out of sight before that monster caught up to her.

Another intersection came into view a moment later. This time she chose left.

This was good. The more turns she made, the more lost she'd get. The more lost she was, the harder she should be to find. Right?

She took another right at the next intersection, but then her luck ran out. Another dead end materialized from the punishing darkness.

She let out a terrified squeak of a cry and turned to go back, but her path was already blocked.

She screamed and backed herself against the wall.

It was over. She had nowhere left to run.

The scarecrow man had found her.

Except…as she blinked away the tears, she realized that the figure standing before her didn't look like the monstrous scarecrow man at all. It just looked like a man.

Except…sort of hazy?

She wiped at her eyes, confused, then squinted into the gloom again.

The figure stepped toward her, brightening in the glow of her flashlight. But not *just* brightening. It became clearer, like a camera lens focusing.

Then, impossibly, Keith was standing in front of her.

Chapter 92

Andrea had definitely found her way *down*, at least… She could only guess at how many floors of this endless labyrinth she'd been flushed past, but she was definitely farther down than she was before.

Given the choice, however, she would've much rather taken the *stairs*.

She was going to have to be careful not to let her guard down again. Apparently Tia wasn't through making her miserable yet. Next time, that raging psychopath might throw her down a hole with no water to catch her.

She still couldn't see a thing, but she felt a little *cleaner*, at least. Maybe it washed off all that crusty, stinking mud. That would be a small silver lining. That stuff was so gross.

After stumbling around in the dark for a while, she'd located one of the chamber walls and was now following it, searching for a way out.

She wasn't sure why, but those darker-than-dark patterns had vanished from her head again. Had she left the murk entirely? Or did that terrifying water slide just leave her too weary and shaken up to use that trick? She still had no idea how this stuff actually worked.

It didn't sound like Olivia's psychic thing was the same as hers. She didn't hear voices. She didn't see things other people couldn't see. According to her, she just had these *feelings* about things. Mostly dread, it sounded like. And panic. Warning her not to go certain places or to run away.

That sounded a lot more useful, if she were being honest. All this ghost stuff ever did for her was get her in trouble.

The wall seemed to go on and on. Where was the exit? She desperately *hoped* there was an exit. She hadn't been dropped into a room with no passages leading out, had she? Although that would be just her luck, she supposed…

The roar of the rushing water was a lot quieter than it was where she fell in, but it was still loud enough to make it hard to hear if anything might be in here with her. She thought of the hound back in that offset passage, the one without its scales slashing. It was only the sound of its footsteps on that torn-up stone that gave her any warning that it was there. She'd definitely never be able to hear something like that in here. The very memory sent a shiver of dread all the way down her body.

Paranoid, she slid her bare toes in a wide arc around her. It felt perfectly smooth and unscarred, thankfully, no sign that the hounds had dug their claws into it.

But she still needed to get out of here and away from that noise. It was doing nothing to ease her headache, meaning she didn't even have the luxury of just sitting down on the floor and resting for a while.

She pushed onward, her fingers sliding along the stone, searching for a corner, her toes still prodding for dangers with each step she took. She wished she could see. This was all so agonizingly *slow*!

She stopped and stood there a moment, motionless, holding her breath, her blind eyes wide in the darkness. Was that a voice she heard just now? Was someone down here with her? Had she stumbled into another place that was haunted?

No… It was just the rushing water. It played tricks on you, made you hear all sorts of things.

She continued on, feeling her way along the wall, searching for a way out of this drenched chamber.

How big was this room? It *sounded* big. She could hear the noise of the water echoing around her. And she was still making her way along the same wall. Was she just going in a circle? It was so hard to tell in the dark, with nothing to use for reference.

She was starting to think she wasn't ever going to find a way out.

Then she felt it. Her fingers slipped off the stone, around a corner.

Cautious, she crept closer, running her hands around it, shuffling her feet along the floor, trying to get a measure of the space.

She slipped around the corner and then crept away from it, reaching out into the darkness for another wall, trying to determine if she'd found a passage or merely another chamber.

There was nothing there.

She crept out a little farther, trying to remember how wide the labyrinth passages were. Six feet? Ten? Twelve? She was never very good at estimating distances. And being in the dark didn't help anything.

It wasn't this far, though.

She was about to turn around when her fingers brushed another wall.

A little prodding revealed it to be another corner, just like the last one. It *was* a passage leading away from the water.

She turned and crossed the empty space again, measuring it.

No. This was definitely wider than a regular passage. She pressed her hand against the wall, then reached up. Even standing on her tiptoes, she couldn't reach the top of it, but that didn't tell her anything. She didn't think she could reach the top of all the other passages, either. Some were tall enough for those freaky sentinel statues to stand in, after all.

Back in the first temple, there were a lot more smaller passages, she recalled. They ducked through a lot of places, even crawled through a few.

She still remembered that one cramped passage where Wayne nearly got stuck. She was so glad she went last. The view she had of Olivia was really embarrassing. If someone had been behind her, she would've been *mortified.* And she couldn't imagine what *Olivia's* view must've been!

She crept forward, still sweeping the floor ahead of her with each step, cringing a little in anticipation of another obstacle like the one above that she stubbed her toe on.

Instead, she felt her toes slip over an empty space.

Frightened that she was standing over another ledge, she crouched down and then flattened herself on the cold floor before reaching down to examine what was there.

Not a sheer drop, she found, but steps.

A staircase leading deeper into the labyrinth.

(*Go down. All the way to the bottom.*)

She stood up and quickly thrust her hands into the space behind her, half-expecting to find Tia standing there, ready to push her again, but there was nothing there.

Satisfied—for now—she pressed her hand to the wall again and began descending the stairs.

Just how deep *was* the labyrinth, she wondered. How far down into the earth did it go? And what sort of terrifying things might be waiting for her down there?

Chapter 93

Gina stood alone in the darkness, her blind eyes wide and filled with tears. The hourglass structure was gone. The terminal, the chamber, the entire glass labyrinth…all of it had vanished. She was back in the stone labyrinth again.

She turned all the way around, scanning her surroundings with her psychic eye. Those same twisting corridors, one after another, disappearing into that queer haze of her muted vision. There wasn't a living creature for as far as she could see. There weren't even any chambers nearby. Everything was narrow and claustrophobic and pitch-black and endless.

She caught no glimpse whatsoever of that other side.

The terminal was activated. She understood that. She'd completed the job she was sent here to do. But in the process…

A great, hitching sob forced its way up and she pressed her trembling hands over her mouth. Great, wet tears rolled down her cheeks.

What had she done?

Nicole…

She left her there. Alone in the darkness.

She had no choice. Even without the supernatural strength of the thing puppeteering her, she was far too small and weak to be a match for someone as fit and strong as Nicole. She would have murdered her.

But that didn't matter.

(*We started this together and we're finishing it together. I won't leave without you.*)

She couldn't hold back the sobs. They poured out of her, overwhelming her.

She left Nicole back there. She abandoned her.
And now she was gone.
(*I trust you.*)
Gina sank to her knees on the cold stone and wept.

Chapter 94

Violet stood there in the dark, clinging to Albert's hand, feeling awkward in addition to all the invasive feelings that were already circling around inside her head.

He was trying to use sex magic to activate his psychic senses, like they described back on the carriage ride. It still sounded like bullshit to her, but she couldn't deny that she believed it. She even watched them do it once. Back in the Denselands, when they came across that castle-looking place. It sounded like there was a child crying inside and they intended to investigate, but he stopped them, claiming it wasn't safe. They were reluctant to take his word for it. It didn't seem right not to make sure. Then he grabbed Brandy and kissed her. It was only a kiss. That was all. They didn't get all handsy or start groping each other. They didn't even get all crazy with their tongues like so many drunks she'd seen making out at parties. They just shared a long, slow, romantic kiss and then Brandy confirmed that there was no one inside. It was weird. But it was kind of cool, too, she had to admit.

This was the same thing, except Brandy wasn't here. *She* was here. There was only the two of them and yet she was somehow a third wheel…

But she didn't dare let go of his hand. She couldn't stop thinking that he'd probably be gone again the next time she reached for him. It just kept happening, after all.

Uncomfortable, but unwilling to give those invasive paranoid emotions any acknowledgement, she focused on the things he told her. About the psychic predator that spirited them away and their pervy shaman's magic phone call to coach them through some sort of magic teleportation spell that somehow sent them both to Nicole and Gina's location. She might not be a genius, but she was plenty smart enough to know that not one part of that story made any sense. And yet she didn't doubt it was true, either. It wasn't any less believable than being spirited away to some apocalyptic wasteland and brutally murdered by monsters over and over and over again without so much as a scar to show for it all.

And then there was that bit about some kind of psycho witch hijacking his brain for a while? What the hell was *that* about?

She glanced around—pointless as it was in this darkness—and wondered how long this was going to take him. Was it something he'd really be able to do? Just think some dirty thoughts and get a mental snapshot of the space around them? A few days ago, she would've called absolute bullshit on all of this, but a lot had happened in that short time.

Her blind gaze drifted down to her hand in his without realizing it. What was he thinking about right now? He assured her that he wouldn't have to get "freaky," as he put it, but what *did* it require? Was he just reminiscing about sexy times with his wife? Or was he dreaming up new things to get himself turned on?

He was probably thinking inappropriate thoughts about *her*. Focusing on the feel of her hand and imagining what *other* parts of her might feel like.

Pervert.

She should snatch her hand away and hide until he went away.

She squeezed her eyes shut and pushed the thought from her mind. No. That wasn't her. That was the room. Albert was a nice guy. And he was very much in love with his wife. Even a stranger like her was able to see that right away.

The last thing she wanted was for them to get separated.

Besides, what would it really matter if he indulged in some kind of perverted fantasy about her if it meant making the magic work and finding the way out of this awful room? What difference would it really make if he never acted on such thoughts? It wasn't like *she* never indulged in a little fantasy now and then.

"Hmm..." he sighed.

"Did you find it?" she asked, eager to move on.

"Not yet. Sorry."

"Oh."

"I was hoping I might find Brandy..."

Like when they were captured by the psychic predator, she recalled. "No luck?"

"I didn't think it'd be that easy."

She had to admit, she rather liked the idea of there being some kind of magic teleporting spell that could bring people together even across this weird darkness. But she still didn't understand how something like that worked. Did both parties have to be intimate? How did Nicole and Gina fit into the equation the first time? That seemed sort of weird now that she was thinking about it.

She found herself imagining that he was thinking not about Brandy, but her best friend in that moment, and forced the thought from her mind. These invasive emotions were trying to paint everything in the worst light possible, attempting to drive them apart, just like he said they would. And she didn't know this man well enough to be sure of anything. She didn't know *anyone* here that well except for Corey. Her mind was using that against her.

She had to remind herself that she wasn't the kind of woman to play the victim. If he made any kind of pass at her, she'd clobber him. It was that simple.

"This is harder than I'd hoped," he sighed. "I need to sit down."

He let go of her hand while he seated himself. He didn't go anywhere, and yet feeling him pull his hand away sent a jolt of anxious fear through her as if he'd snatched it away and bolted. She could hear him right there, doing exactly as he said he was doing, and yet she didn't like being separated even by such a little bit. She quickly seated herself next to him and reached for his hand again.

He took it immediately, thankfully. Then he took her other

hand, too. "Humor me for a minute, okay?"

"Um…? Okay?"

He shifted himself so that he was facing her and squeezed her hands. "I'm gonna just pretend you're her. Nothing weird, I promise. Just, sitting here. Holding hands like this."

"Okay," she said again. "Whatever helps, I guess." Then she frowned at herself. "I mean, not *whatever*, but…you know what I mean."

He chuckled a little. "I know. Believe me, I'm not *that guy*. I promise."

She took a calming breath and closed her eyes. She didn't want to be stuck here waiting for him to find some kind of magical mindset. She wanted to be moving toward the exit. But she had no idea where the exit was, which was exactly why he was doing this.

(*I know things about my environment. I can kind of tell when there's something that other people can't see.*)

That was how he described it back in the carriage. And they could certainly use that sort of sixth sense right about now.

She just needed to be patient.

She needed to trust him.

Chapter 95

He should've known it wouldn't be that easy.

Corey stood up and hurried to the next station. The infection seemed to be contained within the network, but it was spreading faster than he could scrub it. And it was everywhere at once, eating away at the programming in five places while he was fighting with it in another. It was exhausting. And he didn't seem to be making any progress.

Worse still, he'd begun to understand that he hadn't contained the infection at all. He'd only contained *himself.* He had it backward. The café was the prison, not the network. Somehow, he'd built this one room and locked himself inside it. This was a decent strategy, since it wouldn't be able to physically overwhelm him in this place like it nearly did in that server room. But while he was locked up in here, it was free to continue eating away at the stoneworks outside.

What was it doing out there? How was it affecting things?

Were the others in danger?

A sea of popup windows bombarded him, like an army of minions blocking his way, protecting their master who cowered behind their ranks. He slammed them closed, felling them one by one, searching for the browser tabs hidden underneath.

And he had a few weapons of his own to use against this thing. He forced his way into the settings. He deleted the cookies and cleared the cache. He reset the homepage and activated the ad blocker. Simple things, yet effective. Because this was, after all, only a vivid metaphor for his battle with the infection. If it could manifest as a virus, he could fight it by manifesting his own defenses. In the end, it was a battle of wills. Even more, it was a battle of *imagination*. As long as he could conceive a logical retaliation, he could keep fighting.

The problem wasn't a lack of weapons. The problem, he'd quickly discovered, was in the numbers. This thing was replicating and spreading too quickly. He couldn't keep up, much less get ahead of it.

He didn't think the computers' bult-in virus protection would be of any use, but he was surprised. It didn't cleanse the system, but it delivered a decent blow. His own version of whipping out the heavy artillery on a battlefield. A veritable siege weapon at his disposal.

He couldn't help wondering if that equated to the protections already existing within the sentinels' "software" or if it was another of the "tools" he brought with him to battle this thing.

What sort of defenses *did* the machine have, anyway? Shouldn't someplace as highly advanced and mysterious as this have accounted for and shielded against this kind of threat? How was *he* any kind of match for something if even sentinel technology couldn't stand up to it?

There was no end to all the questions he had, and still there were no answers to be found.

In front of him, the computer flashed a fatal error and crashed. In an instant, it was dead.

At the same time, he felt a shudder pass through the room around him. The lights flickered. One of the paintings fell off the wall. And a crack shot down one of the windowpanes.

"Huh," he grunted, looking around. It didn't appear that he was nearly as safe here as he'd first thought. What would happen to him if he lost control completely? Would this entire little existence simply…implode on him?

He really didn't want to find out.

This was going to be a very long night.

Chapter 96

Brandy tugged at a lock of her hair. The water had washed most of the ichor off her body, but her hair, while better than it was, remained greasy and stiff with it. She hated the way it felt, but just like everything else, she was powerless to do anything about it.

She turned and shined her light back the way they came. How long had they been walking this same passage? It hadn't turned or diverged since they climbed out of that frigid water. And all this walking had done little to warm her up. All it was doing was making her bare feet ache.

She couldn't stop worrying about Albert. Where did he go? Was he safe? He'd better not get himself killed out there. They hadn't been married a week yet! (Or had they…? How long had it been since they said their vows? Even time was all messed up out here. Everything was so fucking confusing!)

She couldn't stop thinking about what that awful voice back in that tall grass said to her about Dolly's "new toy."

She rubbed absently at her swollen lip. She was still fuming mad over that nasty little witch. If she ever saw the little slut again, she was a dead woman. She didn't care *what* kind of magic she had.

"So what's your deal?" she asked, needing to take her mind off the witch for a while.

"What?"

"Do you have some kind of secret psychic power, too, then? Or do you just talk to dolls?"

Everett looked down at Dolly, distracted. "Oh… Yeah. Uh… Spirits. I see spirits, I guess."

"So, ghosts and shit?" Nicole said that Andrea was able to see and communicate with ghosts, now that she was thinking about it.

"Not *ghosts* so much. More like *other* kinds of spirits. Like, 'faery folk' or something, maybe? Elves and gnomes and stuff, you know?"

"Huh."

"Like Alice."

She remembered him referring to her as a spirit when he first showed her to him.

(*She's a spirit from the other side of, like,* everything, *I guess, that I kind of turned into a doll and she's been helping me.*)

It didn't make the fact that he was walking around and talking to a doll any less creepy, that was for sure. And besides that… "I thought you said fairies were *bad*."

"They are. Or at least the ones that bullied Olivia in Gutler's Weep were pretty bad. But Alice isn't like them. She's something completely different."

"If you say so." She just hoped that Alice stayed on their side and didn't decide to go full Chucky on them before this was over.

Ahead of them, something different was finally emerging from the gloom.

"Stairs," observed Everett, as if she needed his keen observational skills to tell her what she was looking at. (She was feeling a little tired and cranky. She should probably be careful about what she said. She didn't want the kid to think she just didn't like him. He really did seem like a nice guy.)

"That's good, isn't it?" he went on. "Aren't we supposed to be going up?"

She stared up into the darkness ahead. "That's right…" she recalled. Gina told them they needed to reach the top of the city's central tower. But that was assuming that they were actually under it and not about to ascend into the wrong tower.

Or for all she knew they might be nowhere near the surface and these were only the first of countless steps they'd be forced to climb.

"Alice says we're still going the right way."

She wasn't thrilled about the idea of taking the stairs all the way to the top of a fucking *tower*...but it was certainly better than going the *wrong* way.

With a heavy sigh, she started up the steps. But after climbing only the first four, she stopped and looked back, distracted.

"You okay?" asked Everett, turning to see for himself what was there.

"Yeah. Just...a weird feeling for a second there..."

"What kinda feeling?"

She shook her head. "Nothing. My imagination." But was it? For a moment there, she thought she heard Albert's voice calling out to her.

She wanted to sit down and try contacting him again. She'd escaped the nightmare the ichor plunged her into, so maybe he'd escaped the witch, too. But if he hadn't, then the little whore would only attack her again before she could reach him. Plus, there was no way in hell she was getting herself all hot and bothered in front of this kid. She'd humiliated herself more than enough for one day.

She continued up the steps.

Everett followed close behind, still cradling Creepy Alice in his arm as if she were a baby.

"So does that come in handy?" she asked without looking back. "Seeing 'spirits'?"

"Well, back in Gutler's Weep I could see mushrooms that no one else could see."

"Oh." He saw *mushrooms*. That was a perfectly normal thing to say. Maybe she shouldn't have asked. She felt like her capacity for dealing with weird shit was running low.

"But I haven't seen anything like that since we arrived in the Denselands. Now that you mention it, I guess I'm not all that useful here. Except for finding Alice, I mean."

"I wouldn't go that far." He *did* technically catch her when she fell out of the ichor. (Although she still didn't understand how she just sort of...*dripped* out of the ceiling like he described.)

"But I think I've been doing what I was sent here to do," he added. "Like, I really feel like I was supposed to go to the other side and bring Alice back. I think that might've been the reason the Keeper sent me here."

"If you say so."

"I mean, she's been a big help. She showed me the way out of the dollhouse and helped me save Violet from that priestess. And she got the two of us through the graymother's nest."

"Whatever the fuck *that* is," she muttered.

"Yeah, that's a hard one to explain…"

"Don't bother. I won't understand it anyway."

"Okay."

They fell quiet again, both of them conserving their breath as the stairs carried them higher and higher into the darkness toward whatever fresh nightmares were waiting up there.

Chapter 97

Albert pictured Brandy's face. Her eyes. Her nose. Her ears. Her lips. That mischievous smirk of hers. The way she was always playing with her hair. Her laugh. Her smile. Her voice. Everything about her was perfect, as far as he was concerned. He adored her.

He held Violet's hands, pretending they were Brandy's, pretending she was there right in front of him.

(But not pretending *too much*, of course. He didn't want to get distracted and try to kiss her. He was fairly sure that would turn out the same as when he accidently kissed Nicole. Except he had a feeling Violet would punch a lot harder.)

But he didn't need a kiss to remember what she meant to him. He didn't need any kind of physical contact. He loved her no matter how far away she was. They'd known each other for six years and she still made his heart stutter in his chest on a regular basis.

That feeling was powerful. It was *significant.* He wasn't sure Lyle Shanzer was capable of understanding such a thing, but that feeling of simply loving someone so much was every bit as powerful as the emotions he felt while making love to her. He could use it just the same as he did those other, less savory feelings. Especially when there wasn't something monstrous breathing down his neck.

Thinking of her sent a warm calmness settling through his body. It seemed to wash away those other emotions like a purifying rain.

And it was working. He could see the space around him, the statues that were standing over them, men and women miming out their poisonous paranoid frustrations for them to absorb, driving them apart, destroying their chances of making it out of here safely.

It was a dangerous sort of balancing act, he knew. He needed to see the path, but seeing the things that blocked the path would be disastrous.

He took a deep, calm breath and pushed every thought that wasn't Brandy from his mind.

He'd tried calling out to her several times now, with no luck. And he tried again now, but he still couldn't find her. The best he could sense was a faint sort of flicker of her face in his head, but that was probably only wishful thinking.

He desperately hoped she was still safe out there. He didn't think he'd even want to go home again if she wasn't with him.

The visible space around him was growing. It was like a candle being lit, its flame slowly expanding, widening the radius of its glow, revealing more and more from the darkness.

They were backed into a dead-end space, he saw. And there were other places like this around them. They'd probably been shuffling between those for some time without even realizing it. The actual path forward was fairly narrow. They needed to duck under the outstretched arm of two enraged women aggressively pointing at each other and shouting accusations.

It was curious, the various emotion rooms and the way they affected them. The dangers inherently changed with each one. The sex room had been a sort of trap in and of itself. He and Brandy had been far too distracted to even try leaving. And he had a feeling that the hate room probably would have been similar. They probably would've been thrust into an intense argument and become far more focused on fighting each other than on getting to safety. The only way through was to learn from the first room and cross it blind, in which case that deadly spike pit was waiting to claim them. The fear room, on the other hand, seemed to be designed to either push them back, making it impossible to proceed or else making them panic and driving them into those deadly spikes. Here in the second temple, the sorrow room would've operated much like the sex room, sapping their will to go on, potentially leaving them curled up and sobbing on the floor. Worst case scenario, if it became entirely too much to bear, there was a convenient ledge to jump off of just beyond the door… The anxiety room worked much like the fear room, distracting them with overwhelming emotions and making him careless. This room was a little different. Much like the hate room, it worked to divide those who crossed it together. They could easily become so engrossed in their paranoid fears that they attacked each other, but it was just as easy that they could simply run away from each other and get lost again.

But he couldn't let himself get distracted thinking about things like that.

He needed to think about Brandy.

Of course, thinking about Brandy that first night in the sex room wasn't exactly unpleasant… He didn't want to think *dirty* thoughts while he was holding another woman's hands, but as soon as he remembered the way she kissed him that night, it felt like his psychic eye opened wider.

The layout of the room was becoming clearer. Just like in the anxiety room, he was able to open his psychic eye and see what was around him.

There weren't any spikes in here, fortunately. Nor were there any dangerous drop-offs. It didn't need anything like that.

"I see now," he said, opening his eyes to the same darkness that was there when they were closed. "There *isn't* a way out."

"*What?*"

"I mean, there *is*. But we weren't going to find it stumbling around in the dark." He tried to let go of her hands to stand up, but she held onto one of them. All this darkness must have been getting to her. He could hardly blame her. He let her keep that one and pushed himself up with just the one. "I'll show you."

Still clinging to her hand, he led her toward the bickering women, carefully helped her duck under those outstretched arms and then circled around to the other side.

"Here."

"The door?" she asked, hopeful. She pushed closer to him and reached out, only to find a wall there.

"Not this time," he said. He reached out and grasped her wrist, then guided it a little to the right.

"What's…?" She felt around, struggling with it. "Is this a *ladder*?"

"Pretty much." It was a lot like the one outside the original door back on the burning mountain, where they found the one-armed skeleton and Yggdrasil's seed. It was a series of notches in the walls that acted as rungs. "We have to climb up to leave."

"How the hell were we supposed to find *this* in the dark?"

It was a good question. The answer, he supposed, was probably that they weren't supposed to find it. Anyone who'd made it this far would have to be very careful to be impairing their vision, meaning it would be almost impossible to notice something like this. Only someone like him or Gina could have found the exit without succumbing to the emotions of the statues in the process. And he wasn't entirely sure about Gina. The sorrow room had noticeably affected her even in the dark, he recalled.

"I'm going to climb up first," he decided. "Then I'll help you up. When we get to the top, don't move unless I'm guiding you."

He still couldn't see anything with his natural eyes, but he somehow knew she was giving him a suspicious sort of squint. "Why?"

"Because *that's* where all the traps are."

Chapter 98

The Priestess of Ruin stretched her long legs and settled deeper into her thorny throne of decayed treasures. Blood-red nails drummed slowly upon the splintered remains of relics once considered holy and sacred but were now only moldering and forgotten trash. Her dark eyes narrowed, her lips pulled into a thoughtful frown, she peered across the festering wasteland. Observing… Pondering… *Dreaming*…

Above her, the red sky had grown agitated. It boiled as if responding to her churning thoughts, a supernatural storm brewing, darkening the rotting landscape around her.

This was her domain. This was her power. This was her very existence. She was a cosmic storm of unimaginable destruction, a godly wave of pure atrophy and inescapable ending. Even the impassible wall was unable to contain her. She was here inside it and she was there *outside* it and she was everywhere else as well. She was present and she was past and she was future, then and now and always. Wherever and whenever she wanted to be. All at once. She was here in her favorite chair, settled into the filth and mold of the festering desires of selfish men and women throughout forgotten history. But she was also out there in the City Beyond Memory, watching each and every one of the Keeper's fools as they struggled through that monstrous darkness. And at the same time, she was walking with Andrea as if they were still friends. She was stalking Violet, delighting in her pain. She was manhandling Brandy, amused by her frustration and anger. She was kissing Gina, reveling in her confused fear. And she was also back in the living world, five years ago, watching the first six with wicked delight as they writhed in terror in the first gatehouse, clueless about the even greater horrors awaiting them in the future.

She wasn't merely being obscene when she joked with Andrea about how she was "always touching herself." Every version of herself she ever was or would be was constantly connected, always in contact. Her favorite lies had always been the ones wrapped in their own truths. And it had always delighted her to know that if humans comprehended even a fraction of the truth of the universe around them, they'd be horrified beyond words at some of the things she'd told them right to their faces.

But even a goddess of chaos and decay couldn't see everything. She couldn't predict the Keeper's next move.

Something had changed. He was straying from his usual, boring patterns. She thought it was merely *her* he was reacting to. She'd all but declared war on him, after all. Unable to stomach the sight of yet another world stripped bare of its greatest wonders, she began carving away at the very foundations of his mechanizations. She found and crippled the caretakers guarding the roads to the Denselands. She sent some of the most dangerous remnants in existence to wreak havoc on his chosen twelve. And just like always, the clever little fuck parried her every move. But *unlike* every other time, his designs had grown wild. *Reckless.*

What was going on in that little, swiveling head of his?

She pulled her feet back, raking her naked toes through piles of tarnished, broken, moldy things too far gone to ever shine again.

Everything here was once something that men fought and died over, betrayed each other to obtain and wasted their lives desperately searching for. Few things in this world delighted her more than taking the things that humans lusted after with maddening obsession and watching them rot into dust.

It was no different than what the damned Keeper was doing, really. He'd already scrubbed away most of the world's magic. What would he take away next? Free will? Dreams? Imagination? *Love?* It was better to let it all end now than to witness the birth of yet another travesty of a universe.

She wanted to break the cycle. She wanted to force his

hand. She wanted to bleed as much chaos into the next universe as possible. At least *that* would be interesting. That was her dream. That was the desire that made her squirm in her rotting throne with perverse delight.

But *this*…

The *Murk Serpent*, of all the unexpected things… Had it been here this whole time? Or did the Keeper have it tucked away somewhere in his sprawling compendium? Either way, the mere presence of that snake here in this ancient labyrinth was *extraordinary*.

Her whole body was tingling with excitement. She couldn't remember the last time she felt such a thrill! Even *she* didn't know what she was going to do next!

She threw back her head and let out a guttural, almost *sexual* sort of squeal and dug her fingers and toes deep into the foul decay around her.

At the same time, the roots of the Ruin began to spread, breaking through the rotting boundaries between this world and the space beyond.

The inevitable decay of all things could be delayed, but never stopped. Eventually it found its way into every corner of every world, tearing down whatever the Keeper built. Even his precious compendium, locked away in that convoluted state of existence outside the flow of time itself, wouldn't last forever.

Now would be the time for Ruin.

And it would be gloriously bleak!

Chapter 99

Throughout the ancient City Beyond Memory, the endless stone, untouched by time for ages untold, began to crack and crumble. Statues weathered and fell. The strange, darkness-thriving plants deep in the depths began to wither. Creatures never before plagued by disease suddenly cried out, howling and wailing with sickness. And in the raging storm above, ribbons of ominous red began to snake through the boiling clouds, painting the lightning a bloody hue.

Ruin had arrived.

The end was near.

About the author

Brian Harmon is an independent author of horror fiction, suspense and dark adventure. He grew up in rural Missouri and now lives in Southern Wisconsin with his wife, Guinevere, and their three children.

For more about Brian Harmon and his work, visit
www.BrianHarmonBooks.com

www.ingramcontent.com/pod-product-compliance
Lightning Source LLC
LaVergne TN
LVHW010050110826
845155LV00028B/268

* 9 7 8 1 9 4 5 5 5 9 3 8 9 *